THE CLOUD LEOPARD'S DAUGHTER

1863: When Kitty and Rian Farrell sail their schooner *Katipo III* into Dunedin Harbour, they are on tenterhooks. The new Otago goldfields have attracted all comers, including their friend Wong Fu from Ballarat, who has sent a message asking them for help. To their surprise, Fu reveals he is more than a mere fortune seeker — he is a Cloud Leopard tong master, and when he dies the title will be passed on to his daughter Bao. But Fu's brother wants the title for himself, and has kidnapped Bao and taken her to opium-ridden China, where she will be forced to marry. Kitty and Rian agree to find her, but as they sail closer to their quarry, the stakes jump dramatically. And little do they know that the deadliest threat lies in their midst . . .

Books by Deborah Challinor
Published by Ulverscroft:

KITTY
AMBER
BAND OF GOLD

DEBORAH CHALLINOR

THE CLOUD LEOPARD'S DAUGHTER

Complete and Unabridged

AURORA
Leicester

First published in Australia in 2016 by
HarperCollins Australia

First Aurora Edition
published 2020
by arrangement with
HarperCollins Australia

A catalogue record for this book is available
from the British Library.

ISBN 978–1–78782–315–0

Published by
Ulverscroft Limited
Anstey, Leicestershire

Set by Words & Graphics Ltd.
Anstey, Leicestershire
Printed and bound in Great Britain by
T. J. International Ltd., Padstow, Cornwall

This book is printed on acid-free paper

In memory of my dearest friend,
Mary Ellen Nicholls, 1945–2016.

Prologue

Sydney, November 1856

The moment the gangway hit Queen's Wharf, Amber Farrell shot along it like a rat down rigging, her plait flying, the tail of her shirt flapping loose from her trousers.

'Hoi!' her father, Captain Rian Farrell, shouted. 'Come back here. Where d'you think you're going?'

Amber skidded to a reluctant halt. 'To find Bao.'

'Not on your own, you're not. You wait till someone can go with you.'

Amber's mother, Kitty, appeared at the gunwale. 'And you're not going ashore looking like that. Come back and put on a dress.'

'Ma! It's only Bao. She won't care.'

'Perhaps not, but I do. Come on, back you come.'

Amber looked mutinous, as if she might just turn and run off anyway, but after a long, pointed glare at her parents she sighed and stomped back up the gangway.

'I am sixteen, you know,' she muttered as she stalked past her father. 'I hardly need a chaperone.'

'You damn well do,' he shot back. 'Tahi can go with you, but ask Haunui first. They might have

1

something else planned.'

Amber brightened, and rushed off to find Tahi and his grandfather.

'And get changed!' Kitty called after her. She wasn't having *her* daughter gadding about Sydney looking like a ruffian.

'I blame you,' Rian remarked benignly.

Startled, Kitty asked, 'What for?'

'Her headstrong ways.'

'Me! She gets that from you, not me.'

Amber was soon back, dragging Tahi by the hand, which he clearly didn't mind in the least. Haunui followed, carrying his and Tahi's sea bags. The *Katipo* had picked them up from Paihia a fortnight earlier, where Rian had taken on a cargo of timber, and they would remain in Sydney, when the *Katipo* left, as Haunui had business to attend to on behalf of his iwi. They would make their own way back to New Zealand after that.

Rian eyed Amber and Tahi, suddenly doubtful. 'What if there's trouble? Think you can look after her, boy?'

Tahi puffed out his chest. 'Of course I can!' He nodded at his grandfather. 'Koro's been teaching me how to fight. I'm the best at the taiaha and the mere in the village, eh, Koro? For my age group, anyway. And the best shot with a musket.'

'But you don't have a musket,' Rian pointed out.

'Still the best, though.'

Tahi, Kitty knew, was desperate for time alone with Amber. He'd been in heaven for the past

2

fortnight, cloistered aboard the *Katipo* with her. He utterly adored her and had since they'd met when they were both four years old and she'd pushed him over on the sand at Paihia. Admittedly he'd cried then, but after recovering from the indignity, he'd been charmed by her, and had remained charmed ever since. Now, Kitty suspected, his infatuation had increased, fed by lust as he grew older.

They had so much in common. Both orphaned at a young age and both children of Maori mothers and Pakeha fathers. No one knew who Amber's real father was; Tahi's had been Kitty's uncle, the miserable and unlamented Reverend George Kelleher, whose moss-covered bones had lain undiscovered for years in a cave near Kororareka. And while Tahi felt he knew his mother, Wai, through Haunui's frequent stories, Amber knew very little about her birth mother: the poor mad woman had abandoned her, and as far as Amber was concerned, Kitty and Rian were her parents, and had been since they'd adopted her.

Kitty knew from years of personal experience that two weeks with someone on a schooner was hardly time spent alone, so the prospect of an afternoon in Sydney with Amber would be, for Tahi, extremely inviting.

'Haunui, perhaps you'd better go as well,' Rian suggested.

Tahi hid his disappointment well, but Haunui was also aware of the massive, flaming torch his mokopuna carried for Amber. 'Can't. Got business, eh?'

3

'What about Israel?' Amber asked.

Haunui opened his mouth, then shut it again.

'Israel?' Kitty remarked. 'Do you really think he'd be suitable?'

'Why not? He's tall for his age and looks older. Please, Ma. Pa?' Amber added. 'That's *two* chaperones. Surely that's plenty?'

Kitty glanced at Rian. They did get on very well, the three youngsters — they'd been as thick as thieves for the last fortnight — and Israel had matured a lot lately. He was no longer the scrawny smart-mouthed ginger-haired waif Rian had taken on as ship's boy early in 1855. He'd shot up in height, was filling out, had learnt some manners, and it seemed that hard work had knocked a fair bit of the cheek out of him. And much to Kitty's relief, it appeared that the puppy-like devotion Israel had once had for her had waned, though, on occasion, she worried that he'd transferred it to Amber, as he did tend to follow her around the ship like a lost soul. On the other hand, perhaps he was just lonely for company of his own age. In his eyes, the rest of the crew must seem ancient.

'They're young,' she said. 'Go on, let them have a bit of fun.'

Rian stared at her for a moment, sighed, then bellowed at a deafening level, '*Israel, get down here!*'

Israel Mitchell trotted along from the ship's stern, clearly wondering what he'd done wrong.

'You and Tahi are escorting Amber into town to visit Wong Bao,' Rian informed him.

Israel looked delighted.

4

'I expect you back by . . . ' Rian opened his watch and checked the time. 'Five o'clock this afternoon. You are her chaperones, do you understand?'

Behind her father's back Amber rolled her eyes.

'Yes, sir,' Israel replied smartly.

'Do *you* understand?' Rian barked at Tahi.

'Yes, sir!'

'You do not let her out of your sight, you do not allow her to speak to anyone but Bao, and you do *not* go to the pub. Understand?'

Vigorous nodding from Tahi and Israel.

'Good.' Rian snapped his watch shut and slid it back in his pocket. 'If you're not back by five o'clock, rest assured I *will* come looking for you and I will not be happy.' He turned to say something to Amber but she'd already left and was waiting on the wharf.

Israel and Tahi tore off down the gangway after her, giggling and elbowing each other to get to her first.

'Damn children,' Rian muttered, and stomped off towards the cabin. But he was smiling.

*　*　*

'I thought he was never going to let me go,' Amber declared, marching along George Street and tugging at the neck of her dress. She hadn't bothered to put on a chemise, or even a vest, and was now rather wishing she had.

'Who is this Wong Bao?' Israel asked.

'You know, from Ballarat,' Amber said over her shoulder.

5

'He wasn't at Ballarat, remember,' Tahi pointed out.

Amber spied a stall selling baked potatoes. 'I'm starving. You tell him, Tahi, while I get something to eat. Does anyone else want a baked potato?'

'I do. I'll buy yours,' Tahi offered, just as Israel whipped a half crown from his pocket so quickly it looked like a magic trick.

'I'm flush. We just got our wages. I'll get them.'

Amber waved them both away and trotted off.

'I wish she wouldn't be so . . . well, independent,' Tahi grumbled, staring after her. 'Anyway, Amber met Bao and her father, Wong Fu, on the Ballarat goldfields when we were there in '54. Wong Fu's still mining there, I think. Bao and Amber became great friends but something terrible happened to them and Bao had to go and live with her uncle, Wong Kai, in Melbourne.'

'Something terrible like what?'

'That's their story to tell, not mine. Anyway, she and Bao have stayed in touch. Bao's uncle recently moved his headquarters here and Amber wants to visit her. He's quite a powerful figure, Wong Kai.'

'I know. I was with Mrs Farrell in Melbourne when she did business with him,' Israel said, full of importance. 'When the captain had that trouble with Avery Bannerman and Lily Pearce? Mrs Farrell relied on me then.'

Impressed, Tahi asked, 'You've actually met Wong Kai?'

'Um, not face to face, no.'

'So, not at all, then?'

Turning pink, Israel admitted, 'No.'

'Neither have I. Don't think Amber has, either. I've heard you don't want to get on the wrong side of him.'

Amber returned with the potatoes, juggling them gently, as they were steaming hot. 'Ow. Cheese or plain?'

Israel said, 'Cheese, please,' taking a potato from her topped with a drooping slice of melting cheddar.

Tahi took a great bite out of his, then swore, his mouth hanging open to let out the heat, his eyes watering.

Laughing, Amber said, 'That'll teach you.'

They wandered slowly up George Street. Israel and Amber had left their sea legs behind at the wharf, but Tahi was still swaying a little, unaccustomed to automatically adjusting between walking on a rolling deck and terra firma.

Amber, who'd spent three-quarters of her life at sea, suggested, 'Keep your eyes on the horizon. That'll keep you steady.'

They all looked up ahead, but there was no horizon in sight, only the tall sandstone buildings of the city of Sydney and the busy rush of traffic on the street.

'Do you know where your friend lives?' Israel asked.

Amber took a final bite of her potato, fed the rest of it to a mangy-looking dog who'd been following them, and wiped her hands on her skirt. 'Above a furniture shop owned by a Sun

Lee Sing, somewhere down this end of George Street.'

Tahi pointed to a store front across the street. 'That Sun Lee Sing?'

Grinning, Amber said, 'Probably. Shall we go and see?'

They darted through the traffic across the road, avoiding potholes gouged by wagon and carriage wheels, and comet tails of bullock and horse shit, to the safety of the footway on the other side.

The interior of the store was spacious, dimly lit and crammed with well-made European-style furniture. The smell was of cedar and shellac. A Chinese gentleman wearing European clothing stood behind the counter, working on a counting frame and making notes in a ledger.

'Excuse me, are you Mr Sun?' Amber asked.

'Yes.'

'I'm looking for my friend Miss Wong Bao. I think she might live above your shop with her uncle, Mr Wong Kai.'

Mr Sun stared at her for several seconds, then said, 'One moment.'

He stepped through to the rear of the shop, picked up a mallet and struck a gong with a single, smart rap. Although the gong was small, the sound filled the store. Amber poked her fingers in her ears until it died away. Eventually footsteps could be heard descending wooden stairs from above, then another man appeared, this one in a traditional Chinese loose tunic over trousers. His forehead was shaved and he wore the long plaited queue.

'I know you,' Israel said after a prolonged stare. 'You're . . . um.' Clearly, he'd forgotten the man's name.

The man stared impassively back. 'Good afternoon, Master Mitchell.'

Mr Sun said, 'This is So-Yee, Mr Wong's factotum.'

'So-Yee, that's it!' Israel exclaimed.

'Good afternoon,' Amber said. 'I'm Amber Farrell, and this is Huatahi Atuahaere. You've obviously met Israel. I'm a friend of Miss Wong Bao's. I've come to visit her. Would that be possible?'

'You are Mrs Kitty and Captain Rian Farrell's daughter?' So-Yee asked.

Amber nodded.

'Ah, yes. Your mother spoke of you, as does Bao, frequently. I will fetch her. She will be delighted to see you.'

What a starchy, cheerless fellow Amber thought as So-Yee disappeared back upstairs and Mr Sun returned to his counting.

'How do you know him?' Tahi asked Israel.

'He came with us to Geelong when we rescued the captain. And he killed Mr Chen, the double-crossing bugger! You should have seen it — threw a knife straight into his heart!'

Tahi frowned, confused. 'Which one did the double-crossing?'

'Mr Chen. I never liked him.'

Amber snorted. 'You weren't even there, Israel Mitchell.'

'I was. Well, nearly. I was manning the *Katipo*.'

Feet clattered down the stairs and a young

woman burst through from the rear of the shop.

'Amber! And Tahi! It is true!'

'Bao!' Amber darted forward and embraced her friend tightly, then stepped back to take a good look at her. 'You've grown up! You look wonderful!'

Sixteen now, Bao had grown taller and she'd filled out, no longer the pale little waif she'd been on the Ballarat goldfields. There was colour in her cheeks and Amber had felt substance beneath her hands — muscle and strong bones and vitality. Bao's black hair fell like a sheet of satin to her waist, held back on both sides of her face with small ivory hairclips, and she wore a long, embroidered silk tunic with wide sleeves over loose trousers. Her feet had never been bound and were encased in blue silk slippers to match her tunic.

'So do you. Look at your hair!'

Amber did a little spin so that her long, rum-coloured hair flew out around her head. 'I haven't cut it since I saw you last. Ma says I've got split ends. Oh, it's *so* nice to see you. Can you come out?'

'I am not allowed out without a chaperone.'

'Well, you already know Tahi,' Amber said, 'and this is Israel Mitchell. You can borrow them.'

'My uncle says I must have a grown-up chaperone.'

Tahi and Israel bristled slightly, offended.

'But I have an idea,' Bao said. 'Wait here.' She trotted off again, shouting in Cantonese as she thumped up the stairs.

10

'I bet you wish the first floor had its own entrance,' Israel remarked to Mr Sun.

Without looking up from his counting machine, Mr Sun shrugged. 'I lease premise from Mr Wong, not other way round.'

Bao was soon back with So-Yee in tow. 'My uncle says I may come out if So-Yee comes with me.'

Amber glanced at Israel and Tahi, who looked crestfallen, which made her want to laugh. What did they think they were going to do that would be ruined by So-Yee in attendance? And whether So-Yee was happy accompanying four youngsters on an outing was impossible to tell, as his expression remained utterly inscrutable.

'Where are we going?' Bao asked.

'I fancy tea and cake,' Amber said. 'A tea room?'

So off they went south along George Street, looking for somewhere suitable, So-Yee walking not quite with them but never more than six or seven feet away from Bao. On the corner of George and Market streets they entered a tea room and sat at a table, though So-Yee remained outside on the footway. They could see his back through the wavy glass of the window as he stood, looking out across the street.

A woman came from behind the counter and stared down at Bao. 'You'll have to leave,' she said curtly. 'We don't serve your type in here.'

'What do you mean?' Amber demanded.

'Celestials. Either she goes, or you all do.'

'Say that again,' Tahi said, standing quickly.

'I said, we don't serve Chinese,' the woman

11

said again, slowly and deliberately to Bao. 'Filthy buggers.'

Bao also rose, glancing across at the flies crawling over the cakes and buns arrayed on the counter. 'That is all right,' she said loudly. 'I would prefer not to eat food covered with fly dirt.'

Amber glanced outside: So-Yee was now standing in the open doorway, watching warily. 'Come on, let's find somewhere else,' she said.

'Good idea,' Bao agreed. 'I do not think I like the atmosphere here.'

On the street Tahi said to Amber as Bao marched off, her head held high, 'She's changed, hasn't she?'

'I'll say, and it's not just the way she looks. She's definitely not the Bao I knew at Ballarat. *That* Bao wouldn't have said shoo to a goose. This one I think would wring the goose's neck if it dared to honk back.'

They ended up at a Chinese eating house, displeasing Israel as he didn't particularly enjoy Oriental-style food. Grumbling, he ordered a bowl of plain rice and picked at it as the others talked. Once again So-Yee waited outside.

'I am surprised your father let you come ashore with boys as chaperones,' Bao remarked to Amber.

'We're not boys, we're men,' Tahi said cheerfully as he chased a prawn around his bowl with a chopstick.

'You might be, but he is not,' Bao replied, nodding at Israel.

His face burning, Israel said, 'I am so! I'll be

fourteen in a couple of months.'

Bao snorted.

'And I've been a working seaman for *years*.'

'And I'll be a seaman next year when I turn seventeen,' Tahi said, having finally caught his prawn. He shoved it in his mouth whole and chewed. 'And I join the crew of the *Katipo*.'

'As ship's boy?' Bao teased.

'Not likely. As a proper sailor.'

'You have always wanted to be a seaman?' Bao asked.

'I've always wanted . . . ' Tahi glanced at Amber. 'Yes, I have.'

Bao turned to Israel. 'And you? Sailing is your life's dream?'

Israel shrugged. 'Better than being an ostler's boy, which is what I was doing. I like it.'

'What about you?' Amber asked Bao. 'You won't stay with your uncle forever, will you?'

'I will be returning to my father at Ballarat next year.'

'You've been away a long time. You must miss him.'

'I do. He visited as often as he could when we were in Melbourne, but not now that we are in Sydney. He is too busy. But he writes often.'

'You seem so much better than you were,' Amber said. 'Why can't you go home, well, to Ballarat, now?'

'I am being educated.'

'What do you mean?' Israel asked. 'Letters and that?'

Bao neatly scraped up the last of her rice with her chopsticks. 'Yes, something like that.'

13

'What does a girl need with reading and writing?'

'I can read and write,' Amber pointed out. '*And* do sums.'

'You won't need to do that when you're married,' Israel said. 'Either of you.'

'Well, I'm full,' Tahi said, the tablecloth around his bowl scattered with bits of dropped food.

Amber stifled a burp. 'Me, too. Shall we go?'

Bao waved at So-Yee, who came in and paid the bill.

They spent the next few hours poking happily around in various shops, and watching a dog fight and then a cock fight, then headed back down to the wharves, as Amber didn't want to anger her father by returning late. On the way they encountered a flower-seller, whose wares were arranged on the footway in tin pails containing assorted bunches of blooms.

'Look at those lovely roses!' Amber exclaimed.

Tahi pounced. 'Would you like some?'

'I'll get them,' Israel said.

'No, I will,' Tahi insisted, whipping out his purse.

'Look, if it's — ' Amber began, but both boys ignored her.

Israel's face reddened. 'No, *I* will.'

Bao laughed. 'Such competition! Why don't you each buy a bunch, then Amber's cabin will smell like a rose garden.'

Tahi lunged at the startled flower-seller. 'I'll have some of those pink roses, and some of the yellow ones, please.'

14

'How many?' the woman asked.

'Er, I don't know. Ten of each?'

The woman set about gathering the flowers into a bunch, wrapped paper around the stems, then handed them to Tahi. He paid, then presented them to Amber.

'Beautiful flowers for a beautiful girl.'

Amber went scarlet. 'Thank you.'

Israel was already putting in his order. 'I'll have all the rest,' he informed the shocked flower-seller.

'Of me roses?'

Israel nodded.

'There must be six or seven dozen here.'

Amber drew in a breath. 'Israel!'

'That's all right,' he told the woman. 'I can pay.'

And he did, although Amber couldn't carry them, the bunch was so enormous. They said goodbye to Bao and So-Yee.

'You will keep writing?' Bao asked.

'' Course I will. I really miss you.'

'And I miss you.'

They embraced, the scent of roses heavy around them, then Bao and So-Yee walked away up George Street.

★　★　★

Kitty was leaning on the *Katipo*'s gunwale when Amber, Tahi and Israel arrived back. Tahi walked beside Amber who was carrying a bunch of pretty flowers, and bringing up the rear came Israel labouring under a massive heap, many

15

times bigger than his head, of what were perhaps roses.

He did not look happy.

She hoped this didn't mean trouble on the horizon.

Part One

THE STOLEN GIRLS
AUGUST 1863

I search but cannot find her,
awake, asleep, thinking of her,
endlessly, endlessly,
turning, tossing from side to side.

1

Dunedin, 10th August 1863

The wind changed direction, bringing with it a foetid stench of tidal mud, rotting fish and raw sewage.

Leaning on the ship's rail, a sour look creasing his face, Rian remarked, 'Good God. The stink certainly hasn't improved.'

Kitty silently agreed: the town of Dunedin smelt even worse than when they'd last visited two years back. She most certainly wouldn't be wearing her new cream kid boots into the town.

Amber swung down from the rigging, where she, Tahi and Israel were hanging like a trio of monkeys, landing silently in the deck. 'God, what is that terrible stink?'

'Oh, don't be so dramatic,' Kitty said. 'It's coming from the mudflats.'

Aghast, Amber glanced in the direction of Dunedin's swampy waterfront. 'The town? Where we're going ashore?'

Kitty's eyes met Rian's. At the age of twenty-three Amber was still prone to histrionic behaviour (the result of being spoilt, her father insisted), but in truth she was as tough as old boot leather. Kitty believed she was more easily bored than anything else. She was distracted at the moment, too, and a little on edge, and Kitty didn't know why.

'That's right,' Rian said tersely.

'Well, I'm not traipsing around streets that smell like . . . that,' Amber declared. 'I'm staying on the *Katipo*.'

'You are not,' Kitty said. 'Is she, Rian?'

'She can stay aboard if she likes, but it won't do her any good. We'll be tying up at the wharf later and I can't imagine the smell there will be any better. In fact, it'll probably be worse.'

'How long do we have to stay here?' Amber asked.

'Until our business is concluded,' Rian said. 'A week, perhaps. For God's sake, Amber, it's just a smell.'

'I'm not sniffing other people's shit for an entire week.'

'Language, dear,' Kitty admonished, but without conviction. Amber spent so much time with the crew and they all swore like, well, sailors.

Ignoring her, Amber said to the ship's cook, 'Pierre, can I borrow some of your lavender cologne?'

Pierre, sitting quietly on a coil of rope and watching proceedings with amusement, said, 'Ma chérie, for you a whole bottle.'

'I'm not sure that's a good idea, love,' Kitty said, alarmed.

'Thank you.' Amber glared at her father. 'I'm going to bathe in it so I can't smell anything but lavender.' Then she spoilt her fierce demeanour by giggling. 'I'll pong more like a perfumier's than you do, Pierre.'

'Non, but you must use with the light hand,

chérie,' he warned. 'She is the very special cologne.'

Pierre's 'signature' perfume not only acted as a scent but also deterred mosquitoes and was known to bleach delicate fabrics. As Amber flapped a dismissive hand, Kitty silently cursed Pierre: always so indulgent.

'Ship's boat ahoy!' came a voice from the air.

Kitty raised her gaze to the platform midway up the mainmast, where Israel now perched waiting to alert Rian of the return of the first mate, Running Hawk, and bosun, Gideon. Rian opened his spyglass and trained the lens on a pair of figures rowing out from the shore.

His schooner, the *Katipo III*, stood off in the curve of Otago Harbour, awaiting a berth at the crowded wharf, which extended from the foreshore of Dunedin township like a bony finger infested with a case of particularly spiky warts. Hawk and Gideon had gone ashore several hours earlier to enquire of the harbour master when a berth might become available. They'd been warned in Auckland that docking at Dunedin would be a challenge due to the sheer number of ships arriving there daily to disgorge tonne after tonne of goods, not to mention canny business-men intent on hanging their shingles in the rapidly growing town and miners dreaming of striking it lucky in the surrounding goldfields. The message had been similar regarding accommodation, currently at a premium, which is why they'd decided to sleep on the *Katipo* during their stay.

Until 1861, Dunedin had been home to

around two thousand settlers, a small, rambling town prospering from the literal fortunes of Otago's wool lords. Then, in May of that year, Gabriel Read had found gold forty-five miles inland, and now there were close to twenty thousand people living in and around the town, throwing their rubbish out of windows and tents, sluicing shit directly into the streets, and churning up mud everywhere they went. The place was a shambles — thriving, filthy, overgrown, a ferment of mining and commerce, a magnet for ne'er-do-wells, and a haven for merchants and traders of all stripes.

Rian himself was the latter: the *Katipo*'s hold was stuffed full of house bricks, chests, half-chests and boxes of tea, assorted preserved grocery items, fine wheat, oats, pollard, bran and barley (in casks for the sea journey, not sacks), and the components of a Glasgow-made steam-operated saw mill, all of which Rian knew he would easily sell on in a matter of days.

Gideon and Hawk reached the ship some thirty minutes later.

'Will we hoist the boat?' Rian called down.

Hawk nodded and scaled the rope ladder lowered over the side, followed swiftly by Gideon, the black man's huge, muscled bulk severely testing the ladder's strength.

'Well?' Rian asked.

'The harbour master said there will be a berth available at four o'clock this afternoon,' Hawk replied, sweat adding a sheen to his copper skin. 'There is a schooner leaving port. He warned us the berth is small and the *Katipo* might not fit.'

Rian said, 'We'll make her fit. We're not lugging the entire bloody cargo from here to shore on a lighter.'

Kitty wondered yet again what Rian had found in their private box at the Auckland post office — no, even earlier: he'd been out of sorts since they'd stopped in briefly at Paihia. When she'd asked at the time if he had received bad news, he'd replied with a curt no, but had been impossible nevertheless.

'The schooner departing is only a two-master,' Hawk pointed out.

'I said, we'll get her in,' Rian snapped.

Oh dear, Kitty thought, there goes the paintwork on the hull. She watched Rian a moment longer as he hauled on the ropes with Hawk to raise the ship's boat up from the sea over the gunwale to its cradle above the deck, then said to Amber, 'Go and change into a dress, love, and tidy yourself up.'

Amber's hair was tied back with a piece of black ribbon, her shirt (one of Rian's cast-offs) hung out, her trousers (Pierre's) were rolled up to her calves, and her feet were bare.

'Oh, Ma!'

Kitty sighed: they had this little scene almost every time they made port. 'You are not going ashore wearing trousers!'

'You're wearing trousers.'

'Yes, and I'm just about to put on a dress. Go on, off you go.'

Amber made a face then marched off across the deck and disappeared below. From behind, in her scruffy, loose outfit, she looked about twelve years old, but she was a fully matured young woman.

Tahi climbed down the mainmast and landed lightly next to Kitty. 'Is she in one of her moods, Auntie?'

He'd always called her Auntie. It was a term of respect and endearment, though technically they were cousins.

'Not really. She wants to wear her trousers ashore.'

'You're not *letting* her?'

'Of course I'm not. I've told her to go and get changed.'

As Tahi visibly sagged with relief Kitty nearly laughed. Poor Tahi: he was like a puppet whose emotional strings were constantly being pulled — every one of Amber's moods made him twitch.

'Have you seen Simon and your grandfather?' she asked, knowing Tahi would have had a perfect view of everyone on deck from the rigging.

He pointed past the wheelhouse towards the bow. 'Coiling rope.'

Haunui was in his seventies now, and spent much of his time at home at Paihia, but when the *Katipo* had dropped anchor there the other day, he'd decided to venture down to Dunedin with them 'on a whim'. Except Kitty didn't believe that, because Haunui didn't have 'whims' and he'd been avoiding her since he'd come aboard; he obviously knew about whatever had made Rian so tetchy but she wasn't to be told, it seemed.

The almighty *clank* as the ship's boat settled into her cradle jerked Kitty out of her irritation. She decided Simon and Haunui, and Rian's drama, could wait. She'd do better to make sure Amber really was getting changed. She went below decks and knocked on the door of her daughter's cabin.

'Who is it?'

'Ma.'

Amber was lying on her bunk (still dressed in trousers and shirt), comfortably propped against a pile of cushions, reading *Great Expectations* by that Charles Dickens. She was such a smart girl, always reading, always asking questions, always turning things over in her mind. Kitty often wondered — still — what her real mother had been like before she'd lost her sanity.

She sat on the only chair in the cabin. 'How's your new book?'

'I'm really enjoying it,' Amber said, all traces of her bad mood apparently vanished, though Kitty noted the bottle of Pierre's cologne sitting conspicuously on the small bedside table. 'It's about a seven-year-old orphan called Pip — at least I think he's seven — who goes to visit this mad old jilted spinster, Miss Havisham, who wears a tatty wedding dress all the time and lives in a falling-down house and has an adopted daughter called Estella, who Pip falls in love with, which seems a bit odd for a seven-year-old but never mind, and that's as far as I've got.'

'How strange.'

'Well, I only bought it in Auckland.'

'No, I mean the story. It sounds rather, er, peculiar to me.'

Amber shrugged. 'Clearly you can write what you like when your books are as popular as Charles Dickens's are. I think they're great.'

'I suppose.' Kitty gestured at the cologne. 'You really shouldn't bathe in that, you know.'

'Oh, Ma, I only said that. But you can't deny this place does stink.'

'Yes, it does.' Kitty hesitated, then said, 'Amber?'

'Mmm?'

'Your father has a lot to think about at the moment. Be a good girl and try not to irritate him.'

'Is that why he's being so bad-tempered?'

'Mostly.'

'What's bothering him?'

'I don't know.' But I very much wish I did, Kitty thought. 'What's bothering *you*?'

Startled, Amber blinked. 'Me?'

'Yes, you. I always know when something's on your mind.'

Amber's gaze slid away and a faint blush stained her cheeks. 'Nothing's on my mind.'

She was lying and Kitty knew it. God. Her whole family was keeping secrets from her. 'Are you sure?'

'I just said I was, didn't I?' Amber snapped.

'There's no need to be rude. I'm only trying to help.'

'Sorry,' Amber mumbled.

'Why don't you wear your dark bronze dress with the black trim? Your father likes you in that — it might cheer him up.' Also it was less likely to show the dirt when the hem dragged in the mud.

Amber nodded without much enthusiasm.

'But not your good boots,' Kitty added. 'Wear your old ones. The streets could be rather mucky. They were the last time we were here, remember?'

'God.'

★　★　★

Next door, Kitty let herself into the cabin she shared with Rian and sat on the double bed built against the *Katipo*'s gently curving hull. Then she took off her jacket, lay back and stared up at the ceiling, not really seeing the caulked and shellacked planks, simply relishing the silence and enjoying the rocking of the ship. She adored her life at sea but living in such constant close quarters with ten other people, even though she knew them so well, was very trying at times. Every state of mind and every humour was magnified. When things were good, and they frequently were, they were marvellous, but when they were not, the going could be heavy indeed.

Eventually she sat up, letting out a tiny groan as something in her lower back snagged slightly. She was forty-two now, and had wrinkles around her eyes and a scattering of silver in her hair, but she was still trim and fit and climbed the mainmast rigging every day — to make a point to herself, if no one else. She'd been married to the love of her life for twenty-two years, had raised a child, sailed to every major port it was possible for a European ship to enter, killed two people, and run from the law more times than she cared to count. It was a life she couldn't possibly have imagined when she'd been sent out to New Zealand from England as a silly girl of barely nineteen years, and it was a life she wouldn't trade for anything.

She rubbed the small of her back, then bent and unlaced her boots. Big, heavy things they were, but good on deck in cold weather, and it was bitterly cold today. Hardy little Amber went about on deck in bare feet in all but the coldest of temperatures, but she preferred to wear boots, except when she was in the rigging. No one climbed the rigging with boots on. She stood, opened the flies of her trousers and stepped out of them. A ship was no place for long skirts, especially not the ludicrous crinolines women were wearing these days. They didn't fit through narrow doorways, or on companionways, and were positively dangerous when the wind gusted on deck. She and Amber were happy with a couple of petticoats under their skirts when they went ashore.

She took off her shirt and wondered whether she should wash, sniffed her armpits and decided against it, then stood in her drawers and waist-length camisole before the cupboard, debating which of her frocks to wear. Her favourite cold-weather day dress was the steel blue wool, but it needed mending. She chose the magenta wool skirt and bodice ensemble instead, which would go just as well with her dark grey cape. Actually, Amber was right — it would be so much easier to go ashore in trousers.

As she stepped into first the skirt then a

petticoat, an insistent scratching came at the door. On opening it she encountered the ship's cats, Delilah and Samson, staring up at her, accompanied by Pierre, who was carrying a tray bearing a teapot, cup and saucer.

He grinned, revealing several gold teeth. 'Tea, chérie?'

'Lovely. Thanks, Pierre.' Kitty's younger self would have been astonished to think she would one day stand and chat with a man not her husband while half-dressed, but she and Pierre had been firm friends since their first meeting, and she trusted him implicitly, as did Rian. He trusted all his crew. Mind you, he'd trusted Daniel Royce, too . . . No, that was in the past, and Daniel was long gone now.

The cats slipped in, trotted across the cabin, tails held high like flags, and jumped onto the bed, where they settled themselves comfortably. They were descendants of the famous, somewhat wayward and much missed Boadicea (also known as Bodie), who'd died of old age and bad temper some years earlier.

Pierre tut-tutted. 'Your pere will not be happy with you, mes petites.'

Rian didn't like the cats sleeping on his bed.

Kitty rolled her eyes: Pierre cosseted Delilah and Samson terribly. 'Rian is not their father, and well you know it.'

Rian himself was of the opinion that the cats had been sired by a hyena during a port of call at Mozambique, which was a little unkind. But they were excellent ratters, and that was all they had to do to earn their keep aboard the *Katipo*.

29

Pierre set the tea tray on Rian's writing desk just as a deep, grinding noise rumbled through the hull from the region of the bow: the anchor journeying up from the depths. 'The little tugboat must be on her way,' he remarked.

As was usual these days in well-established ports, a tug would tow vessels close enough to the wharf to allow them to be warped directly into their berths. It saved ships from having to tack endlessly towards the shore prior to tying up, especially on low-wind days, and risking collision with other ships, and also permitted the harbour master to keep an eye on exactly who was entering and leaving his jurisdiction. Exactly *what* was entering port, however, was a different story, and the customs and excise officer's problem, not the harbour master's.

'Hadn't you better get changed then?' Kitty asked.

Pierre prided himself on his appearance and never went ashore looking less than dapper, though he was hardly a classically handsome man. He was barely five feet three, and wiry, and his features had been compared rather unkindly to those of a monkey even in his younger days. Despite his size and looks he was popular with the ladies: probably, Kitty thought, due to his immense charm and his French accent, a product of his Louisiana heritage.

'This be true,' Pierre said. He snapped his fingers at the cats. 'Come on, out you come!'

Delilah and Samson eyed him lazily, yawned, and snuggled down even further.

'Oh, leave them, they're all right,' Kitty said.

She'd pick the fur off the comforter later.

As Pierre closed the door behind him she poured herself a cup of tea, moved to Rian's desk and opened the mirror, an ingenious contraption that, when closed, afforded a slope on which to write, but when pushed upright and opened out provided a three-sided mirror. She undid her plait and brushed out her hair, then leaned forwards, frowning. God, were those more white strands at her temples? That was the trouble with dark hair — everything showed. She hurriedly replaited it and wound it into a bun at the back of her head, then chose woollen stockings for under her heavy boots and reached into the cupboard above her dresses for headwear, pausing for a moment as she considered her lovely little London pork pie hat in black straw. But was Dunedin really the place to sport something so chic? And would it make up for not wearing a crinoline? No, and probably no. She chose instead a bonnet in mid-grey taffeta with a wide ribbon to tie beneath her chin — very necessary today due to the wind. She recalled with regret a lovely bonnet she'd once owned that had ended up floating in the harbour between Paihia and Kororareka, then finished her tea, popped a handkerchief, a jar of lip balm, a tin of pastilles and her coin purse into her reticule, and put on her bonnet. Where was Rian? Surely he wasn't going ashore in the awful old coat he wore around the ship?

Leaving the cats to snooze in peace, she went through the mess room and up on deck.

31

2

The port side of the bow hit the wharf with a hell of a thump. Kitty clutched at the ship's rail for balance. The *Katipo III* was a magnificent schooner, and very swift under sail, but she was rather large. She was the *Katipo II*'s replacement, purchased after disaster struck in Java in 1859 during a spice-buying trip, when a massive tidal wave had smashed every vessel anchored in Batavia's harbour. Fortunately, the crew had been inland and well out of harm's way, but Rian's beloved *Katipo II* had been wrecked and they'd been forced, at great expense, to squeeze aboard a ship owned by the Dutch East India Company and sail to London, where Rian had deliberated for a month over the purchase of a replacement. He'd chosen a four-masted schooner, the largest his crew could manage, excluding Kitty and Amber, though they were both perfectly capable of crewing if required. They'd then waited several months more for the new schooner to be refitted and repainted in Rian's favoured colours — a black hull with a red stripe below the gunwale — and she'd been relaunched as the *Katipo III*.

'For Christ's *sake*!' Rian bellowed at crewmen Mick Doyle and Ropata, who were labouring over the capstan and furiously winding in the warping rope. 'Watch what you're doing!'

Mick's arms went up in an aggrieved gesture. 'Not much choice, so there isn't! The gap's too small!'

'God,' Rian muttered darkly. Then, 'Hawk, bring her stern around!'

A moment later the midsection of the *Katipo*'s hull drifted lazily to within several feet of the wharf, the gangway crashed down and Hawk and Israel thundered across it. From the stern, Gideon heaved the end of a massive coil of rope towards them: Hawk caught it, looped it around a bollard and threw the end back. Tahi ran to join Gideon and between them they hauled mightily on the rope to artfully tuck the *Katipo*'s stern into her berth; a deep creaking ensuing as her timbers ground against the wharf.

'*Christ!*' Rian shouted. 'Go easy!'

Oh, shut up, you bad-tempered Irish sod, Kitty thought. How else are they going to get her in? And do you know something, Rian Farrell? You look every one of your fifty-one years when you behave like this.

He was still a very handsome man — at least she thought so — even though broad bands of silver swept back from his temples now, mingling with his dark blond hair, and his beard grew in more salt than pepper when he couldn't be bothered to shave, which was often, and his face was lined from spending much of his time on deck. But his grey eyes were as sharp as ever, and he was as muscled and almost as fit as he'd been as a young man, though he did favour his good leg these days when he was bone tired. Yes, still very handsome, even with a face like a thundercloud.

Ropata and Mick, dripping sweat despite the cold wind, cranked the capstan, and the *Katipo* moved forwards a dozen or so feet, her long bowsprit now extending over the stern of the vessel berthed ahead of them.

'That'll do! Tie her off,' Rian declared, and marched down the gangway, his coat-tails flapping.

Kitty glanced at crewman Simon Bullock standing at her elbow, as if he might know what was vexing Rian, but all she got back was a mystified shrug. She sighed heavily: this could turn out to be a very disagreeable visit.

By the time they had all disembarked — except for Gideon and Israel, who were staying aboard to keep an eye on things — and were gathered on the bustling wharf, Rian had organised a stevedore crew to unload the *Katipo*.

'Where to first?' Kitty asked him, her gaze taking in the town. The last time they'd been here, Dunedin had looked quaint, despite the mud. That had been during the spring, when the weather had been reasonably warm, though wet, and the bright wooden stores and cottages lining the shore and dotting the steep hillsides had looked rather picturesque.

Now she saw a much larger and messier sprawl of shanties, huts and tents spreading up the valleys like mould, with more substantial two- and three-storey brick and wooden buildings lining the streets near the waterfront. And the smell! It certainly wasn't any better on dry land, and Kitty could see why. The shore in both directions, the road at the end of the wharf, and indeed the wharf itself, were lined with great heaps of rotting fish heads and entrails, and, spilling across the same road, she could see thick brown effluvia overflowing from several creeks and emptying into the sea. Most towns and cities stank, she knew, but this was really quite extraordinary. What must it be like at the height of summer? She glanced at Amber, who glared back at her, only her eyes visible above an enormous handkerchief folded across her nose and mouth. Pierre also had his handkerchief out, and so did Simon.

'Mercantile broker,' Rian replied. 'And then somewhere away from this God-awful stench.' He ducked as a low-flying gull almost took his hat off. 'Christ almighty.'

They were everywhere, the gulls, wheeling and squawking and fighting over the fish guts.

'But Pa, you said before it's just a *smell*,' Amber said.

'What did I say to you?' Kitty reminded her, worried Rian would explode yet again, but he'd already set off along the wharf, followed by the crew.

'Well, he did,' Amber grumbled through her handkerchief.

Kitty's eyes started to water: Amber reeked as though she really had bathed in lavender cologne. 'How much of that scent did you put on?'

'Er, actually, I'm starting to think I might have overdone it.'

Kitty pulled the handkerchief away from Amber's mouth and gasped as she saw the vivid red rash on her daughter's nose, cheeks and puffy upper lip. 'You silly girl!'

'What?'

'Your face! It's bright red and swollen.'

'Is it? It does sting a bit.'

'Have you put it anywhere else?'

Amber lowered her collar to reveal an angry red weal on her throat. 'And some on my chest and elbows and wrists. And my belly.'

Kitty spat on the hanky and began to rub beneath Amber's nose. 'God. Here, wipe it off.'

'Ow, Ma! That hurts!'

'Well, you can't leave it there. What if it's corrosive?'

Amber batted her hand away. 'It won't be corrosive! Pierre wears it all the time.'

'Yes, and look at him.'

They looked at each other then giggled.

'Hoi!'

It was Rian, waving at them from across the street.

'Are you coming with us or not?' he called.

'Coming!' Kitty called back. To Amber she said, 'We'll have to find a chemist and get some balm or something. Keep your hanky over your face or people will stare.'

'So what if they do?'

'They'll think I've slapped you, and I will in a minute. This is all your own fault, you know.'

'That's true,' Amber agreed amiably.

Kitty took her arm and gingerly they crossed the road, mud sucking at their boots and Amber swearing as a passing horse and cart splashed filthy puddle water over their skirts. And now the rain, which had been threatening all afternoon, started — fat, freezing drops that sounded like pebbles hitting the rim of Kitty's bonnet.

'What's wrong with your face?' Rian asked.

'Er, we think it might be Pierre's cologne,' Kitty replied.

Pierre looked mortified. 'Mon Dieu! Did you apply without the diluting?'

Amber said, 'Well, no one said to.'

'Non, chérie, she must be diluted! I said the light hand! Especially for the face. Otherwise . . . ' Pierre did a mime of a person exploding.

Rian did lose his temper then. 'For God's sake, Amber. Why can't you behave yourself?'

Tahi took a step forwards but Haunui settled a meaty hand on his shoulder, stopping him.

'She does behave, most of the time,' Kitty snapped. 'Why don't you behave *yourself*? Why are you in such a damned foul mood? What is the *matter* with you?' She'd had enough of his bad temper.

Embarrassed, the crew looked everywhere but at Kitty and Rian. They were accustomed to witnessing the odd disagreement between them (it was difficult not to, living aboard a schooner), but such altercations weren't usually aired on the street of a busy town.

Rian stood with his hands on his hips, head down, his hat obscuring his face. Perhaps, Kitty thought, he's realised he's gone too far, and he damn well has. At last he let out a sigh, took a letter from his pocket and handed it to her. 'I'm sorry, mo ghrá. Really, I am. It's this. Read it.'

So Kitty did, glancing at the signature first — ooh! It was from Wong Fu, their friend from the Ballarat goldfields.

3rd April 1863
My Dear Friend Rian,
I pray that this letter finds you, Kitty and Amber happy and well. I do not know when you next plan to visit Auckland, Sydney or London, so I have sent identical letters to all of your post boxes in the hope that you take delivery of one sooner rather than later. I have also sent a copy to our good friend Haunui in the Bay of Islands, as perhaps he may have some means of contacting you.
 I have very bad news. Bao has been kid-napped.

Kitty sucked in her breath and stared at Rian, appalled. 'Kidnapped!'

'Bloody hell!' Amber said, and Kitty didn't even tell her off.

'Keep reading,' Rian urged gently.

At first I had no idea who had taken her, but I have since discovered it was my brother Kai himself. He has sent her away somewhere — I do not know where — as part of a 'business arrangement' he has made with another tong master. I have been told that Bao is to marry this man. I am devastated and my heart bleeds for my poor daughter.

Rian, it seems that yet again I must ask for your help. If you are in a position to come to Otago, I will forever be in your debt. You will find me at the Chinese Camp at Lawrence near the Tuapeka diggings, south-west of Dunedin.
Your friend,
Wong Fu

Amber, her skin tinged with grey under her welts, said, 'Oh God, poor Bao.'

'Fu's *here*?' Kitty asked.

'It seems so.'

'I thought he was still at Ballarat. Is that why you wanted to bring the cargo south?'

Rian nodded.

Kitty turned to Haunui. 'And you knew about this and didn't *tell me*?'

Haunui tried to look contrite but couldn't quite manage it. 'We didn't want to worry you.'

'*Worry* me!' Kitty exclaimed. 'Have you any idea — '

'Never mind that, Ma,' Amber interrupted. 'We have to go and see Fu. Now. Today.'

'Where is this Lawrence?' Hawk asked.

They all looked at one another, mystified. The last time they'd visited the region, Lawrence might not even have existed.

Rian glanced at the sky: the rain clouds seemed tethered above the town and the light was going. 'We can't go tonight. I need to find buyers for the cargo and get it off the wharf.'

'No, we *have* to go tonight!' Amber insisted.

'We don't,' Rian said calmly. 'Fu wrote that

letter four months ago. One more night isn't going to make much difference. It won't, Amber. We'll go tomorrow and do the thing properly.'

'Can we sell everything today, do you think?' Kitty asked.

Rian made a sweeping gesture with his arm, taking in the busy street. 'I'd be bloody surprised if we couldn't.'

Princes Street was lined with stores and houses, though excavations through a hill had left some buildings stranded atop high banks and accessible only by steep wooden steps. On other stretches of Princes Street the ground was quite flat, and, at intersections, paved with cobbles, albeit currently awash with mud and animal dung. In unpaved areas, however, the street surfaces were pitted with enormous potholes, though there were sections of muddy footpath outside some stores. None of this seemed to deter shoppers, and there were plenty of stores in which to spend money: bakeries, chemists, drapers offering such luxury items as silks, mohairs and crinoline steels, fruiterers, milliners, ironmongers, grocers, general merchants featuring fine and expensive homewares, butchers, saddlers, fishmongers, blacksmiths, timber merchants, gunsmiths, jewellers and watchmakers, ships' chandlers, furniture emporiums, wine merchants, furriers, vast shops specialising in diggers' supplies, haberdashers, *numerous* hotels, dining rooms, tobacconists, liquor stores and newsagents. For those feeling unwell there were doctors, dentists and, if worse came to worst, undertakers. For the commercially minded there were banks, livestock agents, land agents, surveyors, draughtsmen, a notary public, solicitors, architects, a post office, various mercantile brokers, the offices of the Union Steamship Company, Dalgety Rattray and Co, Bright Brothers and Co, and Cobb and Co, general stables, and, for the down and out, pawnbrokers and loan companies.

Kitty saw his point.

So off they went, Rian, Kitty, Amber and Simon, to find a broker who would take most of their cargo off their hands in one fell swoop (after a short detour to a chemist for Amber), while Hawk and Mick headed off in search of a timber mill that might be in need of a steam-operated saw. The rest of the crew were to investigate the quality of Dunedin's various dining rooms in anticipation of the evening's meal.

★ ★ ★

They met up several hours later at the Provincial Hotel on Princes Street. Kitty ignored the curious, and in several cases hostile, stares following them as they made their way through the room. She'd long ago given up worrying about what others thought about her presence in a public bar.

'How did you go?' Rian asked Hawk as he sat down.

'We approached three mills and received two offers,' Hawk replied. 'One was fair and one was an insult.'

'Go back in the morning and close the deal?'

'The proprietor wants to see the goods first.'

'Fair enough,' Rian said. 'Well, we got rid of everything. Turnbull, Robinson and Co are taking the lot.'

Pierre rubbed his hands. 'Très bon. The beer all round, then? And vin de xérès for the ladies?'

'Sherry? To hell with that,' Amber said. 'Make mine a brandy, I'm freezing.' Her upper lip and nose were now glistening *and* red, liberally coated with a smear of witch hazel and mercury ointment.

Rian waved at a barmaid to attract her attention. She meandered across, her crinoline knocking over two stools as she approached, her hair piled into an elaborate sweep of glossy ringlets and her heavy gold jewellery flashing in the lamplight. Kitty stared at her; the girl looked more high-class whore than barmaid.

Rian ordered beer, brandy, whisky for himself, and asked Kitty what she fancied.

'A small brandy, please.'

'Right away.' The girl smiled: two of her teeth were also gold.

As she swayed off, Amber remarked, 'The pay must be good here for barmaids.'

Mick, Hawk and Pierre laughed.

'The mademoiselle she has more than one job, perhaps?' Pierre said, waggling his eyebrows suggestively.

Rian took off his hat and scratched his head. 'We stopped by Cobb and Co and bought tickets for the coach tomorrow morning. Seven seats. Hawk, Pierre and Simon, I want you to come with us. And you, Haunui.'

Kitty knew he'd chosen his crew members

with the most level heads. And Simon had always been good at dealing with people. As a younger man he'd been a missionary at Paihia and Waimate with the Church Missionary Society, but had suffered a crisis of faith and left in 1845 (though he still ministered occasionally, usually only when someone specifically requested pastoral assistance or had died). He had been sailing with Rian ever since.

'How far away is this place?' Haunui asked.

'Lawrence?' Rian leant back as the barmaid arrived with their drinks and plonked them artlessly on the table. 'I don't know. Girl, do you know?'

'Know what?' she asked, a hand on an ample hip.

'How far away Lawrence is.'

'It's about sixty miles south-west of here, near the Tuapeka diggings. Gabriel's Gully? Takes a day by coach.'

God almighty, Kitty thought, a whole day in a coach.

Rian grunted and handed the barmaid a sixpence for her trouble. She looked at it as though she barely recognised such small change, but dropped it down her cleavage nonetheless, gave the table a quick wipe with a reeking rag and left them.to it.

Rian said, 'The coach leaves from the Provincial Hotel. We're to be there by a quarter past five.'

'In the morning? So *early*.' Pierre looked aghast.

'You're used to it,' Mick said.

'But we are ashore. I am on the shore leave.'

'No you're not, so go easy on the beer tonight,' Rian warned. 'Apparently the coach won't wait for stragglers. So, where are we eating?'

Ropata said, 'The City Buffet. Just opened and advertising a chef who's supposed to be an 'experienced Parisian Artiste'.'

'Sounds all right,' Rian said, though Pierre snorted disbelievingly and declared he'd rather eat at a Chinese restaurant.

The City Buffet was definitely all right, and certainly no mere ordinary. Kitty had the oysters aux natural and pheasant cutlets vol-au-vent with pate de fois gras, Rian chose the pheasant followed by roast sirloin of beef with horseradish sauce, and Amber had hare julienne soup and roast turkey farcie aux truffe. Pierre had four courses: eels en matelote, salmi of whole duck, roast hare and game sauce, and charlotte à la Russe, though he didn't finish any of it and insisted that the eels tasted muddy, the duck was overdone, the game sauce was too gamey, and the cream in the charlotte was off. No one else complained about their meals. Rian laughed and called him a jealous old harpy, but Kitty patted his hand and assured him that his cooking was just as good, which it almost was.

After dinner they went upstairs to the smoking and coffee lounge, though Mick left, announcing his intention to visit the 'Devil's Half Acre', a squalid area of town notorious for its saloons and whores. After a moment Simon slipped out after him, and though they were all aware it wouldn't be a woman whose company he was seeking, no one said anything. They never did.

★   ★   ★

Later that night aboard the *Katipo*, Kitty snuggled into Rian's chest. She could barely keep her eyes open and knew they had to be up very early in the morning, but she had something she needed to say.

'You could have told me, you know.'

'Told you what?'

Astounded, she pulled back and glanced up at his face. He looked relaxed, his eyes closed, which was good: he wouldn't see her hand coming if she chose to slap him.

'About Fu and Bao! Why didn't you?'

'I told you, I didn't want to worry you.'

Kitty sat up. 'No, you just behaved like a bear with a sore head and made everyone's lives a misery.'

'Possibly.'

No apology, Kitty noted.

'But you've got other things to worry about,' Rian said.

Did she? 'Have I? What?'

Rian opened an eye. 'I don't know. Haven't you?'

'Not really.'

Both eyes now. 'And you'd be finding out anyway. I just thought the less time you had to fret about it, the better. Amber, too. Look at how upset she is now she knows.'

'*Stop* trying to look after us!' Kitty exploded.

45

He was always doing this, treating both of them as though they weren't even capable of tying their own boot laces.

Rian looked at her, truly taken aback. 'Stop looking after you? But I can't.'

'We're grown women, you know, Amber and I.'

'I do know that.'

'Good.'

Silence, save for the creaking of the *Katipo*'s timbers, then loud voices and a burst of raucous laughter outside as a party made its way along the wharf to its moored ship.

'Am I forgiven?' Rian asked eventually.

'I suppose.'

He pulled her close and arranged the bedclothes cosily over them. 'So, do you feel better now, knowing that Bao's been abducted?'

No, you swine, I don't. 'Well, hardly.'

'See, I told you you'd worry.'

'But at least I know now what was upsetting *you*,' Kitty retorted. 'God, poor Fu. Poor *Bao*. Imagine not only being kidnapped by your own uncle of all people, but then discovering you're to marry someone you've never set eyes on before.'

'At some point she would probably have had to marry someone she'd never met,' Rian said. 'I believe that's how the Chinese do these things.'

'I know, but at least Fu would have chosen someone decent for her.'

Rian stroked Kitty's hair thoughtfully. 'You know, I'm more than happy to meet with Fu, but I'm not sure how we can help him.'

'Perhaps he just wants advice.'

'Perhaps, but I can't understand why he hasn't gone after Bao himself.'

'But if he has a claim here, wouldn't he lose it if he abandoned it? You know what it was like at Ballarat, especially for the Chinese.'

Lifting Kitty's legs, Rian settled them across his lap so she was nestled over him like a question mark. 'I can't see Fu putting gold ahead of Bao, though, can you? She's more important to him than anything.'

'No, I can't.'

'So why hasn't he?'

But Kitty couldn't answer, because she really didn't know.

★   ★   ★

The Cobb and Co coach clearly did not wait for stragglers. They had been told the interior was fully booked, but there was an empty seat when they departed at exactly half past five. The weather was foul — wet, the rain accompanied by an icy wind, and the sun not yet risen. According to the driver — a chatty, personable man who introduced himself as Ned Devine — the journey would take around nine hours, plus stops for a meal and to water and change the horses.

The interior bench seats accommodated nine, as Kitty discovered when she climbed inside — four at the front facing five at the back. She chose a rear seat as she didn't fancy travelling the whole sixty miles backwards. Rian, Amber,

47

Pierre and Hawk sat next to her, leaving Simon and Haunui to sit opposite beside the only traveller not in their party, an older gentleman who piled several bags in the empty space next to him. There were already two men occupying the box seats outside beside the driver, which apparently cost more than interior seats and were highly favoured. (Surely not on a day like this, she thought.) It appeared that no one, however, had bought a seat on the roof.

Amber's face was looking better, though marred by her expression, which was sour at having to leave a warm bunk on the *Katipo* so early. She was desperately upset about Bao, too, and not bothering to conceal it.

Kitty was sick with worry herself, for both Bao and for Fu. For Bao to be abducted by her own uncle . . . On the other hand, while Wong Kai had once done Kitty a very big favour, she knew how ruthless he could be, and despite her distress and dismay she wasn't entirely surprised to hear what he'd done.

The coach started off with a lurch, all six horses leaning into the harnesses. Kitty's head hit the wall behind her.

'And we're off!' announced the nameless gentleman cheerfully.

Kitty gave him a watery smile that, embarrassingly, turned into a yawn so enormous she thought her face might turn inside out. 'I do beg your pardon,' she murmured from behind her glove.

'You have my sympathies, madam,' he said. 'It's certainly an evil morning for rising early.

Please, allow me to introduce myself. Lawson Trippe, Esquire, at your service.' He half-rose from his seat and offered his hand all round. When he came to Haunui in the corner he exclaimed heartily, 'Ah, one of our dusky native friends!'

Haunui winked at him and gave his hand an extra hard squeeze.

Lawson Trippe, Esquire, sat down again, rubbing his fingers on his trousers. He was a big man with a gut, bushy grey mutton chops and a florid face. His clothes were very well cut, his boots shone, and he wore a heavy gold watch chain with a fob containing a large, glittering red stone. A ruby, Kitty wondered, or glass?

'Travelling to the diggings on business, Mr Trippe?' Simon asked politely.

'I do have some commercial interests at the Tuapeka, yes, though more at the Dunstan. That's where the money is these days. Yourselves?'

'We're visiting a friend,' Simon replied.

'Is that so? A lot of folk have moved on from Gabriel's Gully. I do hope your friend isn't one of them. You might find your journey's been wasted.'

Rian stretched out his legs, sliding his boots under the seat opposite. 'I don't think so. Our friend is settled at the camp near Lawrence.'

'Oh. Oh dear.' Mr Trippe looked crestfallen. 'I think you might have been put wrong, I'm afraid. I believe that's the Chinese camp. You certainly don't want to go *there*.'

Kitty held her breath.

'Oh, I think we do,' Rian said. 'Our friend *is* Chinese.'

49

'Really?' Mr Trippe stared. 'Good God. Well, for heaven's sake, don't take your womenfolk. I've heard some most alarming stories about, well, I won't raise the subject in mixed company, but you men will understand the matter to which I'm alluding. Pardon me, ladies.'

'Do you actually know any Chinese people, Mr Tripe?' Rian asked.

'Trippe. No, not as such, but — '

'Then I suggest you refrain from repeating what is essentially gossip.'

Mr Trippe opened his mouth, then closed it again.

No one said anything for the next twenty minutes. The sun still hadn't risen and it was freezing inside the coach. The door had a glass window, but the window openings on either side and in the opposite wall weren't glazed; their leather curtains were down to keep out the rain, but sadly admitted the cold. Kitty entertained herself by watching her warm breath make little clouds of vapour in the air.

Eventually, Mr Trippe cleared his throat. 'I do apologise for my earlier comment.'

Rian nodded. 'Accepted, thank you.'

Cheering up visibly, Mr Trippe said, 'Did you know that these coaches are American made? Have you travelled with Cobb and Co before?'

Poor old buffoon, Kitty thought. Clearly he can't bear the thought of going for nine hours without talking to anyone.

'We went by coach from Melbourne to Ballarat once,' she said, 'but I don't think it was a Cobb and Co. Was it?' she asked Rian.

'It was, actually.'

'This particular model is the Concord,' Mr Trippe blathered on, 'named by the man who invented it, JS Abbott, who hailed from Concord, New Hampshire. Fascinatingly, it has a most unique suspension system, the coach body sitting on eight leather straps supported by curved iron jacks, which is why the Concord is sometimes referred to as the Jack coach.'

'That *is* interesting,' Simon said politely.

'They say the suspension system provides the most comfortable mode of transport across land known to man, though in my opinion it does rock somewhat.'

At that moment the coach hit a pothole and they were almost hurled off their seats. Amber started to laugh and so did Haunui, though Kitty didn't think any of them would be quite so amused after they'd spent an entire day being similarly thrown about.

Rian retrieved his hat from the floor. 'You were saying?'

'Yes, well, I do feel the roads to the goldfields *could* be maintained with a little more vigour,' Mr Trippe replied.

'We haven't even left Dunedin yet.'

Mr Trippe tweaked the curtain over his window and peered out into the slowly encroaching dawn. 'It appears not.'

'Anyone for the cards?' Pierre asked, producing a pack from his pocket.

'I say, what did you have in mind?' Mr Trippe looked thrilled.

'Vingt-et-un, euchre, whist? Poker?'

Oh, not poker, you poor fool. Pierre, Hawk

and Amber were all extremely crafty players and Kitty knew he wouldn't stand a chance. Unless he was even more crafty, or an accomplished cheat.

Rubbing his hands together, Mr Trippe declared happily, 'I think poker might be just the thing, don't you?'

Oh dear.

Rian shook his head in rueful anticipation, said, 'Wake me up when we stop for food,' settled his hat over his face and slouched even lower in his seat.

By ten o'clock Mr Trippe had lost eleven pounds and signed a promissory note for thirteen more, which they all knew he would never pay because they wouldn't see him again, but no one minded. Simon had just suggested — very tactfully — that they change to some other game that didn't involve gambling for money when the driver stopped to water the horses. Everyone got out to stretch their legs and use the facilities behind the coaching inn, then they were off again along a road that only deteriorated the farther they travelled from Dunedin. The landscape was rugged but it wasn't bereft of civilisation. There were plenty of amenities on the roadside catering to miners on their way to and from the diggings on the Tuapeka and the Dunstan: coaching inns, hotels, stables and, most predominantly, grog shops.

Their next stop was at the Taieri River, where the horses were unharnessed from the coach's shafts and ferried across the water, followed by the coach itself, then its occupants, who froze in the icy wind tearing down the valley from the snow-covered mountain ranges. When they reached Waihola, overlooking the lake of the same name, half an hour later, they stopped for a hot meal (Pierre paid for Mr Trippe's, as he was now out of funds) and to change horses, then carried on to Milton before turning inland.

By that time Kitty was thoroughly sick of JS Abbott's marvellous Concord. The damned thing rocked and swayed like a ship in high seas, except nowhere near as comfortably or soothingly, and despite its unique suspension system it bounced mightily when it hit potholes, ruts and rocks, and she'd hit her head on the ceiling twice now. She felt as though she'd ridden for a week on horseback, and they still had over three hours to go. Rian, however, had managed to sleep almost the whole way. Or he had at least pretended to sleep, possibly so he wouldn't have to talk to Lawson Trippe, who had just not shut up. Neither had Amber or Pierre, both bored silly once they'd grown tired of playing cards. Simon had retreated into his book and Hawk hadn't said much either, though that wasn't out of character. Haunui dozed but every time the coach hit a bump his head whacked against the wall and he woke with a flailing jolt, frightening the life out of Mr Trippe.

But at least the landscape was worth looking at. They'd all decided they'd rather be cold than suffocate so they'd fastened back the blinds to enjoy the splendid scenery. The sky, however, was a dull silver colour and looked ominously heavy, suggesting that snow wasn't far away.

They passed through Waitahuna just before three o'clock in the afternoon, and an hour and a half later arrived at Lawrence, exactly on time.

The town was small, built entirely of wood like most other gold towns — and smelt strongly of pigs.

'Don't you start,' Kitty warned Amber.

'Will you take us out to the Chinese Camp?' Rian asked Ned Devine after they'd farewelled Lawson Trippe, Esquire.

Ned scratched the back of his neck. 'Can't, sorry. I've to ready the coach for the return trip. I've a schedule to keep to, you know.'

'Damn. How far away is it?'

'Half a mile or so.'

Kitty eyed the pile of bags Hawk had just retrieved from the roof of the coach: she didn't fancy hauling those half a mile.

Rian asked, 'Do you know where we can hire a cart?'

'I don't, but someone in the pub's bound to,' Ned replied, pointing across the street to a hotel called the Oasis.

So off they trooped to the pub, where Rian found a man willing to transport them to the Chinese Camp in his wagon for five shillings. By the time they came back out of the Oasis it was snowing lightly, and growing dark.

'God,' Kitty muttered, pulling the hood on her cape over her head. What a thoroughly unpleasant day it had been all round. Her bum and back hurt from being bounced about in the coach, and now they were to be frozen to death crouching in somebody's delivery wagon. She glanced at Simon — hat jammed on, hands shoved deep in his pockets and looking as miserable as she felt — and caught his eye and they burst out laughing. But it wasn't funny, really, and if it hadn't been Wong Fu who needed their help they would probably have stayed the night at the Oasis. Or perhaps not come at all.

She and Amber stood about stamping their feet while the wagon owner, whose name was Henry Turner, went off to harness up his horses, then, when he returned, watched as the men loaded the bags, and climbed into the wagon themselves.

'I'm starving,' Amber said.

Kitty was, too. 'I'm sure Fu will feed us.'

Mr Turner flicked the reins and the wagon set off. Within a minute those sitting in the back, which was everyone except Rian and Hawk, perched beside Mr Turner on the high front seat, discovered that the wagon's suspension was the same as that of the Cobb and Co's 'unique' Concord, except that the side boards of the wagon were only a foot high.

'For God's *sake*,' Kitty muttered, hanging on with a vice-like grip as she was tossed this way and that.

'All right back there?' Mr Turner called over his shoulder.

'Good, eh,' Haunui shouted as he slid off his bag and hit his head on the back of the driver's seat.

The road out to the camp was atrocious, the short trip not aided by the fact that the wagon's pair of carriage lamps illuminated barely more than ten feet ahead, snow swirling down through the weak beams of yellow light. The horses, however, were steadfast, plodding onwards and never losing their footing on the rough and slippery surface.

'You have a good team there,' Hawk remarked.

'Haven't let me down yet,' Mr Turner replied, shrugging deeper into his sheepskin coat. 'Camp should be coming up in a minute.'

And so it did, a cluster of low buildings shrouded in white divided by a rough street. Henry Turner brought the wagon to a halt.

'Will you wait?' Rian asked him. 'I want to make sure our friend's here before you leave.'

Mr Turner nodded and dug a pipe and a silver match safe out of his pocket.

'Stay here,' Rian said to everyone else.

Sore, and with a hideous earache from the cold, and profoundly grumpy, Kitty thought angrily, Don't you order me around as though I'm a lackey, but in truth she was frozen almost stiff and wasn't sure she could move anyway.

Rian disappeared into the snow-dusted camp, reappearing again ten minutes later. 'He's here. Down you hop.'

With much grunting and groaning everyone disembarked, farewelled Henry Turner after arranging with him to pick them up the following day, and walked into the little village. Wong Fu appeared halfway down the empty street, a slight yet surprisingly tall figure wrapped in a heavy coat, the snow whipping around him and lending him the insubstantial appearance of a ghost. Quickly he beckoned them in through

56

the doorway of a small house. They followed, all grateful to at last be out of the snow and wind.

Inside, the room was lit by several lamps, and a hearty fire burned in a brick hearth flanked by a pair of wooden chairs. But Kitty ignored the fire, too shocked by the sight of Fu, who was wiping melted snow from his shaved forehead with a cloth and wringing out his long queue.

He looked sick and as though he'd aged twenty-five years since their last meeting, not nine. She believed he was somewhere in his forties now, younger than Rian anyway, but he could easily pass for sixty. She shot a look at Rian, who raised a concerned eyebrow back, then she stepped forwards and embraced Fu tightly.

'You poor man. We've been so worried since we got your letter. Have you heard anything about Bao?'

'I have heard nothing,' Fu said bleakly. 'Thank you so much for coming here, all of you. Amber, my child, you have grown so, just like my Bao.'

He looked, then, as though he might burst into tears, so Kitty indicated the fire and said, 'Why don't you sit down and warm your feet? They must be like blocks of ice.'

All Fu wore on his feet was a pair of embroidered slippers, now soaking wet. He took a single step towards the fire, then stopped. 'Forgive me, please. You must think me very rude. Did you eat at Lawrence? Can I offer you refreshment? You will of course stay at our village tonight.'

'Er . . . ' Rian began.

57

'It is no trouble and we have plenty of food. Excuse me while I make the arrangements.' Fu opened the door and shuffled out into the cold.

'What's happened to him?' Haunui asked, clearly horrified.

'He looks so *old*,' Amber said. 'He must be so upset about Bao.'

Rian said slowly, 'I suspect he might actually be ill.'

They all stared at one another: this was news no one had expected.

'Why don't you ask him?' Kitty said.

'He'll tell us if he wants us to know.'

Fu returned. 'A meal will be ready in half an hour. We shall dine in my house tonight, rather than in the eating hall. In the meantime, shall we talk?' He indicated a table on one side of the room.

They seated themselves, grumbling about thawing feet and hands, while Fu fussed about moving a kerosene lamp onto the table and setting out tumblers and a bottle of brandy.

Then he sat down himself. 'I will start the story at the most appropriate place, which is, of course, at the beginning.

'You know that after what happened at Ballarat I sent Bao to stay with my brother, Kai. She remained with him in Melbourne and then Sydney for three years, then returned to me when she was seventeen, much recovered. I could have sent her home to Kwangtung Province, but there is a reason I did not, which I shall come to later. I believe she suffered a deep sickness of the spirit after the incident at

Ballarat, exacerbated by the enmity we suffered at the hands of the white miners at Sovereign Hill.' Fu sighed. 'I also believe she experienced some guilt after the deaths of Tuttle and Searle.'

'Why?' Rian asked. 'She wasn't responsible for that.'

'No, you are right,' Fu said shortly. 'But as I say, she was much recovered when she returned to me. My brother is an ambitious, sometimes cruel and often ruthless man, but he does care for Bao. Whatever he did for her was to her benefit. We stayed on at Ballarat until last year, when we were alerted to an invitation in a Melbourne newspaper inviting Chinese nationals to come to Otago. We were wary about this, as we did not want to find the same unpleasant situation awaiting us in Otago that we were experiencing in Victoria, so we asked for certain conditions to be met. We received a written guarantee, the invitation was issued again, and we came. Our job, we discovered on arrival, was to pick over old diggings, as we did in Victoria, and we have been successful. The white miners have moved on from the Tuapeka to diggings farther up in the high country, believing that the gold here has been depleted, but we are still finding plenty.'

'And *is* the situation here as unpleasant as it was in Victoria?' Rian asked, pouring himself a second brandy.

'So far, less so, although the Lawrence Town Council did pass a bylaw prohibiting us from living and doing business in the town, though a handful of us do have businesses there. They gave us this block of swampy land beside the creek to live on instead. In the winter it freezes to icy mud and in the summer it seethes with mosquitoes.' Fu sighed again, but whether it was from frustration, sadness or fatigue it was hard to know. 'But to return to the story of Bao, early in January I received a letter from Kai asking me to send Bao to him in Sydney for a holiday. She did not want to go, so I wrote back to him at the end of that month and told him of her decision. I heard nothing back from him. One day four weeks later, while we were all out at the diggings, she went down to the creek, which is not far from here, to launder clothes, and did not come back. We searched and searched, and went into the town to ask if she had been seen there, and sought the assistance of our Chinese constable-interpreter, and placed advertisements in the newspapers and offered rewards, but could not find her. I, of course, feared the worst. She has grown into a very beautiful and gracious young woman. I thought she had been assaulted and killed, and her body hidden.' He fell silent, rubbing at a spot of spilled brandy on the table top. 'I cursed myself for bringing her here.'

Kitty knew Bao hadn't been assaulted and killed, but she felt his pain all the same. She laid a hand over his. 'You shouldn't blame yourself. You're not responsible for what other people choose to do.'

'I *am* responsible for my daughter's welfare and safety, and I have failed her. Twice.'

'Don't torture yourself, man,' Rian said gruffly. 'How did you find out who took her?'

60

'Late in March I received a letter informing me that she had been kidnapped by Kai's men, taken briefly to Sydney, then spirited away somewhere to participate in a marriage arranged by Kai. I am assuming to China, but China is a very big place.'

'Who wrote this letter?' Pierre asked. 'And it came from where?'

'Sydney, I expect, and it was not signed. Perhaps it was penned by an enemy of Kai's, hoping to cause trouble between us.'

Rian's eyebrows went up.

'How do you know the letter is not a hoax?' Hawk asked.

'Whoever wrote it must have seen Bao at some point. He, or she, describes the earrings Bao was wearing when she disappeared. Pearl and jade drops. I gave them to her when she turned nineteen.'

'Perhaps they were concerned for Bao, and wanted to tell you what had happened to her,' Simon said. 'Not everyone's out to cause mischief.'

'That is true,' Fu agreed.

'But why would Kai do such a thing?' Amber blurted. 'What a . . . *pig*. He's her uncle. He's supposed to look out for her, not kidnap her and marry her off just to settle some business deal.'

'I'm afraid, love, he can do what he likes,' Rian said. Turning to Fu, he asked, 'Can't he? Is he still the headman of your tong?'

At that moment the door opened, letting in a blast of cold air, and three men entered carrying trays of food, setting them on the table along with bowls and chopsticks. Presented were pork and fresh vegetables, duck with cress, some sort of preserved shellfish with pickled vegetables, and plain rice, and Kitty's stomach growled.

Fu waited until the men had gone, urged everyone to help themselves, placed a small piece of duck in his own bowl, and sat gazing down at it.

Finally, he said, 'Kai is not the master of my family's tong. He never was.'

Kitty stared at him, and so did everyone else. She was sure he'd told them that Kai was head of the Wong family association. Apparently it was usually someone of considerable social standing and wealth, and Wong Kai was certainly that. He'd controlled his own little empire in Melbourne, and no doubt was doing exactly the same in Sydney, probably on an even grander scale.

'Then who the hell is?' Rian asked.

'In our family the master is known as the Cloud Leopard,' Fu replied. 'And that is me. I am the Cloud Leopard.'

Astonished, Kitty put down her chopsticks. She glanced at Rian, who looked equally startled. Fu, the headman of his family's tong? But he was so gentle, and gracious, and, well, unassuming. On the other hand, they both knew he'd been responsible for Josiah Searle and Albert Tuttle burning to death after they'd abducted Amber and Bao at Ballarat, so he wasn't *quite* as benign as he seemed. And there was the fact that he led his men with such easy authority and they, in turn, seemed to have followed him without hesitation.

'No offence intended, Fu,' Rian said, 'but I

understood that the master is traditionally a man of wealth.'

'Our association has wealth,' Fu replied. 'We have gold. But we send as much home to our families as we can.' He hesitated, then said, 'And that is part of the problem. Please, eat before the food grows cold.'

While they struggled with their chopsticks, Fu picked at his piece of duck and talked on.

'Kai has always been bitter because our father, Chi-Ping, passed the office of Cloud Leopard to me rather than him. Chi-Ping has never really trusted Kai, believing he has a propensity for corruption that is not in the best interests of the family.'

Well, that's certainly true, Kitty thought, chasing a piece of pork around her bowl with a chopstick.

'Where is your father these days?' Rian asked.

'My grandfather, Kwok-Po, died in Ballarat several years ago, and my father accompanied his remains home to Kwangtung Province and has not returned. Over the past few years Kai has been agitating for change in the family, believing he should assume the role of master. He considers me too parsimonious and says I should pay our men here and in Ballarat more and send less gold back to the family in China. He also believes I should purchase land here and in New South Wales and Victoria. But we do not belong here. We are not wanted and we will not be staying. Once the gold has been mined we will return home.' Fu pushed his bowl away. 'Unfortunately, some of my men have been tempted by

Kai's exhortations for higher pay and, I suspect, are no longer loyal to me.'

'But what's this got to do with Bao?' Kitty asked.

'You'll hand over the reins if he returns her,' Rian said. 'That's it, isn't it?'

Fu shook his head. 'No, it is more complicated than that. I am unwell. In fact, I am dying. And when I do, Bao will become the next Cloud Leopard.'

Kitty was speechless, at both Fu's bad news and his revelation about Bao. Eventually she managed to say, 'Oh, Fu, I'm so sorry. Are you sure? Have you seen a doctor?'

'I have not consulted a European doctor, but I do not need to. I have a cancer of the stomach. I have been taking Chinese medicines and treatments but they are no longer effective.'

'It wouldn't do any harm to see a European doctor, surely?' Rian asked.

'It would not cause harm, but it would be a waste of time. What could a white man's doctor do for me that a Chinese doctor cannot?'

'Very little,' Hawk agreed, who wasn't keen on European medical practitioners himself.

'But . . . Bao?' Amber said. 'A tong master? How can she be the next Cloud Leopard?'

'I don't understand either,' Kitty said. 'Has Kai always known she's next in line after you?'

Fu said, 'Yes. She was chosen when she was born and named accordingly. Her full name is Wong Bao Wan, Bao Wan meaning Cloud Leopard.'

'Yet you said he looked after her very well

when she went to live with him.' Kitty frowned. 'Why would he do that if he knew he'd be overlooked again in favour of her? You'd think, with Kai being the way. he is, he'd do his best to stop her becoming the next master.'

Fu said, 'Kai has always been fond of Bao, and I believe he would not deliberately hurt her.' He shrugged his thin shoulders. 'I expect that nine years ago, when she went to stay with him, he assumed that he would have deposed me by now. But of course he could not tell Bao that, so was compelled to school her in the arts in which a master must be proficient. He was always in a better position to offer her such knowledge.' Fu hung his head. 'I have been remiss. I am afraid I have dedicated too much of my own time and energy to searching for gold to attend to the needs and education of my own daughter.'

Amber said, 'What arts?'

'A high level of pecuniary acumen to manage the family's finances, although Bao has always been very clever with numbers and is a fine scribe and linguist. She speaks Cantonese and English, of course, some of my countrymen's other dialects and now also quite passable Hindi, Bangla and French. She has also been schooled in politics at the family, village and provincial levels, and also the martial arts, at which every master must be adept.'

'You mean *fighting*?' Kitty was astounded. She'd seen exhibitions in Macau and in Shanghai, both bare-handed and involving weapons, and could not imagine Bao having anything remotely to do with either.

'Yes,' Fu said. 'I myself was considered an expert with the staff in my younger days.'

They all stared at him, a skinny, pale, extremely ill-looking man who could barely wield his chopsticks, never mind a fighting staff.

Fu went on. 'And Kai *will* prevent Bao from becoming the next Cloud Leopard if he marries her off. When I die the wealth of the family, currently held in my name as master, will convert to Bao's name for her to safeguard and manage. Providing, that is, that she does not marry, and she both understands and has agreed to this. Should she marry another tong master, however, our family's wealth will automatically be transferred to him and she will lose her status as head of our family, although you can be sure that Kai will have arranged with this man that he himself retain a significant proportion of our family's assets. My wife and I have no other children, so the office of Cloud Leopard will finally become Kai's, and Bao will be left with nothing at all.'

Sitting silently now, Fu closed his papery eyelids. He was so thin that the flickering lamplight rendered his face a death's head.

'Are you sure of all this?' Rian asked.

Wearily, Fu opened his eyes again. 'Not entirely, but I do know my brother. And his ambitions.' Then he said, 'Family is at the heart of everything in Chinese life, but I am dying, I am too weak to travel and I do not know how much time I have. I no longer care much about digging for gold, or wealth, or even my responsibilities as a master. My foremost priority now is my daughter. I want her back.' He paused, then, gripping his hands together so tightly that his knuckles showed white through the skin, he said, 'Rian, I am asking you to find her.'

'Of course we will,' Amber said immediately. 'Pa? Won't we?'

Kitty crossed her fingers. Rian glanced at his men. Hawk, his right-hand man, stared back, the tiniest lift of an eyebrow indicating his approval.

Pierre, garrulous as usual, exclaimed, 'Oui, of course we do it!' He grabbed his chopsticks, dug them into a bowl of rice and theatrically flicked a scattering of grains into the air. 'We sail to China, rescue the mademoiselle and be back before the dinner it gets cold!'

Rolling his eyes, Rian looked at Simon.

Simon gave a nod. 'I think we should.'

'Haunui?' Rian asked.

'Why not? One last adventure for me, eh?'

'Mmm.' Rian tapped his teeth with a chopstick. 'It'll be dangerous, won't it?' he asked Fu.

Fu agreed that it would.

'Kitty, what do you think?'

'Well, of *course* we should go!'

Bursting into tears, Fu covered his face with his hands.

3

The *Katipo* left New Zealand waters three days later, sailing around the southern tip of Stewart Island and heading nor'west up and, across the cold and turbulent reaches of the lower Tasman Sea. The temperature climbed marginally as the mysterious polar wastes of the Antarctic receded but the seas never calmed, churning in the grip of fierce winter gales. Everyone huddled inside layers of clothing and oilskins but it was nothing new: they'd sailed vicious, frigid seas countless times. Pierre served thick, hot stews three times a day to warm their bellies and they washed their meals down with scalding tea laced with brandy.

Amber and Tahi had found their own way to keep warm. A week out from New Zealand, one evening just past midnight, Amber lay in her bunk so galvanised by anticipation she almost couldn't breathe.

When the door to her cabin opened — slowly, slowly, so it wouldn't give out its usual tell-tale squeak — and Tahi crept in, she sat up and threw the bedclothes back for him. He tip-toed over to her bunk, avoiding the deck planks he knew creaked, and slid in beside her. They wriggled down to lie beneath the covers and he grabbed her.

She giggled. 'Your feet are *frozen*!'

'Mmm, you're not. You're nice and warm.' He

kissed her then tugged at her nightdress. 'You should take this off.'

'Well, you should take *your* clothes off.'

While he divested himself of his shirt and trousers she pulled her nightdress over her head and flung it on the floor, then squealed as her warm bare skin pressed against his muscled but goose-pimpled chest.

Tahi put his fingers to her lips, gently pressing them closed. 'Someone will hear us.'

'No, they won't.' The ship creaked and groaned so loudly as she deftly negotiated the Tasman's mighty swells, Amber expected they could bellow both verses of 'Alice, Where Art Thou' and no one would hear.

She slid her hand down Tahi's firm belly: he was eager for her already, but then he always was. This would be the seventh delicious time they'd managed to be together. She'd been counting because she loved it. She loved what they did, and she loved him.

She half-rolled onto him, smothering his handsome face with kisses, shivering as she felt his cool hands slide over her buttocks.

And then the door flew open — swiftly and *very* squeakily this time.

'What the *bloody* hell's going on in here?'

Amber turned so quickly she cricked her neck. 'Pa!'

Her father raised his lantern and Amber saw instantly how utterly furious he was. 'Get out of my daughter's bed,' he said so quietly that the words were almost inaudible.

Tahi scrambled out of the bunk, dragging the

top cover with him, and stood between Rian and Amber.

Rian's jaw worked visibly.

'Go, love,' said Amber. 'He's my father, not yours. Leave it to me.'

Tahi felt behind him and she gave him her hand to squeeze. He wrapped the blanket a little more firmly around him and walked out, not looking at Rian, the pair of them bristling like wild dogs. She wanted to laugh at their posturing, but the sick thump of her heart in her chest made even hysterical laughter unlikely.

In a voice as cold and sharp as a steel blade, Rian demanded, 'Make yourself decent,' and turned away.

Amber struggled into her nightdress, then, in a spirit of defiance, put on Tahi's shirt over the top. Bloody hell!

Her mother appeared in the doorway, a shawl wrapped around her shoulders. 'What's happened? Rian? What's wrong?'

'I've just caught Tahi in bed with our daughter, *that's* what's wrong!'

'Oh, Amber!'

Amber was stung by the hurt and disappointment in her mother's voice, but the moment passed, quickly supplanted by outrage. 'I'm twenty-three! You were only twenty when you ran off with Pa! Why can't I have a lover?'

She watched as her parents deliberately refused to look at each other.

'Tahi's my crewman,' barked Rian. 'I'm not having my daughter consorting with crew.'

'He's *not* crew. He's . . . Tahi. I've known him

forever. He's more or less family.' She shut her mouth because, on reflection, that only made things sound worse.

Rian's jaw worked again and he said through gritted teeth, 'We'll talk about this tomorrow. I can't stand for it right now. But it has to stop.'

Amber glared at him. No, it doesn't, and it won't.

Rian glared back, then handed her mother the lantern and left them to it.

Kitty sighed. 'This is what you've been hiding, isn't it?'

Amber kept silent. If her mother wanted to lecture her she wasn't going to help her do it.

'How long has this . . . dalliance been going on?'

Dalliance? Amber's temper flared yet again. She and Tahi weren't having a *dalliance*! They loved each other!

'I don't know.'

'Oh, don't be so childish. You must know.' Gesturing at the rumpled bedclothes, Kitty said, 'How many times have you been together?'

'Seven, not counting tonight, which Pa ruined.' Alarmed by the look of horror on her mother's face, Amber said, 'What?'

'Have you had your courses lately? Have you missed any?'

'No.'

'No, what? No, you haven't had your courses, or no, you haven't missed any?'

'No, I haven't missed any!'

Kitty let out another huge sigh and sat down on the bunk. 'Well, thank God for that. Most

71

women would have fallen by now.' She frowned. 'You and Tahi *have* actually, er . . . ?'

'Yes, Ma, we have. It wasn't that hard to work out what to do, you know.'

Her mother was quiet for a minute. Amber hoped she was getting ready to leave.

But Kitty hadn't finished. 'You've upset your father very much.'

'Well, he's upset me. And Tahi.'

'I don't think the pair of you realise the trouble this will cause. Tahi will have to leave the ship. Haunui will be heartbroken, not to mention very embarrassed.'

'*Why* will Tahi have to leave? I don't think *you* realise, Ma. Tahi and I are both grown up. We can do what we like. If he goes, then I'm going with him.'

Mother and daughter stared grimly at each other. After several very long seconds, Kitty said tersely, 'Your father's right. This is better discussed in the light of day.'

She left, closing the cabin door firmly behind her.

Amber sat for a moment on the edge of her bunk, then lay down and pulled the bedclothes up to her chin.

★   ★   ★

Kitty set the lantern on the bedside table. Rian was in a chair, his feet up on the desk, a glass of brandy in his hand, his face apparently carved from granite.

'Well, what did she have to say for herself?' he

demanded. 'I suppose she's bloody well expecting, is she? I'll throttle that bloody boy tomorrow.'

Subsiding onto the bed, Kitty pulled the blankets over her freezing cold feet and settled back against the pillows. She understood how furious Rian was, and why, but knew he must be very disappointed, too, as he really was very fond of Tahi. 'Yes, thank you,' she said. 'I could really do with a drink.'

Rian poured her a generous nip and handed it to her. 'Did you know this was going on?'

'Me? Of course I didn't!'

'Is she . . . ?' Rian made a squeamish face and waved in the general direction of Kitty's middle.

'She says not.'

'Would she know?'

'Oh, for God's sake, Rian, she's wilful and contrary, not a mental defective.'

'I've heard said a lot of girls don't know, until it's too late.'

'That's the thing, though, isn't it?' Kitty took a hurried sip of her brandy and winced as it burnt her throat. 'She's not a girl. You might want her to stay twelve years old forever but she's twenty-three. And so's Tahi. They're adults, Rian. And she's right, I was three years younger than her when we . . . became a couple.'

'What's that got to do with anything? And why are you defending her?'

'I'm not defending her, I'm just saying.'

'Well, don't. She's behaved like some bloody little tart and I won't have it, and certainly not under my roof, do you hear me?'

73

He caught her eye momentarily then reached suddenly for the brandy, splashing out another couple of fingers into his tumbler. Kitty knew, in that quick, angry glance, what was going through his mind. He was thinking back to when she'd made a terrible mistake and allowed herself a single sexual encounter with Daniel Royce. Yes, she'd thought Rian was dead, and was swimming in despair so black she'd almost lost her mind, but that hadn't lessened the awful impact when Rian — not dead at all — had discovered what she'd done. He'd forgiven her, and she'd forgiven herself, but it had taken them a good twelve months to be comfortable with each other again.

'Sails,' she said.

'What?'

'Not your roof, your sails.'

Rian scowled at her. 'The boy will have to go, at the very next port.'

'I know. It really is a shame. I said to Amber he would. And she said — ' Kitty began.

'Well, I'm not throwing *her* off my ship. She's my daughter.'

'No, I mean it's a shame because Tahi absolutely adores her. He always has.'

Rian snorted. 'Mooning about after a girl when you're twelve isn't the same as climbing into bed with her when you're twenty-three, though, is it? Especially when she's *my bloody daughter!*'

'Our daughter. No, it isn't, but as I think I might already have mentioned, our daughter is also twenty-three.'

74

'You *are* defending her. You're defending both of them.'

'I'm *not*. I'm simply pointing out the facts. He loves her, Rian, and she's told me she loves him.' Kitty paused for effect, then played her ace. 'She also said that if Tahi has to leave the *Katipo*, she'll go with him.'

'Oh, how bloody ridiculous!'

Knocking back his brandy, Rian crossed his arms and stared into the lantern's flickering flame in sour silence. Finally, he declared, 'They love each other, do they? Well, if that's the case they can bloody well get married. Then they can rut themselves silly every night of the week.'

At last! Kitty thought. For a smart man, sometimes her husband could take ages to arrive at a very obvious conclusion. 'Like we did, you mean?'

A flicker of a smile crossed Rian's face. 'Yes, like we did.'

'How clever of you,' Kitty said. 'And, of course, if they're married we won't have to worry about them running off together and we won't lose her.'

'Exactly.' Rian eyed her suspiciously, then laughed. 'Am I supposed to sit here thinking this was my idea?'

'Wasn't it?'

'Mrs Farrell, I do believe you've just manipulated the crap out of me.'

Eyes wide, Kitty pressed a hand against her chest, fingers splayed.

'You're not just a pretty face, are you?' Rian said. He crossed to the bed and settled beside her. 'But if that boy rejects my girl, or ever hurts her, I'll throw him over the side myself.'

★ ★ ★

Nobody enjoyed the luxury of sleeping in aboard the *Katipo* when she was under sail, so Kitty and Rian were up and dressed when Haunui knocked on their cabin door just after six o'clock the following morning. His hand pressed against the ceiling for balance, as the seas had risen again in the early hours, he found the chair at Rian's desk and creakily eased himself into it.

Kitty had thought, when he joined them at Paihia, that he was finally starting to look his age, but he looked especially weary this morning. His handsome silver hair and beard looked a lacklustre white in the gloom of the cabin, and the patterns of his full face moko seemed to have faded and spread into the darkness of his skin.

'Tahi told me what happened, and I am sorry.'

'I should think so, the randy little bugger!' Rian burst out.

'Rian!' Kitty exclaimed. 'It's hardly Haunui's fault!'

'It is my fault,' Haunui said. 'I raised him. I thought I had done a better job than that.'

'You do know he loves her?' Kitty asked.

'Ae, he always has. But he should have come to me first. Amber's not just some little wahine.'

'Well, I'm glad you realise that,' Rian snapped.

Very calmly, and with infinite empathy, Haunui regarded him. 'Of course I realise that, e hoa.'

Rian rubbed his hands over his face. 'Christ, Haunui. I'm sorry.'

'Amber says she loves him, too,' Kitty said.

Haunui nodded. 'Tahi believes she does.'

'Anyway,' Rian said, 'I'm not having them sneaking all over the ship having secret assignations, so they can damn well get married. Does that suit you?'

'I couldn't ask for a better granddaughter-in-law. But does it suit them?'

'If it doesn't, I'm going to have to let Tahi go.'

Haunui stood. 'I think it will suit. I'll get him and we'll tell him now.'

Kitty went next door to fetch Amber, who was sullen and peaky-looking, informing her that her father had something he wanted to say.

Soon all five were in Kitty and Rian's cabin. Kitty realised Haunui couldn't have said anything yet to alleviate Tahi's discomfort as he seemed nervous under his determinedly grown-up calm. He winked at Amber, and she brightened a little when she saw him. Kitty's heart dropped in her chest: Amber had once looked to her for comfort. And at exactly the same time, tears stung her eyes. They really did love each other.

Rian sat in his desk chair, facing the unfortunate pair, like a king on his throne. Pompous old fart, she thought.

'Amber's mother spoke to her last night,' he said to Tahi. 'So I'll deal with you now.'

Tahi swallowed. 'Yes, sir.'

'I'm very disappointed in you.'

'Yes, sir.'

'You've abused our trust.'

'Yes, sir.'

'I expected a lot more from you.'

'Yes, sir.'

'Did you not give a thought to Amber? To her reputation? Her future prospects?'

Tahi tentatively raised a finger. 'Excuse me, sir.'

'What.'

'Sir, I wish to marry Amber.'

'What?'

Kitty nearly laughed: Rian looked deeply affronted at having his — *her* — clever idea hijacked.

Taking Amber's hand, Tahi said to her, 'I do. I want you to be my wife. Will you?'

'Yes!' Amber's face was radiant. She hugged him. 'Yes, yes, yes! Ma, Pa, is that all right with you?'

'Well, I suppose so,' Rian said.

'Really?' Amber stared at him, shocked. 'Ma?'

'If it's what you both really want, then I'm very happy for you,' Kitty replied.

And she was. Tahi was a delightful young man and if Amber really did love him, and wasn't just suffering from a bad case of lust, then why shouldn't they marry? Then at least any child they might produce would have both a mother and a father, whereas neither Tahi nor Amber had known their true fathers — which was probably a blessing.

'Koro?' Tahi asked Haunui.

Haunui grinned. 'Fine by me, boy.'

'Can we get Simon to marry us?' Amber asked. 'He's a preacher. He could do it today.'

'No,' Rian said. 'If you're getting married you're doing it properly, in a church. I've a mind to stop off at Sydney anyway.'

Startled, Kitty said, 'Sydney? Why?'

'We need to find out where Wong Kai's sent Bao.'

Kitty glanced uneasily at Haunui. 'And how will you do that?'

'By asking him,' Rian replied.

'He won't tell you.'

'Maybe not, but he might let something slip. And while we're there these two can get married.'

'But we'll have to publish the banns and book the church and everything, and that'll take weeks!' Amber complained.

'No, it won't,' Rian said. 'There are ways and means.'

'And what about a wedding dress?' Kitty asked. 'She can't get married in any old thing.'

'Enya can whip something up.'

Kitty gave Rian a withering look. His widowed sister, Enya Mason, was certainly a very accomplished dressmaker, but even she wouldn't be able to make a wedding dress in less than a very busy fortnight without any notice. 'And don't forget we'll need a venue for the wedding breakfast,' she went on. 'We're not settling for cheese and pickles in some pub.'

Rian waved a hand. 'We'll talk to Biddy. She'll know how to get everything sorted.'

That was true, Kitty thought. Mick's mother, Biddy Doyle, a landlady in The Rocks, seemed to know all sorts of people. 'Well, I hope so. Much as I'm delighted to see Amber and Tahi married, we *are* in a hurry.'

'I know,' Rian replied. 'Which is why I'll be

dealing with Wong Kai while you're doodling about organising the wedding.'

Kitty gaped at him. 'Doodling about! You're the one insisting on a church and all the rest of it! And if you're going to see Kai, so am I. You don't know him like I do. In fact, you don't know him at all.'

'No, you're not.'

'Yes, I am.'

''Scuse us,' Haunui interrupted. 'I can smell food. We finished here?'

Kitty realised that she, too, could detect the tantalising aroma of a cooked breakfast. God, she was starving. 'Yes, we're finished, aren't we?'

Rian nodded.

Kitty gave Amber and Tahi each a kiss and a hug. 'Congratulations, my dears. I really am very happy for you.'

As Haunui opened the door for the newly betrothed couple, the entire crew, gathered in the mess room, burst into a hearty round of 'For They Are Jolly Good Fellows'.

Kitty shook her head: you couldn't do anything on a ship without everyone knowing your business.

★   ★   ★

The *Katipo* arrived at Sydney Cove on the twenty-eighth day of August, received immediate clearance from a customs and excise officer as she wasn't carrying a cargo, and dropped anchor. Everyone went ashore bar Gideon, who volunteered to take the first shift staying aboard to keep an eye on things.

Ropata disappeared immediately to send word to his wife, Leena, that he was in town. Their marriage had been a love match and he was resolutely faithful to her, despite the fact she'd refused to accompany him to sea, preferring to remain in New South Wales and raise their five children, the eldest of whom was now fourteen.

The rest of the crew headed off to the pub while Kitty, Rian, Amber, Tahi, Haunui and Mick tramped up steep Essex Lane, intersected by Harrington and Gloucester streets, then turned into Carahers Lane, a narrow street crowded with well-established little cottages and a row of two-storey sandstone tenements. Kitty and Tahi's mother, Wai, had once rented one; their landlady, Biddy Doyle, resided next door.

Mick rapped on his mother's gleaming, blue-painted front door, then opened it without waiting for a response. 'Mam? It's me. I'm home.'

'Mick? Is that you?'

The owner of the voice soon materialised, a heavily built and rather large-bosomed woman with grey hair pulled back in a wispy bun. Her face was wrinkled and time-worn these days but she had Mick's lively dark eyes. She looked like someone's dear old grandmother, but Kitty knew that behind the shawl, the cotton house cap and her address in modest Carahers Lane she was as sharp as an embroidery needle and well known for her business acumen.

'So it is!' Biddy Doyle cried and enfolded Mick in a squashy embrace. 'My boy! Are you well? Has he been well, Captain?' she asked

Rian. She always called him 'Captain', even though she'd known him for decades. 'More to the point, has he been keeping out of trouble?'

Mick was forty-eight, and still an extremely handsome man. He'd never married, preferring to break the hearts of his more naive lovers and sorely try the patience of those with a little more wisdom in every port they visited. His mother despaired of him.

'Lately he has, yes,' Rian replied. 'And how are you, Biddy?'

'Me? Oh, I'm fine, so I am.'

'Been adding to your property empire?'

'All the time. Come in, all of you, I've just boiled the kettle.'

Inside, the house was far more comfortable than its plain exterior suggested. The front door opened onto a small hallway with an exit to the back yard at the far end and a stairway leading to the floor above. Biddy ushered them into a parlour-cum-kitchen. Against the rear wall was a fireplace into which had been set a very modern, black-painted iron stove, which, Kitty imagined, no doubt rendered the little house unbearably hot in summer. In fact it was rather stuffy now. The walls were papered with an attractive floral pattern and the red, brown and oxblood-coloured tile floor was laid with two lush carpets. Biddy's furniture was rather nice, too, and there were framed pictures, little vases, figurines and knick-knacks everywhere.

'You've not got the gas on yet?' Kitty remarked, pointing at the brass and glass kerolier hanging from the ceiling.

'Costs too much,' Biddy replied as she spooned tea into the pot. 'Only them with pots of money can afford to get the pipes connected.'

Well, that's you, isn't it? Kitty thought, amused.

Mick said, 'Mam's frightened of it. She thinks it'll blow her house up.'

When the tea had been served, together with a freshly baked almond cake and a plate of gingernut biscuits, Kitty said, 'Biddy, we'd like to ask you a favour, if we may.'

'Of course, dear.'

'Amber and Tahi are betrothed — '

Biddy's hands flew in the air. 'Oh, my dears! *Congratulations!* And a lovelier young couple I've not seen for many a year!'

'Thank you, Mrs Doyle,' Amber said.

'Thank you,' Tahi muttered, flushing scarlet.

'Yes,' Kitty went on, 'but they're in a bit of a rush. They'd like to be married as soon as possible.'

With a compassionate smile Biddy settled a hand over Amber's. 'Well, don't you worry about it, love. There's nothing to be ashamed of. It's just nature taking her course, that's all.'

Haunui let out a laugh, spraying almond cake crumbs across the table. 'She's not expecting a little one. Not yet, anyway. That's why we want them to hurry up and get married, eh?'

'Then you're probably being very sensible,' Biddy said, helping herself to a gingernut. 'What can I do for you?'

'We're on our way to China,' Rian said, 'on a matter of some urgency, so we can only stop a week or thereabouts here. I want Amber to be married in a church rather than a registry office, so we need to have the banns published, secure the church, organise a venue for the break-fast — '

'Have a dress made,' Kitty interrupted, 'and do all those other things necessary for a wedding that my husband doesn't have a clue about, all in the space of seven or eight days. Can you please help us?'

Chewing on her biscuit Biddy thought for a minute, then swallowed. 'Holy Mary, that's a tall order. Your sister's a dressmaker, isn't she, Captain?'

'She is and I'm sure she'll help.'

'Well, I can do a bit, and I'd be happy to. But you can't publish the banns because these two lovely young folk aren't resident in the parish of Sydney. You have to live here to do that.'

Amber said, 'Shite!'

'Language, dear,' Kitty warned.

'But Ma, what are we going to do?'

'Don't worry, love,' Biddy went on, 'you can be married by licence. It's costly but permission to marry is granted a lot faster. And it's considered to be more prestigious, and it's private.'

'That'll do, then,' Rian said.

Biddy nodded. 'Good. As I said I'm happy to help, but I know who'd be far better placed with venues and pulling strings and the like.'

Kitty's heart quickened. 'Who?'

'Friday Woolfe and her friends. Do you know them?'

'I don't, no. Do you, Rian?' Kitty asked.

Rian's eyes had closed, and he wore an odd,

pained expression. 'Oh, God, not them.'

'You *do* know them?'

Biddy laughed gaily. 'From a long time ago, he does. Have you not told your lovely wife about your Newcastle adventure, Captain?'

'Why would I?' Rian opened his eyes. 'It was a bloody disaster. *And* it was thirty years ago.'

'What adventure?' Amber demanded.

'Yes, what adventure?' Kitty echoed. Why had he never mentioned it?

Waving a hand wearily, Rian said, 'Oh, you tell them, Biddy.'

'In 1833 — or was it 1832? I forget now — Friday Woolfe and some friends of hers chartered the *Katipo* to take them up to Newcastle. One of them — Harrie Downey, her name is — had a baby girl abducted by a mad Englishman named Leary, and they followed him there to get her back.' She grinned at Rian, who rolled his eyes. 'What I heard was that the women locked the captain here and his crew in the mess room of the *Katipo* and stole the ship's boats — ha! — and they rowed themselves ashore. They found the little girl and rescued her, but had to run for their lives when Leary chased them, and sadly Friday was shot in the head. But they got away from Newcastle all right, so they did.'

'But you implied this Friday Woolfe's still alive today,' Kitty said.

'I did and she is. Her head must be made of maple wood. Anyway, so Harrie got her daughter back, and that was the important thing. Such a lovely lass, Harrie. Wouldn't hurt a fly.'

85

While his mother had been speaking, Mick had slumped farther and farther down in his seat, his face reddening.

'What's the matter? Kitty asked him

'Nothing.'

'Nothing!' Biddy exclaimed. 'What that poor girl went through!'

'Jesus, Ma, can you not let it lie? It was years ago! It's done with!'

'If it's done with, why are you sitting there with a face like a beetroot?'

Kitty glanced at Rian for an explanation, but instead he said, 'We don't need that lot, Biddy, surely? Can't you find us a breakfast venue and a church?'

'Oh, don't be so gutless. Friday has a venue *and* the ears of all the right people, so she can probably get the marriage licence pushed through, and possibly even a church and an officiant, knowing her.'

'How?' Kitty asked. 'Is she the governor's wife or something?'

Mick blew tea out through his nose.

'Well, hardly, dear,' Biddy said. 'She's the madam of Sydney's most exclusive brothel. She specialised, herself, in . . . ' she paused, taking in the curious Amber 'some rather particular tastes, but she's just the proprietor now. Not to mention filthy rich.'

Kitty felt a very unwelcome stab of — not quite jealousy, but certainly discomfort. 'Did you know that?' she asked Rian.

'I had heard she was running a place on Argyle Street these days. She was only, er, employed there when I met her. When we took them to Newcastle,' he quickly clarified.

'She's been the madam there for years,' Biddy said. 'Elizabeth Hislop left everything to her when she died, bless the poor woman's soul, and that wasn't long after your little adventure. So go and talk to her. Go on. Tell her I sent you. She does owe you, if I recall.'

'Why?' Kitty asked. Then more persistently, 'Why does she owe you?'

Biddy explained, 'Because if the captain hadn't been where he was in Newcastle to pick up Friday and her friends when they were running from Jonah Leary, she would very likely have died.'

'But I've not even spoken to her since then,' Rian said, 'nor seen her. None of them. Why would I? She was a nightmare to deal with. They all were. And that friend of hers, the princess, Aria, she and I hardly parted on the best of terms.'

'Well, you'd better mind your manners because she's still around.' Biddy pointed a teaspoon at Rian. 'Look, do you want your lass to have a nice wedding or not?'

'Of course I do.'

'Then go and see Friday.'

Rian let out the most enormous sigh.

★ ★ ★

By the time Kitty, Rian and Amber walked into Friday Woolfe's hotel — the Siren's Arms — on Harrington Street the following day, Kitty was

87

absolutely bursting to meet her. By now she knew everything about her that Rian knew, which admittedly wasn't very much, including the fact that her brothel was just around the corner on Argyle Street, and that Mick had been excluded from the legendary Newcastle rescue mission because he'd taken advantage of Friday's friend Harrie Downey, with dreadful repercussions.

The hotel itself was a pleasant surprise. Kitty had been expecting a dingy haunt sailors might patronise but it was rather more refined than that, with highly polished floorboards, marine paintings on the walls, intricately knotted ropes draped artfully about and a pair of brightly painted ship's figureheads flanking the well-stocked bar. It still smelt like a pub, though.

'Morning, ladies, sir. What can I get you?' asked a man polishing a row of glass tankards.

Well, nothing at nine o'clock in the morning, thank you, Kitty thought.

Rian said, 'We've an appointment with Friday Woolfe.'

The man gestured with a tankard. 'Through there, down the hallway, door on the right. She shouldn't be long. But then again, she might. If she is, ring the bell and I'll get someone to bring tea.'

Kitty didn't think that boded well.

They followed his instructions and found themselves in what appeared to be a private room, furnished with a sofa and several armchairs arranged around a narrow fireplace in which someone had recently banked a nice little fire. The gas was definitely on here, as a small gasolier hung from the ceiling rose and two gas brackets were mounted on the wall, all lit and emitting a slightly peculiar smell. They made themselves comfortable and waited. And waited and waited.

Eventually, Kitty asked, 'What time are we seeing Enya?'

'I said eleven in my note,' Rian replied.

'I wonder how rich Mrs Woolfe really is?' Amber said.

'Disgustingly,' a voice said. 'And it's Miss Woolfe, not Mrs.'

Into the room swept two tall and utterly startling-looking women at whom Kitty could not help but stare. For some reason she'd half-expected them to be young, as they would have been when Rian first met them, but they were middle-aged, perhaps in their early fifties. Nevertheless they were strikingly attractive and, as she gazed at them, reminded Kitty of something. After a few moments she realised what: a couple of parrots. The Maori woman in her dark dress looked like a black cockatoo with sleek, shiny feathers, and Friday Woolfe like nothing so much as a rosella in her gaudy gown with her brightly coloured hair.

Her skirt and bodice were a vivid aqua colour with purple and indigo accents, and her wild mass of wavy hair an improbably rich, deep red. Kitty suspected that an awful lot of henna paste was used in Friday Woolfe's toilette. Her face was lined around the mouth and eyes, and she had the very fair skin that generally didn't weather well under the southern sun. She was, however, very tall, and well rounded, her breasts and hips substantial though her waist was still neat, and the extra padding saved her from appearing excessively aged. She was a natural beauty, but the most remarkable thing about her were her tattoos. The sleeves of her bodice ended just below her elbows, revealing multi-coloured ink completely covering her arms to her wrists, and out of her neckline, which wasn't immodestly low, flapped the wings of a bird. Kitty had seen plenty of tattoos before on sailors, but very few on women, and certainly not in this quantity. They were shocking, yet also beautiful. Against Miss Woolfe's coloured skin lay softly gleaming gold, and lots of it: around her wrists and throat, on her fingers, and dangling from her ears.

The Maori woman was also well built, and even taller than Friday Woolfe. She wore the chin and lip moko you often saw on New Zealand women, and her slanted, fiercely intelligent eyes beneath beautifully arched brows were set wide apart, the pupils as black as olives in oil. Few age lines marred her handsome features, and in her otherwise coal black hair — undyed, Kitty guessed — a wide silver streak swept back from her right temple. She was dressed from head to foot in a costume of expertly cut black taffeta (taffeta in the daytime!), as if in mourning, though her jewellery was of gold and greenstone, not jet.

Rian rose, apparently compelled by good manners — and perhaps an element of discomposure? Kitty wondered — but she remained seated despite an awful urge to jump up in the presence of such magnificence. It wouldn't do to lose her dignity, or the upper hand.

'Captain Farrell,' the Maori woman said. 'After all this time we meet again.'

'We do,' Rian replied. 'Miss, er . . . '

'Aria Te Kainga-Mataa.'

Going red, Rian said, 'Yes. Miss Te Kainga-Mataa, Miss Woolfe, this is my wife, Mrs Kitty Farrell, and our daughter, Amber.'

Aria's eyes narrowed as she inspected Amber. 'You are Maori.'

Amber said, 'I know.'

Trying not to stare now at the women, Kitty could see that Aria wanted to know more, but also that she wasn't going to ask. But she didn't have to.

Amber went on. 'My mother was Ngati Whatua and my father was Pakeha. Neither could care for me. Ma and Pa took me in when I was small.'

'Ah.'

Friday rubbed her hands together briskly, the jewels in her rings glinting in the gaslight. 'Well, I'd say it's nice to see you again, Captain, but I don't know if it is yet. Let's face it, it wasn't that much fun last time, was it? Biddy said you need a favour but she didn't tell us what sort, did she,' she added to Aria, 'the shit-stirring old trout.'

Aria's eyebrows merely went up, as though such machinations were to be expected from Biddy Doyle.

'Well, pardon me, but what happened last time

was hardly my fault, was it?' Rian replied. 'And it was you who came to *me* for help then.'

'That's true.' Friday sat down in an armchair, causing the front of her crinoline hoop to flip up and reveal the hems of several petticoats, a pair of heavily tattooed shins, and the fact that she was wearing scruffy old black boots. 'Oh, for fuck's sake!'

Amber burst into smothered giggles.

Lurching grumpily to her feet, Friday flicked up the crinoline from the rear and collapsed again, whereby her skirt settled in a more seemly fashion with a graceful billow. 'You're not wearing a hoop?' she asked Kitty. 'Bloody smart of you, I reckon. Pain in the arse.'

Aria sat on the sofa beside Amber. Kitty noted that *her* hoop didn't flip up.

'Anyway,' Friday went on, 'Biddy says it's time to repay our debt. So, what can we do for you?'

Rian said, 'Amber needs to marry, and in a hurry.'

Both women glanced at Amber's middle.

'No, our daughter is not in a predicament.' Kitty tried her best not to snap. Why did people always think the worst?

'We need the marriage licence pushed through as quickly as possible,' Rian said, 'a church and an officiant, a decent venue for the wedding breakfast, and caterers for about twenty guests.'

'Is there a fiancé?' Aria asked. 'Or do you need one of those, too?'

'Of course there's a damn fiancé. He's a crewman on my ship.'

Friday made a face. 'You poor little thing.

Aren't they all a bit long in the tooth by now?'

'The boy in question is twenty-three,' Rian said stiffly.

'What are you staring at, sweetie?' Friday asked Amber.

'I'm looking for where you got shot. I can't see a scar.'

'Amber!' Kitty was horrified. 'Don't be so rude!'

Friday lowered her head to reveal an abnormally wide parting in her hair. 'Went right along the top of my head, didn't it, Captain? Bled like forty bastards.'

'God, how awful,' Amber said, sounding hugely entertained. 'What happened to the man who shot you?'

'Followed us back to Sydney, had another go at us, shot a peeler instead and swung for it. Bloody good riddance, too. Have you got a frock?'

'My sister here in Sydney's an expert dressmaker,' Rian said.

Friday and Aria exchanged a glance. 'Pity,' Friday remarked. 'Our friend Harrie makes lovely dresses. You remember Harrie, Captain. Charlotte's ma?'

'Charlotte?' Kitty asked.

Rian explained, 'Charlotte was the child who was rescued.'

'What about rings?' Friday asked.

Kitty looked at Amber. 'We haven't thought about rings, have we?'

'Ha!' Aria exclaimed. 'Sarah can make those. She is a very good jeweller.'

Rian's eyebrows went up. 'The Sarah who came to Newcastle?'

'Yes.'

'She's a jeweller?'

'Only the best,' Friday said. 'Have you submitted the marriage application?'

'Not yet.'

'Do it today. The registry's on Elizabeth Street. I can get it approved by Tuesday. What church did you want?'

Kitty frowned. They hadn't thought about that, either. Tahi had been educated by the Church Missionary Society at Paihia but she doubted if he particularly cared which altar he stood before when he married Amber. She herself was vaguely Church of England and Rian was an extremely lapsed Catholic. 'Rian?'

'Church of England.'

'St James's, then? Harrie and James got married there. We'll aim for about ten days away. That'll give you time to get the dress and the rings made. Or sooner?'

'As soon as possible. So you *are* willing to help us?' Rian asked.

'Why not?' Friday said. 'You helped us. But why the rush?'

'If there is to be a, shall we say, 'predicament',' Kitty admitted reluctantly, 'we'd like it to be conceived *after* the ink's dry on the marriage certificate.'

Amber reddened. 'Ma! Will you stop saying that?'

'Also we're on our way to China on urgent business,' Rian added. 'We've barely any time to spare in Sydney. Ideally only a week.'

'A week!' Friday exclaimed. 'Christ, that's cutting it a bit fine.'

'It is,' Rian agreed. 'If you don't think you can manage that we can find someone else to make the arrangements . . . '

'Oh, we can manage it, all right,' Friday said, 'providing *you* don't interfere. I remember you were a great one for interfering thirty years ago. Why don't you go off and, I don't know, do something manly and leave things to us and your wife and daughter to sort out?' She flicked her hand in Rian's direction. 'Go on, hop off, there's a good captain.'

Rian said nothing, though the muscles in his jaw tensed visibly.

Kitty felt her hackles rise. No one ever spoke to Rian like that, certainly not foul-mouthed, middle-aged brothel keepers. But it did seem that the woman was able to get things done. How bloody annoying.

'Actually,' she said through gritted teeth, 'Rian does have more important things to do, and we have another appointment shortly. May we come back this afternoon, just Amber and myself, and perhaps arrange to visit this jeweller you spoke of?'

'No need. I'll ask Sarah to come along, and maybe Harrie, too, though we'll be over at the brothel by then. You don't mind, do you?'

'No,' Kitty said, ignoring Rian's deeply disapproving look.

'Shall we say two o'clock?'

'That will be fine, thank you,' Kitty replied.

'Have you had a bereavement?' Amber asked suddenly, indicating Aria's sombre gown.

'My mother died last year, but that is all right. She was old and I did not like her. Also, I am fond of wearing black.'

Rian stood and collected his hat. 'Thank you for your help. I'm very grateful for your assistance and I believe I will follow your advice, Miss Woolfe, and leave the arrangements to you, my wife and my daughter. After the fact please present your invoice for all costs incurred, with of course your facilitation fee included.'

'Oh, don't be such a starchy old miseryguts, Captain,' Friday said. 'We're friends, aren't we?'

The expression on Rian's face said no, they weren't.

'The price'll be what Elizabeth Hislop paid you to take us to Newcastle — five guineas — plus allowance for inflation. Then we'll be properly even.'

'That's very generous of you, Miss Woolfe,' Kitty said. She'd add up the cost of everything herself and make sure they paid exactly what was due. She didn't want to owe this woman anything.

'You'll have to pay Sarah yourselves,' Friday said. 'But as for the rest, five guineas is fair. You've no idea how important it was to us to get Charlotte back. Absolutely *no* idea.'

'She's well, the child?' Rian asked.

'Very, though she's not a child now. She's a grown woman with a family.'

'Yes, I suppose she would be.'

Taking her lead from her mother and father,

Amber stood. 'Thank you. I'm really grateful for your help.'

For the first time, Aria smiled. 'You are welcome, dear.'

★   ★   ★

While Amber, Kitty and Rian were having their uncomfortable meeting at the Siren's Arms, Haunui and Tahi were wading through breakfasts of enormous beef and oyster pies, fried potatoes and ale in an eating house on George Street.

'You nervous, boy?' Haunui asked as he attacked a slice of potato.

'What about?'

'Getting wed.'

'No. Amber's all I've ever wanted, though I'm happy to leave all the organising to her and Auntie. I wouldn't know where to start. Are you going to eat that bit of crust?'

'Ae. Get your hands off it.'

'I *am* a bit nervous about having Rian as my father-in-law.'

Haunui's bushy grey eyebrows went up. 'He's a good man. And he thinks a lot of you.'

'He didn't the other night.'

'Ae, well, you shouldn't have been in bed with his daughter, should you?'

'I definitely should be marrying her, though.'

'I reckon.'

Tahi sipped his ale and took his time setting the tankard back on the table. 'Even my mother said so.'

Haunui went very still. 'Wai did?'

97

Tahi nodded. 'She came to me, the night Rian caught me and Amber? It took me ages to get to sleep but when I finally did, I dreamt we were walking along the beach at Paihia and she told me I'd marry Amber and everything would work out eventually, but I had to beware of Israel.'

Haunui pushed his pie crust around on his plate, then cut it in half and stared at the pieces. It wasn't that his daughter Wai, Tahi's mother, had appeared to Tahi in a dream that bothered him, it was her message. When Tahi was four he'd dreamt that his mother's bones would be coming home to New Zealand from Sydney, where they'd been buried since 1840, and they had, on the very day he'd predicted, and when he was older he'd had a vision of Rian's whereabouts when Rian had been missing, presumed dead. So Wai revealing herself to her son recently wasn't so unusual, but her comment about Israel was.

'What exactly did she say?'

Gazing down at his own plate Tahi screwed up his face, thinking. 'Just that I should beware of him, and that he isn't who I think he is. Or did she say 'what I think he is'? I've forgotten.' Finally meeting Haunui's gaze, he said, 'I don't know what she meant, Koro. Israel's my best mate. Why would I have to beware of him?'

Haunui had a very good idea why. Tahi and Israel *were* apparently the best of friends, and had been since Tahi joined the *Katipo*'s crew. In fact, they'd got on well even before then, when Haunui and Tahi had accompanied the *Katipo* on short voyages. He, Haunui, had watched

Israel grow from a scrap of a boy to a tall, well-built, pleasant-looking man of twenty-one. His freckles had faded and his hair had darkened to a deep bronze, spoiling Mick's taunts of 'carrot head', which, as far as Haunui could see, had only taught Israel a hard-earnt lesson in stoicism.

But Haunui was also very good at noticing what other folk didn't, and he'd seen the way Israel studied Amber when he thought no one was watching. He'd seen the slow, hot burn of desire in his eyes, and the carefully veiled jealousy when the lad turned his gaze towards Tahi. And while it was true that some of the cheek, cunning and guile had been knocked out of Israel by nearly a decade of sweating away at sea under the guidance of a decent ship's crew, Haunui didn't believe he'd changed that much. He'd just learnt to hide that side of himself better. He didn't trust the boy and neither, he knew, did Ropata.

'Perhaps he cares for Amber, too, eh?'

Tahi looked shocked. 'No, he doesn't. Well, he does, but everyone cares for her. But not in the way I do, he doesn't. He's my best mate. I'd know.' The tiniest of hesitations. 'Wouldn't I?'

Haunui eyed him for a moment, then popped a piece of crust into his mouth. 'Just something to think about, eh?'

'And what did my mother mean by everything would work out *eventually* when Amber and I marry? Was she saying things won't work out straight away?'

In went the other piece of crust. 'I don't know, boy. It was your vision.'

4

Sydney had certainly changed since Kitty had first visited in 1840: it seemed ever bigger and busier every time they called in. The population had increased to nearly one hundred thousand: houses, commercial buildings and warehouses had gone up everywhere, the streets were crowded, and you could buy almost anything you wanted in the shops. Semi-Circular Quay had been reclaimed from mudflats on the foreshore, sewer pipes were now installed along the main streets, and paving had been attempted here and there — though, Kitty noticed, as she dodged the usual potholes and piles of animal dung, without much success.

And still the place stank. Perhaps towns and cities always would. London had the Great Stink a few years ago, and Melbourne wasn't referred to as Smellbourne for nothing.

Marching up George Street beside Rian, she said grumpily, 'I don't think I've ever met such a rude woman in all my life.'

'You've met plenty of rude women.'

'Why did you just put up with what she said to you? I couldn't believe my ears.'

'Because she can get us what we want. Look, I don't like her, either.'

'I'm right, though, aren't I? She *is* a proper cow.'

'I did warn you. I told you she says and does what she likes. She was like that the last time I had to deal with her. I expect it's just the way she is.'

'Are you *defending* her?'

'No, but we want Amber to have a decent wedding, don't we?'

They turned right into Suffolk Lane and entered Enya Mason's dressmaking salon, once a single tiny shop but now three premises joined together to accommodate her expanded business. Enya was the same age as Kitty, and, to the horror and shame of her and Rian's wealthy Irish family, had been transported to New South Wales at the age of eighteen for unwittingly receiving stolen goods. After four years she'd gained a ticket of leave and married Joshua Mason, who'd died two years later, fortunately leaving her enough money to start her own dressmaking business, which had been extremely successful now for some time. These days Enya was quite a wealthy woman. There had been plenty of beaux, but she had never remarried.

The bell over the door rang and Enya appeared from the rear of the salon immediately.

'Rian, girls, how lovely to see you!' she exclaimed in. the lovely, cultured Irish lilt that had never left her. She bustled around the small counter and gave each of them a squashy hug, then whacked Rian on the arm. 'One miserable little note? Why didn't you write me a proper letter and let me know earlier you'd be in town? I could have made some time for you. I'm that busy at the moment.'

Oh dear, Kitty thought.

Rian said, 'Sorry. We didn't know we were coming. Amber's getting married. And no, she's not expecting. Can you make her a dress in a week?'

Enya plonked her hands on her hips and blew a wisp of hair back from her still very lovely face. 'Of course I can. I'll just pull one out of thin air, shall I?'

'Don't be like that.'

'Have you any idea what goes into making a wedding gown?'

'Of course I don't,' Rian said. 'I sail ships.'

'I do,' Kitty said, 'and we really are very sorry, Enya, but we truly are pushed for time.' She explained why, then said, 'If you can't manage it then that's our bad luck. We'll have to find someone else.'

Enya shook her head. 'You will not. If Amber's getting married she's wearing one of my dresses. Come through to the back and we'll sit down over a nice cup of tea and talk about it.'

Rian looked horrified.

'Not you,' Enya said. 'You won't be much help.'

Already halfway out the door, Rian said. 'I'll leave you to it, then. Back in an hour or so.'

In a corner of the workshop through the door in the rear of the salon, Enya bustled about over a small hearth as Kitty and Amber watched four women at work on garments in various stages of construction.

The tea ready, Enya moved several bolts of rather gorgeous silk off a table and arranged cups, a teapot and a plate of biscuits. She sat down, gathered half a dozen sheets of paper and a lead pencil, and looked up at them expectantly, her cornflower blue eyes steady. 'Now, what style did you have in mind? And sit down, will you? You're making the place look untidy.'

Amber and Kitty sat.

Kitty said, 'Something pretty. She spends most of her life in damned trousers. I'd like to see her looking like a proper pretty young woman on her wedding day, at least.'

'A crinoline?'

'She doesn't care for crinolines.'

'I might,' Amber said.

Kitty frowned at her. 'You don't. You said you don't.'

'I might have changed my mind.'

'Shall we start with colour, then?' Enya suggested.

'Black,' Amber declared.

'You are *not* getting married in black!' Kitty exploded.

'Why not? Other people do.'

'Well, you aren't.' What *was* Amber playing at? And then it occurred to Kitty; that Aria person had been wearing a black crinoline. 'That sort of thing might work very well on a middle-aged woman, but it isn't at all suitable for a twenty-three-year-old bride, and that's that.'

'What middle-aged woman?' Enya asked.

'Oh, Friday Woolfe's friend. Aria Kainga someone.'

'Friday and Aria? How on earth did you meet them?'

'It's a long story, but they're helping us to arrange the wedding. Unfortunately.'

Enya poured the tea. 'Why unfortunately?'

'Because I didn't find them to be particularly pleasant, especially that Friday Woolfe. In fact, I thought she was vulgar, vicious and rather spiteful.'

'Friday was?' Enya looked surprised.

'She was a bit rude to Pa,' Amber explained with a grin.

'Well, Aria's always been a little aloof, but that's just her way. And Friday can be loud, and a bit coarse, but you'd not find a more generous soul. She's very well known for her charity, especially the money she gives to women down on their luck, prostitutes too sick to work, habitual drunkards and the like. She's teetotal herself, but not sanctimonious about it like some of them can be.'

'Generous, philanthropic *and* teetotal?' Kitty crossed her arms. 'Good God, what a saint.'

'She is, though, Ma,' Amber said. 'She said she'd organise everything for my wedding. And she *didn't* drink anything.'

Kitty snapped, 'No, but then it was hardly the appropriate time of day for alcoholic refreshments, was it?' She glanced at Enya's grin. 'What?'

Enya laughed. 'She really annoyed you, didn't she?'

Kitty broke a biscuit in half, picked out a currant, examined it for a moment, then dropped it on her plate. 'No.'

'Liar. She did. Why?'

'Oh, she was just so *indelicate*.'

'Indelicate! Kitty, you live on a ship full of sailors!'

'And they're awful, Ma,' Amber said, giggling. 'You know they are!'

Enya put her elbows on the table. 'Look, I know perfectly well what's upset you, and so do you. But I can't help you until you come out and say it.'

Kitty sat in silence, feeling her face redden. She felt a fool. She retrieved the lone currant from her plate and squashed it brutally between her fingers. 'She's beautiful, even now, even if she has got a mouth like a midden. He met her before he met me. Why does he dislike her so much if nothing happened between them on that trip to Newcastle?'

'Because she got the better of him, that's why. And you know how he hates that.' Enya patted Kitty's hand. 'And Kitty? Nothing happened between them. I know that for a fact. He told me.'

'Did he?' But that still didn't feel right to Kitty. And why the hell was she even worrying about this? It all happened decades ago. What was wrong with her? 'Why would he tell you something like that?'

'Because he was, well, I think he was a little discomposed.'

'Discomposed? Because he *didn't* make a conquest? Honestly, Enya, I know Rian can be fairly arrogant at times, but he'd never be put out by something like that. He isn't Mick, you know.'

'He was discomposed, Kitty, because Friday and Aria were — are — lovers.'

Now *Kitty* was discomposed. 'Lovers? As in . . . they're lesbians?'

'Yes.'

'But they're both so beautiful!'

'Oh, stop it! You're being as silly as Rian!' Enya looked really quite cross. 'Don't be so judgmental. You're not normally. They've generously offered to help you, so accept it with good grace otherwise Amber will miss out on the wedding she deserves. Ignore Friday's bad language and her crass behaviour. It's just the way she is. She wasn't gently raised like we were, you know.'

Kitty hoped her expression was revealing less than she suspected it might be. Having flattened all the currants she could find in her biscuit she fiddled with her teacup instead, turning it round and round in its saucer.

'Your mouth looks just like Samson's bum, Ma,' Amber remarked.

Kitty sighed. Yes, she was jealous of Friday, but not because she'd feared that Rian might have slept with her, so long ago — before she had met him. And she was hardly in a position to take the moral high ground, after Daniel. No, what she resented was Friday's apparent ability to so casually dominate Rian. She'd never seen another woman do that, ever, and it angered her. When being so rude to Rian, had Friday not even considered how she, Kitty, might feel? The awkward position in which being insulted, while needing the woman's help, placed her?

She sighed again. The fact is, Rian had been weak. He hadn't stood up for himself and it had annoyed the hell out of her.

Enya poured herself another cup of tea. 'How exactly was Friday rude to Rian?'

Gleefully, Amber replied, 'She told him to hop off and do something manly while we women sort out the wedding.'

'Oh, honestly, Kitty, is that all?' Enya exclaimed, setting down the teapot quite a lot harder than was necessary. 'That's nothing for Friday.'

'It was the way she said it. And she did swear quite a bit.' Kitty felt heat crawl up her face as Enya gazed at her, but refused to look away. 'She made Rian look an idiot. And me.'

'Why you?'

'Because . . . ' Oh God. 'Because he didn't react. He just sat there and took it, like a . . . like a henpecked husband. Like a fool.'

'You're the fool, Kitty Farrell. Has it not occurred to you that he ignored it because he wants Amber to have a nice, albeit swiftly arranged, wedding? Which she won't if you spoil things by refusing to get along with Friday and Aria. Honestly, love, what's the matter with you?'

Kitty stared down at her teacup once again. What *was* the matter? Was she anxious about Amber and Tahi? Well, yes. Bao? Definitely. Distressed about Fu's ill health? Yes, that too. Was she approaching the change of life? Possibly. She'd heard that tended to make some women contrary and moody. But if so, what a time to start. 'I don't know, I really don't.'

'For God's sake, they're just women like you

and me. Look, would it help you to know that Friday came here as a convict? So did her best friends Harrie and Sarah. They were emancipated years ago, but by God they worked for it. Not Aria, though. She comes from some sort of Maori nobility but is estranged from her family, apparently.'

Nosiness getting the better of her, Kitty asked, 'What were they transported for?'

'All for stealing, I believe. I've heard said Sarah's an absolute artist. If you want something pinched, talk to her.'

'Still?' Kitty was shocked.

Enya held out a hand and waggled it. Maybe yes, maybe no. 'So you've actually got something in common with Friday, haven't you?'

'I have not. What do you mean?'

'Well, you and Rian spend a fair bit of time flouting the law, so get off your high horse. Amber, dear, there's a ladder out in the yard. Would you mind fetching it? Your mother might need some help.'

Amber giggled, and even Kitty felt herself smile. 'God, I'm sorry. I really am.' She made a monumental effort and pushed the business of Friday Woolfe's behaviour, and Rian's response to it, to the back of her mind. 'Shall we get back to this wedding dress?'

'I don't *have* to have a black one,' Amber said, conciliatory now. 'What colour do you think would be nice, Ma?'

'White would be lovely, but we'd never get it washed on the ship.' Kitty looked at Enya. 'What do you think?'

'You don't have to take the dress with you after the wedding. You could leave it with me; I'll have it laundered if necessary, and you can pick it up next time you're in Sydney. Do you *want* a white gown?' Enya asked Amber.

'White satin *would* be nice,' Amber replied. 'With lace. I might as well go overboard. I won't be getting married again.'

'I should hope not,' Kitty said.

Enya stood. 'I've got some lovely silk satin, though it's very slightly off-white, and some gorgeous Honiton lace. I'll fetch them.' She shot off through a door and returned just as quickly carrying several bolts of cloth, which she laid on the table. The satin was heavy, the palest of creams, with the lustre of pearls. The lace, a dense pattern of flowers and leaves, had been appliqued to a continuous length of net measuring two feet wide, and the colour matched the satin perfectly.

'Oh, that's beautiful!' Kitty said.

'Isn't it?' Enya agreed, unfolding a piece of the lace. 'You don't often see Honiton in lengths like this now. It's all machine-made lace these days, but this is made by hand. I've been saving it for something really special, and I can't think of anything more special than Amber's wedding dress.'

'It's lovely but it looks very expensive,' Amber said. 'So does the satin. Do you think Pa will mind paying so much?'

Enya looked offended. 'Your pa isn't paying for this. This is my wedding gift to you!'

Kitty opened her mouth to protest but Enya

talked over the top of her. 'Now, back to style. I'd suggest something fairly simple, if we're going to show off the lace. Too many ruffles and bows and it will be overshadowed.'

'That's all right,' Amber said. 'I'm not that fond of ruffles and bows. It isn't really . . . me.'

'What about something like this?' Enya began to sketch, her pencil flying across a sheet of paper with practised ease. 'There's quite a lot of the lace, so we can use it as a border for a veil, too, if you'd like that.'

The design was simple, but exquisite. The bodice was darted and close-fitting with a modest scooped neck trimmed with the lace, and the flared, three-quarter sleeves were pleated at the inner elbows and also bordered with lace. The waist was snug with a band of satin above a widely pleated hoop skirt, trimmed from halfway down with more of the Honiton. Completing the ensemble was the veil, about three feet in length.

Amber's eyes shone, then she laughed. 'Tahi won't recognise me.'

'Do you like it?' Enya asked.

'It's beautiful!'

'Good.' Enya sat back in her chair and blew out her cheeks. 'Do we really only have a week to get it made?'

Kitty felt awful. 'Possibly. Probably. It depends on the church. I'm sorry, Enya, it's such a lot to ask of you. Will your assistants be able to help?'

'We're overwhelmed with orders already.' Enya brightened. 'But I do know one or two very good sempstresses I can probably call on.'

Amber said, 'Didn't Friday Woolfe say she

might invite her friend to our meeting this afternoon, the one who makes nice dresses? With the funny name?'

Enya grinned. 'Harrie Downey? Speak of the devil, though actually you couldn't meet a sweeter person. Harrie's a good friend, and a very fine sempstress. Do you mind if I come to this meeting?'

'Not at all,' Kitty replied. 'We're seeing them at two o'clock, at Miss Woolfe's brothel. We should probably go to the back door.' She paused. 'Or not. Actually, I don't know if I care.'

She and Enya stared at each other, then burst out laughing.

'That's better,' Enya said. 'I don't like it when you're upset.'

Amber said, 'That Sarah person's coming as well. Apparently she's a jeweller?'

'Sarah Green. The whole crew. They're as thick as thieves, those four.'

*   *   *

Friday Woolfe's brothel was nowhere near as sordid as expected; in fact, the house was extremely elegant. They were shown in to what was clearly Friday's office, or perhaps both Friday's and Aria's, as the room accommodated two desks. Harrie Downey and Sarah Green had already arrived. Kitty liked Mrs Downey immediately. A pretty, plump woman, her eyes sparkled with health and good cheer, and she smiled almost constantly. Sarah Green, however, seemed more reticent — small, slender and the sort of person Kitty liked to think of as a

111

'watcher'. Astute and wary, rather than crafty and cunning. Probably.

Enya and Harrie greeted each other warmly as they all sat down in the somewhat crowded room.

'Overcome your fit of pique, Mrs Farrell?' Friday Woolfe asked pleasantly.

'Which fit of pique would that be, Miss Woolfe?' Kitty replied, ignoring a barbed look from Enya.

'The one you were in this morning.'

Kitty made a decision. 'Yes, I have. And I apologise for my behaviour.'

Putting her booted feet up on her desk, Friday said, 'Actually, it's me that should be saying sorry. So . . . sorry.'

Aria, Harrie Downey and Sarah Green all looked at her in what appeared to be shock.

'What?' Friday said. 'I was a bitch to the captain and there was no reason to be.'

'That's never bothered you before,' Sarah Green remarked.

'True, but this was Captain Farrell.'

Sarah said, 'But you've always loathed him. No offence intended, Mrs Farrell.'

'None taken.'

'I know,' Friday said, 'but we do actually owe him. I shouldn't have said it.'

'Then perhaps you should apologise to him,' Harrie suggested.

'Thank you, Mrs Smart-Britches, but there's no need to go that far.'

'Why not? It wouldn't kill you.'

'It would. I've got principles, you know.'

Aria laughed, the sound surprisingly earthy and indecorous from such a patrician-looking woman.

Sarah said, 'No you haven't.'

Friday ignored her. 'Anyway, I shot down to St James's and had a chat to the reverend fellow, who's got a slot on Saturday the fifth, at eleven o'clock. He can do the wedding ceremony then.'

'Christ,' Enya said. 'That's only six days away.'

Kitty gazed at Friday in awe. 'How did you manage that?'

Friday rubbed her thumb and forefinger together in the universal gesture for money. 'Always works. Have you submitted the marriage application yet?'

'Rian's doing that this afternoon.' Kitty had no idea what Rian was doing, but she'd make damned sure the application was lodged before he got his supper.

'And the dress?' Friday asked.

'I'll definitely need help with that,' Enya said. 'Harrie, how busy are you at the moment?'

'Not too busy to lend a hand. Do you have a design?'

Enya gave her the sketch.

'Ooh, lovely. Are these single or double darts under the bust?'

'Double. They give a smoother fit.'

'And you've chosen the fabric?' Harrie asked Amber.

'Off-white silk satin, and Auntie Enya's given me some lovely Honiton lace.'

'Gorgeous! Look,' Harrie said, passing the sketch to Sarah.

Sarah had a look. 'Can you make this in a week, Harrie? It looks like a lot of work.'

Harrie raised her eyebrows at Enya, who replied, 'I was thinking we could ask Nora Barrett to help.'

'Yes, let's,' Harrie said. 'I'm sure with three of us we can get it done. Will you be available for fittings?' she asked Amber.

Amber nodded. 'We're staying . . . where are we staying, Ma? On the *Katipo* or ashore?'

'My house, of course,' Enya said.

Friday said, 'Good, that's settled. Now, rings. Sarah's said she'll make them for you at a good discount you really should take advantage of, 'cos she never offers discounts.'

'That's right, make me sound mean,' Sarah said.

'Well, you are.'

'I'm a businesswoman.'

'Aren't we all?'

'I can't make them for nothing because I have to pay the wholesale price for the gold and the stones, but I can offer you a forty per cent discount because you're Captain Farrell's daughter. That's the best I can do and there'll be no profit in it for me, but that's fine,' Sarah said. 'Do you have a betrothal ring?'

Amber presented her bare hands. 'And I don't want one, either, thank you.'

'Fair enough. What did you have in mind for your wedding ring?'

'I hadn't actually thought about it.'

Sarah took a pencil from her reticule, turned the drawing of the wedding gown over and started to sketch on the back of it.

'Sarah!' Harrie protested.

'What? It's just a drawing of a frock.'

'And you're just doing a drawing of a ring. Scribble on something else.'

'Shut up, you two,' Aria said mildly.

So far Aria had watched the proceedings in, Kitty thought, slightly amused, perhaps even bemused, silence, as though she thought all this fuss about a wedding was a waste of time.

'Will your fiancé want a wedding ring?' Sarah asked.

Amber said, 'I doubt it. He's not that sort of man.'

'What sort of man is he?' Aria asked.

'Well, he's . . . I don't know. He's lovely.'

'Name?' Aria demanded.

'Huatahi Atuahaere. He's Nga Puhi.'

'Same as you,' Friday remarked to Aria.

'Can we get back to the ring?' Sarah said. 'If you don't mind? Now, plain gold, or gem-set?'

Amber frowned. 'I don't know.'

'You don't know much, do you?'

Kitty bristled, but she needn't have.

'Actually, Mrs Green, I know a lot more than you seem to think I do,' Amber declared. 'It's just that I don't care much for jewellery and I really haven't thought about a wedding ring. But I suppose I do need one and I appreciate your generous offer and I'm happy to be guided by your obvious expertise.'

'Oh. Well, good.'

'Ha!' Friday laughed. 'That's put you in your place!'

'Excuse me.' Aria rose and left the room.

Kitty watched her go. 'Have we upset her?'

'Doubt it,' Friday said.

'If you'd like gem-set,' Sarah said, 'birthstones are popular for brides.'

'I don't know my real date of birth.'

'Or garnet or amethyst,' Sarah went on without missing a beat. 'Emerald or sapphire would look nice against your skin colour. Or aquamarine. I have three or four of those at the moment with very nice cuts.'

Amber looked at Kitty, who said, 'It's your choice, love.'

'Aquamarine, then.'

Sarah drew a quick sketch, and showed it to Amber.

'That's pretty. Can you make it so it doesn't stick up and catch on things?'

'I can. I'll get started this afternoon,' Sarah said. 'Do you do any sort of physical work?'

'Of course I do. I'm a crewman on Pa's ship.'

'Are you?' Friday exclaimed. 'Fancy that!'

'Better make it fifteen carat then,' Sarah muttered. 'More hard-wearing than eighteen carat.'

'Do you have bridesmaids and flower girls?' Harrie asked.

Amber looked alarmed. 'Er . . . '

'Because if you don't, I can supply dozens. Charlotte and Lewis's little girls will be happy to step in, and Hannah and Walter Cobley's two. And I have two other daughters who are eighteen and nineteen, and our friends Lucy and Matthew have older girls, too. And what about groomsmen?'

Overcome by a sense that things were slipping — no, being torn — from her grasp, Kitty raised her hands. 'Really, Mrs Downey — '

'Harrie!' Friday barked. 'Shut up. It's not your wedding, it's Amber's.'

Looking only marginally embarrassed, Harrie said, 'Quite right. I beg your pardon, Miss and Mrs Farrell. It's just that I do love weddings, don't you?'

Amber said, 'Thank you, Mrs Downey, but Tahi's grandfather will stand for him, and I'd like Delilah and Samson to attend me.'

Friday made a face. 'Who the fuck are Delilah and Samson?'

That bad language again, but this time it didn't bother Kitty nearly as much. 'You are *not* having a pair of cats as bridesmaids.'

'How *sweet!*' Harrie exclaimed.

Amber demanded, 'Why not?'

'Because it's absurd, they won't be allowed in the church, and they'll run away and get into trouble.'

'Knapped, you mean?' Friday said. 'Bloody cats, they're always doing that. Bloody kittens everywhere.'

'Ma, this is my wedding!'

'You're not having Delilah and Samson!'

'We'll elope!'

Already very close to the end of her tether, Kitty finally reached it. 'All right then, dear, you do that.'

Amber laughed. 'I knew you'd say that.'

'Is that what you really want?' Kitty asked. Because perhaps it was.

'Ma, I just want to marry Tahi, as soon as possible. I don't want a lot of fuss. And then I want us to find Bao. If I could have my way *she'd* be my bridesmaid, but I can't have that, can I?'

'No. I'd love Bao to be your bridesmaid, too, but everything's happening in the wrong order for that.' Kitty thought for a moment, then said decisively, 'Right. The church has been booked, the marriage application is being lodged today, the dress and ring are organised. So all we need to do now is find a venue for the wedding breakfast and buy Tahi a decent suit of clothes.'

'You can use the private lounge at the Siren's Arms for the breakfast,' Friday offered, 'which we can also cater. We have a very good cook and a decent wine cellar. Can't help you with the groom's wedding clothes, but.'

God, was there no end to this woman's generosity? It was . . . unnerving. 'Thank you very much, Miss Woolfe.'

'Friday,' Friday corrected.

'You will of course add the cost of that to the final account?'

'I've already said how much our fee will be.'

'Yes, well, thank you.' Five guineas with a bit extra for inflation wasn't going to cover the cost of everything Friday Woolfe was offering.

'I'm not looking forward to taking Tahi shopping,' Amber grumbled.

'Haunui can do that,' Kitty suggested.

Aria reappeared carrying a long and heavy-looking parcel wrapped in a bed sheet. She laid it across the arms of a chair and removed the sheet, revealing an extraordinarily beautiful cloak patterned with dense horizontal bands of kiwi and pheasant feathers woven into a base of flax fibre as soft as linen, with a wide taniko hem.

'This is a kahuhuruhuru made for my father, who died ten years ago. It was sent to me after my mother also passed. It is Nga Puhi so it is fitting that your fiancé wear it on the occasion of his marriage.'

'His grandmother was Hareta Atuahaere,' Kitty said, rashly letting out a secret she'd kept for decades and wondering why.

'Wife of Tupehu? He is Tupehu Atuahaere's moko?'

'No, he's the grandson of. Haunui Atuahaere, Tupehu's brother. Tahi's mother was Haunui and Hareta's daughter. She died here in Sydney in 1840, when Tahi was born.'

'Ah.'

No judgment whatsoever in that single little word, Kitty noted.

'Hareta was my great aunt,' Aria went on. 'I did not know her well. She left our hapu when she married Tupehu. I believe I only met her once.'

'So you and Tahi are related?' Kitty asked. Goodness.

'It seems so.' Aria reached into her pocket and brought out another parcel, this one wrapped in a square of silk and tied with ribbon, and offered it to Amber. 'Perhaps you would like to wear these?'

Opening the little packet, Amber gasped as she uncovered a tall, thin hair comb exquisitely carved from bone, and a pair of feathers Kitty recognised as those of the New Zealand huia bird.

'Ma, look! They're lovely! And only a princess can wear huia feathers. Haunui told me that.'

'Not with the veil,' Enya said quickly. 'The teeth on the comb will ruin it.'

'Then I won't have a veil. You don't mind, do you?'

Kitty thought Enya looked as though she did mind, but she very graciously said, 'It's your day, sweetheart. You can wear whatever you like.'

Amber beamed at Aria. 'Thank you, Miss Aria. And for the cloak. I know Tahi will appreciate it.'

'Won't he look like a chook, with that over his suit?' Friday commented.

'Shut up, Friday,' Aria, Harrie and Sarah said in unison.

★   ★   ★

As soon as Kitty and Amber left the brothel they belted along to Elizabeth Street — nearly as commercially busy as George Street these days — to the General Registry of Births, Deaths and Marriages, where they found Rian, Haunui and Tahi in the act of applying for a marriage licence. Kitty immediately felt guilty for doubting Rian, and wondered why she had. He'd never let Amber down before.

'Fancy seeing you here,' Rian said. 'How did your meeting go at . . . er . . . ' He eyed the dour-looking clerk examining a sheet of paper, his red ears almost visibly flapping. 'With our new confederates?'

'Very well.'

'No fisticuffs?'

'Don't be cheeky. No, everything's been arranged.'

'Good.'

The clerk stamped the paper so vigorously that everything on the counter rattled, then announced pompously to Tahi, 'You may expect to hear whether your application has been successful within eight to ten days.'

Or two, according to Friday, Kitty thought, her fingers crossed.

'Right, then, I'll see you back at Enya's,' Rian said.

'Why, where are you lot going?'

Rian looked at her. 'I don't know what Haunui's doing but I'm off to find Wong Kai to see what I can get out of him about Bao.'

'By yourself? He won't talk to you, you know.'

'How do you know he won't?'

'Because he's . . . difficult. I've dealt with him before, remember.'

'No, I don't specifically remember,' Rian said. 'I was indisposed, if *you* care to recall.'

Kitty hesitated; she was treading on very delicate ground here. At the time that Rian had been abducted and was seriously injured, prompting her to call on Wong Kai for help, she'd recently taken her comfort with Daniel Royce.

'Well, he is,' she said. 'Very difficult. He helped us then, but only because it suited him. He's a snake, Rian, and we should treat him like one.'

'I'm not scared of snakes.'

'You should be.'

'Time to go, boy,' Haunui said to Tahi.

121

But before they could move, Kitty asked, 'Will you take Amber back to Enya's, please?'

For a moment Amber looked as though she might protest, but in the end she merely took Tahi's hand.

Kitty and Rian watched them go.

'The Chinese quarter, then?' Rian said.

★   ★   ★

The 'Chinese quarter' wasn't an exclusively Oriental trading precinct, but an area on lower George Street near the wharves where more Chinese-operated businesses could be found in Sydney than anywhere else.

'Where will he be hiding?' Rian wondered aloud as they stood outside a draper's and tailor's owned, according to the brightly painted shingle above the shop front, by someone called Lau Chi Ho.

'He won't be *hiding*,' Kitty said. 'He'll be around here somewhere, squatting like a big fat spider in his fancy rooms counting his money.'

'Is he fat?'

'No, actually he isn't. He looks a lot like Fu.'

'Shall we ask in the draper's here? They all seem to know one another's business.'

While Rian liked Wong Fu very much, and a handful of other hong with whom he'd established good commercial relationships in Hong Kong, Shanghai and Macau, he was, in general, wary of the Chinese. In his opinion they could be secretive, suspicious and extremely wily. He did, however, remind himself that that could apply to businessmen of all stripes, including himself — perhaps it was the impenetrability of their languages that bothered him. The *Katipo* crew had enough smatterings of different European languages to eavesdrop successfully on many vendors' and buyers' conversations, but they had no hope of that with the Chinese. And the Chinese had a genuine reason for mistrusting and resenting Europeans: they were mistreated everywhere they went beyond their homelands, and had suffered for decades from the influx of opium forced onto their people by the bloody British.

'We can try, I. suppose.'

Rian followed Kitty into the store, which smelt of cotton and something else he couldn't place. A Chinese man wearing smart European clothes stood at the counter folding a length of fabric.

'Good afternoon,' Kitty said. 'We're looking for a gentleman named Mr Wong Kai. Would you know where we could find him, please?'

The man stopped his folding and looked at Kitty for a long, calculating moment. 'Good afternoon, madam. He has rooms above Sun Lee Sing's furniture store. But you will need to speak to Mr Sun first.'

'Of course. Thank you for your help.'

Outside, Kitty and Rian passed a laundry, a fruit and vegetable market, a Chinese herbalist, three boarding houses for Chinese men, a shop advertising services such as letter writing, grog shops, cook shops, several general stores selling imported Chinese products, and what were clearly a couple of gambling dens before entering Sun Lee Sing's emporium.

'Mr Sun?' Kitty asked as they were approached

by yet another Chinese man wearing better clothes than Rian owned.

The man bowed.

'We're looking for Mr Wong Kai and were directed here,' Kitty said.

'A business matter?'

'You could say that,' Rian replied.

'One moment.'

Mr Sun went to the back of the store and struck a small gong, which reverberated right through Rian's head, then stood in repose, as still as one of his pieces of furniture.

Eventually another man appeared, this one wearing traditional Chinese dress.

'Oh,' Kitty said, sounding surprised. 'Hello, So-Yee.'

'Good afternoon, Mrs Farrell, Captain Farrell. You wish to speak with Wong Kai?'

Puzzled, Rian looked at her. 'Who's this?'

'You won't remember him. He was there when we rescued you.'

Rian felt his shoulders tense; Christ, that annoyed him. It made him sound so pathetic. And no, he didn't remember the man, the sour-looking bastard.

'He works for Wong Kai,' Kitty went on. 'And, yes, please, we do need to speak to him,' she said to So-Yee.

'Come.'

They followed him through to the back of the store, upstairs and down a long corridor, seeing no one. So-Yee knocked on a door and ushered them in.

A man sat behind a vast, highly polished desk

on a chair that was, Rian thought, ridiculously close to a throne. He looked so much like Fu that he had to be Wong Kai.

He didn't get up, though he did say, 'Mrs Farrell, how delightful to see you again.'

'Good afternoon, Mr Wong,' Kitty said. 'It's good to see you again, too. This is my husband, Captain Rian Farrell. Rian, this is Mr Wong Kai.'

Rian nodded. 'Mr Wong. Please accept my belated gratitude for your help when, er, I required it.' The words stuck in his throat, but they needed to be said.

It was Kai's turn to nod, as if saving abducted people from crazed criminals was all in a day's work. He gestured with a lazy hand. 'Please, sit. I trust you have recovered from your travails in Ballarat and Melbourne?'

'Well, I should have,' Rian said. 'It was nine years ago.'

'Indeed.'

'You've cut your hair,' Kitty remarked.

Rian gave her a look: it seemed a very intimate thing to say.

She met his gaze. 'The last time Mr Wong and I met he wore his hair in the Manchu style.'

Many Chinese still did shave their foreheads and wear the long braided queue, but more and more, Rian was noticing, were cutting their hair into European styles, as Kai had done.

'You haven't joined the Taipings, have you?' he asked.

Kai smiled a bit unpleasantly and with such ease that Rian wondered whether he ever smiled any other way. 'You understand that the queue is a symbol of subjugation to the. Manchu rulers of the Qing dynasty? And that failure to wear the hairstyle is punishable by beheading?'

'Yes, actually,' Rian replied, regretting his comment now.

'What do you know about the God Worshipping Society?' Kai asked.

Understanding that he was referring to the Taiping rebels, Rian said, 'Not much.'

'They have been at war against the Qing dynasty for thirteen years. They were formed by a man named Hong who believes he is the brother of your Jesus Christ.' Kai spread his hands in a 'what can I say?' gesture. 'He. has based his new dynasty, the Heavenly Kingdom of Great Peace, on Christian precepts and declared himself Heavenly King. They have outlawed prostitution, slavery, foot-binding, the subjugation of women, adultery, gambling, opium smoking, and the use of alcohol and tobacco.'

Kitty asked, 'You don't agree with outlawing slavery, foot-binding and the subjugation of women?'

Kai shrugged. 'Who am I to attempt to change the customs of a thousand years? That is the emperor's job. Or God's, which in our culture is the same thing. The Taipings' God, however, knows no mercy whatsoever. Their army is a million strong and they have raged through the south-eastern provinces of China. Twenty million people have lost their lives.' He sat back. 'No, Captain Farrell, I have not joined the Taipings. I have adopted a European hairstyle and clothing because the businessmen I treat with find a

European countenance to be more acceptable. But you did not come here to talk about the God Worshipping. Society, did you?'

'No, we did not,' Kitty said. 'We'd like to talk about your niece, Bao.'

Kai remained silent.

'We were recently in Dunedin, where we saw Fu,' Rian said. 'He told us that Bao was sent away by you without his permission, and that she's to marry someone as part of a business deal. Is he correct in assuming that?'

Kai eyed him for a long moment. 'This is family business, Captain, and Chinese family business at that. Fu is a weak man. And ill. He should not speak of our affairs outside the family.'

'The tong, you mean,' Kitty said. 'This is to do with you gaining power, isn't it?'

Kai brushed an invisible speck of something off his immaculately cut, pure linen waistcoat. 'If I may be so forthright, Mrs Farrell, that is not your affair.'

Rian saw the set of his wife's jaw and leant back in his chair, waiting for the explosion.

'Yes. It. Is,' she said, her voice frosty enough to blacken the leaves of the hardiest of plants. 'We're very fond of Bao and so is my daughter. We're extremely concerned for her, and for Fu. He's asked us to find her and return her to him, so we would appreciate you telling us where she is, please.'

Kai laughed. 'I am afraid I cannot do that.'

'Cannot, or will not?'

'All right, *will* not, if you insist.'

Kitty took a second to smooth the fabric of her skirt, her head down, lips pursed. Then she said, 'You know, Mr Wong, when you and I did business in Melbourne, I thought the deal we struck concerning the gold was fair. And of course I'll always be grateful for your assistance regarding the matter of Avery Bannerman.' She looked up. 'But you didn't do that for me, did you? Bannerman and Lily Pearce were rivals and you had to get rid of them. You don't do anything if it doesn't benefit you, do you? You're as selfish and greedy as Fu is kind and wise. It's no wonder he's the Cloud Leopard and you're not.'

Kai's face remained impassive as he said, 'Captain, please control your wife's behaviour.'

'Haven't been able to so far.'

Kitty crossed to Kai's desk and leant over it as far as she could reach. 'Where is she, Kai? Who's got her?'

Alarmed now, Rian also stood.

'China isn't that big, you know,' Kitty went on. 'We know she must be there somewhere. We'll find her.'

Unperturbed, Kai replied, 'Are you sure my brother's intelligence is correct? She could be anywhere. And China is *very* big.'

Rian took Kitty's arm. 'We should go. This isn't getting us anywhere.'

Kai said, 'Yes, please do leave. And if you persist in trying to find my niece, you will very much regret it.'

Outside in the hallway So-Yee was waiting to escort them back downstairs, which he did in silence. In the doorway of Sun Lee Sing's furniture store, where they all stood blinking in the sunlight, he said suddenly, 'I am very fond of Bao. She is in Hong Kong. If you locate a man named Yip Chun Kit, also known as the Frog, you will find her.'

Rian and Kitty stared at him. Kitty said, 'You sent Fu the letter!'

'Yes.'

'Why didn't you tell him Bao had been sent to Hong Kong?' Rian asked. 'Would have saved us all a lot of time.'

So-Yee fixed him with a hard look. 'When I wrote the letter I did not know. But now you do. She has faith in you, and so must I. Please bring her back.'

Rian met So-Yee's gaze for a moment, then gave him a firm nod.

5

It rained a little on the morning of Amber and Tahi's wedding day, but no one cared. Amber looked gorgeous, with a veil after all, arranged to safely accommodate Aria's comb and huia plumes, and Tahi a very suitable consort in the feathered cloak fastened over his new morning suit. The cats, Delilah and Samson, did attend the ceremony, though not as bridesmaids despite the satin ribbons they wore around their necks. Pierre and Simon sneaked them into the church in wicker baskets, though the cats gave themselves away by yowling during the consecration. Nonplussed, the reverend stared intently into the small congregation, who gazed resolutely back while Amber giggled into her bouquet of cream daffodils.

Rian gave Amber away and Kitty was her maid-of-honour, wearing her indigo velvet skirt and a tightly-fitting jade brocade jacket made by Harrie Downey. Haunui was Tahi's best man, squeezed into a suit of clothes, hired for the occasion, that were really not big enough. He spent half the service wriggling about trying surreptitiously to encourage the seat of the trousers out of his backside

Pierre was, as usual, splendidly attired. He wore a cream satin brocade waistcoat embroidered with tiny sprigs of forget-me-nots over a white linen shirt, a navy blue velvet coat and off-white trousers and reeked of lavender scent, and received the usual hectoring from the crew for it, which he nobly ignored. The standard of dress went down from there, terminating in Mick, whose best trousers had a tear in the knee and who'd spilled rum on his shirt even before they'd arrived at the church.

'That went well,' Rian said to Kitty as they exited St James's after the ceremony.

'It did,' she replied happily. 'Isn't she beautiful?'

They looked fondly at Amber standing with Tahi and Israel. She was laughing uproariously at something, her head thrown back, her glorious hair tumbling down her back. Tahi was gazing at her, and so was Israel. But who wouldn't? Kitty thought. She was such a bright and vivacious girl. Then Israel thumped Tahi on the back, so hard in fact that Tahi took a step forwards, then said something that must have been equally funny because they all laughed like hell again. Then Israel waved to Mick, gave Amber a quick peck on the cheek, and trotted off.

'I hope he doesn't feel too left out,' Kitty said. 'Who?'

'Israel, now that Amber and Tahi are married.'

'For God's sake,' Rian said, 'it's a ship's crew I'm running here, not a bloody schoolyard. Are you ready to go? I'm starving.'

Friday and Aria provided a truly delicious wedding breakfast at the Siren's Arms, including soup, oysters, fish, poultry, joints, several game pies, boiled and roasted vegetables, fancy jellies, pastries and tarts, a wedding cake with two sugar cats prancing across the top (decorated by Harrie), ale, spirits and French wine, some very fine pekoe tea and good percolated coffee. Even Pierre approved.

It was fortunate the breakfast was held in a private room, as several crew members drank far too much and would have been thrown into the street had they been drinking in a public bar. Friday and, to a considerably lesser extent, Aria found their antics entertaining and came in periodically for a look and to check whether anything more was needed.

'God, would you look at that,' Friday said in wonder as she watched Pierre doing his special rendition of a sailor's hornpipe. 'The things you see when you haven't got a gun.'

'That one over there looks like he is about to vomit,' Aria grumbled.

'Where?'

'That one, with the torn trousers.'

'Mick bloody Doyle. Never mind. It'll wash out.' Friday shook her head. 'And I thought I made a fool of myself on the jar.'

'You did.'

'But not like this.'

'That is what you say.'

'Come on, let's leave them to it.'

Kitty watched them go, slightly embarrassed by the crew's dreadful behaviour but not really caring. They were enjoying themselves and there wouldn't be time, or the opportunity, for relaxing once they were on their way to Hong Kong. In any case it wasn't all of them. Hawk didn't drink much and neither did Gideon, and Simon only needed three ales or two glasses of wine before he fell asleep. She closed her eyes painfully as Pierre launched into the first verse of 'Hanging Johnny', then opened them to a roar of laughter.

Israel was doing his drunken best to climb up onto a chair.

'I'd like to ma — . Christ!' Over backwards he went, taking the chair with him.

Cheers and vigorous banging on the table.

He reappeared, grinning, righted the chair, grabbed Simon's tankard of ale and laboriously clambered up again. 'I'd like to make a speesh to my bes' mate Tahi here, who jus' got married. Yes. Tahi an' Amber.' He raised the tankard to the ceiling, slopping beer down his arm and all over Simon, and said it again together with everyone else. 'Tahi's my bes' mate. An' so's Amber. May the bes' man win an' he has. You b'long together. What a han'some couple. Um, what else? May your life be full of luck an' happiness.'

Another cheer went up.

Kitty glanced at Haunui: he wasn't smiling.

'Tahi's my bes' mate,' Israel said again. 'An' Amber. The mos' beau'ful girl in the whole wide worl'.' He looked down, wobbling dangerously. 'Shoulda been me, eh Tahi? But you deserve her 'cos we're mates. May the bes' man win. Tahi an' Amber!'

'Tahi and Amber!'

'Get down before you fall down,' Hawk said.

Israel tipped his head back and poured the ale down his throat, then flung the empty tankard at the wall. Being pewter, it bounced.

'I said sit down!' Hawk ordered.

Simon gripped Israel's hand and helped him slide into his seat.

'Shoulda been me,' Israel muttered again as he subsided face first into a half-eaten plate of jelly.

'He'll have a sore head in the morning,' Rian said to Kitty.

'And so will you if you don't stop drinking.'

'It's not every day our daughter gets married.'

'I damn well hope not.'

After the breakfast, Mr and Mrs Atuahaere retired — with unseemly haste, Kitty and Rian thought — to Enya's home for a 'rest', while everyone else stayed on at the Siren's Arms for a few hours more. At the end of the afternoon Friday and Aria presented Rian with an invoice for six guineas, for food and alcohol, venue hire and services rendered.

Kitty whipped the invoice out of Rian's hand and examined it. 'This is a ridiculously low amount. It's less than Amber's ring cost, and Mrs Green gave us a huge discount.'

Friday shrugged. 'It's what we agreed. We're happy with it.'

'But — '

'No buts, Mrs Farrell,' Aria said. 'Your daughter and new son-in-law are charming and we were pleased to be of assistance, but this specific figure pertains to a debt thirty years old. Once settled it will be cleared. We always pay our debts.'

Rian withdrew his purse from his coat pocket, counted out six sovereigns, and set them on the table. 'I take it we're square now?'

'We are,' Friday replied, and offered her hand.

Rian shook it. 'Lovely doing business with you.'

Friday squeezed his. fingers as vigorously as possible. 'And you, Captain.'

Kitty said quickly, 'Thank you for all your help, ladies. We appreciate it. Amber and Tahi had a lovely day.'

'Let's just hope they're not making a baby as we speak, eh?' Friday said. 'Not a lot of room on a ship for a baby.'

Kitty could only agree.

★   ★   ★

While Kitty, Rian and Enya went back to Enya's, the rest of the crew walked — or staggered — the short distance from Harrington Street down to Semi-Circular Quay to the *Katipo*, the sun just beginning to dip below the ridge behind them. The waterfront was still busy with lumpers, stevedores and provedores bustling backwards and forwards servicing the many ships tied up along the wharves before the light went.

Dodging a horse and dray piled precariously high with recently unloaded bales of cotton, Hawk led the way towards Queen's Wharf, casting an occasional glance over his shoulder to make sure his drunken charges were still all present and correct. Yes, and there was Gideon, wearing his usual patient expression and stolidly bringing up the rear.

On Queen's Wharf itself Hawk slowed as something caught his eye, a slim shadow dropping off the side of the *Katipo*'s gangway. The shadow melded with several others skulking against the ship's hull, then resolved into the shape of three Chinese men emerging into the light of the fading sun and walking along the wharf.

Hawk grabbed the arm of the closest as they approached. 'What were you doing on my ship?'

The man stared at him then shook him off, saying something in Cantonese.

'I saw you, one of you was on my ship,' Hawk insisted. 'What were you doing?'

The man looked at his companions in apparent confusion, then back at Hawk, and shrugged.

'Do not act like you do not understand!' Hawk felt himself losing his temper. 'I saw one of you on the gangway!'

The man spoke again in Cantonese, and gave another exaggerated shrug.

'Perhaps he really does not understand,' Gideon suggested.

Mick said, 'Let's beat the shite out of him. That'll loosen his tongue.'

'Shut up,' Hawk snapped. 'Gideon did you see someone on the gangway?'

Gideon, ever honest, replied, 'No, but I was not looking.'

Hawk glared at all three Chinese then forced himself to step aside. They'd been up to no good, he damn well knew they had. They stared back at him for a second then moved off, and disappeared into the crowd.

★   ★   ★

The crew were above deck preparing to set sail as the high tide turned. It was early morning and most were suffering from the horrors. They grizzled and grumbled their way around the ship barely speaking.

Not Haunui, however.

'E hoa!' he called, despite his thumping head, as Ropata jumped the last few feet down from the base of the main mast.

His friend approached, looking seedy. 'I am never drinking wine again. It does not suit me.'

In heartfelt agreement Haunui blew out his tattooed cheeks, turning them into small balloons. 'You remember what I said to you about that one?' he asked in Maori, nodding towards Israel, who was sweating away farther along the deck coiling a massive length of rope.

Ropata nodded. 'Did you see him yesterday?'

'I did. Staring at Amber the whole time. And you would have thought Tahi was his own son getting married, he was that happy for him.'

'Too happy?'

'Far too happy. He drank too much and in his cups he let his true feelings show.'

'Just a little. He is not stupid,' Ropata said.

'He is not that clever, either, but he is cunning. I am worried. I do not trust him. He is planning something.'

'What?'

'How should I know? But I feel it.' Israel glanced towards them. Haunui waved cheerfully and switched back to English. 'Leena seems well, eh? It was good to see her at the wedding.'

'She is well. And so are the kids.'

'If she was my woman I wouldn't be at sea all the bloody time.'

Ropata made a face. 'You know what it's like. Once the sea gets hold of you . . . '

Haunui nodded, because he did, sort of. He sniffed. 'You know, boy,' he said, even though Ropata was in his forties, 'you stink like a brewery.'

'So do you.'

They grinned at each other.

★   ★   ★

Two men, standing in the shadows of a warehouse, watched keenly as the slack in the rope between the tug and the *Katipo* tightened and the big schooner began slowly to move away from Queen's Wharf.

'How far ahead of you will you allow him to sail?' Wong Kai asked his companion.

'Not far,' Lo Fang Yi replied. 'His ship is fast. It would not do to let him out of sight.'

Kai eyed Lo Fang. He was tall for a Chinese, and favoured the queue and traditional loose trousers and tunic of a professional sailor. He had worked for Kai on and off for some years, owned a fast European-style schooner himself, and Kai knew he was utterly ruthless and loyal only to whoever was paying him.

'And if he sees you?'

'What if he does? Many vessels sail the route north-west up through the Pacific. He is committed to sailing to Hong Kong, yes?'

'To China. He is not aware that my niece is in

Hong Kong. I do not know at which port he intends to land.'

'Then he will have to tolerate being followed.' Lo Fang Yi paused, then added, 'Until the time comes for us to no longer follow him.'

★　★　★

Lo Fang Yi was right: ocean-going traffic was fairly busy following the route between Australia's eastern seaboard and around New Guinea and the Philippines, mostly shipping engaged in trade with China's eastern ports, Japan and, less frequently, Russia. But by the time the *Katipo* had entered the Coral Sea and was approaching the Solomon Islands, the crew had noticed that one vessel in particular was tailing them somewhat persistently.

On a warm, windy morning Mick shouted down from the crow's nest, 'She's there again. Have a look.'

Rian shut one eye, raised his spyglass to the other and had a good long stare at the ship rocking smoothly along some distance behind them, then handed the glass to Hawk.

As Hawk lowered it Rian asked, 'What do you think?'

'Did you see the flag?'

Rian had; a yellow rectangle with a bright red disc in the centre. A sun? 'Looks vaguely Chinese to me, but China doesn't have a national flag.'

'Pirates?'

'This far from the motherland? Wouldn't think

so. Chinese privateers usually stay pretty near their own coast. And it's a schooner, not a junk.'

'That does not mean they are not pirates.'

Rian said, 'Christ, do you want them to be?'

Hawk said nothing, ignoring his little outburst.

Squinting at the ship, reduced to a dot now without the benefit of the spyglass, Rian muttered, 'I wonder if they're working for Wong Kai, if it's a Chinese vessel.'

'Why would he send someone after us?' Hawk snorted. 'Does he think he can stop us?'

Rian took the glass off Hawk and had another look. 'It's not a gun ship. At least, I can't see any gun ports without a view of the side.'

'It is too small for a gun ship. Unless there are cannon on deck, but I did not see any. Did you?'

'No. Did you notice it anchored in Sydney Harbour?' It was the sort of thing to which Hawk usually did pay attention; if the ship were armed it wouldn't have been permitted to moor in the cove.

Hawk shook his head.

'God.' Rian rubbed his hand across his face. 'Well, we'll just have to keep a bloody good eye on her then, won't we?'

* * *

Amber wrinkled her nose. 'Do cats make a noise when they fart?'

'What? I wouldn't think so. Their bums are built wrong,' Tahi replied, then gagged slightly. 'God, they make a stink, though.'

140

Laughing, Amber clambered over him and opened the porthole, then shooed Samson and Delilah off the bed towards the cabin door, which she flapped vigorously behind them.

'What's Pierre been feeding them, I wonder?'

'I doubt it's their dinner making them smell like that,' Tahi said. 'It'll be all those rats from the hold.'

'I don't think they actually eat many of those. You've seen the bits all over the deck. Would you, if you could have Pierre's cooking?'

'I'm not a cat.'

To be honest Tahi wasn't all that keen on Samson and Delilah, even if they did earn their keep regulating the ship's rat population, but Amber absolutely adored them and he was more than willing to tolerate whatever made her happy. He now had the two things he loved most in life — Amber and the sea — not counting his koro, of course. He loved Haunui very much as well. And to think he was married to Amber because Rian caught them in bed together. What was that saying Pakeha people had? Every cloud has silver inside it? Surely this cloud had so much shiny silver it must fall right out of the sky.

Amber jumped on the narrow bed, landing astride him and nearly making him do a patero of his own. That would be extremely embarrassing. They hadn't been married nearly long enough for him to be doing that in front of her.

'So!' she said, leaning down and kissing his forehead, the ends of her hair tickling his face.

'So what, Missus?'

'So where's my treat?'

Tahi wriggled his hips. 'Same place it always is, waiting for you.'

Amber grinned.

Tahi did too, but perhaps not quite so enthusiastically, and hoped she didn't notice. They'd been having sex morning and night since the wedding and his ure was actually getting quite sore, and though most of him might not need a rest from love-making, he suspected that bit of him did. He'd asked his koro and then Mick about it, and they'd both laughed at him. But he couldn't help himself — Amber need only smile at him and he was ready. Even just the scent of her hair was enough to set him off. It was . . . feral. He felt like some sort of animal on heat. It was fantastic.

And he knew Amber was just as delighted with him as he was with her, even if it was boastful of him to think that. But he did know it, in his heart and in his belly. And she'd told him on their wedding night she didn't want to share him, not even with a child, which is why every day first thing she took extra care with her women's paraphernalia that would stop a baby from taking hold. He never looked while she did it because it was anything but his business, so he never knew quite what she was doing, but she said between her mother and Aunt Enya she had things pretty well organised. He hoped so. One day they'd have a family, but not yet. For now he was happy just to practise.

'I want to ask you something first.'

'What?' Amber looked excited.

'How do you think Israel's been?' Tahi was

worried. His friend seemed a bit . . . moody lately. Perhaps even jealous.

'Israel? What do you mean? I don't want to talk about Israel. Not *now*.'

'I just wondered if you'd noticed anything, I don't know, *different* about him.'

Amber sat back on Tahi's thighs and crossed her arms. 'Not really. He's been a bit quiet. I just thought he was . . . ' she thought for a moment' . . . giving us room to be man and wife, I suppose. Why?'

'I'm not sure.' Tahi thought, Israel *couldn't* be jealous, surely? He'd always known about his love for Amber. He'd never hidden it. Perhaps he needed to talk to his friend.

But not now. Amber was right; behind closed doors was for him and her.

★   ★   ★

Tahi was dreaming. He and Amber were walking, though he didn't know where. Not in a city, and he didn't recognise the landscape. She was telling him all about Bao, which was silly, because he already knew Bao. He told her so, and she turned her beautiful face to him and said, 'Oh, that's right. I forgot.'

And that hurt his feelings because he never forgot anything about her, and he had to remind himself that this was only a dream, and you couldn't control what happened in dreams.

And then she said, 'You know, Tahi, I hate to ruin such a lovely day . . . ' which was odd, because it had been daytime a moment ago, but now it was night ' . . . but I think something bad's coming.'

He glanced around, and even though it was dark he could still see, and nothing looked wrong. 'What do you mean, bad?'

She shrugged in that way she had that mostly he thought was adorable — what was that word? Whimsical? — but was sometimes a little bit annoying. 'I don't know, do I? Just bad.'

They walked on. After a while they came across Pierre, Simon, Mick and Ropata, sitting around a little table eating beef and piccalilli sandwiches and playing poker.

'Hey,' Tahi said. 'Something bad's coming.'

But they couldn't seem to hear him, or see him for that matter, and kept on playing.

Amber took his arm. 'Never mind. Come on, we'll be late.'

'What for?'

'Hong Kong.'

'But aren't we all going?'

'Bao hasn't got time to wait for them to finish playing cards. She needs to be rescued,' Amber said, and ran off.

'No! No, wait!' Tahi ran after her, but the faster he ran the slower he seemed to go, but that was all right because Amber didn't appear to be getting much farther ahead, either.

The sun came up then, and when he shielded his eyes he saw it wasn't the sun but a great, gleaming, bronze and gold dragon rising up over the horizon, like a taniwha snorting monstrous jets of fire and smoke. He called over his shoulder for help but there was no one there;

Pierre and the others had vanished.

The dragon came closer and closer, hovering above them, filling the air with heat and soot. Tahi screamed out, 'Run, Amber, run!' but she just stood there staring up at the huge creature, apparently mesmerised by its shining scales, massive beating wings and emerald eyes. He tried to move towards her but his feet were melting into the ground and now his hair and skin were catching alight.

Amber, though, wasn't on fire. She stood in a circle untouched by flame and still the dragon descended until a scaly claw reached down and snatched her up; with a thunderous flapping of wings and a swirl of smoke and searing heat, the thing turned and disappeared up into the sky.

'No!' Tahi screamed after it. 'No!' Then he fell face first onto the suddenly cold ground as darkness crept over him.

He lay there for days — or was it only seconds? — until a voice told him to get up.

'Mama?'

'You cannot lie there forever, child.'

He rolled over and sat up. His mother appeared as she always did when she came to him: a neat-figured sixteen-year-old girl with black hair to her waist and beautiful dark eyes. It was strange to think that he was already seven years older than she would ever be. This time, though, she was wearing the feathered kahuhuruhuru that Aria Te Kainga-Mataa had lent him on his wedding day.

'The taniwha took Amber, Mama.'

'Well, then, get her back.'

145

He stood up, relieved to discover that his feet were no longer melted. 'I don't know how,' he admitted, ashamed because now she would think her father had raised a heahea.

'Do not be a fool, child. Follow them.'

He winced. She *did* think he was being an idiot. 'But he's a powerful taniwha. I'm just a seaman.'

She came to him and touched his cheek with a hand that felt like ice on a winter puddle. 'You are not 'just' a seaman. You are my son, the mokopuna of Haunui and Hareta, and the descendant of countless esteemed rangatira. You have friends and you have the sight. You can do anything you wish to do, so do not whinge.'

He put his hand over hers and it went right through so that he felt the skin of his own face. 'But a taniwha, mama!'

'You must ask the cat for help. The cat will help you.'

She started to fade. He opened his mouth to beg her not to go, but now he was flat on his back again, utterly unable to move, and the words wouldn't come out. Try as he might all he could manage was the faintest exhalation of air. He wanted to shout out for her, for Amber, for anyone, but he couldn't even move a finger, never mind make a noise. His mind was racing but his body was as unresponsive as a corpse's.

Was he dying?

Was he already dead?

But if he was, surely he wouldn't still be breathing? He stilled his lungs, feeling his blood pound in his head, and moments later he awoke.

He reached out a hand, felt Amber sleeping peacefully beside him, and almost wept with relief.

★   ★   ★

The following day Tahi sat down with Israel in the lee of the cabin and asked if they could talk.

'What about?'

'Dunno, really,' Tahi replied, though he did.

Israel pulled up his knees to make a little shelter, stuffed tobacco into his pipe, lit it and drew hard. 'Who d'you think's on that ship?' he asked, jerking his head towards the *Katipo*'s stern.

'Rian says it's Wong Kai's men.' Tahi didn't smoke, so, for something to do, he picked at a small hole in his trousers.

'Might not be, but.'

'Who else would it be? Who else knows we're headed for Hong Kong?'

'Could be just anyone going the same way,' Israel said.

'They're sticking pretty close if they are.' Tahi glanced into Israel's eyes, then looked away again. 'Do you really think so?'

'Nah. I think it's Wong Kai's men.'

They sat in silence for a few minutes. Finally Tahi said, 'It's a bit strange.'

'What is?'

'Being married.'

Israel didn't reply. Tahi wanted to see what his face was doing but thought it better not to look. 'I'm used to being by myself, especially at night,

147

and now . . . I'm not.' God, that hadn't come out the way he'd meant it to. 'I mean, it's good, but it's strange.'

'Having to spend your nights in bed with a gorgeous girl like Amber? Sounds like torture.'

Tahi did look then. A cheeky grin spread across Israel's face and he elbowed Tahi in the ribs, quite hard.

Relieved, Tahi said, 'No, it's not quite that bad.' And then felt deeply disloyal to Amber.

Israel laughed. 'Look, I said at the wedding you're a lucky bastard, and I meant it. She's a lovely girl and you've always wanted her, haven't you? I'm happy for you. For both of you.'

'She thought — we thought — you were a bit quiet. Now, I mean.'

'Just giving you time to get used to being married.' Israel sucked the life out of his pipe again. 'Don't worry, it'll wear off.'

'I was worried you might be . . . well, I don't know.'

'Jealous? Bugger off. I couldn't be happier. You're me best mate even if you have gone and got yourself hitched'

Hawk shouted out then for help trimming a sail.

Tahi got to his feet. Israel looked up at him and for a moment Tahi stared down at his bronze hair, greenish eyes and the golden hairs on his bare arms.

'Yeah,' he said. 'You are.'

★   ★   ★

148

The crew observed the mystery ship tailing them day after day as they sailed up towards New Guinea and between the southern-most tip of the long skinny isle of New Ireland and Bougainville Island, north-west of the Solomon chain. Keeping sight of her was easy while the weather remained clement, but once they moved beyond the relative shelter of land they met the full force of the Pacific Ocean. In one respect conditions were favourable as both the current and south-east trade winds were assisting them in the right direction, however typhoon season in the tropics was also imminent.

One morning, as they were sailing north-west through the Philippine Sea, Gideon interrupted Rian at the mess table and, in his perfect English, calmly advised that the wind was picking up and that a bank of sinister black clouds was amassed on the horizon.

'North, or west?' Rian asked.

'Nor-west.'

'Bugger.'

Bugger was right, Kitty thought. A typhoon coming straight in off the open sea could be terribly vicious.

'Can we make it to land before it hits?' Rian asked. 'How far away are we?'

'I do not think so,' Gideon replied. 'Neither does Hawk.'

Rian stuffed a piece of bacon into his mouth and followed Gideon up the companion ladder.

Kitty glanced at Amber, who said, 'I'm going up for a look, too.'

'I'll be up in a minute,' Kitty said.

She was both frightened and exhilarated by the awful, wild power of storms at sea. The *Katipo* was well built and sturdy, and Rian a very capable captain, but she was frequently astonished, not to mention extremely thankful, by the fact that whenever filthy weather descended upon them, they always popped out the other side of it relatively unscathed.

Gathering up an armful of breakfast dishes she carried them into the galley. 'You should probably put the stove out, Pierre. Gideon says there's a typhoon coming.' Just as she finished saying it she noticed that the stove door stood open and the flames had already been doused.

'I know, chérie, I can feel her.' Looking crestfallen, Pierre pointed to a tray of half-baked buns. 'Look at my sweet rolls, they be ruined. By the time the storm passes the yeast will be over and done with and there will be no rising!'

How typical of Pierre to be more upset by a spoilt batch of buns, Kitty thought, than a dirty great typhoon bearing down on them. 'Do you need a hand to secure everything in here?' she asked.

'I be fine. Just see to the cats, eh? Tell Rian I be on deck shortly.'

Kitty went in search of Samson and Delilah, found them in her and Rian's cabin, and shut them in. Then she ventured up on deck, grabbing at her hair as the wind whipped it wildly around her head. Overhead the sails snapped and billowed. The air, smelling of salt and metal, was warm and heavy with the threat of rain, and though the Philippine Islands were somewhere off to port, there were no birds at all in the ragged, yellowing sky. On the horizon, at a distance of about three miles, towered a colossal wall of steel-grey cloud.

The ship lurched in response to a sudden swell, and Kitty grabbed for the rail. As though the sea heaving was the signal for the turmoil to begin, the wind roared across them with a noise like a steam locomotive at full power and a fat raindrop drove into her cheek. She felt like she'd been shot. Within seconds the rain was pelting down.

'Get below,' Rian shouted. 'Take Amber.'

Still gripping the rail, Kitty glanced around the deck, noting that the crew had already battened everything down. She didn't want to go below, too fascinated — mesmerised, almost — by the approaching storm. But she did grab Amber's arm and urge her towards the cabin door, where they crouched.

'I said get below!' Rian bellowed at them before he turned back to the crew, ordering, 'Box off! Now!'

Kitty watched as the crew struggled to set the sails, attempting to turn the stern of the ship into the storm. They didn't need to be told what to do, of course, being as skilled and experienced as Rian, but someone had to be in charge. It was how a well-run ship operated.

'Brace up all the lower yards then go free!'

Kitty knew he'd be heading for land in an attempt to outrun the storm. She stood to peep over the cabin roof in the hope of glimpsing the islands that lay to the west, but saw nothing but

151

a wall of driving rain and almost had her hair torn off by the wind. Swearing and ducking down again, she grabbed at Amber as the ship listed heavily and they both slid on their knees across the drenched deck, stopping only when they collided with the bulwark. Kitty winced as a long scratch on her calf seeped blood through a rip in her trousers. Seeing the expression on Rian's face as he started towards them, she indicated to Amber that perhaps they really should go below.

Rian lost his footing, coming to a crashing halt on his arse several feet away. 'For fuck's sake!' he roared, his face scarlet. 'Get below!'

Kitty nodded and crawled towards the cabin door, but before she and Amber reached it came a noise, audible even above the pounding rain and shrieking wind, that froze her blood; the unmistakable sound of the belly of the large main course sail tearing. She whipped her head around in time to see the mizzen course go as well, and then the fore course, which was very odd. A few seconds later, the spanker at the bow tore apart. The wind roared through the new gaps and the *Katipo*'s speed dropped dramatically.

Scrambling to his feet Rian bellowed, 'Take in the lot! We'll go bare.'

Kitty knew, as she wrestled with the cabin door and stepped carefully onto the companion ladder, he had no choice, if he wanted to save the remaining sails. They would just have to bob wildly about wherever the typhoon took them and pray it wouldn't be to the bottom of the sea.

Amber slammed the door shut behind her and came down the ladder backwards. They were both utterly drenched.

She sat at the mess table, her feet braced wide for balance, wringing out her hair. 'Pa's going bare poles,' she said, her voice raised almost to a shout over the creaking and groaning of the *Katipo*'s beleaguered timbers.

'It's safest,' Kitty replied as she inspected the scratch on her leg. She'd survive. And going bare *was* safest, in theory.

'We look like drowned rats.' Amber gasped. 'Oh Christ, where are the cats?'

'Shut in our cabin.'

Staggering across the room like a drunk, Amber shoved open her parents' cabin door and peered into the gloom. 'I can't see them.'

Kitty joined her, holding onto the wall for stability. She couldn't either, though she could certainly smell cat shit, the poor, frightened little beggars. Rian wasn't going to be pleased. She got down on her knees and peered under the bed, and there they were, huddling together in the farthest corner, two pairs of eyes gleaming out at her. 'Come on, chickens, out you come.'

No, they were staying where they were. She didn't blame them. 'Where have they shat?'

'Don't know,' Amber replied. 'Let's worry about that later.'

They shut the door on the cats and retreated to the mess table, feet hooked around bench legs to stop themselves from sliding and hands gripping the edge of the worn table top.

After a few minutes Amber said tentatively, 'I

hope they're all right up there.'

'Try not to fret, love. They'll be down as soon as the sails are furled. We've been through this before.'

Amber nodded. The cabin around them clanked, grated and squealed as though in mortal pain. Eventually she said, 'I know.'

They settled in to wait.

★   ★   ★

The typhoon passed after about an hour, leaving the sky the colour of an aquamarine, with only ragged streamers of white cloud following the storm inland. Kitty felt faintly sorry for whichever unlucky Philippine settlements it might strike, but any such sentiment was dwarfed by her immense relief at the fact that the *Katipo* was still afloat and everyone aboard. You so often heard stories about crew getting washed overboard during storms and she dreaded it one day happening to them. The sails had sustained extensive damage, however, which couldn't be repaired on board, and the most convenient ports where new sails could be reliably purchased were Manila and Cebu, the Philippine archipelago's oldest city. Manila would have been the preferred option as it was due north, towards China, but it lay in ruins, having been razed by an earthquake four months earlier.

'It's a fair distance out of our way,' Rian said.

'It is,' Hawk replied. 'But we will not be going anywhere at all if we do not replace the sails.'

Mick unrolled the charts depicting the

Philippine Islands and pointed with a blunt finger. 'We're here. If we sail through the San Bernardino Strait then straight down the middle here past the Visayas, we can duck into Cebu that way. It's all sheltered, so it is.'

Rian said, 'If it's sheltered there won't be enough wind to get us there, not with half our sails missing.'

Hawk stuck his own finger on the map. 'The winds come from this direction once you get past Biliran Island. There will be enough, this time of year. And we are not missing half of our sails.'

Pointing himself, Rian asked, 'Aren't you forgetting Mactan Island? It's like the doldrums going through the channel there.'

Now there were fingers everywhere.

'So?' Mick shrugged. 'We'll tack ourselves silly, or pay someone for a tow if we have to.'

Hawk said, 'Mick is right, Rian.'

Rian burst out, 'Look, I just don't want to stop in Cebu, all right? I don't want to stop at all.'

Kitty asked, 'Why not?'

'We do not have a choice,' Hawk said.

Cocking his thumb Rian jabbed it over his shoulder. 'Had you not noticed?'

'Yes,' Hawk replied.

All four turned to look at the ship sitting out on the horizon. Mick swore.

'I was hoping the typhoon might have dealt to them,' Rian said, 'but apparently not.'

Hawk remarked calmly, 'We cannot voyage in open sea with three sails missing. You know that. We must replace them.'

'They'll follow us in,' Rian said. 'I don't want

them anywhere near us.'

'We do not even know who 'they' are.'

'I've a damn good idea. And I hate Cebu. It's full of Spanish Catholics.'

Mick laughed. 'They do own the Philippines.'

'Like the English own Ireland?'

That shut Mick up.

Kitty liked Cebu. She'd liked Manila, too. So many of the buildings there had been beautiful — grand churches and lovely elegant mansions with iron lacework as pretty and as delicate as the mantillas and shawls the Spanish women wore. But now, by all accounts, the famous Walled City was nothing more than a great pile of dust and rubble.

'How long will it take to buy new sails?' she asked

'No time at all to buy 'em,' Mick said, 'but we'll need half a day to rig the buggers. We could be there overnight.' He looked at Hawk for confirmation.

Hawk nodded. 'One night ashore at the most.'

Rian sighed. 'One night, then.'

Kitty said, 'Good. We need to give the cabins and everything in them a good airing. They're dripping.'

No ship was completely watertight above the Plimsoll line, and the rain and high seas of the typhoon had poured in through cracks in the decks and soaked everything below.

'We're not leaving the ship unattended,' Rian said quickly.

'I didn't say we should,' Kitty replied. Honestly, sometimes Rian must think she was really stupid. 'But the bedding's wet, all of it. And some of our clothes. I think we should find a hotel for a night.'

'Gideon can stay aboard,' Rian said. 'And you, Mick.'

Mick opened his mouth, then shut it again.

Throughout the entire discussion, from the corner of her eye, Kitty had been watching Tahi. First he'd climbed the fore mast and had a good poke around at its torn sail, then gone up the mizzen, and now he was descending from the main mast.

Wiping his rope-greased hands on his trousers he approached Rian. 'I think the sails that ripped were tampered with.'

Rian scowled at him. 'What?'

'It looks to me as though the canvas has been cut with a knife in places and weakened.'

'Sabotage? All four of them?'

Tahi nodded. 'Maybe not the spanker. That might just have failed because the others did.'

'The Chinese we saw on the wharf,' Hawk said flatly. 'I knew they'd been aboard.'

'Wong Kai's men,' Rian muttered.

'But they couldn't have known a typhoon would hit us,' Mick said.

Rian said, 'Obviously they took a punt. Typhoons hit everyone in these waters at this time of year. Fortunately for us it didn't pay off.'

Very fortunately, Kitty thought, and sent up a little prayer to whoever — or whatever — it was that looked over them while they were at sea.

It took the *Katipo* a day and a half to tack down to Cebu, though they didn't need a tow past Mactan Island. The night they spent aboard was somewhat unpleasant, however, on clammy mattresses under damp sheets that were already beginning to smell. The weather was warm and humid, and Kitty wondered whether the bedding would dry at all. That was the trouble with sailing in the tropics. Perhaps it might be easier to replace the lot. Cebu was a good-sized city and the region's trading hub, so its merchants would stock all manner of goods.

The mystery ship did follow them as they wove their way down through the Visayan islands towards Cebu. It lost them briefly, but had reappeared again by the time they'd sailed around the point on which sat the little triangular Fort San Pedro and tied up at a crowded wharf. Through his spyglass Rian, tight-lipped, watched it furl its sails and dock some distance away along the foreshore.

'I told you they were following us,' he muttered to Hawk.

They fielded the usual nosy and officious visit from customs officials then disembarked, leaving Mick and Gideon behind, and entered the city.

It stank somewhat, despite the fresh sea breeze, but the wide, palm-lined streets were attractive, and the architecture, formal public gardens and shopping precincts impressive. The farther you went from the shore, however, the more the city fell into disarray, as though Cebu had been constructed specifically to be viewed from the sea. The northern and western reaches, bordering the market gardens, were positive slums.

It was a very busy city, perhaps not as grandiose as Manila had been with its walled citadel, but still distinctly Spanish in architectural aspect. The streets were crowded with pedestrians, horsemen, carabao carts (and what a mess carabao made!), the carriages for hire known as kalesas, and privately owned dainty cabriolets and heavier carriages; and many races were in evidence, including Chinese — great numbers of them — English, the Cebuanos (the island's natives), and the ruling Spanish. You could tell Spaniards anywhere. Kitty was quite envious of the women's dark beauty, though they did tend to look like bad-tempered birds of prey when they aged. And their clothes! The beautiful flounced skirts and lace bodices with enormous, bell-like sleeves, and gorgeous flower-embroidered and beaded shawls and the brightly painted fans they flicked so artfully. They looked like jewels gliding about the Philippines' lush greenery.

While Rian and Hawk went off to look for replacement sails, Ropata and Pierre were dispatched to book a hotel for the night. Kitty and Amber, with Simon as their minder, flagged down a red, yellow and green-painted kalesa and directed the driver to Colon Street in the Parian district, for centuries the centre of Chinese commerce, even before the Spanish arrived, and still known as a marketplace for all sorts of quality goods and services.

'What are we looking for?' Simon asked, fanning his face with his hat.

'New bed linen.'

'For the whole ship?'

'Well, it's not going to dry in this weather, is it?' Kitty said.

'True, it is quite humid.' Simon sniffed his own armpit and made a face. 'It'll cost a packet, linen for everyone. Can't we just send the wet stuff to be laundered?'

'No. It's well overdue for replacement. I'm sick of mending sheets — and reminding people to cut their toenails. In fact I might even get new mattresses if the price is right.'

'We need a bigger one anyway, if we're extending our cabin,' Amber said. Ropata occupied the berth next to hers, but had offered to move into Tahi's vacated cabin so the wall could be taken down. 'You should see the way Tahi sleeps,' she added to Simon, and grinned. 'On his back like a huge starfish.'

'That's quite enough, thank you,' Kitty said, her hands over her ears. 'I don't want to hear about your private life.' Unless it was to be informed that Amber's courses were arriving regularly. She didn't want to be a grandmother for quite some time yet.

'Linen or cotton?' Simon asked.

'What? Oh, good quality cotton. Really soft linen will be too expensive, even here.'

They got out of the kalesa at the top of Colon Street, a long and narrowish road bordered by two-storeyed wooden buildings housing commercial premises on the ground floor and accommodation above, and spent a couple of hours wandering in and out of the shops. Rain threatened once more, the air felt as dense as a damp flannel on the face, and Simon and Kitty were tormented by mosquitoes, but Amber, for some reason, was not.

'I wish the weather would break,' Simon complained, blotting sweat off his brow and neck with his sleeve.

'I don't,' Amber said. 'Then we'll just be hot and sweaty *and* covered in mud.'

'I think I've seen what I want anyway,' Kitty said, 'back that way.'

So they retraced their steps to a draper's emporium stacked to the ceiling with bolts of cloth and manchester, and Kitty made a bulk purchase of twenty sets of sheets made from Egyptian cotton, and nine linen ticking-covered, horsehair-stuffed mattresses, two of them double-sized.

'Er, I hope you don't expect me to carry these back to the ship,' Simon said. 'I might get two on my head, if I take my hat off, but not nine.'

'Oh, don't be so stupid,' Kitty snapped. She was sick of shopping now, and her feet hurt. 'We'll pay someone with a cart and one of those stinking great carabao beasts to shit its way back to the wharf.'

The Chinese draper, who had affected to speak barely any English while transacting the sale of the sheets and mattresses, smiled down at the counter.

Half an hour and a kalesa ride later and Kitty, Amber and Simon themselves arrived at the *Katipo*.

'Is Rian back?' Kitty asked as she clomped down the companionway into the mess room.

Pierre and Ropata and the rest of the crew were sitting at the table eating cheese and

161

pickles. 'Non, chérie, but they should not be far away now,' Pierre replied.

How did Pierre know that? Kitty wondered crossly. Rian could be anywhere. 'Did you book a hotel?'

'Oui.'

'Well, we don't need it now, I actually bought all new linen. And mattresses. They should be arriving soon so if you could all strip your bunks, please.'

Pierre exchanged a look with Ropata. 'But the hotel, she is booked.'

'Then unbook it.'

'We had to pay a good-sized deposit,' Ropata explained. 'And we can't get it back.'

Kitty stared at him for a moment. 'Is it a nice hotel?'

'Very fancy. Eh, Pierre?'

'Magnifique.'

It would be wasteful to spend so much money on a deposit and then not turn up, Kitty thought, wondering if the hotel had a guest bathroom with a proper bath. 'Perhaps you're right. We can't cancel now.'

Rian, Hawk and the new sails arrived half an hour later, Rian in a cheerful mood because he'd purchased the sails at a good price with the cost of delivery thrown in. There were approximately four hours left of daylight and he wanted to fit them as soon as possible.

Then the new mattresses and linen turned up — 'How much?!' Rian exclaimed — and while he and the crew were fitting the new sails, Kitty and Amber set to exchanging the old bedding for new. The ever-present smell of mould tinged with sweat and brine — so ubiquitous it was barely noticed any more — immediately faded from the sleeping quarters. Pierre went off with the boy who'd delivered Kitty's purchases, his cart piled high with old bedding, to sell the used linen at the rag market, and by the time he returned the sun was touching the horizon and the new sails were almost rigged. It hadn't rained after all, ratcheting up the humidity, and everyone was suffering because of it.

Moods were improved, however, once they settled in at the Hotel de Oriente, minus Gideon and Mick, left aboard the *Katipo* clutching their short straws. The hotel truly was 'magnifique', built in the usual overblown Spanish style with gothic charm and opulence oozing out of every plastered inch. Pierre, ever conscious of Rian's budget, had booked them all two to a room, which no one minded, such was the standard of accommodation. Kitty was delighted and very pleased she hadn't insisted they all stay aboard ship, trying out their new bed linen. And yes, there was a bathroom on every floor of the hotel, which made three in total, each containing a white-painted tin bath almost big enough to float in without touching the ends. The cost of a hot bath was extra, however, but she didn't care — she was having one. Sadly, the outdoor privies smelt as foul as privies did anywhere, and Kitty hoped she wouldn't have to spend too much time in the Hotel de Oriente's.

Dinner that evening in the hotel's dining room was an occasion. Although the hotel's owner was presumably Spanish, and the maître d' certainly was, the rest of the staff were Chinese or Cebuano, and the food — dishes described on the menu as paella, pisto, jamon serrano, tortilla, empanadas, croquetas and (according to Pierre who spoke a bit of Spanish) something with baby octopuses — all had a distinctly Oriental flavour to it. Delicious, though. Unfortunately Rian lost patience with the maître d's somewhat theatrical fawning and flouncing among the tables and called him a prancing nancy-boy, which was when they discovered he actually spoke very good English. It was all right for Simon to be the way he was because he never flaunted it, but Rian considered that if you were different, or different in that sense, at least, you should keep it to yourself.

But apart from that, Kitty thoroughly enjoyed her evening out. Pierre didn't criticise the food, no one drank too much, she had a delightful if slightly envy-making time eyeing what the wealthy ladies of Cebu were wearing, and was very much looking forward to her hot bath even if the thermometer/barometer arrangement in the hotel hall said it was still eighty-four degrees Fahrenheit.

★　★　★

'God, it's hot,' Amber grumbled to Tahi as she opened the door to their hotel room with one hand and yanked off her bonnet with the other. 'Bloody thing,' she said and hurled it at the bed.
　'What's the matter?'

164

'I hate it. It makes my head itch.'

'Then don't wear it.'

'All right, I won't. Oooh, you darling, did you do this?'

'What?'

Amber indicated the vase of spectacular purple, pink and yellow orchids, the carafe of wine and two long-stemmed glasses on the nightstand beside the bed.

'Um, actually, no.'

'Oh.' Amber looked for a note but there wasn't one. And then she realised: this was the first night she and Tahi would spend together not aboard the *Katipo* since the evening of their wedding, so this was rather like a honeymoon. It must have been her mother; it was definitely the sort of thoughtful thing she would do. 'Ma,' she said, and grinned.

'That was nice of her,' Tahi said. It was, but a little embarrassing.

Amber lifted the carafe. 'Want some?'

Nodding, Tahi drew the drapes then sat on the bed to unlace his boots, grunting slightly and stifling a burp as he bent over.

'That'll teach you for having two helpings of pudding.' Amber tasted her wine. 'Hmm, quite tanniney. Bracing.' She waited until Tahi had kicked off his boots, handed him a glass and lay down beside him.

'Should you be putting your boots on the bedspread?' Tahi remarked.

'Why not? I'm paying for it.'

'Your father is.' Tahi sampled his wine. 'God, tanniney's right. You know, my little bellbird, you can be really quite arrogant sometimes.'

'I know. You love me anyway, though.'

'I do.' He took her free hand in his. 'And I always will.'

'I know that, too.'

'Do you love me?'

Amber leant over and kissed him. 'Until the end of time.'

6

The following morning in the dining room Simon's stomach rumbled audibly. 'God, I'm hungry. Where's our food? I could eat a maggoty ferret.'

'Never mind your stomach,' Kitty said. 'Where're Amber and Tahi?'

Mick smirked. 'Probably still upstairs playin' tunes on the old one-holed flute.'

'For God's sake, Mick.' Rian scowled at him.

'Well, you were young once, so you were. You know what it's like when you're that age.'

Kitty dropped her napkin on the table. 'I'll go up and see what's keeping them.'

'Wait, I'll come with you,' Rian said.

The others looked at one another. After a moment Haunui, then Hawk, left the table as well.

Upstairs Kitty knocked on Amber and Tahi's door. No response. She knocked again then cautiously tried the handle. The door opened into semi-darkness, releasing a waft of stale air.

'Good morning,' Kitty called. 'Amber?' She stepped inside, blinking against the gloom, followed by Rian. A figure lay sprawled across the bed. Kitty moved closer. 'Amber? Are you awake?'

But it was Tahi, lying on his side, almost fully dressed and apparently still asleep.

A feeling of dread began to stir in the pit of Kitty's belly.

'Where the hell's Amber?' Rian asked.

'The bathroom? Out in the privies?' Haunui suggested as he and Hawk entered and gazed down at the bed, but Kitty didn't think he sounded hopeful.

Rian prodded Tahi's hip. 'Tahi?'

Nothing. Kitty looked about; Amber's bonnet lay on the end of the bed, but other than that there was no sign of her.

Haunui shook the lad's shoulder vigorously. Tahi muttered incoherently. His eyes fluttered but failed to open. Haunui hauled him into a sitting position and bawled into his face, 'Boy! Wake up!'

Then Haunui slapped him. Tahi's head whipped to one side and his eyes snapped open. He stared uncomprehendingly at his grandfather for a long moment, then leant over the side of the bed and vomited on the floor. Everyone leapt out of the way.

Rian levered him upright again. 'Where's Amber?'

Tahi coughed and wiped his mouth on the hem of the bedspread, then looked around wildly. 'Don't know,' he rasped. 'I . . . I must've passed out.'

'Were you on the jar last night?' Rian demanded.

'This carafe is almost full,' Hawk declared, sniffing the wine from the nightstand. He frowned and sniffed it a second time.

Tahi shook his head. 'We only had a glass.' He

168

coughed again, cleared his throat noisily and spat. 'Amber said you left it for us.'

'Left what?' Kitty said.

'The wine. And . . . those.' He nodded at the orchids.

'I did not.'

Hawk took the tiniest sip from the carafe, then passed it to Haunui who did the same.

'What's that funny taste?'

Hawk scowled viciously. 'I think laudanum.'

Kitty's belly plummeted to somewhere near her boots and cold sweat prickled across her skin.

'Laudanum?' Rian almost shouted. 'They've been drugged? But . . . ' He turned on Tahi. 'When was the last time you saw her?'

'I . . . we . . . ' He rubbed his hands across his sweaty face. 'She lay down beside me. I . . . can't remember after that.'

'Well, bloody well try, man!'

Tahi looked wretched. 'There's nothing *to* remember! She poured us some wine . . . I think we lay down, and then you woke me. Oh *God!*' He put his face in his hands. 'I *saw* this, in a vision.'

Incredulous, Rian stared at Tahi, then yanked his hands away from his face. 'You what?'

'In a vision. I saw Amber being taken.'

Far more calmly, Haunui asked, 'Who took her, boy?'

'A taniwha. A dragon.'

'Oh, for fuck's sake!' Rian exploded.

Thinking that Rian might hit Tahi, Kitty stepped between them. 'Stop it, Rian. This isn't

Tahi's fault. He was drugged, that's obvious. Look at the poor boy!'

Kitty watched as her husband made a massive effort to rein in his runaway fear and anger. Clearly this wasn't Tahi's misdeed, or even blunder.

'This is Wong Kai's doing,' Rian said, his voice as harsh as steel across stone. 'I'll guarantee it. It'll be those bastards on that ship. I'm going down to the docks.' He stormed out, Hawk and Haunui on his heels.

Tahi lurched off the bed after them, took several staggering steps off course towards a chair, then fell over it. On his knees on the carpet, he groaned and clutched at his head again. 'What's wrong with me, Auntie? This is worse than being drunk.'

Kitty helped him to his feet. 'It's the laudanum. You've had too much.'

Tahi retched, but hardly anything came up this time. 'I feel awful, as though my head's full of cotton.' He gave the tiniest of sobs then looked mortified. 'Oh God, please don't tell anyone I did that. My beautiful little bellbird. I let them take her, Auntie. I just lay there asleep and let them take her. I'm so sorry.'

Kitty did her best to soothe him, though she would have preferred in her despair and rage to burn the city to the ground.

The door slammed against the wall as Israel — red-faced, his eyes wild — charged in. 'Is it true — Amber's been kidnapped?

Kitty could only nod.

Israel kicked viciously at a chair, toppling it.

'Who? Who's taken her? I'll *kill* them!' Then he rounded on Tahi. 'Where the bloody hell were you? Why didn't you stop them?'

Already beset with fear and guilt, Tahi sprang towards him, fists raised.

'That's enough!' Kitty ordered. 'It wasn't his fault, Israel. He was drugged.' She pointed at the carafe. 'They both were.'

Letting out a huge sigh, Israel ran his hand through his hair. 'Sorry. I'm sorry. But who could have taken her?'

'We think Wong Kai's men,' Tahi replied flatly.

★   ★   ★

Rian, Hawk and Haunui, together with Pierre and Ropata, raced into the street outside the Hotel de Oriente, hailed a passing kalesa, jammed themselves into it and urged the driver to take them down to the docks as fast as possible. The poor horse, when they arrived, was lathered in sweat from ears to tail. They searched and searched, running along the foreshore and out to the farthest ends of every wharf, but the mystery ship was nowhere to be seen. It, and presumably Amber, had gone.

★   ★   ★

The *Katipo* left Cebu immediately. The tide was in flood and the wind was on-shore, neither ideal for setting sail, so Rian paid an extortionate fee for a tug to tow the schooner out through the channel past Mactan Island, until she could sail

171

under her own power up through the islands and traverse the San Bernadino Strait out into the Pacific Ocean. At no time did they sight the mystery ship, which was terribly frustrating. Was she ahead of them and sailing for China? Had she harboured somewhere else in the Philippine Islands, or had she turned back for New Zealand or Australia? With a possible twelve-hour lead on them, she could be anywhere. Rian, however, convinced that the ship was crewed by Chinese, believed it was bound for China, and nothing would change his mind. Of course, China's eastern seaboard was immense and she could be heading for any number of ports.

'Hong Kong,' Rian said when Hawk tried to discuss the matter of their destination with him.

'Why?'

'Because they're going to bargain with her.'

'How do you know that?'

And Rian had snapped, 'Wouldn't you cut a deal? Use your head, man. They'll give Amber back if we agree not to look for Bao.'

'I will use my head if you use yours, instead of letting your heart rule your actions.'

'Bollocks. I never let my heart rule my actions.'

Hawk gave a snort of disbelief. 'You do not know who is crewing that ship, you do not know where it is heading, and you do not know if Amber is aboard. Also, they do not know that we know Bao is in Hong Kong, therefore they will not assume that we will head there.'

That brought Rian up short. Then he said, 'They must realise there's a good chance we will,

Hong Kong being a Crown colony where we can appeal to the British authorities. And you don't know the answer to any of those questions, either.'

'You are right, I do not.'

'Then shut up and let me get on with it. She's my daughter, not yours.'

They stood together on the deck in silence, the wind lifting their hair and the sunlight bouncing off the crystal blue sea so that they had to squint. Not far from the *Katipo* a pod of half a dozen dolphins breached, hurling themselves high into the air and landing with almighty great splashes. Tiring of this after several minutes they swam in closer and settled down to ride the *Katipo*'s bow waves.

'I'm sorry, Hawk,' Rian said. 'I didn't mean that. I know you care about Amber as much as Kitty and I do. And Tahi, too, I suppose.'

'You suppose? You could perhaps talk to him. The boy feels bad enough without thinking that you believe it is his fault.'

'But I don't.'

'Then tell him.'

Sighing, Rian went in search of Tahi, who'd found himself a quiet spot on deck and was repairing a small tear in an auxiliary sail. Rian watched him quietly for a moment. Usually he was very handy with a needle and a sailmaker's palm, but not today. Today he'd forgotten to grease the twine with beeswax and his stitches were uneven and the tension all wrong. Realising at last that he was being observed he glanced up, his face a study in nervous misery, looking as

173

though he expected to be told off.

Rian squatted in front of him, suppressing a grunt as his knees cracked like pistols going off. 'I wanted to say you're not to blame for Amber being taken. You're lucky they didn't put enough laudanum in that wine to kill you both. Thank Christ you didn't drink all of it.'

Tahi looked relieved but still desperately unhappy. 'I feel so useless. So . . . *stupid*.'

'Yes, well.' Rian expected he'd feel quite stupid and useless himself. 'This vision of yours, this dragon. Who, or what, do you think it . . . ' He searched for the right word. 'Symbolised?'

He was aware of Tahi's visions and although he wasn't sure he believed in them he knew Haunui did, as did Pierre, Ropata, Gideon and Hawk, and he suspected Kitty did, too.

'I thought . . . At first I thought it might be Israel.'

'Israel?' Rian was shocked. The ship rolled and he planted his hands on the deck for balance. 'Why Israel?'

'Because, well . . . ' Tahi shrugged. Rian thought he looked unexpectedly shifty. 'But now, it being a dragon, I wonder if it meant a Chinese. It's a Chinese crew on that ship, isn't it?'

Rian nodded. '*I* think it's Wong Kai's men.'

'Which means if we forget about Bao, they'll return Amber.'

It wasn't a question, Rian noted, but a statement of fact. He'd done well to work it out. 'Something like that, I expect.'

A shadow fell across the deck: they both glanced up to see Israel standing a few feet away.

Rian hoped he hadn't heard what Tahi had just said about him.

'Well, I vote we forget about Bao,' Israel said. 'We can't look for them both.'

'Forget about her? No!' Tahi protested. 'Amber wouldn't want us to — I know that for a fact. *I* don't want us to. And what about Wong Fu?'

'He'd understand, wouldn't he, especially when we tell him Amber's your wife now.' Israel nodded at Rian. 'And with her being your daughter.'

Rian said, 'Bao is *Fu's* daughter, and we made him a promise.'

Tahi looked up at Israel through narrowed eyes, and Rian felt a distinct and uncharacteristic crackle of animosity pass between the two young men.

'Bao's your friend, too,' Tahi said sharply. 'And we don't abandon our friends.'

''Course she's my friend,' Israel agreed. 'All I'm saying is maybe there aren't enough of us to look for them both. So who's more important?'

'Christ, boy,' Rian said, 'what a terrible bloody question to ask.'

Israel stared down at him. 'You don't think Amber is?'

Rian didn't answer.

'Because I do,' Israel said.

Rian looked at Tahi, who exclaimed angrily, 'It *is* a terrible question, and a stupid one. We have to find *both* of them.'

'That's right,' Rian said, and after a moment patted Tahi's shoulder. 'Good lad.'

It took nine days of good, swift sailing for the *Katipo* to reach Hong Kong. By the time she did, everyone's nerves were in complete tatters, as they'd not seen even a glimpse of the ship they assumed Amber was aboard. Rian, earlier so determinedly confident, was beginning to doubt himself, wondering if the ship had in fact weighed anchor in some secluded little Philippine bay, or simply turned back for the Antipodes. But why would her captain do that? Surely, if he had Amber, he'd use her as a bargaining agent?

And if *he* didn't have Amber, who did?

Despite her fear and tension, Kitty couldn't help feeling a little thrill of enchantment as the *Katipo* sailed slowly into Victoria Harbour. The sun had not long risen, the morning air was warm and heavy with moisture and cloud sat low over Mount Victoria, wreathing the jade green peak in a pale, shifting gauze of mist. They'd come in through the West Lamma Channel, between Lantau and Hong Kong islands, so that Kowloon, part of the Chinese mainland, now jutted into the harbour to their left and the long sweep of Hong Kong's shoreline extended to their right.

The way the island's city of Victoria sat at the base of Mount Victoria always amused her. It looked, to her, as though the houses and emporiums and the great mercantile establishments, the warehouses, the shacks and the endless clutter of Chinese stores and markets had once been tidily arrayed up the steep slope of the mountain, but some giant of a housewife had flapped the lot like a tablecloth and they'd all landed in a heap along the shoreline, leaving only the grand English mansions farther up the mountain to benefit from the ocean's cooling breezes.

The city was an ant's nest, a population of more than a hundred and twenty-four thousand crammed into a space at the foot of Mount Victoria not much more than four miles long. Most inhabitants were Chinese — mainly Cantonese and Hakka — some of whom travelled regularly between Hong Kong and the mainland, and others of whom were merely passing through on their way to goldfields around the world, jammed like sacks of rice in the stinking holds of ill-maintained ships. The British colonial government — masters of Hong Kong after the island was ceded to Britain after the First Opium War — turned a deliberately blind eye. The Chinese occupied one end of the city, though in separate enclaves as the two clans didn't mix, and the remainder of the population, foreign merchants, occupied the other. Kitty much preferred visiting the Chinese precincts as they were more colourful and goods were much cheaper.

In the main the foreign merchants were British and American, bankers and importers and exporters, perhaps the most notorious being the firm Jardine Matheson and Company, famous for smuggling opium into China. But to be fair, they were only one of a good handful of

European companies who'd made absolute fortunes from the misery of others. They'd also built churches in Hong Kong; and schools; the polo, cricket and jockey clubs; the racecourse at Happy Valley; beautiful botanical gardens; and the elite Hong Kong Club, to which Rian had never been invited.

The many wharves and the waterfront were crammed with vessels, predominantly tea clippers but also a good smattering of other European cargo ships, both sail and steam-powered, numerous ocean-going and coastal junks, and countless smaller sampans nipping about like backswimmers. Kitty was in awe of the big junks with their soaring prows and sterns, and flared orange sails like dragon's wings. They looked quite delicate but she knew the sturdiest could run with the sharpest of gales and withstand all but the most vicious of storms.

Rian, as usual, was on deck peering through his spyglass. 'There she is!' he exclaimed.

'Where?'

'Third wharf along. The red and yellow flag.'

Sick with disappointment because she'd thought he meant Amber, Kitty snatched the spyglass off him and raised it to her eye, seeing quite clearly through the glass the ship that had been following them tied up among a line of other ships at a wharf near the Central Marketplace.

'Hawk!' Rian bellowed, seeing a gap. 'Furl the sails and get ready to warp in. There's a berth at Pedder's Wharf. Israel and Ropata, take the boat and hurry up!'

In Hong Kong you didn't wait for permission

from the harbour master to dock: it was so busy and crowded that if you did wait you could be sitting out in the harbour for ever. You just found a spot and zipped in.

Ropata and Israel ran to lower the ship's boat over the side. If some other captain had also spotted the berth the victors would be the crew who reached the wharf first. Ropata rode down in the boat, his teeth rattling in his head as it hit the water, then Israel half-climbed, half-jumped down after him and they took off, rowing for all they were worth.

There *was* another ship's boat heading for the wharf. Israel and Ropata doubled their efforts and got there first by two boat lengths. The defeated crewmen swore foully: Ropata grinned and Israel raised two fingers. They climbed up to the platform and wound the rope attached to the *Katipo* around a bollard, then Ropata rowed back out to the ship with the loose end. The boat was hauled back up, secured, then the rope fed through the capstan near the bow. Gideon removed his shirt, windmilled his arms to get the blood moving, spat on his hands and put his back into winding the handle on the capstan. Nothing happened for some moments except for the sound of his bare feet squeaking against the deck as he scrabbled for purchase, but then the *Katipo*'s slow up and down bob subsided and she began to move towards the wharf. Sweat popped out on Gideon's furrowed black brow, his teeth showed white in a grimace of toil and his huge muscles bulged, the sinews in his neck and shoulders standing out like ropes. But as the ship picked up a little speed she gained a momentum of her own and it seemed that he would not, after all, explode from his efforts.

The last part of the *Katipo*'s mooring was completed in a flurry of rope-tossing, easing in and tying up, then Rian was on the wharf and rounding everyone up.

'Simon, you stay here with Kitty. Everyone else come with me.'

No one needed to ask where they were going.

'You're not leaving me behind!' Kitty exclaimed.

'I am. It might be dangerous.'

'Oh, bollocks to danger.'

'You're not coming, Kitty. And someone has to watch the ship.'

'I bloody well am coming. Simon can stay here by himself.'

'I said no!' Rian almost shouted. 'Just behave, will you?'

Kitty felt her face redden. 'Don't treat me as though I were five years old!'

'Then stop acting like it.'

The crew looked everywhere but at her and Rian.

'She's my daughter, Rian. I'm worried *sick*.'

'So am I, and I don't want to have to worry about you as well. Look, we'll be back before you know it.'

Kitty could see she was beaten. This time. She marched across the gangway onto the *Katipo* with such ill-tempered vigour that the spring in it almost launched her into the air. 'Damn you,' she muttered as she passed Simon, standing on the deck.

'Me?'

'No, not you, him.'

She thumped down the companionway into the mess room then to her cabin, where she flopped on the bed beside Samson and Delilah, who barely stirred. It was hot in the little room but she dared not open the windows as the cats would get out and escape.

Instead she lay on top of the bedspread, said out loud every swear word she knew, then wept.

★   ★   ★

Rian and the crew marched along the waterfront to the berth at which he'd seen the ship. Striding along the wharf itself, their boots made quite a noise on the planks as they approached.

He stopped alongside the ship and shouted, 'Ahoy, the vessel flying the red and yellow ensign!'

Several heads peered over the gunwale.

'Get your captain,' Rian ordered. 'I want to speak with him.'

The two Chinese sailors stared down at Rian for quite a while, looked at each other, then disappeared for so long he thought they weren't coming back. He felt inside his jacket for the security of his revolver, just in case. Finally another figure appeared, this one a man with far more bearing than the previous two. He wore a queue, and his tunic appeared to be of silk.

'Good morning,' he called down in Cantonese.

Rian understood the greeting, but refused to

181

make a fool of himself by trying to converse in the man's native tongue, of which he had only a basic grasp.

'Do you speak English?' he asked.

'Yes.'

'Are you the captain of this ship?'

The man nodded. 'I am Lo Fang.'

'Will you come down here and speak with me, please.'

The man hesitated, then said something to someone out of sight. A moment later the gangway was lowered on chains, hitting the wharf with a resounding crash, and he descended. He was taller than Rian, which made Rian step back so he wouldn't have to look up at him. His loose moss-green silk trousers matched his embroidered tunic, and Rian thought, I bet you didn't sail all the way from Sydney in that pretty outfit.

A noise from above made him lift his gaze and he saw, lined up along the gunwale, approximately two dozen of Lo Fang's crew, the barrels of the rifles they held just — but deliberately — visible.

'I'm Captain Rian Farrell of the *Katipo*,' he said. 'I believe you have my daughter aboard your ship.'

Lo Fang, whom Rian guessed was somewhere around forty years of age, cocked his head in polite bemusement. 'Pardon me, Captain Farrell, but I do not know your daughter.'

'I think you do. She's the one you, or your crew, drugged with laudanum and abducted from the Hotel de Oriente in Cebu ten days ago.'

Lo Fang's expression became concerned. 'Kidnap is a serious business, Captain. Have you alerted the authorities?'

Slimy bloody bastard, Rian thought. 'I don't need to. I know it was you who took her and I want her back.'

Lo Fang remained silent.

'If it's money you want I'll pay.'

'I do not have your daughter.'

Rian noted that Lo wasn't looking solicitous now. 'Then let me come aboard so I can see for myself.'

'No.'

'Then I'll bring the police and they can look.' This wasn't a hollow threat. The Hong Kong police were well known for being as rough and ready as the characters they were paid to keep in order.

Lo Fang shrugged in a way that made Rian want to punch him. 'Bring whomever you wish, Captain. You still will not find your daughter.'

Then he turned and walked back up the gangway. At the top he clicked his long, bony fingers and it rattled up behind him, closing with a bang.

Resisting the urge to draw his revolver and shoot at every head he could see sticking up over the gunwale, Rian counted to ten instead. Killing people wouldn't get Amber returned to him: not at this point, anyway. He turned on his heel and stalked off, followed by his grim-faced crew.

★ ★ ★

Rian sat at the mess room table with Kitty, Pierre, Haunui, Hawk, Simon and Tahi, staring into a glass of brandy. He'd been very subdued since talking to the Chinese captain that morning, and Kitty didn't have the energy to jolly him along.

They'd discussed trying to sneak onto Lo's ship themselves and searching it, paying someone else to do it, and actually calling in the police as Rian had threatened (though he didn't want them involved if possible as he distrusted all law enforcement), but no potential solution was ideal and all could result in harm to Amber. And there was also Bao; they would need to start looking for her as soon as possible.

Miok came belting down the companionway. 'There's a fellow here says he's got something to tell you. D'you want to see him?'

'Concerning what?' Rian asked.

Mick shrugged. 'He's Chinese, but. I *think*.'

They all trooped up on deck. The 'fellow' had made himself at home sitting on a crate and smoking a pipe. He wore traditional dress, plus an enormous bamboo hat, the like of which you usually saw on heads in market gardens or the goldfields, not in the city. It was jammed so low on his head no one could see his face.

'Captain, Captain,' he said in heavily accented English when Rian appeared, and bowed from the waist and extended a hand, though he didn't bother to rise.

Rian didn't shake it. 'You wanted to see me?'

'I have information for you.'

'About?'

'Your child. Your daughter?'

Kitty stifled a hopeful gasp as Tahi demanded, 'Where is she?'

Rian shushed Tahi with a hand. 'What's your name?' he demanded. 'And take that damned hat off.'

'I have no name today. And I must remain a ghost. You will understand when you hear what I have to say.'

'I'll be the judge of that.'

Kitty flinched, wishing that Rian would refrain from being quite so aggressive when he was upset. It brought out the worst in people.

As it was, the man said nothing.

They all stared at him. Or rather, at the brim of his hat.

Simon suggested, 'Perhaps some compensation might be in order?'

Rian heaved out an almighty sigh and Kitty felt like slapping him. He should know by now that you didn't get anything for nothing in this world, and in particular anything worth having.

She said, 'Mr Ghost, it would honour us if you would allow us to make a financial contribution towards the welfare of your family. What amount might you find satisfactory?'

As if he'd been waiting for this offer all along, the man named a figure in Chinese currency that roughly equalled three guineas. It was a reasonable amount of money, but Kitty knew she — and Rian — would pay ten times that if the information led them to Amber.

Rian nodded and Simon disappeared into the cabin to fetch the money from the ship's safe.

'The information?' Rian prompted.

'Financial contribution first.'

A stony silence fell. Simon returned, the money was handed over, counted, and slipped into a pocket.

Then Mr Ghost lifted his head, revealing his chin and nose, which looked like any Chinese man's chin and nose. 'I am a seaman, Lo Fang Yi is my captain. You are right. We did kidnap your daughter from the hotel at Cebu. She was well treated while she was with us — '

'*Was?*' Tahi interrupted. 'Where the hell is she now?'

'Tahi,' Rian warned, though he too appeared badly startled.

His hand shooting up briskly, the palm out, Mr Ghost declared, 'I will finish. She was well treated while she was aboard our ship. As we approached Hong Kong, passing the west coast of Lamma Island, we were beset by Chinese pirates and she was taken from us.'

Feeling as though she'd just been struck, Kitty folded her hands over her head and it took her a moment to realise that she was making a high, keening sound. White-faced, and apparently shocked out of his anger, Rian drew her arms gently down, enveloped her in a one-armed hug and murmured, 'Don't fret, mo ghrá. We'll get her back.'

Will we? she wondered. Will we really?

'Who are these pirates?' Hawk asked.

Mr Ghost seemed to deflate slightly, as if overwhelmed by the task of having to describe them. 'Their captain is rumoured to be great-grandson of the infamous pirate queen Cheng I Sao, who commanded a confederation of eight hundred armed war junks and many thousands of pirates, and went into battle with the heads of her enemies tied around her neck by their queues.' He paused then said, 'Fortunately, in these modern times, this no longer occurs.'

'Does he have a name, this captain?' Rian asked, the edge back in his voice.

'He is Lee Longwei. Sometimes he is known as the Dragon.'

Tahi breathed in with a sharp little hiss. Everyone looked at him. 'My vision. The dragon?'

Pierre said, 'In the vision, where, the dragon, did he go with Amber?'

'I don't know! Just up in the sky.'

Mr Ghost made a noise that might have been a chuckle, or it might not. 'Lee Longwei does many remarkable things but he does not fly.'

'What do you mean, remarkable?' Hawk asked.

'He is feared by all the other pirates in the China Sea, and by your Royal Navy.'

'It's not *our* Royal Navy,' Rian said. 'We don't consider ourselves English.'

'As you wish,' Mr Ghost said, bowing his head in acknowledgment. 'Lee Longwei also never loses a battle — of any kind. Possibly that is because he is ruthless, and fearless, and will never back down. He is young in age yet has the wit and authority to command over a thousand men and close to fifty war junks. But here is perhaps the strangest thing. He refuses to

187

smuggle opium ashore from the country traders' ships anchored out at sea. A pirate with morals — when the situation suits him.'

'But don't your pirates make half their money smuggling opium? Pirates, and these fellows paddling about in their little waka?' Haunui asked, flapping a vague hand over the side of the *Katipo*.

'Some do, some do not. Many Chinese do not agree with the importation of opium to our lands.'

'Do you?' Simon asked.

'I do not and I curse the day tobacco and opium smoking were ever introduced to China, almost as much as I curse the day you English arrived.'

'Don't call me English,' Haunui said.

'Hush,' Kitty urged. 'Let him finish.' She had a feeling that if Mr Ghost were allowed to say his piece, he might be better disposed to give an opinion on what he thought might happen to Amber.

'We beg your pardon,' Rian said. 'You were saying?'

'My people have been debased and ruined by the opium forced upon us: we have suffered and lost two wars and our great Qing dynasty has gone into irreversible decline, just so gweilo in England can drink our tea, from our porcelain, wearing gowns and waistcoats made from our silks. That is the rape and exploitation of a people of the highest order.'

Shocked, Kitty stared at the man. That had been a brutal thing to say. But the more she thought about it, the more she realised that he'd summarised the situation very succinctly. Her cheeks burnt, even though she knew she wasn't personally responsible for any of it and was uncomfortably familiar with the story of the East India Company's exploits in China. In fact she agreed wholeheartedly with Mr Ghost. That was the trouble with guilt if you were inclined that way — you could feel shame for things that had nothing to do with you.

'Why would Lee Longwei take our daughter from you?' she asked. 'What would he want with her?' She dearly wished Mr bloody Ghost hadn't used the word rape.

Mr Ghost was still for a moment, his ridiculous hat casting a long shadow across the deck. Then he gave a small shrug and said, 'Perhaps he will hold her for ransom.'

'We've got money, we can pay,' Rian said. 'How do we find him?'

Mr Ghost's hat swivelled left and right and Kitty really wanted him to take it off. Something about the way he spoke — the schooled and grammatically correct words he used — reminded her of someone she couldn't quite place. She realised he was shaking his head.

'It may not be money he will want.'

'Well, we don't have anything else,' she said, her own temper fraying now. 'What do you mean?'

Another shrug. 'Not all ransoms concern money. But I am only speculating and I will say nothing else.'

'For God's sake!' Rian snapped.

Tahi took a step forwards, his fists clenched.

Haunui settled a calming hand on his shoulder.

'You can't just not tell us anything more. Why won't you?' Kitty demanded.

A sigh very close to impatience. 'Because I do not know. I am making a guess, a supposition, a deduction, a prediction, a — '

'You most certainly are the human thesaurus, monsieur,' Pierre interrupted. 'Do you know the meaning of 'a beating'?'

Mr Ghost presented his hands, palms up. 'I am merely offering my opinion based on what I know of Lee Longwei.' He stood. 'I have finished here.'

'Wait!' Rian said. 'A man named Yip Chun Kit. Can you tell us where to find him?'

A brief hesitation, then out came the hand again. 'Another guinea. For the family.'

Rian had that much in his pocket, and passed it over.

'He has a large house here at the base of the mountain, near the racecourse. Ask anyone.' He paused, then added, 'My kinsman, So-Yee, sends his compliments. Good day.'

'So-Yee?' Rian echoed, as they watched the Chinese man walk down the gangway and disappear into the crowd milling along the pier.

'I do not understand,' Hawk said.

'I think I do,' Simon remarked thoughtfully.

Kitty nodded. 'So do I. So-Yee. I was racking my brains trying to work out who he reminded me of. Similar voice, same use of words. Perhaps So-Yee knew Kai ordered Lo Fang to abduct Amber on the voyage here. Perhaps the business with the sails was part of that.'

'Well, it's bloody lucky we didn't end up in Davy Jones's locker because of it,' Rian said.

'And maybe So-Yee asked his kinsman in the hat, whoever he is,' Kitty went on, 'to keep an eye on things and tell us what happened.'

'Why would he do that?' Tahi asked. 'So-Yee is Bao's secret . . . what's the word?'

'Advocate,' Simon suggested.

Tahi nodded. 'Bao's advocate, not Amber's.'

'I suspect he doesn't want us to be distracted from what he considers to be our most important task,' Kitty said, 'which is rescuing Bao. In other words, the sooner we find Amber, the sooner we can focus on Bao.'

Pierre whistled. 'The man has the heart of ice!'

'Well, yes and no,' Kitty said. 'He can't be that hard-hearted to take such a risk for Bao and Amber.'

An expression of dawning comprehension spread across Pierre's weathered face. 'Aah, So-Yee is in *love* with Bao!'

'I don't think so. He's extremely fond of her but I think it's more a matter of his undying loyalty to Fu.'

'If he's that loyal to Fu what's he doing working for Kai?' Rian asked.

'Spying,' Kitty said simply.

Part Two

THE FRAGRANT HARBOUR
OCTOBER 1863

My love is as a fever, longing still

7

Wong Bao Wan sat in a red sandalwood chair, her back supported by an embroidered silk velvet cushion, staring out of the window at the garden beyond. The stiff, oiled paper covering her windows was rolled up today — it was rumoured that only the Empress Dowager Cixi had glass in her palace, including an entire conservatory — but when Yip Chun Kit was angry with her, which was often, he forbade her from lifting the paper, so that her rooms were suffused all day with a sickly yellow light. Her apartment in his courtyard house was lavish, but it was still a prison. She'd only been permitted out to bathe, visit the privy, or walk in the confines of one of the house's two beautiful gardens — and never on her own; her personal female servant, Po, even attended her on visits to the privy. And she was aware that her apartment was guarded at night.

She knew very well why she was here and what her uncle, Kai, expected of her, but she would never submit to Yip Chun Kit. He was a domineering, unpleasant and physically unattractive man and she'd discovered not long after she'd arrived that his servants called him 'The Frog', but it wasn't his flat head, bulging eyes and extraordinarily wide mouth that repelled her. In fact it wasn't him at all: she simply didn't want to be in Hong Kong, not while her father was so ill, and she was livid with Kai for having her abducted and brought here. She suspected her father was dying, though he hadn't actually told her so — wanting, she presumed, to stop her from worrying, but she could see what was happening to him. If he did die before she returned home, Kai would very much regret his actions.

The servants here lived in fear of Yip Chun Kit. She'd tried to befriend them but realised now if she made accomplices of them it would mean their certain death when she did manage to leave. No, she'd come to understand that quite possibly her greatest ally in this household was someone who, in theory, should be her worst enemy. Not Chun himself, but his primary concubine.

Her name was Lai Wing Yan. She was stunningly beautiful and in her early twenties, with eyes almost as round as a European's, which Chun prized, a mouth like a rosebud, silky black hair that fell to her waist and milky skin. Chun preferred all his women to possess a pale complexion and insisted they never venture outside without a parasol. She was tiny — Bao wondered how she fared beneath Chun's bulk — and had very delicate feet, though they weren't bound. Perhaps she was of Hakka or Manchurian origin: their women didn't bind their feet, which possibly blighted her slightly in Chun's eyes as a prospective wife. In which case he shouldn't be physically interested in her, Bao, as her feet were in fact on the large side. But then, he wasn't, was he? It was her authority and her family tong's wealth that he wanted.

Wing was terribly competitive and enjoyed nothing more than setting Chun's wife, Yip Tan Ling, and the other concubines against one another. And now, of course, that included Bao. Wing was jealous because, according to servants' gossip, so far she hadn't been able to give Chun a child, and it was her one aim to become primary wife, which would never happen while she remained barren. Tan had provided three children, while the other two concubines, Yu Peijing and So Mei Yan, had popped out two apiece. And now she feared that Bao, who came with a very significant dowry courtesy of Kai and wasn't unattractive herself, would prove to be a font of fertility and supplant Tan, ruining Wing's chances of becoming favoured wife.

Yu Peijing and So Mei Yan weren't threats to her, Bao had decided. They were unlikely to achieve the status of Chun's wife, not with Tan already firmly in place and Wing snapping at her heels and secretly trying every fertility treatment known to Chinese medicine, and they seemed content with their children, their luxurious accommodations in Chun's compound, and happy to tolerate his attentions once a week.

Tan was a problem, if not in the same direct fashion as Wing. She clearly knew that Bao was about to supplant her, disliked her intensely, and took every opportunity to demonstrate the fact. She glided about on her smelly pig-trotter feet, her face powdered white, her shaved eyebrows replaced by an alarmingly angled false pair

197

drawn on higher up, and her rouged lips puckered in a sour moue. Bao suspected she actually loved Chun, and had no wish to upset the woman. Without Bao telling her directly, however, Tan couldn't know that, and Tan refused to speak more than a few words to her. She wouldn't believe Bao anyway, such was her apparent belief in Chun's irresistibility to all women.

Bao saw and spoke with the other women quite often during her visits to the gardens. Chun's women were present so often when she was there that she had initially wondered if they, too, were prisoners. They weren't, though. Yu Peijing told her that sometimes they went to the markets and to the shops on Queen's Road and Wellington Street, and at other times they took the children, all under the age of ten and currently being raised in Chun's compound but not destined to live there forever, to the public gardens or up to Victoria Peak if it was especially hot.

Bao, however, was stuck in the house, and had been for months, and it was driving her mad. Chun was a tong master himself, and a very wealthy hong, and his courtyard house was large to accommodate his women and children, his parents, several other family members, and his servants. It was constructed in the traditional style: a walled compound with one entrance with two garden courtyards surrounded by single-storey buildings, like a capital H with the top and bottom closed in. It was built of the best timber and tile, well appointed, with plenty of bathing rooms and privies, lavishly furnished, and the gardens were havens of serenity, but none of this meant anything to Bao. What were silk sheets, exquisite cloisonné vases and a lotus pond when her father was dying in a damp country at the bottom of the world?

In any normal Chinese home she'd simply be able to walk out the door, but this wasn't a normal home. Included among Chun's servants were four bodyguards, big men who, judging from their size and facial features, were from the north. When Po wasn't trailing around after her, one or other of these men was keeping a very close eye, which was unnerving and irritating. She had not even been able to send a letter to her father as Po had been too frightened to smuggle it out of the house for her. He would know where she was, though. So-Yee would have seen to that. He appeared loyal to Kai, but he was far more loyal to her and her father.

Po appeared, flitting quietly across the polished wooden floor in her slippers.

'Miss Wong, Mr Yip wishes to attend you.'

Oh, go away, Bao thought. 'What does he want?' she snapped in Cantonese without turning around.

Looking slightly aghast at, and frightened by, Bao's rudeness concerning Yip Chun Kit, Po said, 'He would not tell *me* such a thing, Miss Bao. He only asked me to tell you. He will be here in five minutes. Would you like me to comb your hair?'

'No.'

'Will I prepare tea?'

199

Bao turned around and gave her a big bright smile. 'You can prepare what you like, Po. I could not care less.' Then she felt mean. It wasn't Po's fault she worked for a crooked, pompous racketeer. She sighed. 'Yes, make some tea. Please.'

Po scurried off, her short indigo robe flapping and the cotton fabric of her trousers swishing.

Bao stared out the window again, then lifted a cheek and deliberately farted. The previous evening's meal had been duck gizzards with hoisin sauce, rice and hundred-year-old eggs, and she hoped the smell would linger until well after Kit arrived.

It did but he didn't seem to notice. He bustled in without knocking, by which time she'd moved from the window to the futon in her small private reception area, as she absolutely refused to receive him in her sleeping chamber.

'Good morning, Bao,' he said. He'd addressed her in this casual manner since she'd arrived, apparently thinking it was acceptable to dispense with formalities as, in his mind, they were betrothed. 'Are you well today?'

'Yes.'

'Good.'

He looked around, perhaps deciding where to sit. Bao scattered cushions across the futon, making it clear he wasn't welcome there, so he squeezed his considerable backside into a chair. As he subsided a strong waft of sandalwood incense and stale garlic crossed the gap between them, confounding Bao's olfactory passages.

'Is there tea?' he asked.

'Po is bringing it.'

Chun smoothed the front of his robe over his fat thighs. 'I have a surprise for you, which I am sure will delight you.'

I doubt it, Bao thought.

Po tapped, peeped around the door as though terrified of interrupting something intimate and wheeled in a trolley containing the tea accoutrements. These included: a porcelain brewing tray; two matching, very ornate and heavy silver teapots decorated with a dragon motif that wound its spiky way around the pot in relief, the head forming the spout and the tail the handle, both balanced on silver burners to keep the water hot; two silver canisters with the same dragon pattern containing the teas; two porcelain cups (small and delicate, without handles) painted in red, orange and bright blue enamel featuring yet more dragons; an embroidered tea cloth; a tea pick; a strainer; a tea scoop in the shape of a scallop shell; and a miniature hourglass, all also in silver. Dragons were generally a motif reserved for emperors and persons of royal heritage, in theory at least, and Bao thought Chun had a cheek filling his house with such items as he was clearly neither.

'Which tea would you prefer, Mr Yip?'

'Green.'

'And yourself, Miss Bao?'

'Red, thank you.'

Nervously, Po tested the temperature of the water in the teapots with a finger, clearly burning herself quite painfully, then decanted several scoops of tea leaves into each and turned the hourglass over. She poured the green tea first as it required less time to brew, using the tea strainer to trap the leaves and filling the room with a fresh, grassy aroma. When a minute had passed, she reached for the pot containing the red tea, but Chun beat her to it.

'You may go now,' he ordered.

Surprised, she bowed slightly and left them, sucking her scalded finger.

'Stupid girl,' Chun muttered.

Grunting slightly, he eased himself out of his seat, grasped the cane handle of the teapot and poured, the tip of his tongue sticking out between his moist, red lips. He spilt a lot of it across the brewing tray, but some went into Bao's cup. She knew she should knock on the table between them to express her gratitude and respect for the fact he had poured for her, but couldn't be bothered. She wondered if that was the surprise.

Evidently delighted with himself for condescending to carry out such a menial task, Chun took a sip of tea and sat back. 'So,' he said.

'Yes.' Then, 'Are we waiting for something?'

'We are.'

Bao had no choice but to drink her tea and try not to stare at him. He really was an unattractive man. He was, she suspected, very vain about his appearance and today he was wearing an ankle-length gown of sky blue silk fastened by button and loop across the right breast and beneath the arm. He also wore a coral-coloured sleeveless waistcoat over the robe, as sumptuously embroidered as the robe itself. If he was fat and ugly but possessed of a pleasant nature she wouldn't have minded him. She certainly still would not marry him, but she wouldn't mind him.

She rolled her eyes as he reached down to his groin and had a good rummage about, but then she realised he was retrieving something from the little drawstring pouch attached to his belt. He withdrew a small, carved white bottle with a coral stopper — white jade? Bao wondered — tipped a scattering of finely ground brown powder onto the back of his hand and sniffed it violently up each nostril. Then almost sneezed his head off.

Another knock at the door.

'Enter!' Chun shouted as he wiped his streaming nose with the tea cloth.

Two women appeared, laden with what appeared to be several cotton garment bags and assorted other containers.

'Put everything over there.' Chun indicated the futon. 'This is the bride.'

'Good morning, miss,' the women said in unison, bowing low then placing their parcels carefully about the place.

Bao felt a very unpleasant sense of foreboding creep from her belly up into her chest and throat.

'I have had your wedding garments made,' Chun announced.

Oh *God*!

'At great expense,' he went on, 'but the ensemble, I think you will find, is very beautiful. You will be pleased.'

He said it, Bao noted, as though it were an order, not a prediction. He clicked his pudgy fingers and the women opened the first garment bag and lifted out a high-necked robe that fell to the hips in cherry-red velvet silk covered with exquisite embroidery everywhere but on the shoulders and across the upper bust and back. Apart from the red silk background the dominant colours used in the embroidery were varying shades of blue, green, orange, pink, purple and gold, all hues that harboured specific meaning, as did the animals and flowers represented. The second garment bag contained an ankle-length skirt to match the robe. The outfit was indeed very beautiful.

'Very lovely,' she said, more to please the women than anything else.

'And the headdress,' one announced, unable to keep the excitement from her voice.

Out came a *very* large and ornate headdress of gilt copper, kingfisher feathers, coral and pearls, and a matching clip for the back of the hair when it was put up, both of which were jaw-droppingly beautiful. Bao leant forward for a closer look: the workmanship was outstanding. Chun smirked.

The headdress was followed by a long pair of coral, turquoise and gold ear pendants, a heavy silk gauze veil, which Bao knew was to be worn over the face until the moment of the wedding ceremony, and a pair of gold velvet shoes.

'Are you impressed?' Chun asked.

'I am,' Bao replied. She knew that everything would fit too, as she'd been measured for a new wardrobe when she'd arrived. She hadn't had much with her except the clothes she'd been wearing when she'd been taken from the Chinese Camp, and a couple of outfits Kai had paid for when Lo Fang Yi had stopped briefly in Sydney. 'But I still will not marry you.'

Chun's self-satisfied expression rearranged itself into one of impatience, then anger. He clicked his fingers at the women again and they scuttled out.

He said, 'You are so sure you have a choice in the matter.'

Again a statement, not a question.

'We all have choices in life.'

'Not you. Your uncle and I have a contract. If you refuse to marry me he will not become head of your tong, and Kai *very* much desires to become your family's . . . what do you call it?'

'Cloud Leopard.'

'Yes. Very quaint.'

'It is,' Bao agreed amiably. 'As a tong master yourself, what are you known as? I heard that people call you the Frog.'

Chun's eyes bulged, his throat worked and his face darkened with anger, thereby unfortunately adding to his froggy looks. 'I have had men whipped for less.'

'Then whip me.' Bao shrugged, almost but not quite apologetically. 'I still will not marry you.'

Chun leant forwards and slammed a hand down on the low table between them. 'Do you not understand! It is too late. The process has begun. The three letters and the six etiquettes are already well underway.'

'Are they?' Bao didn't even look at him.

Instead, she examined the end of her long plait for split ends.

'Yes. *I* do not object to the marriage proposal; *you* do not — '

'I do so!'

'You do *not*! My family does not object, and neither, of course, does your guardian, Wong Kai.'

'He is *not* my guardian. My father is my guardian.' And he will have sent me help, she thought fiercely. He will not have left me to extricate myself from this unpleasant situation on my own. Even now someone will be looking for me.

'Your father is too ill to partake. The matchmaker is overseeing the process, an astrologer has matched our birth dates propitiously, and a practitioner of suan ming has predicted a fortuitous future for us. The betrothal and gift letters have been sent and the wedding letter has been drafted.'

'I have not been consulted regarding any letters.'

'Why should you? You have said repeatedly that you are not interested.'

That was true, Bao thought. He had her there.

'Anyway, the betrothal gifts have already been presented to your family, and accepted.'

Ah, the bride price. She hoped she'd cost Yip Chun Kit a lot. 'Who accepted the gifts on behalf of my family? Kai is in Australia.'

'An emissary in Hong Kong chosen by your uncle.'

Who could that be? Bao wondered. Someone

with their foot firmly in Kai's camp and eyes assiduously trained on her, no doubt. Was he — or she — here in Chun's compound? That was an unwelcome thought.

'The wedding gifts have also been presented to your family. Foodstuffs and the like, plus jewellery for yourself, which will be held in safekeeping by Kai's emissary until I feel the time is appropriate to grant them to you.' Slyly he added, 'The jewellery is beautiful and very valuable. I chose it myself. Coral and silver ear pendants, a hair ornament of gold and kingfisher feathers, a pair of heavy gold bangles embellished with pearls and coral, an amethyst and white jade necklace, and a moss jade and snow seed pearl necklace, all made by a craftsman trained by the Empress Dowager Cixi's assistant jeweller.'

And all to no end, Bao thought, as she couldn't care less about jewellery.

'And,' Chun went on, 'the wedding date itself has been chosen. We will be married two weeks from today, on Monday the twenty-sixth of October. The stars are very auspicious for that date and augur well for a long and happy life for us.'

Bao hoped Chun wasn't paying his astrologer much: he didn't seem very accurate. And two weeks didn't give her long to formulate and implement a plan of escape.

'What does Tan think of all this?'

'My wife? It is irrelevant what she thinks. She has always known I will take a second wife, and perhaps even a third.'

'I do not believe she is very happy about it.'

'It is not her place to be happy or unhappy. It is my responsibility to my father's brothers to provide them with heirs, as one cannot produce children and the other seems able only to father daughters. For that I need wives. You are an ideal candidate as you come with such an attractive dowry.'

'You mean my family's money, which Kai will share with you when he becomes Cloud Leopard, because of course, as your wife, I cannot retain the office as tong master?'

'That is correct. But I do not think you will find life here onerous.'

No, because I will not be here. 'Lai Wing Yan is also unhappy. She wants to be your next wife.'

'I am aware of that. But a wife must bear her husband children. When she bears me a child, I may reconsider her status.'

'What if she never does?'

Chun's fat shoulders rose then fell. 'There are plenty more where she came from.'

'What if *I* could not bear you a child?'

'You have your dowry. I can take more wives.'

'And if you were to grow tired of me?'

'I am tired of you now, to be frank. You are being very recalcitrant.'

'What if we were to marry, and I forced you to divorce me?' Failing to bear him a son was out as a reason; he'd already commented on that. Bao focused on remembering the other grounds he could cite to divorce her. 'I could commit adultery or behave in a lewd manner. I could demonstrate jealousy concerning your women.'

208

But Tan and Wing were both openly jealous of her, and Chun didn't seem to mind that. 'I could be rude to your parents, gossip publicly, commit theft, or catch a vile disease.'

Chun laughed. 'Then you would just have to spend your time alone in your apartment, missing your lover, gossiping to yourself and suppurating from your various sores and orifices. I would not divorce you, Bao. I would not risk you seizing the office of tong master from Kai once your father has gone. Kai tells me you are a far more capable — and dangerous — woman than you appear.'

Yes, I am, Bao thought, and you should not forget that, Yip Chun Kit, though it would be far better for me if you did. She stood, gathered together the garments and accessories that made up her wedding costume and dumped the lot in his lap. 'I appreciate the time and workmanship that have gone into these, but I will not be wearing them so please take them away.'

'I think not, Bao. It is my wish that you become my wife, and you are not in a position to deny me.'

But Bao had already returned to her chair by the window and was busy watching a fork-tailed sunbird darting about the branches of a plum tree.

⋆ ⋆ ⋆

Yesterday had been a terrible day, as far as Kitty was concerned. In her head, while at sea between Cebu and Hong Kong, she'd concocted a

209

scenario in which they would locate and confront whomever had abducted Amber from the hotel and agree with them to not look for Bao in exchange for Amber's return. Once they had her back, safe and sound of course, they would renege on their part of the bargain and merrily begin the search for Bao, find her unharmed, and sail with her back to New Zealand.

The idea of Amber instead in the hands of a ruthless pirate king was sickening, literally, and every time she thought of it, which was at least once every few minutes, she felt alarmingly light-headed or had to swallow bile.

She hadn't slept much, and knew Rian hadn't either, and had had to resort to a hefty dose of laudanum to finally drop off. Now, this morning, she felt as if her head were stuffed with cotton, which didn't bode well as she, Rian, Simon and Hawk were off to try and talk to Yip Chun Kit. While they were doing that Haunui, Tahi, Pierre and Gideon would talk to ships' crews along the waterfront in the hope of news of Lee Longwei's whereabouts. Kitty was laden with guilt — she felt she should be looking for Amber, not Bao, who was at least not being held by an actual, and notorious, pirate — but they'd made Wong Fu a promise and she intended to keep it.

Having got directions to Yip Chun Kit's house as easily as Mr Ghost had predicted, they hired an ox cart and driver to take them across the city to the foothills of Mount Victoria. The cart was unsprung and extraordinarily uncomfortable, but the city of Victoria, despite its considerable population, lacked any carriages for lease. The few carriages on the island were privately owned, mainly by the British. Sedan chairs were available for public hire, and were slower than walking, but much less effort for the passenger if their destination was the summit of Mount Victoria.

Shaken and bruised, Rian, Kitty, Hawk and Simon dismounted creakily from the cart and gave the driver instructions to wait. He nodded benignly, fed his ox a great wodge of hay from a sack beneath his seat, packed a long pipe with tobacco and lit it.

As was customary, the front wall of Yip Chun Kit's house sat very close to the street, with his servants occupying those apartments most likely to experience any ambient noise. The best apartments, Kitty knew, would be at the rear of the property, and would house Chun and his immediate family. It was difficult to gauge from the street the lavishness of his home but judging by the length of the front wall, the compound was substantial. A single gated portico sat off-centre in the wall, in accordance with the principles of feng shui, which vaguely irritated Kitty, who felt the door should be in the middle. It looked odd, off to one side like that. Untidy.

Rian banged the knocker, the head of a ferocious-looking lion dog with a ring in its mouth. A flap above the knocker flipped up almost immediately and a pair of suspicious eyes peered out.

'Er, good morning. Is this the residence of Mr Yip Chun Kit?'

211

The eyes stared unblinkingly for a moment, then an unseen mouth rattled off a long sentence in Cantonese.

Rian looked at Simon. 'I didn't get any of that. Did you?'

'Something about an appointment?'

'No, we don't have an appointment,' Rian said slowly. 'But we'd like to speak to Mr Yip. Would you tell him that Captain Rian Farrell has a business proposition for him? A very lucrative proposition.'

'That is a waste of time if he cannot speak English,' Hawk pointed out.

'I think he can,' Simon said.

Another mistrustful stare and the flap rattled shut. They waited. A pair of sedan chairs carrying white women went past, the bearers with the long poles on their shoulders labouring and sweating under the weight of their passengers, followed by an ox and cart a few minutes later that coated them liberally with road dust.

'Perhaps he's not coming back,' Kitty said.

Simon wiped his face with a handkerchief then blew his nose. 'I suspect he will.'

'How do you know?'

'From his eyes.'

'Oh, don't be so stupid. All we could see were his eyes.'

'Yes, but they registered quite a lot of interest when Rian said his name.'

'What rubbish you talk sometimes, Simon.'

'Well, occasionally, but not always,' Simon replied benignly.

Rian took Kitty's hand and squeezed it. 'Just

wait, mo ghrá. I think he will come back.'

Eventually the door in the wall opened and a tall, very well-built Chinese man wearing a sour expression indicated that they should enter. 'Mr Yip see you. Please follow.'

'I told you he could speak English,' Simon whispered to Kitty.

'Is it the same man?'

'If it isn't there must be more than one fellow employed here tall enough to look through that flap in the door. See how high up it is?'

It was true, the flap was set higher than the eye level of the average Chinese person. Yip Chun Kit must have some serious concerns about his personal safety. But then he probably would, being a hong, a tong master and quite possibly not a very nice man. What decent man would collude with someone like Wong Kai to abduct a young woman and marry her to deny her her power and steal her family's wealth?

Following the tall Chinese through a beautiful courtyard, they didn't see another soul. Passing beneath a carved archway, its roof surmounted by writhing dragons, they emerged into a second even more sumptuous and wonderfully perfumed garden. Again they saw no one. On the far side, their guide trotted up a short terrace of steps, opened a door then beckoned them to enter.

They found themselves in an anteroom furnished with an ornately carved bench and a low table on which sat an exquisite cloisonné urn nearly three feet high.

'Wait,' the big Chinese man said.

Kitty sat on the carved bench, which wasn't any more comfortable than it looked. Somehow a small stone had found its way into her boot: she untied the lace, removed the boot and decanted the stone onto the flagged floor. Of course, at that moment their guide returned.

'Mr Yip see you now.'

Damn. She jammed her foot back in its boot and stood, conscious of her trailing bootlace, then followed the others into the next room.

Yip Chun Kit was ensconced in a high-backed chair carved with dragons chasing their scaly tails and phoenixes and the like — almost a throne, really — and she immediately thought, oh dear, he does look like a frog. We *must* get poor Bao away from here. His English, though, was very good.

Introductions were made, a short discussion ensued regarding the voyage to Hong Kong and how lucky they'd been to secure a berth at Pedder's Wharf given the busyness of the waterfront, and if Chun knew who they were he didn't show any indication. In fact he was most gracious and offered tea. Kitty's heart sank. Taking tea in China wasn't like taking tea in England, where you simply boiled the kettle, tipped some leaves in the pot then poured yourself a cup. Here, taking tea was a ceremony and could take quite some time depending on the participants and the context. But to decline the offer of tea was the height of rudeness and she knew that Rian wouldn't dare, even though he wasn't fond of green tea in particular. However, he surprised her.

'Before we accept your kind offer,' he said, 'perhaps I should clarify exactly why we're here.'

'Ah, yes.' Chun nodded towards the big man who'd taken up position near the door. 'My man, Tsang Ho Fai, said you have for me a very lucrative business proposition? I have to say I cannot wait to hear it.'

He smirked and Kitty realised then that he knew exactly who they were.

'Well, here it is,' Rian said. 'I want you to hand over Wong Bao Wan now. We're here at the direct request of her father, Wong Fu. There won't be a wedding, Wong Kai won't be the next Cloud Leopard, and there certainly won't be any money in it for you, do you understand?'

Chun looked vastly amused. Kitty felt like slapping him.

'I am afraid I do not. I have never heard of this . . . What is her name?'

'You know exactly who I'm talking about,' Rian said. 'And I know she's here somewhere, if not in this compound then somewhere in this city. So I suggest that you save yourself some trouble, go and fetch her, and we'll be on our way. Kidnap is a capital offence, you know, and this is a British colony.'

Spreading his chubby hands in a parody of bemusement, Chun said, 'That is as may be, however I still do not know of this Miss Wong.' Then he raised his groomed eyebrows and a forefinger as if he'd just had the most marvellous idea. 'But if I meet her I will tell her you are looking for her.'

'No need, we'll find her soon enough,' Rian

replied with forced good humour. 'And no thank you, we don't want any of your tea. I'd rather drink boiled grass clippings.'

He gave the shallowest of bows, less than the effort you'd put into glancing down at your boots, took Kitty's arm and marched from the room, followed smartly by Simon and Hawk.

'Keep your eye out for Bao,' he said out of the side of his mouth as they crossed the inner courtyard. 'If she's here she'll know we are, but I'm betting she's locked up.'

Simon said, 'Kidnap's not a capital offence, is it? It's only a misdemeanour.'

'He won't know that, will he?'

'He might.'

Glancing over her shoulder Kitty saw that Tsang Ho Fai was following them. She gave him a little wave.

Through the archway and into the front courtyard, then out onto the street. Behind them the door shut with quite a bang.

'Bad-tempered sod,' Rian said.

True to his word the driver of the ox and cart was still waiting. The ox stared at them through mournful brown eyes as it chewed yet more hay while the driver lay along the seat, conical hat over his face, his skinny ankles revealed by too-short trousers. Kitty thought the ox probably ate better than its owner.

Hawk rapped on the cart to wake the man without giving him a fright. He sat up quickly, swivelled on the seat, put his hat on and grabbed the reins.

'Where now?'

'Back to the docks. And there's an extra shilling in it for you if you hurry.'

That was a generous bonus, Kitty thought, and was guaranteed to garner more bruises: when an ox trotted all hell could break loose. But she was glad to be heading back to the waterfront. They'd done what they could about Bao for now and, as Rian had said, if she was at Yip Chun Kit's compound, at least now she would know they were looking for her. They would make a plan to do what they could to help her escape. In the meantime there might be news about the whereabouts of Lee Longwei, and therefore Amber. Even just knowing where she was would make things better. Well, a tiny bit better, at least.

★ ★ ★

Bao bent to inhale the scent of a newly unfurled peony, a perfume which reminded her achingly of her father. Peonies were his favourite blooms.

'Be careful the entire flower does not disappear up your nostril.'

Bao didn't need to look to see who had spoken: only Lai Wing Yan would say something so insulting to her.

Over her shoulder she replied, 'Do you have to be so rude?'

'No. I choose to be.'

Bao turned and faced Wing. It was true that in comparison to Wing's finer nose, Bao's nostrils were more full, but they'd always been perfectly serviceable. She could breathe through them,

217

blow them and even pick them quite comfortably, if she felt like it. About to suggest that perhaps Chun liked Chinese-looking noses, she bit her tongue as annoying Wing further wouldn't be productive at this point.

Instead she said, 'Tan is looking very eye-catching today.'

Wing gave an inelegant snort of amused derision. 'Ha! Eye-catching? That is one word for it, I suppose.'

'Two.'

'What?'

'Eye-catching is two words.'

Wing flapped a dismissive hand at her and they shared a few moments studying Chun's wife as she tottered along the garden's gravel path on her tiny feet, followed by her personal servants. She wore a beautiful gown of embroidered sage green silk, too much jewellery for a walk outdoors, heavy face powder, and her hair had been shaped into elaborate knots at the back and sides of her head and decorated with artificial flowers.

'She dyes it, you know,' Wing remarked.

'Her hair?'

Wing nodded. 'She is older than Chun by five years, but brought a huge dowry with her when they married and at the time Chun needed money. Delivering her last child nearly killed her. A pity it did not.'

'If she had died, would he have married you?'

'I am Chun's primary concubine. Of course he would have.'

She said it so quickly that Bao wasn't sure

even Wing believed it.

'She is jealous and frightened of you,' Wing went on. 'She does not want to be wife number two, hence the extra effort she is making.'

'And are you jealous of me?'

Wing's eyebrows shot up. 'Me? Jealous of your big feet and tea-coloured complexion and the muscles in your arms like a man's? Ha! That is a joke.'

'My feet are not *that* big. They are just not dainty.'

'Chun will soon see what a mistake he has made and you and Tan will end up walking around and around the garden bemoaning your lot while he spends his time with me.' Wing picked a chrysanthemum, pulled a handful of petals off it and let them fall to the ground. 'I do not even know why he wants to marry you.'

Far better you don't, thought Bao. She looked around for Po but the girl was well out of hearing distance, gazing into the lotus pond. The day before, when Rian and Kitty had come, she, Bao, had been locked in her apartment and hadn't seen them but she'd heard the gossip from the servants and from Yu Peijing and So Mei Yan. She'd overheard the servants talking and had gone to Peijing and Mei, with whom she was on reasonably friendly terms, and pumped them for details. They hadn't wanted to tell her anything at first, and she'd realised they'd been warned not to speak to her about the matter, but they were terrible gossips and eventually the story of Kitty, Rian, Simon and Hawk's visit had come out. No one had encountered them directly but everyone had been peeping through their windows and had compared notes later. Even Tsang Ho Fai had gossiped, boasting about how he'd put the fear of the gods into the gweilo visitors.

Also, last night someone had slipped a note beneath her door written in beautiful Cantonese characters which read:

Wong Bao Wan,
Your English friends Captain Rian and Mrs Kitty Farrell came to the house today, looking for you. Chun lied and said you were not here. If you wish to leave you must try to get a message to them. Their ship is moored at Pedder's Wharf. Do not dally.

It hadn't been signed and there was no other indication of who had written it, but Bao suspected Tan. The confident strokes and curves had the same elegant formality she did, and the sentiment behind the message was certainly hers. Had Wing written it, Bao was sure the message wouldn't have been half as polite.

'Can I trust you?' she asked.

Caught between suspicion and curiosity, Wing eyed her. 'Not really. Why?'

'I do not want to marry Chun.'

Wing sniffed the remains of the chrysanthemum and made a face. 'Then tell him.'

'I have, repeatedly.'

'Tell your family. Tell your father, or the matchmaker.'

'My father is in New Zealand on the

220

goldfields, the matchmaker is in Chun's employ, and . . . Well, it is complicated. I have no one to represent me. The decision has been made. I am to marry him in two weeks.'

'Two weeks!' Wing looked stunned.

'Yes. I have even seen the wedding costume.'

Wing's pretty mouth twisted into something very ugly, but she remained silent. In her fist the chrysanthemum was crushed to pieces. Noticing what she'd done, she dropped it and wiped her hand on her gown.

Bao said, 'The thing is, I would rather die than marry Chun, so I must leave.'

'Leave this house?'

'Yes.'

'But I have seen Chun's men outside your apartment door at night. I know you are not permitted beyond the compound walls. You cannot leave.'

'I can, with your help.'

'Why should I help you?'

Bao was disappointed. She'd thought Wing quite a lot smarter than that.

'Do not look at me in that manner,' Wing snapped. 'I do not like you. The worst thing I can do to you is not help you so that you have to stay here. Had you thought of *that?*'

'Would you really cut off your silly little nose to spite your face?'

Looking absolutely horrified, her hand cupped over her precious nose, Wing demanded, 'What do you mean?'

Bao sighed. She'd forgotten the idiom was an English one, not Chinese. 'Would you really see me marry Chun rather than help me escape, just because you do not like me? I mean, the reason you do not like me is because I am supposed to marry Chun, yes?'

'Yes,' Wing answered slowly.

'So if you help me escape, your problem goes away and so does mine.'

A short silence fell while Wing thought it through. Then: 'How involved would I need to be?'

'Not very.'

'Would there be any risk to me?'

'I can arrange things so that there is not. Well, hardly any.'

'When were you thinking of going?'

'I need a day or two to get ready, with your help, so possibly the day after tomorrow.'

Another silence. Then: 'All right, I will help you. But only to get rid of you.'

'Of course.'

'And if you do get away and I am blamed, I will say you threatened me with my life.'

'Naturally. You can say whatever you like. I will be long gone.'

Wing nodded, apparently satisfied. 'What will you need?'

So Bao told her.

8

There had been no word the day before of Lee Longwei's whereabouts, a dearth of news that had crushed Kitty. She didn't know whether to scream, weep, hit out at something or collapse on her bed with her pillow over her head. Rian was just as upset and as usual his tension manifested as a foul mood, resulting in everyone doing their best to avoid him, except Hawk, Pierre and Haunui, who were impervious to his temper. Poor Tahi, too, was in a state, his jaw tight, his face drawn and his eyes bleary from lack of sleep. Israel was also horribly on edge, pale-faced and hair-triggered. They were *all* tired, and desperately worried about Amber and Bao.

Kitty couldn't remember ever feeling this awful. No, that wasn't quite true. Once, when Amber had been a little child, a young woman named Amiria — not much more than a girl herself — had taken her and Kitty had had to hunt her down and take her back. That had been pretty damned terrible. And the time that Amber and Bao had been abducted by Searle and Tuttle at Ballarat had been hideous, too. In fact, counting Lo Fang's and Lee Longwei's deeds, this was the fourth time in her life Amber had been abducted, which, if the present situation wasn't so terrifying, would be ridiculous. It was almost, Kitty thought in her lowest moments, as though she were being made to pay for plucking Amber from the streets of Auckland when she'd been tiny, and daring to presume she and Rian could raise her as their own. But would God really do that? She'd asked Simon, who should know, having been a missionary. Would He really punish her for taking someone else's child?

'Don't be silly,' Simon said. 'Of course He wouldn't. That isn't the sort of thing God does. If he bothers to do anything at all.'

'Then why do I *feel* like I'm being punished?'

'I don't know. Let's try and concentrate on finding Amber rather than brooding over our . . . selves, shall we?' Simon had replied.

That had given Kitty a shock. 'Are you calling me self-indulgent?'

Simon had looked shocked then. 'No. God, no. I just don't think it pays to dwell on why things happen. Don't look for hidden meanings when there aren't any. Look, you did nothing wrong when you took Amber off the streets. I was there, remember. You've raised her beautifully and given her a wonderful life. Why would God or anyone else punish you for that? Don't waste your time worrying about the past. Worry about now if you have to, but don't make it any worse than.it needs to be.'

Kitty had felt a little better after that conversation but of course her fear and distress remained. This time it felt as though Amber really had been snatched away and hauled up into the sky by the creature in Tahi's vision, never to be seen again, which was absurd, yet not. There were different degrees of gone — gone for the day, gone for a week, gone forever — and Amber felt very gone. Even when Rian had been caught in a flash flood on the Ballarat goldfields and everyone was convinced he'd been killed and his body lost downriver, she hadn't felt this empty. She'd known then he was still alive, and so had Tahi.

Now, she finished setting the mess room table, then went into the galley.

'Pierre?'

'Oui, ma chérie?'

'Will you do a reading?'

Pierre tipped the fat from a roast leg of pork into a metal bowl to keep for later, then wiped his hands on his linen apron. 'For Amber?'

Kitty nodded. 'And Bao.'

'You know Rian don't like it.'

'Bugger Rian. *I* don't like not knowing what's happened to our daughter.'

'Have to be just the bones. I don't have the snakes here.' Pierre frowned, adding twenty extra wrinkles to his already incredibly lined forehead. 'Or the little snakes, do they like Hong Kong?'

'I've only seen bigger ones, though they were dead and hanging up in the marketplace, and I've heard a lot of them are quite venomous. I really don't want one of those loose on the ship.'

Pierre looked comically alarmed. 'Samson and Delilah will have the heart attack! No, we stick with just the bones. After supper, oui? I will need half an hour or so to prepare the dollies.'

'Good. Let me talk to Rian.'

Chuckling, Pierre said, 'Heh. Mick will shit.'

Rian wasn't the only one aboard the *Katipo* not entirely comfortable with Pierre's eclectic mix of Louisiana voodoo and Catholicism.

Kitty managed one slice of pork at dinner, even though it was expertly roasted with delicious crackling, half a potato and seven green beans, and Simon and Pierre only picked at theirs because they, too, were the sort of people whose appetites were affected when they were upset, but everyone else took deliberately small servings out of respect for the missing girls, then sat staring miserably at their empty plates, which annoyed Kitty.

'For God's sake, eat, would you? They wouldn't want you all to starve just because they're not here.'

There was a mad rush then for the pork and vegetables, and a palpable lifting of the mood around the table. It was a pity Kitty was going to have to flatten it again.

'Rian?'

'Mmm?' Said through a mouth stuffed full of potato.

'I've asked Pierre to do a reading for Amber and Bao. You know, with his bits and pieces.'

Mick crossed himself.

Rian eyed her, chewing slowly. He swallowed and took a sip of ale. 'You know what I think of all that.'

'I do.'

'I'm not having any snakes on this ship.' Rian turned to Pierre. 'You've not brought any aboard, have you?'

Pierre shook his head so violently his plait

226

flicked from side to side. 'With the cats? I think *not!*'

'Hmmph.'

And that was all Rian said.

Mick muttered, 'Holy Mary, Mother of God.'

'You don't have to watch,' Haunui said. 'You big lily-liver.'

'Don't you call me lily-livered! I'm not scared of a few stones and tatty old bones, so I'm not!'

'Good. You can sit right next to Pierre then, eh?'

'I bloody well will!'

'Settle down,' Rian warned.

Pierre stuffed a last forkful of pork into his mouth and rose. 'The table can someone else clear her, please. And the dishwashing. I must prepare.' And off he went to his cabin.

An hour later they were ready, sitting around a freshly scrubbed mess table. The overhead lanterns were all lit and another sat on the table itself. From a velvet bag Pierre took out a carved marble rooster, a string of multi-coloured beads, a small statue of a monkey, a dried chicken's foot (which Kitty was sure she could smell) and a handful of dark red polished stones. After arranging these items very carefully in a large square, he placed a crude doll dressed in a silk robe and with a long black plait hanging from its head in the top left corner.

'This be Bao's reading,' he said.

He took a second small velvet bag, loosened the ties and blew a long, steady breath inside it, shook the contents energetically so that they rattled, then tipped them onto the table, exactly in the middle of the square. Out came a cascade of dry, brown bones from a human hand.

Once again Mick crossed himself.

'Hmm,' Pierre said as he studied the pile.

'What do they say?' Kitty asked.

Pierre held up a finger to silence her. Then, he moved the Bao doll from the top left corner to the bottom right, squinted with one eye, and said, 'Ah.'

'What?' Kitty demanded.

'She be near, and she be joining us soon.'

Rian frowned. 'What do you mean?'

'What I say.'

'Do you mean she'll escape from Yip, or we'll rescue her?'

'Dunno. The bones just say she be with us soon. They not be a book, you know.'

'Well, that's good news, isn't it?' Simon declared, grinning. The most formally religious of them all, strangely he had no trouble accepting the rituals and predictive powers of Pierre's gris-gris.

'Do Amber now,' Kitty said, desperate for news. 'Please.'

Pierre carefully set the Bao doll aside, collected the bones and dropped them back into their bag. Producing another little doll, this one wearing tiny cloth trousers and a shirt and with long, very realistic hair, he placed it inside the square.

'That hair looks just like Amber's,' Tahi said, astonished. 'How did you do that?'

Which is exactly what Kitty was thinking. The doll didn't particularly look like Amber but the hair rendered it . . . macabre.

'I pick it out of her hairbrush,' Pierre said. 'It make the divination work better.'

Tahi reached out towards the doll, then snatched his hand back. 'Can I have it, Pierre? The doll? When you've finished?'

Mick gave a great, theatrical shudder. 'Holy Jesus, are you sure, there? I wouldn't be touching it with a barge pole.'

'Non, I pull it apart after this. It be . . . ' Pierre screwed up his face as he sought the right word. 'Tainted.'

'The hair, then?' Tahi asked, sounding close to desperation. 'Can I just have the hair?'

Feeling near tears herself, Kitty patted his hand. 'Don't worry, love, we'll find her. We will, really.'

Pierre blew into the bag of bones again, gave them a vigorous shake, and decanted them into the centre of the square. Squinting, he studied them for a long moment, leant to the left, then the right.

'*What?*' Kitty almost shrieked. 'What can you see?'

'Hush, ma chérie. I am looking.'

Pierre placed the Amber doll in the bottom right corner of the square, removed a small bone from the middle of the pile, nodded once and sat back. 'Oui, Pierre *thinks* he understands.'

'Well?' Rian prompted sharply.

'The lwa show me the Dragon. He hate the British.' Pierre cocked an eyebrow. 'Ha. Who do not?'

'What the hell is a lwa?' Mick muttered.

'Keep quiet,' Rian snapped. 'What else?'

'The Dragon use Amber so the British swallow all the opium in China.'

A short, confused silence. Then, from Simon: 'Surely that can't be meant literally?'

'You got all that from a pile of old bones and a dried up chicken's foot?' Israel scoffed.

Pierre gave him a dirty look. 'Pierre's bones and beads and little precious things, they are *symbols*, and only the voodoo priest — that be *moi* — knows their secrets. This be a riddle. The lwa like the riddle.'

'The lwa are voodoo spirits,' Hawk explained to Mick.

'But you could have just made that up,' Israel insisted.

Pierre sat back and crossed his arms. 'Oui, but why? Tell me that.'

'Ae, why would he make it up?' Haunui demanded, fixing Israel with a very hard look.

Kitty watched Israel gazing back at Haunui, and wondered what had got into him. Whatever it was seemed suddenly to have captured his tongue because he remained silent.

Haunui set his beefy forearms on the table and leant forwards, the lantern light picking out the moko on his face. 'Come on, boy, explain yourself. Why would he make it up?'

'I . . . ' Israel swallowed. 'That's not what I really meant to say.'

'Well, what did you mean?' Rian asked.

'I *meant* that maybe he just read the signs wrong.' Israel waved a hand towards the bones. 'It seemed a funny thing to say. You know, the

230

British eating all the opium in China.'

'I just pass on the message,' Pierre remarked.

Kitty glanced around the table and saw that no one else believed Israel, either.

'And Pierre, I mean the bones,' Israel went on, 'well, they didn't tell us anything about Amber, did they?'

'Was there nothing else?' Tahi asked Pierre.

'Oui, there was but *someone* they butted in while I was doing the telling.'

Everyone was suddenly alert again, staring at Pierre expectantly.

'I think on the Dragon's junk. The bones they say a ship.'

Kitty's sense of disappointment was so overwhelming she could taste it.

'We already know that,' Hawk said.

'But *where?*' Tahi persisted. 'Where is she?'

Pierre just shook his head, looking as distressed as Tahi obviously felt.

'And was that all?' Kitty asked. 'Will we get her back? You saw we'd get Bao back.'

'Oh, oui, Amber, she come back.'

'Well, why didn't you say that at the start?' Rian barked. 'For God's sake, Pierre!'

'But somebody die.'

'Who?'

Pierre said, 'The lwa they don't see that bit.'

But they all knew he was lying.

★　★　★

Tahi went up on deck for some fresh air, not really aware he was being followed until Israel

231

joined him as he leant on the gunwale and stared down into the murky waters of the harbour, moonlight picking out the clumps of rubbish bobbing against the ship's hull and the warm air intensifying the stink of sewage, seaweed and rotting fish.

'That was a bit unkind, what you said to Pierre,' he remarked.

Israel rubbed his face wearily. 'I know. I wish I hadn't now.'

'Well, why did you?'

'I don't know. I suppose . . . I just don't believe in all that mumbo jumbo.'

'It isn't mumbo jumbo. It's a . . . craft.'

'Pretty strange one.'

'Well, he's usually right with his predictions. I suppose you don't believe in my visions, either.'

Israel shrugged and said nothing. A dead and bloated dog — possibly — floated slowly past in the water below.

Eventually Israel said, 'Look, I'm sorry.'

Tahi eyed him. Israel looked as bad as he felt — as though he hadn't slept for a month. 'What for?' He knew, though. He knew very well.

'For being an arsehole. For blaming you when Amber got taken at Cebu, and for suggesting we forget about Bao, and for . . . for generally just being an idiot. You don't need that, you need a mate.'

Tahi grunted, not willing to let Israel off the hook quite so easily. 'It hasn't helped.'

'Yeah, well, I honestly am sorry.'

Staring down at the water again, Tahi let a minute tick by before he asked, 'Why?'

'Why what?'

'Why *are* you so angry?'

'Well, isn't it obvious?' Israel sounded perplexed. 'First that bastard Lo Fang snatches her, then some bloody pirate! 'Course I'm angry! We all are, aren't we?'

Tahi turned to face him. It was about time he said this outright. 'Amber, you mean? My wife? *My* wife, not yours.'

Israel's head jerked back, just a fraction, but it was there — Tahi thought he might as well have slapped him.

'What are you talking about?' Israel looked horrified. 'Of course she's *your* wife. But we're mates, aren't we, the three of us? I'm just worried. I'm worried *sick*. I'm worried for her and for you. Jesus, Tahi, look what it's doing to you. You look like a man on his way to the gallows.'

Relenting slightly, Tahi said, 'So do you.'

Israel ran a hand through his hair, making it stick up like a cockatoo's. 'Well, I bet none of us are getting much sleep.' He sighed. 'Anyway, that's all. I wanted to say. That I'm sorry for being such an arsehole. You're my best mate and, well, whatever I can do to help, I will.' He stuck out a hand. 'Friends?'

Tahi looked at it for a second, remembering the quote 'Know thine enemy.' Was that from the Bible or somewhere else? And was Israel really his enemy? Then he shook. 'Friends.'

★　★　★

233

Lai Wing Yan paused at the door of her apartment, opened her parasol and arranged it low over her head to keep the autumn sun off her face. She was off to the Central Marketplace to do some shopping and wore good town clothes, a long skirt of embroidered duck egg blue silk with a matching high-collared short robe, silk shoes with six-inch wooden soles, and carried two embroidered cloth purses, one for money and one for her fan. Her hair was arranged into a large, smooth knot at the back of her head and her face was heavily made up with white powder, rouge and brow pencil and lip stain, as was customary when a woman of standing went out in public.

As she headed off across the courtyard with her servant, Ka, hurrying along behind her, she encountered Tan, taking the morning air.

'Good morning, Wing.'

Wing bowed a greeting, but didn't stop to talk.

'Off into town?'

'We are going shopping,' Ka said.

'More silk for costumes, I expect,' Tan replied acidly. 'Enjoy yourselves.'

Ka exchanged a long-suffering glance with Tan's servant and hurried on after Wing.

At the front gate Tsang Ho Fai sat on a stool, peeling a piece of fruit. The gate was always guarded, as though Yip Chun Kit were frightened of being attacked, which was not out of the question given his unsavoury business practices, or perhaps that his women or servants might abscond.

'Where are you going?' he asked as Wing and Ka approached.

'The Central Marketplace to do some shopping,' Ka replied.

'I was not talking to you. I was asking Princess Pretty Feet here.'

Wing altered her stance so that the hem of her skirt fell over her shoes, and lowered her parasol even further. 'Shopping, as Ka said.'

'Hmph. As if you do not already have enough fripperies.' Wing ignored him.

Groaning as if it were the most almighty effort, Ho got to his feet and unlocked the gate. 'Am I calling the chairs?'

'Yes,' Wing replied as she stepped out onto the street.

Ho shouted to a houseboy, who ran off to alert the bearers. In no time at all two sedan chairs and four liveried bearers appeared. Wing settled herself into a chair and gripped the arms as the bearers lifted it and balanced the poles on their shoulders. She looked behind to make sure Ka was ready in the second chair, gave Ho a little wave, commanded, 'Central Marketplace,' and off they went.

The trip seemed, to Wing, to take forever, travelling as they were at a snail's pace, but they finally arrived at the marketplace, which had been busy and crowded with shoppers since just after dawn. The bearers parked their sedan chairs outside the market and went off in search of food — which the market had in abundance — while Wing and Ka made their way towards the rendezvous point.

She was there, waiting for them, the real Wing. Bao breathed a deep sigh of relief.

'Did you have any trouble getting away?' Wing asked.

'No, everything went smoothly, even when I had to speak in your voice,' Bao replied. 'Although I do not know how you can wear this powder on your face all the time. It feels disgusting.'

She'd spent several hours that morning with paints and powders disguising her face to look like Wing's, and using ash from burned incense to recontour the shape of her nose. Even her hands had had to be whitened to match Wing's delicate pale skin. If that girl had done half a day's manual work in her life, Bao would be astounded. She had also borrowed a costume of Wing's, very similar to the one Wing was wearing now. And Wing's shoes! They were far too small and killing her! Wing never wore flat shoes, so Bao hadn't been able to today, either.

'Only barbarian women go about with a naked face,' Wing said sniffily.

'You do, in Yip's house.'

'In public, I mean.'

Bao bent down and prised off the murderous shoes. 'You can keep these, too. They were so tight I would not be surprised if my toes fell off.'

Examining one, Wing said, 'Look, you have burst the stitching. This is my second best pair!'

'Sorry. I will have to pay you back one day. And for the costume.'

'I do not want paying back,' Wing said. 'I just want you gone.'

'And I am very happy to oblige. You are sure no one saw you leave the house this morning?'

'I am positive. I crept out before dawn when there was no one on the gate and I hired a sedan chair. I did not use ours. You disposed of the powder and rouge you did not use?'

Bao patted her purse. 'It is in here. I will take it back to the ship with me. And I cleaned up after myself very well.'

The plan was for Wing to return to the compound with Ka. With luck, Bao's means of escape would remain a mystery.

'Thank you for your help, Wing. And you too, Ka.'

Ka smiled nervously, but Wing just nodded.

'And if something does go wrong when you get back — '

'I will blame it all on you,' Wing said.

'I am sure you will. But if you need help, and you can get away, come down to Pedder's Wharf. My friends' ship is called the *Katipo*. You will be safe with us. Both of you.'

Wing gave her a disconcerted look. 'But you do not like me. Why would you help me?'

'Because I can.'

Bao made her way out of the marketplace and headed for the waterfront. She was hungry but too impatient to reach the *Katipo* to stop and buy something to eat. What if, for some reason, they'd gone? What if they'd believed Chun when he'd told them she wasn't at his house? She had other choices — she could work her passage back to New Zealand on another ship — but even just the thought of the *Katipo* having departed left a bitter tang of disappointment in her mouth.

She most certainly could not stay in Hong Kong, not while her father was so ill in Dunedin. She must get back there to be with him in what were likely to be his final days. She would never forgive herself if he died there alone, in a country that had never welcomed him and in which his bones could never rest in peace. And she would not return to her village in Kwangtung Province without him, either.

Her mother had passed some years earlier and she was the only child her father had chosen to take to the goldfields with him. Possibly because she was the next in line to be Cloud Leopard, but also, she liked to think, because he loved her so much. He had taught her everything, to read and to write in Cantonese, and the Mandarin language of governemt, as well as English, to calculate, and to read the heavens — not the traditional arts of the Chinese scholar, but skills that would help her build a comfortable and honourable life for herself.

And, of course, there had been Kai. He had taught her the martial arts so that she might keep herself safe, and she'd proved a very capable pupil. On one hand she found Kai's contribution to her education ironic, given that he had no intention of allowing her to become Cloud Leopard, a role he so passionately coveted for himself, but on the other she understood his reasoning because she knew he cared for her wellbeing. Of course he was in the main working in his own interests, and to fulfil his most cherished ambition, but he genuinely believed he was doing a good thing, sending her off to marry a man like Yip Chun Kit. Chun was rich, he would provide for her and give her children, and she'd never have to worry about anything.

But it wasn't what she wanted, and it wasn't what her father wanted, either.

Bao glanced down at her feet: they were filthy now and looked incongruous sticking out from beneath the hem of her silk skirt. She was dying to wash her face. She looked around. Where was she? She didn't know Hong Kong very well at all. She couldn't see the sea but she could smell it and see and hear gulls.

She kept walking and finally, as she rounded a two-storey building, she saw dozens of bare masts in the near distance and the long finger of a pier. She dashed across the street, dodging ox carts, sedan chairs and the occasional rider on horseback, and down towards the shore, the smell of fish, smoke and something rotten filling her nostrils. Her hair fell out of its arrangement as she leapt across a pothole, its accumulation of water filmed with rainbow-coloured oil.

It made sense to her that Pedder's Wharf might be at the end of Pedder Street, so she walked along the edge of the waterfront, hoping she'd chosen the right direction. Here the ground was paved and, as she approached two very grand, three-storey stone buildings with archways and open verandahs on each floor, one on either side of a sort of open plaza, she encountered an actual street sign declaring *Pedder Street*. Extending from directly in front of one building was a lovely big wharf. She almost laughed out loud.

She stepped onto the wooden boards, her bare feet making no noise at all, and hurried along, peering at the names painted onto forward bows. She'd read plenty about the *Katipo III* in Amber's letters but never seen the ship. Then she spotted her, a beautiful craft painted black below the high-water mark with a red stripe above. She stood for a delicious moment, contemplating her means of returning to New Zealand and her father, and happily looking forward to seeing her friends, then ran across the gangway.

'Hello!' she called. 'Is anyone home?'

Mick Doyle popped up from behind the cabin, blanched and looked about to faint.

'Mr Doyle?' Bao rushed over to him. 'Are you all right?'

'Holy Mary!' Mick exclaimed, clutching his chest.

'It's me, Mr Doyle, Bao.'

'Jesus God, I thought you were a ghost, so I did.'

Gideon thumped down onto the deck from the mizzen mast, grinning hugely. 'Miss Bao?'

'Mr Gideon, how lovely to see you.'

'You escaped! We knew you would.'

'Did you?'

'Pierre read the bones.' Gideon cast an eye along the wharf. 'Does Yip know you have absconded?'

'He will soon.'

'And he will expect you to come here?'

'He must know that I know you are here for me.'

Gideon looked thoughtful, but not unduly

worried. 'Mmm. I will set a watch. Come below. Rian and Simon have gone to see the governor about you and Amber being abducted, but Kitty and most of the others are here.'

'Well, there is no — ' Bao stopped, staring at him. 'Did you say that *Amber* has been abducted?'

'Yes, it is a long story. Come below. Kitty will tell you.'

Bao followed Gideon down the companion way, her skirts gathered in one hand, the most awful sense of dread and guilt filling her belly. In the mess room she greeted the crew, who were, to her embarrassment, delighted to see her, then Kitty appeared from her cabin, holding a piece of embroidery.

'Bao?'

Bao ran to her, to be embraced in a hug of such ferocity that she knew Kitty was also hugging her missing daughter. Bao quite understood.

'Oh, my love,' Kitty said, 'I'm so pleased to see you. Did you escape? Are you all right?'

'Yes, yes, I am unharmed. What has happened to Amber?'

Kitty sank onto the bench before the mess table. Bao sat beside her.

'Are you sure you're all right? Do you need food or anything to drink? Pierre, some tea perhaps?' Kitty looked around. 'Where's Pierre?'

He was already in the galley putting together a tray in between mopping his eyes. He was very fond of Bao and she looked tired and thin, and he hadn't liked the state of her dear, scratched, dirty bare feet.

'Please tell me about Amber,' Bao said again.

'Oh God,' Kitty said. 'We went to see Kai in Sydney, about you. He warned us off and told us not to come after you, but we took no notice. So-Yee told us on the quiet you were here in Hong Kong.'

'Oh, good old So-Yee,' Bao exclaimed.

'I know,' Kitty agreed. 'A ship followed us and we had to stop in Cebu after a storm and our sails ripped, we think thanks to Kai, and Amber was taken from our hotel there. She and Tahi were drugged. They're married now, you know.'

For a moment, Bao was delighted. She'd always known the two would marry one day. They were perfect for each other. She shot Tahi a huge, beaming grin, but his answering look of misery wiped the smile off her face. He was in awful pain, and she immediately felt it, too. 'Who stole her?' she demanded.

'The captain of the ship following us, Lo Fang,' Tahi said. 'It was my fault.'

'It was not,' Kitty insisted.

Bao nodded. 'He works for Kai. He took *me* from our camp. Swine. And they are here, in Hong Kong?'

'They were.'

'Well, I will get her back. I know how to manage a man like Fang.'

Hawk, Tahi and several of the other men exchanged doubtful looks. Bao saw but wasn't offended. They didn't really know her now, as a woman.

'That's not the end of it,' Kitty said, her voice wobbling on the last words.

Bao braced herself for more bad news.

'Fang's ship was raided by pirates before it reached Hong Kong and Amber was taken by *them*. Their captain is Lee Longwei, also known as the Dragon.'

The hairs on Bao's neck and arms prickled. She had heard of Lee Longwei: stories of his barbarous and bloody conduct had reached as far as the Chinese working the Australian and New Zealand goldfields.

Kitty burst into tears, flapped a hand at Bao when she reached for her, blew her nose on the piece of embroidery and struggled mightily to compose herself. 'I'm sorry. It's all been a bit much, really. We've just felt so . . . useless. We were sure you were at that frog person's house but couldn't get to you, and some strange relative of So-Yee's implied to us that Longwei would probably try and ransom Amber but possibly not for money — but *what for*, though? — and Pierre's bones said something bizarre about the British swallowing all the opium in China, and we haven't got a clue where Longwei is despite asking everywhere. Rian's even gone to speak to Sir Hercules Robinson. You're safe now, which is wonderful, but it seems our only hope is the British government. Amber's a British citizen, being a New Zealander, so, in theory anyway, the governor here should be able to help us.'

'What strange relative?' Bao asked. 'What bones?'

As Kitty started to explain Pierre appeared, first with a tray bearing tea and several plates of cake and biscuits, and again with a large bowl filled with hot water and a pile of clean, soft cloths.

'Cloths for the face, then for the feets,' he explained. 'And maybe Bao she borrow some of Amber's clothes?' he added, indicating Bao's beautiful but impractical costume.

'If you do not mind,' Bao said, looking first at Kitty, then Tahi for permission. 'I am more accustomed to wearing shirts and trousers than this sort of thing.'

'So's Amber,' Tahi said. 'She won't mind. I'll sort something out for you.'

While Bao scrubbed at her face and then her feet, Kitty explained about the visit from Lo Fang's crewman, and the reading Pierre did for both Amber and Bao. After a short interruption during which Gideon sent Mick and Ropata back on deck to keep an eye out for any sign of Yip Chun Kit or his men, Bao, in turn, described her escape from Chun's compound, not neglecting to mention that she'd offered the *Katipo* as a haven should things go wrong for Wing and Ka. 'I hope that is all right with you. But I do not think that anything will go wrong. Wing is very duplicitous. I expect she can lie her way out of anything.'

Footsteps on the deck above alerted them to Rian and Simon's return. A second later they clattered down the companionway.

'Bao!' Simon exclaimed.

'Hello, Mr Simon. As you can see I have escaped Yip Chun Kit's clutches.'

'Christ, that's a relief,' Rian said, giving Bao a quick, slightly uncomfortable hug. 'Pierre said you would.'

'What did the governor say?' Kitty asked.

244

Rian threw his hat at the table before he sat down: it skidded off and landed on the floor. 'Pompous arsehole. He said Bao being held against her will by Yip Chun Kit was a Chinese matter, not a British one, but that's irrelevant now, isn't it, given she's managed to escape. This ship sails under an Irish flag, and Ireland, though it always pains me to say it, is part of the United Kingdom. If Chun comes aboard to try and take Bao back, we will have the protection of the authorities. Won't stop him causing trouble, though, will it?'

'And Amber?'

'Robinson said her abduction *is* a British matter, but he doesn't have the military resources to go hunting down pirates, of which there are thousands in Chinese waters, looking for one missing girl.'

A resounding silence filled the cabin.

'What?' Israel said, his face suffused with angry blood. 'But she's a British citizen! He's the bloody governor. What the hell's he doing here if it's not to help British citizens?'

Haunui said cheerfully, 'You lot should make up your minds.'

'What?' Israel demanded again, even more sharply.

'One minute you don't want to be English, next minute you do, when you think it'll work in your favour. What a pack of Hippolytes.'

Rian smiled. 'You mean hypocrites.'

'Ae, them.'

Simon said, 'Hippolyte, I believe, was the queen of the Amazons in Greek mythology.'

'Yes, it is hypocritical,' Rian said, 'but this is

245

Amber we're talking about. Bugger principles. In any case he said he couldn't, or wouldn't, help.'

'Chatte,' Pierre muttered.

'Possibly a good thing,' Hawk remarked. 'If he sent soldiers chasing after Longwei there would very likely be a skirmish and Amber could be hurt, or worse. We do not want that.'

Rian said, 'He did say that the Tongzhi Emperor and Empress Dowager Cixi are visiting Hong Kong very soon, and suggested I try and get an audience with the empress dowager. Well, there's no point speaking to the emperor, is there? What sense would I get out of a seven-year-old? Robinson seems to think Cixi may possibly have the pirates' ear.'

'Why would she?' Bao asked. 'The pirates do not abide by Chinese law.'

'It's worth a try.'

'Also I do not think you will get an audience,' Bao said. 'Chinese protocol is extremely strict — the emperor and the empress dowager are godly, and, please do not be offended, but I do not think they or their advisors will consider an Irish sea captain worthy of an interview.'

Rian laughed outright this time. 'You're probably right, especially when you put it like that. But I've got contacts here, compradors who owe me a few favours. I'll have a word.'

Bao knew how powerful the compradors — very wealthy Chinese merchants who acted as intermediaries between other Chinese vendors and European traders to facilitate commerce — were in Hong Kong society, so he very well might succeed.

'Now,' he said as he helped himself to a biscuit, 'tell me how you got away from the Frog.'

So everyone's stories had to be told again, then Bao ducked into Tahi and Amber's cabin to change clothes. Kitty followed her.

'Do you mind if I come in?'

'Of course not.' Bao opened the fastenings over her right breast and beneath her arm and slipped off her robe, revealing a short, soft undergarment with shoulder straps like a chemise. She wriggled into Amber's shirt and closed the buttons.

'Are you really all right?'

'Yes, I am fine.'

'I don't wish to pry, and you can tell me to mind my own business, but — '

Bao managed a smile. 'No, I was not forced to lie with him, if that is what you are worried about. I would have broken his arms, scratched out his eyes and bitten off his tongue had he tried.'

Kitty looked taken aback. 'Oh. Well, that's all right then. I must say, you seem very . . . competent these days.'

Bao undid her skirt and let it pool at her feet. She deliberated for a moment over her bamboo fabric drawers, then stepped out of those as well. They'd only bunch inside the trousers. Though she might keep them — they were lovely and warm. 'You do not like the way I am now?'

'Oh, no, I didn't mean that. It's just that you used to be so — '

'Well, I have grown up now. And I have learnt

many things.' Bao pulled on the trousers, closed the buttons and faced Kitty. 'But I am the same Bao. I still love my father, I still love my friends, I am still loyal, and I know right from wrong. My father has taught me that.'

'Yes, I know. Your father is a lovely man.'

'It will sadden me enormously if I do not spend time with him before he dies. But it will break my heart if I never see Amber again.'

Kitty embraced her again. 'You're a good girl, Bao.'

'Thank you. And please, do not worry. We will find her.'

⋆ ⋆ ⋆

As it happened, they did not need to find Longwei — he found them. Or, his emissary did. Two days after Bao arrived at the *Katipo*, a Chinese man appeared on Pedder's Wharf asking to speak to Captain Rian Farrell. He was directed to the *Katipo*, and received on deck. The day was coolish and overcast, the crisp winds of autumn driving scudding clouds overhead.

The man was tall, well built and apparently lacking an eye. Over the socket he wore a black silk eye patch onto which had been embroidered a blazing red eyeball, with an indigo blue iris and a gold pupil. It was most disconcerting. In Cantonese, he announced himself as Ip To, Longwei's second-in-command. Rian, who could only pick out a few words, studied him warily.

Bao translated.

'Longwei wishes to meet with you,' he said. 'You must come to him, and you may speak with your daughter.'

'I want her back.'

'You may have her in exchange for executing a task specified by Longwei.'

Rian didn't like the word 'executing': it stank of the gallows. So they'd been right, the strange fellow with the hat and Pierre and his bones.

'Ask him what task,' he said to Bao, though he suspected he already had a vague idea, and it was absurd.

Bao spoke, listened, then reported: 'He will not say. He says that is for Longwei to discuss with you. We are to go to Hung Shing Yeh Bay at Lamma Island tonight to meet him.'

'Who's to go? All of us? Won't that worry them?'

Bao said something to Ip To.

'He says it does not matter. They number in the hundreds.'

'And where's this Hung Shing Yeh Bay?'

Bao spoke again, listened. 'He says to get a map.'

Ip To bowed, then strode down the gangway and off along the wharf.

'Surly bastard,' Mick said.

Rian did have a map of Hong Kong and its surrounding waters — no sea captain would be without maps of the ports he regularly entered — so he fetched it and opened it out across the mess table.

Hung Shing Yeh Bay was a remote area on the western side of Lamma Island, which itself was to the south-west of Hong Kong. The bay was well away from prying eyes and no doubt an ideal place to lie low. Rian didn't know the waters around the island, however, and they would have to be careful, especially at night.

They left within the hour, estimating it would take approximately four hours to sail around to Hung Shing Yeh Bay, depending on the wind. If they were lucky they would arrive before full dark.

They weren't lucky. The wind picked up once they left Victoria Harbour and, despite tacking aggressively, they were carried slightly off course towards the northern reaches of Lantau Island to the west. By the time they'd managed to regain their bearings the sun was already sliding down the sky, and a velvety, star-studded darkness had fallen when they rounded a headland and crept into the bay, Rian worried that they would hit some submerged hazard. On the far side bobbed a collection of huge lanterns, or so it seemed. As they neared, it became clear that the lanterns were in fact fires burning on the decks of junks, the flames illuminating the furled orange sails.

'They'll go up like a box of matches if they're not careful,' Haunui said.

Rian shook his head. 'I expect they know what they're doing. Furl the sails!'

The crew ran to gather in the sails and secure them. The *Katipo* slowed and the anchor was lowered. Rian peered through his spyglass, though it wasn't much use in the dark.

'Will we lower the boat?' Hawk asked.

'Both of them.'

The chains began their painful clanking as both ship's boats went out then over the side, landing with identical flat splashes in the sea. Hawk threw down the rope ladders, then hesitated. 'Weapons?'

Rian scratched his nose. Arriving armed to the teeth might not be a good way to open negotiations, but he didn't want to appear an easy mark, either. 'Knives, and don't bother concealing them. And I'll have my revolver.'

Hawk went down the ladder, a thump signalling that he'd reached the boat below. Kitty was next; as she turned to climb down she caught Rian's eye and dared him to say something. He didn't: he desperately didn't want her to go but he wasn't going to tell her she couldn't this time. Bao went down after her, then he joined them. Israel, Gideon, Pierre, Ropata and Tahi climbed into the other boat. Mick and Simon were staying behind. It wouldn't do to come back and find the *Katipo* overrun by pirates.

As they rowed towards the fires, the flames got more distinct, and it became clear that about a dozen junks were harboured in the bay. The sound of music reached them — drumming and some sort of reed instrument? — and also the smell of roasting meat.

From the darkness a small sampan appeared on their right and a voice challenged them in Cantonese. Bao replied, then said, 'That is one of Longwei's men, checking who we are.'

'Did you say we're expected?'

'Yes. He said to look for the junk with the dragon flag.'

As they drew closer Rian realised how big the junks were. They were ocean-going ships, not the usual smaller coastal vessels, with towering prows, massive sterns and masts that soared above their decks and cabins. He could see now that the fires had been lit in great iron braziers the size of washing coppers, though he certainly wouldn't risk lighting one on the *Katipo*.

Longwei's men began to line the bulwarks to stare out at them as they glided past, some lighting long torches and holding them aloft, and the music stopped. The only sound now was the slap of small waves against the junks' wooden hulls.

The biggest ship of the lot was a beautiful vessel, with a steep and elegant curve between a stern and prow that seemed impossibly high from sea level. She carried three masts, the sails of which were currently furled, and Rian could see that they were shaped and rigged in such a manner that when she was at full sail and standing up they would resemble wings. Her masthead was the carved and brightly-painted neck and head of a ferocious-looking dragon, its ugly, fang-filled gob open and reaching beyond the bow as if to devour everything in its path. That she was a war junk was plain to see from the row of ten portholes. Carronade, Rian wondered, or cannon? Cannon had the greater range. From her main mast fluttered a flag on which reared a red dragon on a yellow background. So, they'd found Lee Longwei.

Not daring to stand in the boat in case he ended up in the water and made a fool of himself, he called up to the men on the junk, 'This is Captain Rian Farrell of the *Katipo*. We're here to meet with Captain Lee Longwei at his request. May we come aboard?'

There was a stony silence from above, then a rope ladder was thrown down, narrowly missing Rian.

They tied the boats to the bottom of the ladder, then ascended one by one, Rian going first. As he stepped through the gap in the bulwark he was met by a young man, perhaps in his mid to late twenties, of average height for a Chinese person, wearing the plain tunic and trousers of a seaman. His forehead wasn't shaved and he wore his hair long, hanging unbound down his back. He was handsome, too — Rian supposed: he wasn't a particularly good judge of that sort of thing. He was a little taken aback: he'd expected some kind of monster. At the man's shoulder stood Ip To, arms crossed, unsmiling.

The man stepped forward, his hand out. 'I am Lee Longwei. Thank you for agreeing to meet with me, Captain Farrell.'

Rian's first thought was, As if I wouldn't, when you have my daughter. His second was to wonder where Longwei had learnt to speak English so well.

He shook the man's hand briefly. 'I'd like to see my daughter. Now.'

'You will, then we will discuss business.'

'We don't have any business,' Rian said. 'The only business that you and I have is the return of my child.'

Kitty pushed forward. '*Please* may we see her?'

Longwei looked at her with what might have been real compassion, but Rian wasn't fooled.

'Are you Amber's mother?' he asked.

'Yes, she. is,' Rian replied. 'This is my wife, Mrs Farrell.'

Longwei cocked his head, looking first at Kitty, then Rian. 'Amber's skin is a different colour from yours.'

'Oh, for God's sake, we adopted her,' Rian snapped.

'You adopted a child of a different race?'

'Yes. So?'

'Interesting.'

Scuffling broke out among the *Katipo* party, then Tahi shot forward, fists clenched and his face red. 'Amber's my wife and if you've hurt her, I swear I'll kill you.'

'I have not hurt her,' Longwei replied calmly. 'No one in my personal crew or in any of my squadrons has hurt her. She has been well treated here. You may ask her that yourself. Who wishes to speak with her?'

Everyone did, and said so loudly. Bao clapped her hands then spoke rapidly to Longwei in Cantonese. The conversation appeared to degenerate into an argument and there was a fair bit of voice raising and arm waving.

Then she said, 'I have explained to Longwei how important Amber is to us all, but he will not allow everyone to see her. I believe he fears that all of us together will steal her back.' She glanced around at the twenty or so swarthy and battle-hardened pirates standing about on the deck of the junk and rolled her eyes. 'So he has said only four may go below to talk to her.'

'Kitty and me,' Rian said immediately.

Tahi said, 'And me.'

'And . . . you, Bao,' Kitty said, remembering what Bao had told her in Amber's cabin. 'After all, you're her best friend.'

Bao turned pink. 'Thank you. I appreciate that.'

Longwei led them below, through a whiffy-smelling corridor, into a mess room, then through to a door to a cabin that was obviously his own. Rian, thinking the worst, was incensed.

Longwei shook his head. 'I have been sleeping with the crew.' He knocked on the door.

A grumpy voice shouted, 'Oh, *now* what?'

Rian and Kitty exchanged a delighted grin: that was their charming daughter, all right.

'Miss Farrell, your family are here to see you.'

Silence, then the thump of running feet and the door was wrenched open. 'Ma! Pa! And Tahi!' Amber launched herself at them. 'Aaaah, and Bao! What are you doing here? Did Ma and Pa rescue you? Have you come to rescue me?'

Rubbing his lip where Amber had accidentally clouted him, Rian blinked back tears of, well, relief. She didn't appear harmed in any way, though she did smell a bit garlicky. He glanced at Longwei, only to see the man thoughtfully eying him. He's evaluating how much I care about her, he thought, to assess exactly what he can get me — us — to do to get her back.

'Are you all right?' he asked Amber.

'I'm fine, though I'm bored and I'm sick of

eating Chinese food. I'm dying for one of Pierre's pies or a nice plate of stew,' Amber said, her arm around Tahi's neck.

'You've been treated well?'

'Very. What's going on? You know, this is the *fourth* time I've been kidnapped and I'm only twenty-three. It's *ridiculous*. I want to go home.'

Longwei said, 'Not yet, I am afraid, Miss Farrell.'

'What do you mean 'not yet'?'

'You father has agreed to do a job for me first, in exchange for your release.'

About to say, no I haven't, Rian realised he couldn't, not in front of Amber. 'Can we talk?' he asked Longwei.

'Certainly. This way please.'

Longwei led Rian back to the mess room and they sat down at the scrubbed table. 'Would you care for tea?'

Rian said yes, though he didn't actually want any. They sat around waiting for the tea things to be organised, then he waited some more while Longwei went through what Rian considered to be the tedious performance of preparing and pouring it. It seemed odd to him, a cut-throat pirate bothering with such a fancy and, in his opinion, effeminate ritual, and all for a drink that tasted like something a lady might pour in her bath. He preferred good, strong black tea, like you got in the colonies.

He said so.

'Then ask for it,' Longwei said, 'though black tea is called red tea in China. There are many varieties.'

'Where did you learn to speak such good English?'

'I attended Westminster School for Boys in London for some years. It did not suit me, or I did not suit it. And, of course, I am not a Christian.'

'And now you're a pirate.'

'Yes.'

'The most feared pirate in China?'

Longwei took a sip of his tea. 'So they say.'

'You don't strike me as deserving that reputation.'

'You have not crossed me. Yet.'

Rian sighed. 'What is it you want me to do?'

'The Chinese are being ravaged by enslavement to opium. It is a black blight on our nation and the British are entirely responsible for forcing it onto our shores.'

Not *entirely*, Rian thought. You could also blame the Turks, the Arabs, the Portuguese and other European traders, not that he was sticking up for the British because the British East India Company *had* been responsible for most of it. And there were plenty of corrupt Chinese here helping to distribute it. But saying so wasn't going to achieve anything.

'You do understand the dire extent of the situation here, don't you?' Longwei asked.

Rian nodded.

'Have you ever been a country trader?'

'I have not,' Rian answered truthfully.

'Yes, that is what my sources tell me.'

Feeling nettled and disgruntled, Rian stared at him. Had the cheeky little bastard been poking into his affairs? 'Did you deliberately target my daughter?'

'No. Her capture was the fortuitous consequence of a regular raid, but I am not one to pass up an opportunity.'

Rian shook his head. It really had been a matter of being in the wrong place at the wrong time. Bigger seas, a different prevailing wind, and Lo Fang's path might not have crossed Lee Longwei's and Amber might have arrived in Hong Kong. But would it have changed anything? She still would have been someone else's prisoner. He sighed. 'What do you want?'

'I want the importation of opium into China stopped.'

'I'm sure you do.'

'And I want you to stop it.'

Rian felt an urge to laugh. The idea was just . . . farcical. 'With all due respect, one man can't stop an entire commercial venture that's been operating for over a hundred years. Two hundred, if you count the earlier traders. It would be impossible, you must know that. And why me?'

'I know who you are. I have spoken to the compradors. You are a wily and persuasive man and you know how the English think.'

Well, at least he hasn't accused me of *being* English, Rian thought. 'So do you. You went to school there.'

'That does not mean I grasp the English view of life, or they mine. You can talk to the British authorities. You can make them see what they are doing to my people. Our resistance is broken after the two wars, and now we have the civil war of the Taiping Rebellion. I have heard it said that our opium inebriates number more than twenty-five million and that there are British plans to *produce* opium here, on home soil. That will surely be the death of us. The British already control Chinese customs and excise in Shanghai as a result of the Taiping Rebellion, and will soon manage everything that comes into, and is exported from, China. Speak to the customs authorities in Shanghai. Speak to the country traders. Speak to the British governor. This lethal trade must be stopped.'

It was a lovely speech, Rian thought, but the plan was still ludicrous. 'I already spoke to the governor two days ago, about Amber.'

'Speak to him again, and this time raise the issue of opium imports.'

Rian thought for a moment. 'I was considering seeking an audience with the Empress Dowager Cixi when she visits Hong Kong shortly.'

Longwei looked more than a little discon-certed. 'To what end?'

'I was hoping she may have some influence over persons such as yourself, the pirate factions, I mean, and could therefore possibly help me to get my daughter back. Now, of course, I don't need to speak to her.'

'I doubt she would concede to speak with you, a gweilo sea captain,' Longwei said. 'And no, she does not have influence over the pirate factions. She certainly does not have influence over me.' His voice became bitter. 'I detest her.'

'Why?'

'She has betrayed China.'

This was interesting, Rian thought. 'In what way'

'You have heard of the Treaties of Tianjin?'

'Of course.'

'They were signed by the Xianfeng Emperor, three years before he died. By then Cixi was the Xianfeng Emperor's favoured concubine because she was the only one of his women to have borne him a son. It is strongly rumoured she convinced the Xianfeng Emperor to sign those treaties.'

Rian hadn't heard that. 'Perhaps she just wanted the fighting to stop.'

'Perhaps she is colluding with the British, and now she is the empress dowager and co-regent with the Xianfeng Emperor's former senior consort, the Empress Dowager Ci'an, though in all affairs she wields more power than her co-regent.'

'Yet you don't want me to talk to her about the opium?'

'What would be the point? The treaties have been signed. Cixi has her Summer Palace and her jewels and her silks and her precious son. Only the British can make new policies concerning China's opium trade. The two wars have proven that. So go and speak to the British customs officials at Shanghai, and to the country traders.'

'Look, what if I fail? It's a distinct possibility, you know,' Rian said, not bothering to hide his sarcasm.

Longwei's gaze was frank and unwavering. 'Then I am afraid you do not get your daughter back.'

Rian returned the stare, his temper rising. 'Well, that's bloody unreasonable, isn't it? You ask me to do the impossible and when I fail, which I must, I lose my precious daughter?'

'And my country continues to lose its precious assets, her people. You lose one, we lose millions.'

'But it's not Amber's fault. It's nothing to do with her. It's nothing to do with me.'

'Is it not?'

As Rian glared at Longwei he had a horrible feeling — almost physical, like little worms nibbling at his chest with blunt teeth — that in some way China's misfortunes *were* at least to a tiny degree his fault, but he couldn't quite work out how. 'What will you do with her?'

'You will never know. You will simply never see her again.'

Rian thought that was the most evil thing he'd ever heard and it stunned him. He slammed his hand onto the table, upsetting both little teacups. 'Look, it's your fault the bloody stuff's coming ashore. It's your lot smuggling it in from the country traders sitting out at sea. Why don't you call your bloody pirate mates off? Surely that'd be the easiest thing to do?'

Longwei remained unperturbed. 'You speak as though all Chinese pirates belong to one friendly organisation. Did all British privateers work as a united party? I have no control over pirates who do not belong to my squadrons, Captain, and members of my squadrons do not smuggle opium.'

Leaning across the tea-spattered table, Rian said in a deathly quiet voice, 'If you harm even a single hair on my daughter's head, I'm warning you, I'll hunt you down and I'll kill you. Do you hear me?'

Longwei shrugged. 'I would expect you to say no less.'

'Then we understand each other.'

'I have one further question. Who is the Chinese girl with you?'

Very tempted not to answer, Rian sat with his mouth shut for almost a minute, then decided that cooperating might help Amber. 'Her name is Wong Bao Wan. Her father's in New Zealand. Her uncle arranged a marriage in Hong Kong for her, which she didn't want, so we came here to collect her and return her to her father.'

'She is very opinionated.'

Rian wondered what Bao had said to him. He stood. 'How do I get a message to you?'

'There is a stall at the Central Marketplace that sells only char siu pork. Leave your messages there. They will always get to me in good time.'

9

The Tongzhi Emperor and the Empress Dowager Cixi arrived in Hong Kong to great fanfare later that week. To Rian's surprise he and Kitty were granted a very brief audience with her of two minutes, in a receiving line of dozens of Hong Kong's British residents.

'Well, we don't need to see her now, do we?' he said, screwing up the hand-delivered invitation.

'Hadn't you better tell the governor?' Kitty suggested. 'He probably went to a lot of trouble to get you on that receiving list.'

Muttering, Rian reluctantly smoothed out the invitation, scribbled a note on the back and gave it to the messenger, who trotted off. He was back a little over two hours later, with a sealed note from Governor Robinson. It said:

Dear Captain Farrell
Please be aware that I moved Heaven and
Earth to obtain an invitation for you and
your good Wife to attend the Tongzhi
Emperor and Empress Dowager Cixi's
reception at Flagstaff House. I would be
grateful if you could honour the effort
made on your behalf. It is essential that, as
Colonial caretakers, we on a Diplomatic
level in no way cause offence to the

Emperor, the Empress Dowager or their
Advisors.
H. Robinson (Sir)
Governor, Hong Kong

Hmm, Rian thought, no valediction. Clearly Hercules wasn't happy. Perhaps they'd better go.

Kitty wore her best dress, her steel blue wool, which she'd mended, with her best bonnet and the forget-me-not brooch Rian had given her at Ballarat. She knew she hardly looked the height of fashion and that her costume couldn't compare with the dazzling clothes worn by the other British women waiting to be received by the empress dowager, but she didn't care. She wasn't here to show off.

They waited for ages in a very crowded antechamber of the governor's residence, Flagstaff House, for their names to be called by a footman dressed like an organ grinder's monkey. Unfortunately, it was while they were milling about in the antechamber that Rian noticed Yip Chun Kit, also presumably waiting to be presented to the emperor and the empress dowager.

'No, don't look at him,' Rian said, pulling Kitty behind a potted palm. 'I think it might be a good idea if we left.'

Fanning her face with the black lace fan she'd bought in Cebu — it was horribly hot in here and the air almost solid with the female guests' perfumes — Kitty replied, 'The governor won't be happy.'

'Bugger the governor. I'm not having a scene

264

with Yip. It didn't occur to me he'd be here.' Rian scowled. 'Though it should have, I suppose.'

'Is there another way out?' Kitty asked, looking around. 'That door over there next to the red velvet curtains, where does that go?'

'Let's find out.'

Rian took her hand and they weaved their way across the room, but just as they'd almost reached the far side the crowd parted and left them in full view of Yip Chun Kit, who immediately spotted them and rushed over, knocking folk out of his way, his face rapidly turning a mottled purple colour.

'Wong Bao Wan, where is she?' he demanded.

'I recently asked you the same question, if you care to recall,' Rian replied smoothly. 'Is she not with you?'

Yip Chun Kit looked livid. 'No, she is *not*. She is aboard your ship.'

'Is she really? I don't think so.'

'Do not play games, Captain Farrell. She is my property and I am preparing to fetch her back as we speak.'

Kitty burst out, 'She is *not* your property! How dare you!'

'You're not doing any such thing,' Rian said. 'English law trumps Chinese law in Hong Kong, and if Wong Bao *were* on my ship she'd be under my protection and the aegis of the British government. You're wasting your time.'

Yip opened his mouth to retaliate, but just then his name was called to enter the ballroom. He contented himself with waving his fist under

Rian's nose, turned on his silk-slippered heel and strode off.

'That was unpleasant,' Kitty muttered, fanning herself even more energetically and smiling at those nearby who were continuing to stare.

'A little awkward,' Rian agreed. He waved over a servant and helped himself to two glasses of fruit juice from a tray. 'I knew we shouldn't have come. And I'm not bowing all the way in there. I don't do bowing.'

They'd been told they must approach the emperor and the empress dowager in a position of submission, that is, slowly and with their heads deeply bowed. Kitty wondered how they were supposed to achieve such an entrance without bumping into anything or, worse, walking straight into the empress dowager herself.

And then finally, after a further hot, stuffy half hour, their names were called and they were in the ballroom, and there was Cixi surrounded by dozens of Chinese and British officials, sitting on a throne-like chair and wearing the most glorious silk costume Kitty had ever seen. In bright yellow patterned with gold thread it fell loose from her neck to her ankles and had very wide sleeves and deep borders of maroon, green and black. The robe had a tasselled hem also of gold, and Cixi wore a long rope of pure white pearls looped several times through the robe's front fastening. Her black hair was pinned up and pomaded, and she wore an extraordinary and weighty headdress of pearls, precious stones and silk flowers. On her feet (unbound as she

266

was Manchu) were six-inch-high bejewelled platform shoes, and on the small and ring fingers of both hands she wore six-inch-long gold filigree nail protectors. She also wore rings, pearl and jade bangles, and pearl earrings.

Her face was tastefully made up with white powder, rouge, and just a touch of lip colour. It was unlined and she didn't look as if she smiled often. Kitty decided she might be in her late twenties.

She certainly wasn't smiling now.

She stared down at them rather imperiously, waiting for their names to be announced.

Beside her sat her young son, the Tongzhi Emperor. His costume was almost as ornate as his mother's and, although he held himself with the bearing of royalty, Kitty could see that underneath it all he was just a little boy. She wondered if he'd rather be outside playing on the grass.

At last, Governor Robinson got round to it. 'Your Highness, Captain and Mrs Rian Farrell.'

Cixi's finely arched eyebrows went up slightly, but that was the only indication she'd heard.

Rian nodded his head slightly, the closest he could force himself to a proper bow. 'Your Highness, thank you for receiving us. I beg leave of you to make a request. It is my wish that you formally appeal to the British government to cease importing opium to China.'

Kitty gaped at him. Where the hell had that come from?

A dreadful, ringing silence fell across the room. All British eyes turned to Rian.

Kitty felt her face begin to burn.

A Chinese official translated for Cixi, and a shocked murmuring came from the Chinese.

Cixi stared at him, her expression unreadable. Then she said a single word.

The official translated back. 'Next.'

Rian and Kitty were then personally, and rapidly, escorted from Flagstaff House by a livid-faced Governor Robinson.

'For God's sake, Rian,' Kitty whispered, 'what were you thinking?'

He shrugged. 'Lee Longwei seems to know everything that goes on here. I thought it might help with Amber. I took a punt.'

Outside the governor hissed at him, 'You're a disgrace to the British nation, Captain Farrell. You have just embarrassed yourself, the emperor, Madam Empress Dowager, her officials, and every British citizen here in Hong Kong. I would greatly appreciate your immediate departure from the colony.'

'I'm sure you would,' Rian replied as he and Kitty walked off.

'Well, she could hardly agree to it, not there in front of everyone,' Kitty said, 'even if she did want the opium trade stopped. It was hardly the place and time to raise the matter, was it?'

'Not really.' Rian ripped off his silk cravat and stuffed it in his pocket. 'God, this whole bloody thing is hopeless.'

'With Longwei?'

Rian nodded. 'I can't talk to Robinson again, obviously, not after *that*, and the country traders will be spread across the ocean between here and

West India, and anywhere else in the world they might be contracted to ship. It would take months, if not years, to track them all down. And what would I say to them? 'Look, would you mind not transporting opium to China any more? There's a pirate there who doesn't like it?' What would be the point? Opium's their most lucrative cargo. And as for telling the British customs officials at Shanghai to stop letting the stuff through, I'd probably spend the next ten years in gaol.'

'So we're not going to Shanghai?' Kitty asked.

Rian stopped walking and turned to her. From his expression she knew they weren't. She knew it anyway. Approaching the British customs officials would be a complete waste of time, like all of Longwei's demands.

'Is it a game he's playing?' she asked. 'Giving us these silly, impossible tasks and sitting back to watch us fail?'

'I don't know. I really don't.' Rian stared at his boots for a moment. 'I'm sure he does want the opium trade to stop — he does seem to hate it — but it's hopeless. He must know that. They've lost two wars trying to stop it.'

'He's not . . . mad, is he?' This was a horrible thought, and one that had been nibbling unpleasantly away at the back of Kitty's mind. If he was mad, anything could happen to Amber.

Rian started walking again. 'You'd assume so, given what he's told me to do, but I don't think so. At least, he doesn't *seem* mad when you talk to him. And could a mad man successfully command a fleet of fifty ships and a thousand men?'

'Possibly, yes. You couldn't be sane, could you, to choose to make a living from sailing around plundering and murdering?'

'I'm not sure if people like Longwei see the death they cause as murder. More like collateral damage. Does the British government consider the death of Chinese from opium addiction to be murder? I wouldn't think so.'

'Are you sticking up for him? He has our daughter, Rian!'

'No, I'm not. I'm just trying to understand him. If I didn't know better I'd say he was trying to tackle the situation with diplomacy. Which, in my experience, is very unpirate-like.'

'*Do* you know better?'

Looking slightly surprised to admit it, Rian said, 'No, I don't, actually. I don't know better. But perhaps I should. He had a formal education, you know. In England.'

'Did he?' Kitty was obscurely pleased — that at least solved the mystery of Longwei's excellent English.

'I gather he disliked it there.'

'Oh. Did his parents send him?' Kitty wondered what a pirate's parents could possibly be like.

'No idea. I didn't ask.'

They walked on a little farther. The weather was pleasant, not too warm, and neither considered hailing a sedan chair. Being transported by the power of another human was nothing like riding in a coach and Rian hated them, and they made Kitty feel like some kind of grand, white-skinned queen and left her feeling vaguely shamed.

'So we're not going to do all those things he's asked?' Kitty said.

'No.'

'Will he find out?'

'Probably.'

'Then what *are* we going to do?'

'Let me think about it.'

★　★　★

Israel sat at the mess table, his hands wrapped around a mug of tea that had grown cold, listening in appalled amazement to Rian recounting what had happened at Flagstaff House.

If he'd been there, if *he'd* been given the task of speaking to the Empress Dowager Cixi and her kid, he wouldn't have cocked it up the way Rian so obviously had. No, he wouldn't have even bothered with the opium business, because who cared if a million more Chinese lay around and smoked themselves to death. Cixi probably didn't either. They were useless anyway, once they got a taste for it. *He* would have got straight to the point and demanded that she send her navy — what there was left of it — after Lee Longwei to capture him and his motley bloody crews and bring them and Amber back to Hong Kong, and hang the bloody lot of them.

Not Amber, of course. He hadn't seen her when they'd gone to Hung Shing Yeh Bay, much to his annoyance, but Tahi had said she looked well. He was probably lying, too ashamed to admit his wife had been raped by Christ knew

271

how many filthy, stinking pirates. No, that wasn't true, he knew it wasn't, and thank God, too. Kitty and Bao had both said she'd seemed fit and, if not happy, then at least unharmed. He believed Kitty, and had always liked and admired her, ever since he'd met her in Melbourne when he'd been a scruffy boy working in a hotel stable, though he wasn't so keen on Rian. The rest of the crew thought the sun shone out of his arse, but they couldn't see what he, Israel, could — that he was a bad-tempered Irish bastard who thought he was better than he was — because he usually got them out of the shit. *Usually*, not always. Sometimes it was his fault they got in it and it was Hawk who sorted things. Or Miss Molly Simon, or even Kitty. He did like the way the crew worked together like a family, which he'd never had himself, but sometimes he felt like he was on the outside of it and he could never work out why.

What might have happened if Rian had really died at Ballarat and Kitty had married Daniel Royce? He'd liked Daniel. He'd been a really decent man and it'd been terrible when he'd died. He'd thought he might bawl himself to death, but then he'd only been eleven. Kitty had liked him, too. If she hadn't she wouldn't have done what she did with him. When Rian had been found not dead, and hadn't done everyone a favour by dying of his wounds, Israel had hoped they'd have an enormous fight and Kitty would leave him and go off with Daniel, and he would go with them, and there *had* been a fight, lots of them, but quiet icy ones, and instead

Daniel had died and eventually things just went back to normal.

For a few years they'd sailed the seas and Amber had been all his, though she hadn't known that because he'd been too embarrassed to say anything to her. During that time, he'd mutated from an ordinary boy with carroty hair to an unattractive youth with pus-filled pimples, long skinny limbs, hair like a red squirrel's, and awful-smelling sweat. It had been a nightmare though Amber, who'd gone from pretty girl to glorious beauty without so much as a day of acne, hadn't seemed to notice. But he'd eventually decided why would she? She had to look at Pierre's ugly, wrinkled face, Gideon's terrifying coal black one, and Hawk and Ropata's colossal noses every day. But by the time he'd grown even taller, and his body had filled out pleasingly, and the pimples had vanished, his hair had turned a decent colour and he no longer smelt like cheese and filthy socks, Tahi was sailing with them.

Tahi had become his best friend. They were similar in age and they had a fair bit in common. Tahi's mother had died giving birth to him and Israel could barely remember his; Tahi hadn't known his father and Israel's had shot through soon after he was born; and they were both in love with Amber. Israel, however, had kept that last shared particular to himself.

He didn't feel Tahi deserved Amber. For a start, just because you'd known someone most of your life didn't mean you were the one they married. He understood that Tahi and Amber had been friends since they were about four or some ridiculous age — how can a boy even *be* a proper friend with a girl at the age of four? — but that was like saying kids that grew up in tenements next to one another should get married, and most of them didn't, did they?

Also, he'd spent more actual time with Amber than Tahi had. He'd joined the *Katipo* early in 1855 and Tahi hadn't come aboard until 1857, which meant that he, Israel, had spent two whole years more than Tahi virtually living with Amber, so he knew her better. He knew what made her laugh, though not what made her cry — she hardly ever seemed to cry — and what annoyed her (lots of things), and what she liked to eat. He could make her happy: he knew he could.

And it wasn't that he didn't like Tahi — he did, most of the time. But he was in the way and when something got in the way, well, you just had to move it. Tahi was odd, though, with his visions and strange dreams. Pierre was the same. Israel didn't like that sort of thing. They said Tahi got it from his mother. He often wondered if Tahi could see what was going on in his head, but had decided he mustn't be able to because he'd never said anything. He'd always been good old cheerful, friendly, Tahi.

There'd always been this assumption that they would get together, Amber and Tahi, which had privately enraged Israel, but he'd been happy to bide his time until a chance came for him to step in and take her off him. Tahi, though, had actually shown some balls and started sleeping with her. And then Rian had caught them at it and now they were bloody well married.

It had definitely been a fly in the ointment and had upset him badly to the point that he might have let things slip a bit, and he suspected those two old busybodies Haunui and Ropata might have noticed he wasn't happy about the wedding. He was particularly wary of Haunui, the interfering old woman. Being Tahi's grandfather he was always flapping his big brown ears and poking his nose in where it wasn't wanted, and Israel had caught him watching him sometimes when he thought he wasn't looking, with one of his 'I know what you're up to' looks on his ugly, tattooed old face. I bet you bloody don't, Israel had thought. Haunui would have talked to Ropata because they were as thick as thieves and anyway Maoris always stuck together, and probably Tahi as well, though Tahi had never said anything. Israel steered clear of Haunui and Ropata now, but they'd been watching him, he knew it.

But it didn't matter whether Amber and Tahi were married or not because the perfect opportunity had just landed in his lap. Rian was never going to be able to stop opium coming into China, that was obvious. The idea was possibly one of the stupidest Israel had ever heard. Lee Longwei must be mad.

He had a much better plan, and while Rian and the rest of them were sitting around with their thumbs up their arses, he was going to put it into action and rescue Amber himself.

But he wouldn't be bringing her back to the *Katipo*.

Israel adjusted the sail on the sampan, wondering if perhaps he should have chosen a bigger vessel. The wind had picked up even though it was still early morning and was tossing the little boat about on the waves as though she were no more than a cube of balsa wood. Too late now, he supposed. He eyed the low, dark clouds to the north, hoping that the wind stayed due west and wouldn't swing around to the south. The last thing he needed was rain. He was following the western curve of Hong Kong Island as closely as he dared without running aground, negotiating Sulphur Channel between Green Island and Hong Kong, and calling on Saint Nicholas, patron saint of sailors, for guidance. He was a good sailor, had paid attention and worked hard aboard the *Katipo*, but a sampan was an odd little vessel and he was about to strike relatively open sea.

Also, he was worried that Longwei and his crews might have moved from Hung Shing Yeh Bay and that he was making this perilous bloody trip for nothing. He knew there was a way of getting a message to him, and that it would have been smart to do that before he'd come, but asking Rian how to pass on a message was out of the question, and anyway he couldn't wait. He had to do it now, before Rian decided to make some sort of move himself.

Sailing out of the channel the full force of the wind hit the sampan and sent it scudding across the top of the waves. The tiny boats really weren't built for the open sea. Everything was soaked and Israel could feel an unpleasant rash developing on his backside, but it was a small price to pay.

The bit he was dreading was crossing from the south-western aspect of Hong Kong Island to the northern tip of Lamma Island. If he managed — survived — that, he should be fine, following the western coastline of Lamma Island around to Hung Shing Yeh Bay. And if he got all the way there, they should be able to get all the way back.

He was quite shocked, and a little exhilarated, by the speed of the sampan. He had to tack frequently and was worried about the strength of the thing: it might just fall apart in the middle of the ocean, unused to such violent activity. He'd not had time to examine how it was made, he'd been in such a hurry to steal it.

The wind from his back died off a little as he rounded the end of Hong Kong Island and headed for open sea, but then he was hit from the east by another stiff breeze, so had to adjust the sail again and pull hard on the tiller constantly. His arms would be killing him tomorrow. He thought of tying the tiller, but then worried about having to change direction suddenly. He settled down on the hard wooden seat and steered towards Lamma Island. The fact that he could see it helped.

Nothing untoward happened during the crossing, except that several fish leapt into the sampan. Israel left them there; he watched them flop about on the bottom boards, gasping, their movements slower and slower until they finally died, then he tossed them overboard.

When he reached the northernmost tip of Lamma Island he veered to the west and followed the coast around to the headland concealing Hung Shing Yeh Bay. His arms could barely move, his ears and lips were frozen, and his backside felt as though it were on fire. If Lee Longwei wasn't there, he didn't know what he'd do. He'd . . . well, he'd have to turn around and go back, he supposed.

But Longwei and his men were in the bay, not looking quite so impressive and piratical in the daylight, but fearsome enough. And not the fabled fifty junks, either, only about a dozen. Knowing that Amber was aboard one gave him new strength and he turned the sampan so that the wind filled her sail and headed towards them.

He was met some distance out by two men in a ship's boat. One called to him in Chinese.

That's no bloody use, is it? Israel thought. He couldn't speak a word.

He shook his head and called back, 'No speak Chinese.'

Another question in Chinese.

Again he shook his head. 'No! Only English!' He wondered what he could say to make them understand. 'Rian Farrell? *Katipo*?'

By this time he'd sailed past them and they were having to row to keep up. They didn't look happy about it. One had drawn an ancient-looking pistol.

'Amber!' he shouted. 'Amber Farrell!'

The one with the pistol nodded, then pointed to the junks.

Hoping this meant he could continue, Israel sailed on, his shoulders involuntarily hunched, half expecting to feel the bite of a ball. Nearing the junks he furled in and allowed the sampan to drift. Lee Longwei was leaning casually on the bulwark of the largest ship, observing his approach. Israel saw that just above the junk's waterline near the bow was painted a large, garish eye and the name *Kaili*, something he hadn't noticed during his last visit.

Seeing that he was in danger of banging into the junk's hull, Israel reached for the oars and turned the sampan so she came side on. He maintained the position, looking up at Longwei, waiting for the ladder to be thrown down. It wasn't. Longwei was, however, joined by half a dozen others, all staring over the bulwark at him.

He started to feel stupid. Eventually he called, 'Permission to come aboard!'

Lee Longwei called back, 'Why?'

Taken aback, Israel thought, You arsehole. 'I want to talk. I have a proposition.'

'Captain Farrell does, or you do?'

Ah. 'The captain does.'

'Then why did he not come himself?'

'He's . . . indisposed, so he sent me.'

'In a sampan?'

There were smirks and guffaws from the audience.

'That's right.' And it's damn near killed me.

'And who are you?'

'Israel Mitchell. I was here the other night with the captain.'

'I know you were here then, but who *are* you?'

279

Israel scowled. What the hell was that supposed to mean? 'I'm *Katipo* crew. I've sailed with Captain Farrell for nine years.'

Another long stare. Israel suspected that wasn't the answer Longwei was looking for. Finally he flicked his hand and the rope ladder came tumbling down, clattering against the hull. Israel tied the sampan to the bottom rungs and shinnied up.

'Thank you,' he said as he crested the bulwark. He didn't feel like saying it but decided it would pay to keep on the right side of Longwei. 'Is there somewhere private we can talk?'

'Here will suffice.'

'I'd rather talk alone.'

'Is your message from your captain so sensitive?'

Israel blinked, having forgotten he'd said he was here on Rian's orders. 'Er, yes, it is actually.'

'We can speak below, but Ip To will be in attendance.'

Nodding, Israel said, 'That'll do.' It would, too: the Chinese cove with the eye patch was big but he looked thick-headed and apparently didn't speak a word of English.

Longwei led the way down to the mess room. It wasn't as big as the *Katipo*'s mess room and it stank like a bloody Chinese market at the end of a hot day, but it seemed reasonably clean.

'Would you care for tea?' Longwei asked.

'Not if it isn't proper English with milk,' Israel said as he sat down. 'I can't stand the Chinese stuff.'

Longwei spoke to Ip To in Chinese, and the big man disappeared somewhere. The pirate looked back at Israel. 'So, this proposition from Captain Farrell?'

'Ah, well, yes.' Israel scratched the back of his salt-itchy neck. 'Actually, it is my idea, not Rian's. He went to see that Empress Cixi woman and she gave him short shrift and the governor won't talk to him now, either. So he's pretty well buggered.'

'Has he gone to Shanghai?'

'Shanghai? No.'

'Then what is he doing?'

'I don't know.' Though Israel did know. Rian and the others were coming up with a plan to get Amber back, but they'd never think of one as good as his.

'Then what is this proposition of *yours*?' Longwei asked.

'Look, you want the opium trade stopped and we want Amber back, right?'

'I think that has been made reasonably clear.'

'Right. Do you know who William Eastwood is?'

Longwei thought for a moment. 'No.'

'I've been asking around about who does what in this hole of a town. He's a partner in Jardine Matheson and Co here in Hong Kong. Eastwood only arrived last year. He's twenty-eight, a Scotsman and a bachelor, and my sources tell me he's especially keen on pretty girls with a bit of a dusky tint, if you get my meaning. They say he's been going through the Chinese girls like a hot knife through butter.'

Longwei winced slightly.

Israel went on. 'I thought, if he met Amber, he'd be hooked. You have to admit she's beautiful.'

'You would prostitute her?' Longwei looked mildly shocked. 'To what end?'

'Christ, no. What do you think I am? No, we let him see her, just long enough to tempt him, then we tell him we can arrange a private meeting with her. You know what I mean. Then we lure him somewhere secluded, using Amber as bait, then kill him. We make sure it looks like Cixi's people are responsible, and the British will knock Cixi off her throne.'

Ip To arrived then with Israel's tea and set the delicate little cup on the table. Israel sniffed it. It looked like normal tea, but God only knew what was in it.

'How will that stop the import of opium?' Longwei asked.

'You told Rian you thought she was colluding with the British. Maybe whoever comes after her will make more of an effort to end the trade. And, you know, with Eastwood working for Jardine Matheson, the biggest importers of the lot, it sends a message, doesn't it?' He tailed off.

'It is more likely to start another war.' Longwei drummed his fingers on the table. 'If you accost Eastwood and present the girl like a bag of rice for sale, he will be suspicious. It seems an odd thing to do.'

Israel scoffed. 'Oh, for Christ's sake, we're men of the world here. He must get that all the time if he's made a habit of wenching and no effort to hide it. He'll just think I'm her fancy man. I'll get myself a decent suit of clothes. Don't worry, I'll look the part.'

I'm not worried, he thought, because I'll be doing no such bloody thing.

'And you are expecting me to release the girl?'

'Obviously. Well, the plan won't work if you don't.' Israel sipped his tea: it tasted all right though the milk was a bit strange. 'I'll need her to bait the hook, then to reassure him when he arrives at wherever we decide to kill him. Before we kill him, I mean.'

A muscle in Longwei's jaw clenched and Israel sat back a little. 'Do not keep referring to 'we'. I will not be doing any of the killing. I will not be present at all. This is your plot. How do I know that if I release her you will not just sail away?'

'Because I give you my word that we won't, and I'm good for it.'

'You understand that I have people on the wharves in Victoria, and in the markets, and on the streets?'

'Er, I do now.'

'I will know of every move you make, and if you fail or renege I will take the girl back.'

Bugger, Israel thought. Surely that's a bluff? Then his heart thudded wildly as he realised Longwei had agreed to his plan. 'So I can take her?'

'Yes.'

'Now?'

'Yes.'

'Let me talk to her in private first. There're some things she needs to know.' A few small lies he needed to tell, so he could get her off the ship without any cats getting out of bags.

★   ★   ★

When Ip To returned from escorting Israel to Amber, Longwei summarised his conversation then said, 'It is possibly the stupidest plan I have heard in my life, if he truly intends to go through with it. The man must be mad.'

'Do you believe he actually will?'

'No. I suspect he is here without Captain Farrell's knowledge and wants the girl for himself.'

Ip To said, 'But she is married.'

Longwei gave him a withering look. 'That is why he is here alone. He will be in my cabin telling the girl a pack of lies.'

'It will be a relief to get rid of her.'

'Yes, it will, though unfortunately that may not last long. She may be lovely to look at but she is very bad-tempered and she talks endlessly. I pity her husband. We should have left her with Lo Fang and let him suffer her. That would teach him for taking her in the first place.' Longwei sighed. 'I had hoped that her father might make some headway talking to the British, being the sort of man that he is, but my expectations have come to nothing. He has not gone to Shanghai, I gather he is no longer in favour with the governor, and, to be fair, dealing with the country traders was always going to be beyond the captain's capabilities. Beyond anyone's capabilities, except perhaps the British law-makers'. But then again, it was only a test. I did not really expect him to actually achieve anything.'

'A test of what?'

'His character. Of who he is, of what he stands for.'

Ip To scowled. 'Why?'

'Because my sources tell me he is a man of integrity and ability, and I might have need of him one day.'

'But if it was a test, he failed.'

'Not necessarily. He did not dismiss outright my request when I presented it to him.'

'Only because he thought you might return his daughter if he agreed to it.'

'Well, of course. And I know that privately he considered the task hopeless, but aside from that I sensed in him an empathy for the plight of our people, which is refreshing to say the least, not to mention exceedingly rare in a white man. So while he failed to execute the task, he has passed the test. And when this Mitchell fails, as I am sure he will, and we have the captain's daughter back, I think we will resort to old-fashioned ransom for money, which the captain will no doubt pay, and we will put the funds towards our cause.'

Ip To grunted unhappily. 'I do not understand why you let Mitchell take the girl if you are so sure his plan will fail. What is the point?'

'The point is that I make the decisions and you do not. And I want to see what Farrell does to retrieve his daughter from his crewman. It is all part of the test.'

'Ah.' Ip To suddenly gave a deep chuckle. 'I do

not particularly like Captain Farrell, but he did at least attempt to speak to the Empress Dowager Cixi. I would like to have been there.'

'Yes, although I did not ask him to do that, did I? And in such a public forum. Rather brave of him. As I said, he has a certain integrity. And that is why we will follow this Mitchell. I do not want any harm to befall the captain's daughter.'

'You are growing soft.'

'No, I am keeping my word.'

'And an eye on that Chinese girl.'

'Two, actually,' Longwei said. 'As, unlike you, I have two.'

Ip To scowled.

'And send a ship after that ridiculous little sampan when they leave. But not too close. I would not be surprised if it sank.'

★ ★ ★

Amber scampered down the *Kaili*'s ladder and settled herself in the bow of the sampan.

'It's not very big, is it? Is it safe on the open sea?'

'It got me here in one piece,' Israel replied as he untied the rope and pushed off with an oar.

'It'd better get us back. I'm dying to see everyone.'

Israel flinched, glad he was facing away from her. How the hell was he going to tell her? Perhaps he could just say they'd gone to Shanghai to talk to the customs officials there, or even back to New Zealand. But no, that wouldn't work. It had to be what he'd decided, and he was dreading it.

'How is everyone?' she asked.

He nodded noncommittally. 'Mmm.'

As he turned the sampan and set out rowing, she waved back at the *Kaili*. 'They weren't all that bad, you know, for pirates. I quite liked Longwei.'

'I don't trust him.'

'He let me go, didn't he? He can't be all bad.'

Israel didn't answer, too busy trying to hoist the sail. To the north, above the green hills of Lamma Island, the rain-sodden clouds were gathering, looking like they were getting ready to release a deluge. Should he wait? What if Longwei changed his mind? No, they'd go. Providing they weren't caught in the stretch between Lamma Island and Hong Kong they could always go ashore.

He eyed Amber, huddling in the bow. 'Will you be warm enough?'

She shrugged. He didn't know what she'd been wearing when she was taken from the hotel at Cebu, but someone had given her a pair of trousers, a tunic and a pair of those odd Chinese shoes, which looked at least one size too big. Her hair was tied back, though it continued to whip all over the place. As he watched she pulled a square of cloth out of a pocket and secured it around her head, knotting it at the back. And she still managed to look lovely.

'If you get cold,' he said, 'tell me. You can have my coat.'

'I'll be all right.'

She probably wouldn't, not when they got out into the open sea. He should have thought and brought blankets, but they would only have got wet. Or oilcloth. That would have done the trick. She could have sat there in the bow wrapped up in a big length of oilcloth with her hair streaming out like his very own living figurehead.

He checked his watch and saw it was twenty minutes past one o'clock. If everything went well they should be back in Victoria Harbour before sunset. The wind filled the sail and they fair raced along, even in the bay, and it wasn't long before they rounded the headland and headed north. As soon as they did, a smaller junk from Longwei's squadron raised her sails and very slowly began to tack. Eventually she picked up enough speed to turn in a large arc and bear towards the headland herself.

★   ★   ★

Everyone was disconcerted by Israel's disappearance, but not necessarily for the same reasons. Kitty, Pierre and Simon were of the opinion he'd gone off to drown his sorrows over Amber's continued absence — well, they were all missing her and worried sick — while Mick thought he was probably in a brothel. Rian and Hawk were angry as he had, in effect, deserted his post, and Gideon, though concerned, was annoyed because he'd have to take Israel's place on watch if he wasn't back by nightfall. Haunui, Ropata and, increasingly as the day wore on, Tahi, suspected he'd gone after Amber himself.

'What makes you think that?' Rian asked when they told him.

'Because he's in love with her,' Haunui said.

'Who said?'

'I do. It's obvious.'

'Not to me it isn't.

'You don't notice that sort of thing.'

'Then why should you?'

''Cos I do. And I'm right. The boy's been pining after her for years.'

'Look, no offence intended, Haunui, but you haven't even been aboard most of the time Israel's been with us.'

'But I have,' Ropata said. 'And he's right. Israel thinks he's keeping it to himself, but he does stare at her a lot and he's always making excuses to be wherever she is.'

Rian said, 'Not easy to get away from each other on a ship this size.'

Haunui nodded at Tahi. 'And when they were married, the boy just about turned himself inside out trying to act like he was happy for them.'

'Did he?'

'But he wasn't.' Haunui shook his head. 'He was rotten with jealousy.'

'But he's supposed to be your best friend,' Rian said to Tahi.

'I thought he was. He acted like he was. Maybe he still is — '

'He isn't, boy,' Haunui interrupted.

' — but he wants my wife,' Tahi finished, then realised he was talking about Rian's daughter. 'That is, I mean to say he wishes Amber were his wife, not mine.'

'Why didn't you do something about it?'

'I didn't know. I couldn't be sure it was

289

happening. He was just the same old Israel. Well, until recently.'

'You didn't notice any of the staring and trying to get her alone and what have you?'

'It . . . I don't know.' Tahi's face reddened. 'It wasn't like that. We've just always been friends.'

'You didn't notice it either, Rian,' Haunui said. ''Cos I don't think it *was* like that. I doubt even Amber noticed.'

'When *were* you sure it was happening?' Rian demanded.

'Hold on, Rian,' Haunui said, a hint of admonishment in his voice. 'The boy here hasn't done anything wrong. It's the other one needs a bloody good talking to.'

'More than a talking to,' Ropata muttered.

'When Koro said something, and after the vision,' Tahi said. 'The visions always tell the truth.' He frowned. 'Though I got Israel mixed up with Longwei.'

Rian let out an enormous, angry sigh. 'And you think he's gone to try to get her back himself?'

Haunui nodded. 'Might have. He was a bit sour after you and Kitty came back from talking to the empress. Reckoned he could have done better himself. And then when we decided we wouldn't be going to Shanghai . . . ' He shrugged.

'But Longwei wouldn't hand Amber over to someone like Israel. He's just a boy. He'd appreciate that if I was going to send someone on my behalf I'd send Hawk, or you.'

'Depends what lies Israel told him.'

'Does he lie?' Rian realised who he was talking about, what he'd been like as a lad. 'Of course he does.'

'The thing is,' Haunui said, 'if that's what he's done, where will he take her? If he wants her for himself he won't bring her back here, will we?'

Rian stared at him, the full horror of the situation sinking in. Would he ever get his daughter back? 'Where *would* he take her?'

'At least we know he won't hurt her,' Ropata said.

'That's easy for you to say!' Tahi exploded. 'He probably won't beat or kill her, but what about the rest? She's my *wife*!'

Haunui rested a calming hand on his shoulder. 'Settle down. She knows how to take care of herself.' To Rian he said, 'To Australia, maybe? England? America?'

'Bloody well anywhere, you mean?'

'You settle down too, eh? We'll find them before they get far. Don't worry.'

★ ★ ★

Kitty and Bao were sitting on the deck, trying to make use of the natural light — which was rapidly fading due to a bank of nasty-looking black cloud piling up overhead — to do some mending, and pretending not to hear the raised voices below. Kitty couldn't really concentrate anyway, when she had far bigger things to worry about than holes in socks.

A disturbance on the wharf made her look up just in time to see two Chinese women running along the boards, one trying not to fall off high platform shoes, both carrying an assortment of baskets and bags. They skidded to a halt in front of the *Katipo*, back-tracked slightly, then clattered across the gangway and along the deck, bowing quickly to Bao, then disappeared down the companionway.

A moment later Rian shouted, 'Kitty!'

'Who was that?' she asked Bao.

'Ah. Those were the two women who helped me escape from Yip Chun Kit's compound. I offered them sanctuary? Perhaps I should have reminded you. I am sorry.'

'Oh, well,' Kitty said as she put away the undarned socks. 'Let's go and see, shall we?'

Below decks Lai Wing Yan and Ka stood on one side of the mess room and Haunui, Tahi, Ropata and Rian stood on the other. Pierre hovered in the galley doorway, flour in his pointy little beard and a tea towel in his hand.

Wing's hair had fallen out of its elaborate arrangement and long strands hung down her back and over her shoulders. Her face powder had smudged, revealing flushed skin beneath, and one of her eyebrows had rubbed off. Poor Ka now held all the luggage, out of which spilled badly packed folds of silk and satin, her frightened eyes peeping above the pile.

'You said we could come if we needed to,' Wing said to Bao in Cantonese, her voice high and panicky.

'What happened?'

Ka burst into tears. Mortified, she drew the end of a garment over her head.

Bao clapped her hands at the men. 'Out, please. They need privacy.'

Meekly Rian and the others trooped up the companionway. Pierre made to follow but Bao stopped him.

'Not you. We need tea, please.'

'But I don't know the special Chinese tea.'

'Then make ordinary tea. It's the same thing anyway. With lots of sugar. Do you need food?' she asked Wing and Ka. 'What would you like?'

'Cake,' Wing said.

'She would like cake,' Bao translated for Pierre.

'Cake for les dames Chinoises,' he declared, delighted to be able to feed someone in need, and scurried into the galley.

Kitty divested Ka of her overflowing bags and baskets and led her to a seat, patting her arm as she sat down. 'Don't worry, you're safe here,' she said, hoping that they would be. What on earth had so frightened these girls?

'Excuse me!' Wing stood glaring with her pale, manicured hands on her shapely hips.

Bao, and Kitty, stared back. Bao hadn't realised Wing could speak English.

In Cantonese again Wing announced, '*I* am the premier concubine and *I* am the one to be escorted to the seat, not my servant!'

Ka shot to her feet, looking horrified.

'No, stay where you were,' Bao commanded.

Ka sat again.

Wing barked, 'Get off that seat!'

Ka did.

'Stop it!'

Everyone turned to Kitty.

'Stop being so awful to her. She's not a . . . a puppet!

'Then Wing should not treat her as one,' Bao said. Addressing Wing, she said, 'You were premier concubine in Chun's house but you are here now and you will find things are very different.'

'She is still my servant,'

'Perhaps she is not.' Bao switched to Cantonese. 'Ka, do you wish to remain as Wing's servant?'

Ka looked very much as though she wanted to say no. 'Yes. Miss Wing is a good mistress.'

Bao pulled a face that made her look like a duck. 'Well, we will see.'

Pierre appeared bearing a tray piled high with teapot, cups, and plates of recently baked cake and pastries.

'Sit down, ladies, and Pierre will serve the treats.'

No one moved.

Confused, Pierre raised a wiry eyebrow at Kitty.

'Ka — ' she pointed to her, 'is Wing's servant. Ka sat first and now Wing's upset.'

Pierre said, 'Pfft. If you do not all sit down, the tray I will take her away and no one will have the lovely cakes.'

Bao and Kitty sat, then Ka did, right on the edge of the bench. A few moments later Wing followed, sighing theatrically. Pierre poured the tea, served them each with a slice of cake and a pastry, bowed, and went up on deck.

'Tell us what happened,' Bao said.

'It was so frightening. We had to run for our lives and we did not know if your ship would still be here.' Wing's arms went up, a pastry in one hand. 'It was like leaping across a precipice during the very blackest of nights, unable to tell whether — '

'Could you just tell us what happened?' Bao interrupted.

Wing deflated slightly. 'Oh. When we returned from the Central Marketplace no one seemed to notice that the woman who left with Ka was not the woman who came back. I encountered Chun in the front courtyard garden, and spoke to him, as I went to my apartment to rest but it was not long before Chun realised that you were not in *your* apartment. The gardens were thoroughly searched, then the privies and bathrooms, then every room in the compound, including his mother and father's.' She smirked. 'They did not like that, I can assure you. It became clear to him that you had escaped. We could all hear him shouting and throwing things about. Your apartment was examined from top to bottom but nothing was found. You must indeed have been successful at hiding the evidence of your face-painting.' She paused to shovel a large mouthful of pastry into her mouth in a very unlady-like manner, chewed for quite a while, then eventually swallowed. 'Mmm, this is delicious. Does that little man bake these himself?'

Kitty nodded.

'You are very lucky. I am surprised you are not fatter.'

'And then what happened?' Bao prompted.

'Chun personally interviewed every single person in the compound about what they were doing that day, and what they had seen or heard. It took him two whole days to do so.'

'And?'

'And nothing. Nobody knew a thing.' Wing grinned. 'It was as though you had become a ghost and slipped through the compound walls. But *then*, this afternoon, Ho remembered that the woman, that is, you who were me, who left with Ka to visit the Central Marketplace on the day you escaped, was wearing earrings of pearl and jade.' She made a disparaging face. 'It *would* take him that long to remember, not being the cleverest man. And he remembered because they were familiar to him, but he could not remember why they were familiar. But Chun knew. They are your earrings.'

Kitty glanced at Bao's earlobes: she was wearing them now. She always wore them.

'I had forgotten all about my earrings,' Bao said.

Wing took another bite of pastry and said through it, 'A servant overheard Ho telling Chun, and he told Tan's servant, who told Ka, who ran to tell me. As I spoke directly to Chun when Ka and I returned from the Central Marketplace, I knew it would not be long before he realised I must be involved. I had thought of telling him you had given me the earrings, but of course, I could not produce them. So we ran.'

'How did you get out of the compound?' Bao asked.

'A window in my apartment. It opens onto the lane beside the compound.'

'The only window I had looked out over the garden.'

'*I* was not a prisoner.'

'And did you get away unseen?'

'I think so.'

'Does he know where you are?'

'I said nothing to anyone about this ship.'

Bao spoke to Ka in her own language, and she answered by shaking her head violently.

'Then I expect you are probably safe for now, but I do not think you can stay in Hong Kong. Where is your village?'

Wing looked appalled. 'In northern Kwangtung Province, near the border with Hunan, but I am not going back there. I am no longer suited to village life! And it is too close. Chun may find me.'

'You have to go somewhere.'

'Yes, we do. I am considering Australia.'

Oh God, Kitty thought, Rian's going to love that.

10

The sun had almost set by the time Israel and Amber arrived back in Victoria Harbour. Israel was exhausted and he suspected Amber wasn't faring much better. The rain was just starting, fat drops exploding onto the oily surface of. the harbour's rubbish-strewn waters as he furled the sampan's sail and rowed towards the shore.

'Why are we landing at this end? Amber asked. 'Isn't the *Katipo* berthed at the other end? Pa said we're at Pedder's Wharf.'

Israel was landing as far west and away from the *Katipo*, and from where he had nicked the sampan, as he could. 'I'll tell you when we get ashore,' he said. 'Just give me a few minutes.'

'Is something wrong?'

Pretending he hadn't heard her Israel kept rowing, averting his gaze. He was absolutely dreading what was coming next. When the sampan hit solid ground he leapt out, his legs stiff and sore and refusing to behave, and dragged it up onto the sand, then took Amber's hand to help her disembark.

She wouldn't let it go. 'There is something wrong, isn't there? Tell me, Israel.'

At the very last moment Israel lost his nerve. 'Well, I didn't want to disappoint you but the *Katipo* isn't here. They've gone up to Shanghai to talk to the British customs officials.'

'Customs? Why?'

'Did no one tell you?'

'Tell me what?'

'Longwei wanted your father to talk to certain people about the opium trade. It was a condition of your release.'

Amber dropped his hand. 'And they've *all* gone? Tahi as well?'

Israel nodded.

'When they knew I'd be coming back?'

'They shouldn't be long.'

'When did they leave?'

Christ, now he was just digging himself a deeper hole. 'This morning.'

'Shanghai's bloody days away from here!'

'I know, I'm sorry. I've got money, though. We'll find somewhere to stay and wait for them.'

'Why didn't Tahi collect me from the pirates? Why did it have to be you?'

That hurt. 'Look, I don't know, all right? I just do as I'm told.' Israel took her by the arm. 'Come on, we need to find lodgings.'

He thought she might cause a fuss but she came willingly enough. She must be tired. He was: he was bloody knackered and his clothes were yet again soaked with seawater. He could murder a bath. They walked for about ten minutes into the city until he spied a lodging house he thought looked respectable. Not one for Chinese, of course, but one with a sign outside saying *British Patrons Welcome Only*. The woman behind the counter — some bint from Liverpool who fancied she was classy — didn't even blink when he told her he and his 'wife' wanted a room for five nights. He didn't know if they'd need it that long, but better to be safe than sorry. And quietly, leaning across the counter so Amber wouldn't hear, he registered as Mr and Mrs Irwin Marshall, because you couldn't be too careful.

'Excuse me,' Amber said to the woman. 'My husband's made a mistake. He snores terribly so we always sleep apart, so that's two rooms we'll be needing, thank you.'

The woman smirked and selected two keys from the board beside her. 'That's ten shillings all told, breakfast included. Bathroom's on the ground floor, extra for hot water, request in advance, privies are out the back.'

'God,' Israel muttered, worried about preserving his finances, the reason he'd asked for only one room. In London you could get the same for half that amount, if not less.

'I'd love a bath,' Amber said.

Israel sighed. 'How much for that?'

'Sixpence,' the woman replied. 'I've to boil the water in the copper, you see. It'll take an hour or so.'

'One for my wife, please.'

'Right you are.'

The rooms were adequate. The linen was clean, the furniture dusted and the chamber pots recently rinsed. Israel knocked on Amber's door. She opened it a crack.

He asked, 'Is your room all right?'

'It's fine. What will we do for food?'

'I'll go out and pick something up.'

Amber sat on the bed and brushed at the

saltwater stains on the front of her tunic. Her clothing still hadn't quite dried.

'Do you need something else to wear?' Israel asked. It pained him to see her looking so drab, even though she did often get about the *Katipo* in trousers and a man's shirt. He certainly needed a few bits and pieces. Unable to pack a bag for fear of alerting the others to the fact that he was leaving, he'd simply walked straight off the *Katipo* with nothing but the clothes he was wearing, his hat and his purse.

'Do you mean a dress?'

'Well, you can't go about wearing trousers, can you? Not a white woman.'

'I'm not white, and I can if they're Chinese ones.'

'You can't — people'll think you're one of those half-caste girls. What are they called?'

'Eurasians.'

'Them.'

'So what if they do?'

Israel turned his hat around in his hands, lost for a reply. 'Look, I'll bring back some food and some clothes for you. Will you be all right by yourself?'

'Why wouldn't I be? I'll have a lie down and then my bath, when it's ready.'

'Make sure you lock the door.' Israel had noted that the lodging house appeared to be almost fully occupied — by men.

'I will.'

'All right. Back soon, then.'

'Bye.'

Amber laid down, tucked her arms into her

chest and drew up her knees. Israel watched her for a moment then left, worrying that she'd fall asleep before she'd locked the door.

★   ★   ★

Israel's purse was heavy in his jacket pocket and he was grateful for it. He was carrying all the money he had, a significant sum, but he had a fair amount to buy and he knew Amber wouldn't be happy with anything cheap. He wouldn't want to give her rubbish anyway.

The streets of Victoria were still busy as many of the shops remained open until the nightly curfew sent the Chinese indoors. There were also several early evening markets, which sold not only food but well-made clothing and all sorts of other items including household goods, fruit and vegetable plants and livestock. He might find some of what he wanted there, but not a European-style dress. For that he'd need a draper, perhaps? A tailor? He didn't really know where to start. He did know that generally you — well, women — couldn't just waltz into a shop and buy a costume. According to Kitty and Amber, you had to have your dresses made because of things like measurements and what have you. He, on the other hand, *could* buy a jacket or a shirt from a shop, if he wasn't too bothered about the fit, but he always had to have his good trousers made because he was tall and he didn't particularly like his ankles on show for all to see. But recently Kitty and Amber had been blathering on about the new 'ready-made' dresses you could just buy, though Kitty said the fit would never be right. Perhaps he could find one of those? After all, Hong Kong was full of little Chinese men hunched over bits of material stitching away, wasn't it?

He was on Wellington Street now, where there were plenty of tailors, which he knew because Pierre, being such a dwarf, sometimes went there to get his going-out jackets and waistcoats made. Instead of shingles above their shops, here in Hong Kong the tailors hung robes on poles to advertise their trade, which he thought wasn't a bad idea. Though it could be mistaken for washing hung out to dry, he supposed.

He wandered past a couple, hesitant to enter because it was a bit of a strange request, a man asking for a woman's gown, and irritated by the fact that there were no windows to look into. Fancy being so uncivilised you couldn't make glass. Then, after gazing at a tailor's dummy in a doorway for nearly a minute, he realised what he was looking at. It was wearing a dress! He darted in.

A woman stood behind the counter sorting buttons into little baskets. She was maybe middle-aged, had her hair pulled back in a plain bun and wore the usual Chinese tunic. Some cove, her husband probably, with a skinny queue that fell all the way to the back of his knees, was up a ladder piling bolts of cloth on a shelf.

They both stared at him.

'Evening,' he said. For good measure he took off his hat.

The woman nodded and the man backed

down the ladder, wiping his hands on his trousers when he reached the ground.

'I was looking at that dress on the tailor's dummy,' Israel said.

Another silent stare. Don't tell me they can't bloody well speak English, Israel thought.

'Pak!' the woman shouted.

A young man appeared through a curtain behind her. She said something to him that sounded to Israel like a monkey in a temper, and the boy stepped around the counter and bowed.

'Good evening, sir. May I be assistance to you?'

'That dress on the tailor's dummy, how much is it?'

'I so sorry, sir, it not for sale.'

'Why not?'

'It for display purpose only. To showcase family business.'

The woman interrupted with a question: Pak answered her.

'Have you got any more?' Israel asked.

'Unfortunately no, sir.'

'I'll give you a good price for it.'

Pak spoke to the woman, whom Israel assumed was his mother. She in turn spoke to the man who stood quietly, his hands hidden inside his voluminous sleeves. He gave a short, sharp answer.

'My father say can only sell for fifteen pounds sterling.'

Fifteen pounds! For Christ's sake. That was nearly a quarter of his yearly wage. They were having him on. He looked the dress over again. It

304

was pretty, though, even he could see that. It was a lovely greenish-blue colour, like you got on a peacock, though of course it could be quite different in the light of day, with embroidery all over the top and around the hern, and had a round neck and fitted sleeves. He peeked behind it to make sure it hadn't been made for a woman the size of a cow and gathered in with a peg.

'What's it made of?

'Silk from only best cocoons.'

Israel crossed his arms. 'Fifteen pounds is far too much. I'll give you three.'

Pak looked aghast. His mother fired a question at him and shook her head violently when he replied.

Pak's father stepped forward and held up his hands, digits splayed, then again with three fingers.

'Thirteen?' Israel asked Pak.

A nod.

'No. I'll go to five.'

Pak relayed the offer.

Up came the hands again, plus just one finger this time. Israel sighed. This might take all night. 'Six.'

Eventually they settled on eight. The dress was removed from the dummy, wrapped in paper and tied with string. Israel also bought two plain shirts for himself and handed over the money feeling quite pleased. He was sure Amber would like the dress and although the purchase had definitely dented his finances, he still had quite a lot left.

From Wellington Street he made his way onto

Queen's Road. As he was about to cross the street to enter a market, he witnessed something even he found disturbing. On his right a sedan chair was approaching carrying a white man, who was leaning comfortably back, elbows on the arm rests, a valise resting on his lap. In the gloom the bearer at the front stumbled, went down on one knee, and the chair tilted forwards, spilling the valise onto the dusty ground. In an apparently instant rage, and before the bearer even had time to regain his footing, the passenger launched himself from the chair and set about him with an umbrella, whacking the Chinese man repeatedly around the head with the handle end and finishing his performance with several kicks to the man's torso. Then he snatched up his valise and marched off, broken umbrella dangling from his hand, and hailed another sedan chair.

Israel wondered whether he should offer to help the wounded bearer, who was now sitting up and spitting out what might be bits of broken teeth, but decided not to: he had his mate there and anyway it wasn't any of his business. He crossed the road and went into the market.

He still had such a lot to purchase. Within half an hour he'd bought toilet items for himself, plus a hairbrush with an ivory handle, soap, a facecloth (towels were supplied at the lodging house), a toothbrush and tooth powder, hair ribbons, and a very beautiful ivory and painted paper fan for Amber. He couldn't really afford fripperies, but he knew she'd like it. He also purchased, much against his better judgment, a suit of basic Chinese women's clothing for her, and a pair of flat shoes. The suit consisted of a short robe that closed under the arm and down the side, and a pair of baggy trousers, both of which he thought were bloody ugly but the material, cotton he presumed, was a nice dark rose colour. To his ongoing disappointment he had no idea what sort of underthings she favoured but thought he might allow her some money so that, when she'd settled down after he'd given her the bad news, she could buy her own.

It was then that he had a horrible thought. What if she was close to her time of the month? If she was she'd need rags, which he knew all about because a row of them always flapped from the *Katipo*'s rigging once a month and they all knew what they were but no one ever commented, and he couldn't let her out while she was weeping and wailing so he'd have to buy them for her. Did you buy or make them? he wondered. Surely you could make them. But from what? God. Who could he ask? Not Amber: he'd die of embarrassment.

He left the market and followed Queen's Road back towards the lodging house, laden with parcels. The feeling of dread he'd had when they'd arrived back from Lamma Island was creeping up on him again like a fox stalking a rabbit, and this time he knew he couldn't postpone the inevitable with a lie. And then it struck him. No, he couldn't put if off forever, but he could for at least a few more days.

Enormously relieved to have come to this conclusion he strode happily on, then stopped in his tracks as a flaw in his new plan revealed itself. If Amber wasn't going to be prostrate from grief, how was he going to stop her from running around the city? She was bound to bump into someone from the *Katipo* or see the ship tied up at the wharf. Bugger.

He walked on, thinking hard, and when he came to a Chinese apothecary he stopped again and went in. The stink was unbelievable. He left his shopping in a pile on the floor and prowled around, his handkerchief over his mouth and nose, looking for what he wanted.

Most of the smell was coming from fly-covered animal parts displayed on a table near the rear of the shop. Bear paws, dead snakes, bones, organs in congealed blood, dried seahorses, horns, the hides of some scaly animal, and various other articles he couldn't recognise. Having spotted them he gave the table a wide berth.

One wall of the little shop was covered from floor to ceiling with cabinets piled on each other containing tiny drawers, all labelled, naturally, in Chinese. On another table was arranged a display of plasters and pellets, pills and powders, teas, wines and oils, behind them a pyramid of packets and tins presented in the most beautiful and eye-catching packaging. Together with a set of brass scales and a mortar and pestle, on the counter sat bowls containing dried plant materials, and a row of jars in which floated more innards (presumably animal).

There was, however, also quite a range of European preparations for sale, obviously intended for the British population, though Israel couldn't see many English ladies choosing to shop here. There were medicines even he recognised, such as Freeman's Chlorodyne, Beecham's Pills, Congreve's Elixir and what have you. He thought about the Freeman's Chlorodyne, which he'd used himself, not that he'd had cholera but it was good for stopping the shits, but suspected he might need something that worked to its full effect more quickly.

'Do you have tincture of opium?' he asked the man behind the counter, hoping he could speak English.

A stupid question really, in China.

A nod.

'Give me about eight ounces. No, better make it ten. Er, what strength is it normally?'

''Bout three and one half ounces opium to one and a half pint alcohol. You want stronger?'

Israel hesitated. 'Just a little bit.'

'What for?'

'My wife. Very bad stomach.' Israel rubbed his belly.

'I do little stronger.'

The man turned away and busied himself preparing the tincture. On finishing he wedged a cork in the bottle, wiped it down, applied a written label and named his price. Very reasonable, Israel thought as he paid.

'Thank you.'

'Two teaspoon only,' the apothecary said. 'Is strong. If no good, bad luck. No more 'til four more hour.'

Israel took the bottle. He'd be the judge of whether it was too strong or not.

Amber wondered where Israel was; he'd been
gone ages.

She felt awful — despondent, frustrated,
perplexed and bloody well annoyed. How could
Tahi have just sailed off and left her like that?
Why hadn't he collected her from Longwei's
ship? And if not him, why not her father? It all
seemed very strange. And her mother could
easily have stayed here in Hong Kong: they
didn't need her to sail to Shanghai.

She pulled her legs up and looked idly at the
skin on her knees, surprised she hadn't turned
into a prune, she'd been in the bath that long.
Some man had knocked on the door half an
hour back and when she hadn't responded had
hammered like hell until she'd shouted at him to
go away. Then Mrs Whittle, the woman from
behind the counter, the owner, had come along
and told her through the door her time was up,
and she'd had to promise to get out.

She supposed she'd better. The water was cold
now, anyway. She set her hands on the edges of
the bath and pushed herself up, surprised as
always by the way she felt so much heavier after
a long soak. It was as if she got in weighing eight
stone and got out weighing ten. Perhaps, if you
were in water long enough, you absorbed some
of it.

Suddenly feeling dizzy she bent over and
gripped the enamel until the feeling passed.
When had she last eaten? This morning?
Cautiously she stepped out and reached for her

towel, which was threadbare but clean.

Another knock came at the door.

'Yes, all *right*! I'm getting out now, if you don't mind!'

'It's me, Israel.'

'Oh.' At last. 'Just give me a few minutes and I'll come to your room.'

'Don't be long. I've got food. It'll get cold.'

Amber dried herself, swept her damp hair back off her face, then dressed in the stiff, saltwater-stained clothes she'd been wearing all day. In her hurry to leave the *Kaili* she'd left behind her few possessions, including the dress she'd had on the night Lo Fang's men had abducted her from Cebu, which was no great loss as it was quite the worse for wear now, but it did mean she had barely a stitch to her name until the *Katipo* returned. Her chemise top and drawers were still serviceable but, frankly, they needed a good wash.

Israel let her into his room, which smelled divine. 'Mmm, I'm starving. What did you get us?'

He nodded towards two covered ceramic bowls sitting on a chest of drawers. 'I could only find Chinese food.'

'Which you don't like.'

Israel shrugged. 'Noodles with chicken and beef, and some sort of sauce. I had to buy the bowls.'

'Did you get cutlery?'

'No, but there're chopsticks.'

Amber made a face. She wasn't the most adept with chopsticks, especially when it came to rice and noodles. They ate in messy silence.

'What are you thinking about?' she asked.

Israel was staring into his bowl, scowling. 'What? Nothing.'

'Didn't look like nothing.'

'Well, it was. Have you finished?'

Amber showed him her empty bowl.

'I bought some things for you,' he said, going red.

'A toothbrush, I hope.'

'Yes, and a few other bits and pieces.' He handed her the parcel containing the toiletries he'd chosen for her.

She opened it. 'This is really thoughtful of you, Israel, thank you. Oh, and look at this. How lovely.' She flicked open the fan and fluttered it.

'And this,' he said, giving her another package.

Feeling a little embarrassed Amber opened that too, revealing a tunic and trousers, and a pair of shoes.

'I thought you didn't approve of me wearing Chinese clothes?'

Israel shrugged yet again. 'I hope the shoes fit. I had to guess the size.'

'Well, they're very nice. Pretty colour. Thank you.'

Israel reached behind him. 'And one more.'

Oh, for God's sake, Amber thought, really embarrassed now. She left the parcel sitting on the bed between them.

'Go on,' he said. 'Open it.'

Stifling a sigh, she did. It was a dress, a really pretty one. 'God, Israel, where did you find this?'

'Don't you like it?'

He looked so crestfallen.

'It's lovely. It really is. But I can't accept something like this from you. It isn't . . . Well, what will Tahi think?'

For a second Israel looked quite . . . wild. Startled, Amber stared at him. He stared back.

A sensation of uneasiness crept slowly but very surely across her. She and Israel were friends, and crewmates, and nothing more. They never would be. He knew that. He was Tahi's best mate. She did need clothes but why would he buy her such a fancy gown? Surely any old thing would do? And the Chinese outfit was perfect.

Finally he said, 'You needed clothes and now you've got some.' He poked at a parcel on the floor with his foot. 'I got clothes too, see? Shirts.'

For some reason the fact that he'd also shopped for himself made her feel better. 'Didn't you pack a bag?'

He wouldn't meet her gaze. 'I did but the bloody thing fell overboard off the sampan.'

Amber knew she'd hurt his feelings. He was trying to cheer her up, and she'd bitten his head off. 'I really do like the dress. It's beautiful. Thank you.'

'You're welcome.'

He smiled and she felt even better still. Well, relieved, at least.

She said, 'I'll wear it tomorrow when we go out.'

'Out? Why do you want to go out?'

His smile had slipped and again he looked like the weight of the entire world had settled on his shoulders. What was wrong with him?

'Well, we can't sit around here all day, can we? We'll be bored out of our brains doing nothing.'

'I thought we could, I don't know, play cards or something. Anyway it looks like it's going to rain.'

'So? We'll buy ourselves umbrellas. I don't *want* to sit inside all day, Israel. I've been locked inside for weeks. I've been a *prisoner*, remember?'

Israel nodded. 'I know. You have. Let's talk about it in the morning.' He brightened. 'I did buy one more thing.'

Christ almighty. What now?

He felt about under the bed then produced a bottle with a flourish. 'Brandy, for a nightcap. Fancy one?'

'I'm not going to bed yet!' Amber declared, though she easily could. She was exhausted.

'I am, I'm knackered. Fancy a drop anyway?'

Why not? she thought. Every muscle in her body was complaining after being hurled about in that stupid little sampan. What the hell possessed him to hire such a tiny boat when he could have chosen any number of bigger vessels? Brandy might be just the thing to ease her aches and pains. 'Might as well.'

Israel took a tumbler from the bedside table and poured in several fingers of brandy. Then he had a good look around the room. 'Can you see another tumbler?'

'No, but there's one in my room. I'll get it.'

'Go straight there and do *not* speak to anyone in the hallway.'

'Yes, Pa.' Amber picked up the cotton robe and trousers Israel had given her. 'I'll get changed into these while I'm at it and sleep in them. They look so comfortable.'

'Damn. I forgot to get you a nightgown.'

Flapping a hand, she said, 'Never mind. We'll get one tomorrow.'

She sauntered from Israel's room into hers, tempted to linger and chat loudly with anyone who came past but no one did, and got changed, leaving her dirty clothes in a heap on the floor. Then she collected the tumbler from her bedside table, and took her time wandering back. That'd teach him for ordering her around. When she sat down in his room he gave her the full tumbler, took the empty one and poured himself a few nips.

She took a sip, then another, then frowned. 'What sort of brandy is it?'

He looked at the label. 'It's cognac, actually. Martell. Why?'

'Tastes . . . really funny.'

'Off?' Israel tasted his. 'Seems all right to me.'

Amber took another sip, then shrugged. 'Who else does Pa have to talk to, apart from the people in Shanghai?'

Israel looked at her blankly. 'What do you mean?'

'You said it was a condition of my release. He has to talk to some people.'

'Oh! Right. Well, he's already been to see that empress dowager woman.'

'The Empress Dowager Cixi? Really? How did that go?' Amber took another drink.

'Not very well. Apparently she more or less ignored him and he annoyed the governor while he was at it.'

'Good old Pa. Who else?'

'Ah, the country traders?'

Amber raised her glass again. 'Christ, all of them? That'd take months, if not years. They're all over the place. What's he supposed to be talking to them about?'

'Stopping the opium trade.'

'Tall order. Not a surprise, though. Longwei hates it. There was a crewman caught with opium on one of the junks when I was there and Longwei had him flogged then hanged as an example to the others.'

'Hanged! Bloody hell, did you see it?'

'No, but I heard about it.' Amber swayed. 'What's happened to the lamp? It's gone all flickery.'

'More brandy?'

'Just a little.'

'Pass your tumbler.'

Amber did.

'Why don't you try on your new shoes?' Israel suggested.

Amber moved to the edge of the bed, leant forwards to pick up the shoes, and found herself sliding to the floor. She sat there for a moment, wondering what had happened. The shoes lay near her bare feet but, honestly, they seemed miles away. Israel's hand, huge like a giant's, appeared in her peripheral vision, bearing her drink. She leant to the side so she could see it properly then reached for it, marvelling at how long her hand took to move from her lap to the tumbler.

'Careful,' she heard Israel say. 'Don't drop it.'

The tumbler was the most beautiful thing, the patterns cut into the glass at its base catching and reflecting the lamplight and turning it into an enormous diamond. 'Pretty,' she said, then wondered if she'd spoken aloud or only thought the word. She must be so tired.

She drank, feeling the brandy burn its way smoothly over her tongue and down her gullet, seeping into all the nooks and crannies of her chest, heating her heart and lungs and stomach, and wrapping her tubes and bones in comfortable, soothing warmth. She felt like she could sit here forever.

'Amber?'

'Mmm?'

'Don't fall asleep there.'

Israel's voice seemed so far away.

'I won't.'

*　*　*

When she awoke in the night, her mouth was dry, her head pounded and she didn't know where she was.

'Tahi?' she croaked.

'It's me, Amber, Israel. You're not well.'

'Not . . . ?'

'Here, take this. It's medicine. It'll make you feel better.'

A strong arm helped her to raise her head and the cold edge of a spoon pressed against her lips. She opened her mouth, and swallowed.

'Good girl.'

Soon she was asleep again.

317

Rian was in one of his testier moods.

'Why can't they find their own bloody passage to Australia? I'm sure she's got plenty of money stashed in all that stuff she brought aboard.'

Kitty winced. 'Please, Rian, keep your voice down. They'll hear you.'

Though, to be honest, she wasn't sure she cared. Ka was a charming girl, and at eighteen she *was* only a girl, but a little bit of Wing, who was perhaps ten years older, went a *very* long way. However, they'd been a great help to Bao, and were now in trouble themselves. She and Rian, as Bao's friends and surrogate family, were also obliged to assist. Unfortunately, Rian didn't quite see it that way.

'No they won't.'

'They will,' Kitty insisted.

They would, too, their cabin being directly off the mess room, which, Kitty knew, was where Wing and Ka currently were. Wing was fiddling about organising her cosmetics, while Ka was making repairs to a gown that had been damaged during the dash from Yip Chun Kit's compound. Simon had very kindly offered his small cabin to the two women, and was bunking in with Pierre. Wing had initially requested Amber and Tahi's cabin, which had caused a small ruckus.

Kitty had said no, she couldn't have it.

And Wing had asked, 'Why not?'

'Wing,' Bao had said warningly.

'Because that's my daughter and son-in-law's cabin.'

'But your daughter is not using it,' Wing had said bluntly.

Outraged by the cheek of the woman, Kitty had replied, 'No, you're right, she isn't, and that's because she's currently a prisoner of Lee Longwei, China's most infamous pirate. Did no one tell you?'

'Yes, I have been told. But it is a big cabin and I am accustomed to having commodious quarters. Surely the husband can share with someone else?'

'No, he can't, and you're out of luck,' Kitty had said. 'That's Amber's cabin. No one uses it except her and Tahi.'

'But — '

'I said no!'

Wing had burst into rapid Cantonese aimed at Bao, who had fired a long volley back. Wing launched into a further tirade, but Bao had cut her off. This had been followed by an extended sulk from Wing, but no further mention of Amber's cabin.

Now, Kitty said, 'It wouldn't be safe for them to travel to Australia by themselves. Bad enough two European women on a ship without a male escort, never mind two Chinese women. They'd be treated appallingly. The crew, the other passengers, everyone. And I don't think they do have any money. Well, Wing says she doesn't.'

Rian took his feet down off his writing desk, removed a sock and inspected an itchy patch on one foot. 'That woman is a liar by trade. And speaking of trade, she could earn plenty of money on her back.'

319

'Rian! That's not very nice.'

'True though. It's what she did in Chun's house, if you recall.'

Kitty supposed that was true. 'But only with him, though.'

'What's the difference?'

'If it were me, I'd be thinking, quite a lot, actually. I'd much rather just have one customer I shared with other concubines than, say, five a day, six days a week. Not to mention he's rich.'

'It would save remembering names, I suppose.'

'Do you think they do? Remember the names?'

'How would I know?'

To be honest, Kitty didn't particularly care to know whether Rian knew the answer to that question or not.

'Anyway, I bet she does have a bit of money stashed away,' Rian said, pulling his sock back on. 'You wouldn't jump out the window with your best clothes, your jewellery and all that face paint, and not stop long enough to grab your purse, would you?'

'Shall I get Bao to ask her?'

'She probably already has and been fed a pack of lies. Bao has standards. She'd expect them to look after themselves if they could.'

'Well, you go through their belongings, then.'

'I'm not ferreting through a load of women's things! You do it. And I'm not sure that Ka girl has anything. Probably too busy packing the other one's wardrobe to grab anything for herself.'

'I'm not going through their things, either. If she says she hasn't got any money, we have to believe her. So we have to take them to Australia.'

Rian moved from the desk to the bed and took Kitty's hand. 'We can't. What if we stopped off at Sydney or Melbourne, then arrived in Dunedin to find we were a day or two too late and Fu had died? How would we feel then? How would Bao feel?'

'Well, terrible, of course. But, Rian, he could have died already. And we don't even know when we'll be leaving Hong Kong because we don't know when we'll get Amber back.'

Rian nodded, closed his eyes for several seconds, then opened them again. 'I'm going out to see Lee Longwei again, see if I can do a deal. I'll offer him money first and if that doesn't work I'll ask him what he needs. Weapons, maybe? A man like him's always on the lookout for the latest armaments.'

Kitty nodded, though her heart thumped just at the thought of it. Smuggling spirits and tobacco was one thing but running guns always made her nervous.

'We won't have to bring them in through Hong Kong customs and excise,' Rian reminded her. 'We can meet him offshore.'

'But we'll have to collect them from somewhere, won't we?'

'There are plenty of shiny new Colts and Remingtons lying around in North America at the moment, because of the war. They won't miss a few dozen, and they won't notice them going missing. Don't worry, mo ghrá, we haven't been caught so far.'

'No, we haven't.' Kitty swallowed. 'Not yet.'

'And, look, if it's going to take a while, we can send Bao back to New Zealand on another ship. The other two can go with her.'

'But I don't *want* it to take a while. I want her back now.'

'I do, too, love. But it might. And when we come back from talking to Lee Longwei, we're not mooring back here. We'll find a spot farther along the coast or out in the harbour. While we only had Bao aboard we had the protection of the Crown, technically anyway, but we're not Wing and Ka's guardians. They're Chinese nationals and they're absconding from what to all intents and purposes is their employee. Or quite possibly even owner.'

'Yip Chun Kit?'

Rian nodded. 'And that's Chinese business, not British, in which case Yip is perfectly at liberty to come aboard armed to the teeth and take them back. But he can't if he can't find us.'

'No,' Kitty said.

But, oh dear, Hong Kong was such a very small place.

★ ★ ★

It was raining quite heavily, dripping off the rim of Israel's hat and running down his neck inside his new shirt; he grimaced and turned up the collar of his jacket. In Australia or England — England especially — the weather would be considered miserable, but here it was actually quite nice. The rain had washed the buildings and the leaves of all the lush plants clean, and misty cloud had settled on Mount Victoria like the meringue on one of Pierre's fancier puddings. He couldn't smell any of the nice perfumed flowers, but imagined they were probably getting the crap battered out of them by the rain.

He hoped Amber was all right. He'd dosed her again before he'd come out and she'd gone straight back to sleep. It certainly worked well, that opium. When she'd woken earlier this morning she'd had no idea where she was, or who he was, and had even squatted over the po for a wee, which had been incredibly embarrassing because he'd had to hold her on it so she wouldn't tip over. He'd not thought about all that when he'd given her the opium. He hadn't looked, though, and had tried to ignore the sound of the wee as it had gone into the po, and he'd prayed — *prayed* — she didn't need to shit as well. And she hadn't. And then he'd wondered, should he clean her off? He knew she and Kitty left bits of old cloth in the head on the *Katipo* for that, but was that just for when they had a crap? Anyway, he wasn't about to do something that intimate to her, especially when she wasn't even aware of it. He was saving that sort of thing for when they were in England and they could be together properly. He wanted it to be right.

He was heading for the shipping office to buy two berths to England. He didn't care which ship they went on as long as it had a couple of decent cabins and was leaving soon. The shipping office was quite close to the wharf where the *Katipo* was tied up, which was all right as he wanted to make sure she was still there. They wouldn't leave Hong Kong without Amber, he knew that, but they might return to Hung Shing Yeh Bay and have another go at freeing her themselves. And then there'd be a problem.

He walked on through the rain, dodging sedan chairs, carts, people and puddles until he came to the long and busy expanse of waterfront. Work never stopped there for inclement weather, save for the most violent of storms. He saw with some relief the *Katipo* was still in her berth, so made his way to the shipping office.

He had to wait in a queue, which was annoying, but finally found himself at the front of it.

'What ships are sailing for England in the next few days?' he asked the British clerk. 'I'm looking for two cabins.'

'What port are you bound for?'

'Any. I don't care.'

Putting on a pair of spectacles, the clerk consulted a large black ledger. 'On Tuesday the *Ann Marie* sails for Liverpool, Wednesday the *Hannibal* to London and the *Aurora* to Portsmouth. Thursday the *Grenadier* to Bristol. Any of those suit you?'

'Nothing sooner? Nothing on Monday?'

'The clerk looked again. 'Only two ships departing for San Francisco and New York. You possibly don't want to go there at the moment.'

Israel took off his hat and scratched his head,

324

then quickly jammed the hat back on in case someone he knew saw him. 'One on Tuesday then.'

'The *Ann Marie* to Liverpool?'

'Does it have proper accommodations?'

The clerk reached behind him to a pigeonhole containing hundreds of slim folders. Opening one he perused its contents. '*Ann Marie*, three-masted barque, general cargo, crew of eleven, four cabins suitable for use by passengers.'

'That'll do.'

'Two cabins, wasn't it?'

'Yes.'

'Names?'

Israel hesitated. Should he give their real names or false ones? Put on the spot, he couldn't think of anything made up. Sweat broke out on his brow.

'There's a queue behind you,' the clerk pointed out, unhelpfully, Israel thought.

Suddenly recalling the name he'd given at the lodging house, he blurted, 'Mr and Mrs Irwin Marshall.'

'I'll need a Christian name for Mrs Marshall. In case something untoward happens. For the record.'

'Er, Abigail.'

The clerk wrote the names down in the black book next to *Ann Marie*, then told Israel how much the fare would be. He nearly fainted. To hide his embarrassment he lowered his shocked, red face and dug around in his jacket for his purse, then handed over the money. He now had only about twenty-five pounds left — hardly enough to outfit himself and Amber for the trip to England then start a new life once they arrived there.

In return the clerk gave him a receipt, said good day, then peered around him at the next person in line.

Israel felt . . . pillaged. But then he'd never had to pay to travel by sea before. How did ordinary people manage it? Of course, ordinary people didn't book themselves cabins, he supposed. They went steerage.

He felt he needed a stiff drink after such a shock, and thought longingly of the brandy in his room at the lodging house. Or perhaps he'd stop in at a hotel and get himself a decent glass of rum. There were plenty of hotels in Hong Kong that served proper English spirits and he'd probably been to most of them. How long would that last lot of opium he'd given Amber take to wear off? He'd fed her quite a hefty dose. And speaking of feeding she'd need to eat. What could he give her that she could swallow easily without choking? She didn't seem to be in charge of her facial muscles. Or many other muscles, now that he thought about it.

He left the waterfront and walked along Queen's Road until he came to a little pub he knew quite well, the Red Lantern, and went in, pleased by then to be out of the rain. It wasn't until he'd bought himself a rum and a plate of fried shrimps and found a seat that he realised, with a shock that almost stopped his heart, that if he wanted to avoid the *Katipo*'s crew, the last place he should be lounging about was in a seamen's public house. What was he thinking? He scanned the room, which was half full, but to his immense relief, didn't see anyone he knew. No one from the *Katipo*, anyway. He knew the barman, and he definitely knew a couple of the Chinese girls who worked out of the pub, Lily and Iris.

He'd been with Lily several times when they'd been in port in the past and Iris once. Iris he hadn't thought much of. She'd been a bit disinterested, lying there staring at the ceiling, and he'd had the horrible feeling she was mentally writing her shopping list. And she'd called him an orang-utan, because of the colour of his body hair and how much he had. It wasn't orange, it was bronze. And how would she know what an orang-utan looked like? There weren't any in China, were there?

Lily was much nicer. She could speak a bit of English and was respectful and had good manners, and even smelt nice. Not like Iris, who reeked like the Central Marketplace. He'd decided Lily must wash a lot and not eat that Chinese food all the time, which is what any smart prostitute should do if she expected a white man to pay good money for her.

He took a decent-sized swallow of his rum and looked across at the girls again. Lily waved, then got down off her stool and made her way over.

'Morning, Mr Mitchell. You want Lily today?'

'Not today.'

She sat down anyway. 'You been good? I been good.'

'I've been busy.'

'Busy like bee.' Lily giggled.

Israel had a thought. 'Lily, what do you know about opium?'

Lily shook her head so violently her earrings nearly fell out. 'Opium very bad! Lily never touch. Is bad!'

'But what do you know about it?'

'Nothing. What you mean?'

'What happens if a person has too much of it?'

'In one time?

'Mmm.'

'They die.'

Israel felt quite uneasy. 'Well, how much is too much?'

'Depend on person. Depend on opium.'

'Well, what if they were taking it as medicine, say for a headache?'

'What?'

Putting his hands to his head, Israel made a pained face. 'A headache.'

'Ah.' Lily shrugged. 'Same opium. Person still die.'

Israel drank and thought for a while. 'Would you like some shrimp? They're only going cold.'

'Not like shrimp.'

'So how would you tell if you . . . ? How is it possible to tell if a person's had too much? What are the signs?'

'Like big doll, all floppy. And breathing wrong, too slow, not deep enough, like this.' Lily demonstrated someone barely inhaling. 'Then no breathing at all, and die.'

For someone who knew nothing about opium,

Israel thought, she knew quite a lot. But Amber wasn't the way Lily had described. She'd managed to squat on the pot. He must be getting the dose right.

He finished his rum and shovelled in a couple of handfuls of shrimp. 'Right, Lily. I've got to go now.'

'Where you going?'

'Along the west end. Don't be so nosy.'

She stood. He smiled up at her but she didn't smile back.

'You try be careful, Mr Mitchell. Is not nice, killing people.'

11

Israel turned off Queen's Road to take a shortcut through the narrower streets that would get him to Wellington Street a little bit faster. He wanted to buy Amber a nightgown: she couldn't spend the next few days wearing nothing but that robe and trousers, even if she was only asleep in bed. He'd send them out to be washed and pressed, along with the clothes she'd had on before.

That Lily had turned out to be a cheeky bloody little whore after all. What did she mean *he* should be careful? He wasn't going to kill anyone, least of all Amber. Obviously she was perfectly fine.

He stopped, listening carefully. For a second he'd thought someone was following him: but no, the footsteps had gone. He set off again, making his way past the tiny, closed-in back yards of Chinese houses. There was laundry hanging everywhere, dripping wet, rabid-looking dogs slinking about and skinny cats perched on walls giving him the evil eye, and the stink from open drains and middens was horrific, even straight after such a downpour. In a way he felt sorry for the Chinese, banned by the British from living anywhere on Mount Victoria and doomed, therefore, to live down here in the squalor, but it was squalor of their own making.

He stopped again, sure this time that someone

was behind him. He turned and had a good look. An old woman was feeding chickens in a yard nearby but it couldn't have been her — her feet were bare. And there were two little kids, one without britches and the other wearing the strangest little hat with ears on it, sitting on a gate staring at him, but he didn't think it had been them, either. As he stared back at them they began to rock backwards and forwards, making the gate squeak.

Now he was just scaring himself. He turned again and stepped straight into the solid figure of Ip To. Stifling a shout he leapt back, his fists up.

Ip To batted away his hands, grabbed him by the collar and hauled him along the lane to the junction where it joined with a wider street.

'Help,' Israel shouted as he swung wildly. 'Help!'

A few curious Chinese faces appeared in back yards but no one came to his aid. The two small children followed, cheering.

Lee Longwei stood at the junction, his arms crossed, his face calm. Israel felt the pressure on his neck relax as Ip To let go of his jacket.

'We meet again,' Longwei said.

The children came close. Longwei dug in his pocket, handed them some money and said something in Cantonese. Or was it another dialect he spoke to them? Israel could never tell the difference. They ran off, delighted.

Tugging his shirt and jacket back into shape, Israel said, 'What do you want? I thought we had a deal?'

'We do. I am here to make sure you are

fulfilling your side of it. Because, as we agreed, if you don't I will be compelled to take the girl back.'

'I am fulfilling it.'

'Has she been introduced to Mr Eastwood yet?'

'Last night, as a matter of fact.' Israel flinched inwardly. God, why had he said that? He should be playing for time.

'And did he like what he saw?'

'Very much.'

'A tired and hungry girl wearing a man's trousers and a tunic stiff with dried seawater? That does not sound very alluring to me.'

Israel was getting a bit sick of Lee bloody smartarse Longwei. He wasn't the only one who could think on his feet. 'It wouldn't be, but that isn't what he saw. As soon as we arrived back we took a room at a lodging house. Amber tidied herself up and I went to town and bought a decent suit for me and a very nice gown for her. She wore that. She looked beautiful.'

Longwei's eyebrows went up. 'Well, well. And have you arranged a rendezvous for Mr Eastwood?'

'I have. He'll be meeting Amber at the Lotus Pond Gardens.'

'When?'

'Tuesday night.' They'd be on the *Ann Marie* and heading for England by then and Longwei wouldn't matter a bugger.

'Mmm.' Longwei looked thoughtful. 'Why meet at a public garden, I wonder, when Mr Eastwood has a perfectly comfortable and no doubt well-appointed home?'

Shit. 'How should I know? I asked him and that's what he wants. Maybe he fancies having her outdoors. There's no telling when it comes to some men's tastes, is there?'

A slow nod from Longwei. 'As you say. And the exact time?'

'The time?' For God's sake! 'Eight o'clock.'

'So, eight o'clock this coming Tuesday at the Lotus Pond Gardens.'

'Yes.'

'Well done, Mr Mitchell. And how do you plan to kill Mr Eastwood?'

'That's my business, isn't it?'

'I suppose it is, yes.' Longwei smiled. 'Then I will leave you to it.'

Oh, thank Christ for that, Israel thought.

★   ★   ★

Haunui was out for a walk. He didn't like being cooped up on the *Katipo* for too long. Sailing was good, but he liked to feel solid ground beneath his feet when he could. He was terribly sad, too, about Amber, and for Tahi, who was suffering badly, and he wanted time to himself to get his thoughts in order. He was also worried about Israel; not for his safety but because he thought his disappearance was ominous. Where had the little swine gone? He couldn't shake the feeling that the boy was floating around somewhere, very much up to no good.

He hadn't shared his worst fears with Rian, as Rian and Kitty were also suffering, missing their beautiful daughter, shuffling round like old people. He wished he could help them but he was as impotent as they were. Lee Longwei was a powerful man, with far more warriors at his disposal than Rian had. They couldn't attack him, and Rian's attempts at reasoning with him, and doing his bidding, had also failed. He, Haunui, didn't know much about the matter concerning the opium coming into China, but he did know one man couldn't do much to stop it by himself. The British were formidable opponents, as he'd seen with his own eyes over the last few years at home in New Zealand. If they couldn't take what they wanted by tricking people into signing devious and deceptive treaties they declared war, which they won because the Queen had all the warriors and guns she could possibly need, and then they took everyone's land off them, which was worse even than having to go to war. Without land or access to the sea or rivers, a hapu or iwi couldn't survive. There was no food and no place to live and raise families. It must be the same, he thought, for the Chinese.

He thought about going to a pub and having a few ales, but decided that wasn't really what he wanted. He felt empty, spiritually as well as physically, and when he felt like that what he needed was food, and the crew all said the best place for food in Hong Kong was the Central Marketplace. It probably wouldn't take him long to walk there, and he would have to walk as he certainly wasn't riding in one of those chair things. He was too heavy and he'd end up with his arse through the seat, dragging on the ground.

He marched along the road, enjoying the clean, rain-washed air and smiling at everyone he passed, which meant a lot of smiles. He liked to be friendly, it made him feel good, and better to be friendly than a grumpy old bugger. He received a few smiles back but not many. Most people (except for other Maori) were frightened of him, but he was used to that. It was probably the moko covering his face, his bushy beard, his general size and the fact that he stood at six feet six inches, and he'd decided long ago not to take it personally.

At the market he wandered around appreciating all the delicious food aromas that filled the air. He liked the way the Chinese prepared their food. He'd never tried it before they'd met Wong Fu at Ballarat, but since then he'd eaten it at every possible opportunity. He decided he'd fashion himself a banquet, so went from stall to stall selecting his favourite dishes and a few he hadn't tried before, then sat down on a patch of ground out of the way, arranged his bowls before him, and tucked in.

The meat, vegetable, rice and noodle dishes were as good as he'd hoped, but the sea cucumber he found a bit bland. So were the chicken legs, and rubbery, too, but the sauce was nice and spicy. The shark fin soup was very good, the duck tongues he probably wouldn't bother with again, and the hundred-year-old eggs, while stinky, were interesting — sharp and piquant, like well-ripened cheese. They'd probably make him fart, though. Leaning back on his hands, surrounded by empty bowls, he decided he felt much better, but now he did need an ale. He returned each bowl to its respective stall, thanked the stall-holder, and went in search of a pub. The Red Lantern, he thought — he'd been there the other night with the crew and quite liked it.

The pub was fairly busy but, standing at the counter, he was served immediately. He usually was — one advantage of being big and ugly, he supposed. He took his ale to a corner and leant against the wall, looking around. A little bar girl trotted up to him.

'You come with *Katipo*?'

'I did,' Haunui said.

The girl reached up and touched his face. 'Lily remember pretty lines. You just miss him.'

'Who?'

'Mr Mitchell.'

Haunui stared at her. '*Israel* Mitchell?'

Lily nodded.

'In here? Today?'

''Bout half hour.'

'Do you know where he went?'

Lily's pretty little face turned sour. 'He say west end. He rude to Lily.'

Haunui emptied his tankard of ale in several huge swallows and handed it to Lily. 'Well, I think you're lovely.'

'You just big bear!' Lily replied, giggling.

Haunui left her there, smiling to herself. At the door he let out a burp so loud, long and reverberatingly resonant that it rendered the pub silent for several seconds. Proud of himself, he stepped out into the sunlight, wondering which path Israel would have taken west. And what the hell was he doing there anyway? Was he holed up or just on his way to do business?

He thought Queen's Road, being the main thoroughfare, probably ran all the way west, though he could be wrong, of course, as he didn't know Hong Kong well at all. Even if it did, the chances of walking along Queen's Road and spotting Israel were fairly small. It was pretty well impossible to find a person when that person was also on the move.

But he would try, because he suspected, as he'd said to Rian, that if he found Israel he'd find Amber as well. He had no evidence at all to support this — she could still be shut in Lee Longwei's cabin on his junk on the other side of Lamma Island — but his gut was telling him he was right. Tomorrow they'd be returning to Hung Shing Yeh Bay so Rian could talk to Longwei again, and they'd find out then where Amber was — or, rather, where she wasn't — and he'd know whether his intuition was accurate. If only Tahi could have his visions at will, then he could order one and they'd know more. But there'd been nothing from him, which was a surprise, because it was usually in times of stress and upset that he had them. And the poor boy was *bloody* upset at the moment.

He'd been walking for about fifteen minutes, and noticing that he was getting a blister on his right heel — bloody boots, his feet weren't built for Pakeha footwear — when some distance ahead he saw a figure exit from a side street onto Queen's Road and stride off in a westerly direction. The figure was tall, a head and shoulders above everyone else so probably a white man, and wearing a hat that looked like Israel's.

Haunui bellowed, '*Israel!*'

Without even turning to look the man erupted into a sprint, tearing down the road, knocking several people over in his hurry and disappearing up the next side street.

Haunui took off after him, darting around the bystanders fussing around the unfortunate pedestrians on the ground, and raced into the side street just in time to see his quarry turn the corner at the end. Haunui followed, starting to puff now and feeling his heel burn as though a hot coal had fallen down his boot. At the corner he saw that whomever he was chasing, and surely it was Israel, had made a mistake as the street ahead was long and unbroken by intersections. The man was pelting down the middle of it, his coattails flapping, a parcel clamped under one arm.

'*Stop!*' Haunui shouted as he put his head down and lumbered after him.

But he was old, he'd just eaten an eleven-course meal, and his boots were hurting him. Slowly the gap between them widened.

Then the man ducked to the right and hopped over a fence. By the time Haunui reached it all he could see of him was his hat bobbing along, some distance ahead, behind a wall in a narrow lane running parallel. Then that, too, disappeared.

Haunui swore and, panting heavily, perched on the top rail of the fence, which creaked ominously. He'd lost him. While he sat there, trying to get his breath back, an old lady came out of a nearby house and hit him with a broom, berating him ear-piercingly in Cantonese. He didn't know what she was saying but he imagined she didn't want her fence broken.

'Sorry, whaea,' he said, getting off it.

He sat down in the middle of the street, fortunately not a busy one, and took off his boots, noting that he'd developed blisters on both heels now. Tying the laces together he slung the boots around his neck then stood again and took careful note of his surroundings. The sea was quite close to the west, and the harbour also nearby, so that probably meant that the man/Israel's bolthole was located in a fairly limited area, providing that was where he was going.

Which was useful to know.

*　*　*

Israel could taste blood in his throat, but he was fairly sure nothing was bleeding in there. It was just that metallic taste you got when you'd been running hard. He'd nearly died when Longwei had yelled out to him. He'd thought the bastard had finished with him and then he bloody well follows him and makes a scene in the middle of the street! He'd dared not stop to talk to him. The first time had been bad enough. He'd told so many lies now he was losing track of what he'd said to whom. And he had to keep changing them because things weren't going to plan. If people would just behave the way he wanted them to it would all be a lot easier.

He let himself into Amber's room and stood above her, looking down. She was so pretty when she was asleep. Her complexion and hair were lovely, though her lips looked a bit pale. He felt her hands. Hmm, they were a bit cold. Her wedding ring had slid around so that the stones were under her finger. He turned it the right way, thought for a moment, then slipped it off and put it in his jacket pocket. She wouldn't be needing that any more.

How was he going to get her into the nightgown without compromising her modesty? It was a nice one, pale blue embroidered silk from neck to ankle with long, loose sleeves. The woman in the shop where he'd bought it had said they were made for the European market and were all the fashion. It had made *another* hole in his purse but it was worth it. Perhaps he could talk to the *Ann Marie*'s captain and see if he had any work available on the voyage to England. He didn't mind being a rigging monkey for a month or so, or even swabbing decks.

He turned down the bedclothes, undid the fastenings on Amber's tunic, then arranged the sheet so he wouldn't see anything when he wriggled the tunic off her shoulders and arms. Then he slid the nightgown on over her head and, with much difficulty, manoeuvred her arms into sleeves. God, she was just like a big doll. He froze, staring at her, watching her breath. It *seemed* normal. In fact she was breathing quite deeply.

Suddenly she moaned and flung out an arm, backhanding him right across the nose, making his eyes water. He sat back, his hands over his face. Christ, that had hurt. He dabbed at a nostril, checking for blood, but there wasn't any. He didn't blame her, though: she didn't know what she was doing.

When he'd recovered he folded the bedclothes all the way down, then recoiled at the smell. She'd wet the bed. For God's sake! He'd put her on the po this morning. How could she produce so much pee when she wasn't even drinking anything? And what was he going to do? He could hardly hand the dirty sheet over to Mrs Whittle and tell her his 'wife' had peed in the bed. He'd have to replace it. More bloody money gone.

He tugged the damp, stained sheet out from beneath Amber and dropped it on the floor, then rolled the nightgown down to her knees. Grabbing the hems of the trousers she was still wearing he pulled them off and left them with the sheet. He checked his watch and noted that she'd had her last dose of opium three hours ago, which gave him an hour to duck out and buy some new bed linen. Then, when she'd come round a little, he'd feed her. Rice, probably. She should be able to manage that. But nothing to drink.

This was turning out to be much trickier than he'd expected but it was only for a few more days. Then he'd have to give her the bad news, on Monday night, probably, and they'd be off to England on Tuesday.

Not long now.

★ ★ ★

The following day the *Katipo* set sail for a second visit to Lamma Island. When Rian and Kitty had discussed how much of their personal capital they were prepared to offer Longwei to get Amber back, they'd both agreed: all of it. They had a business and could start again, but there would never be another Amber. And if Longwei preferred guns, or tobacco or whisky or diamonds, then they'd sail to whatever part of the world was necessary and bring it back. No request of Longwei's would be too excessive, outlandish or dangerous because that was Rian's skill — quietly shipping cargo that other captains wouldn't touch with a barge pole.

'Do you really think Israel disappearing has something to do with Amber?' Kitty asked.

Rian did, unfortunately. He was kicking himself for being so blind. How could he not have seen that the boy had been lusting after her all this time? What an old fool he was. He'd known that Tahi was keen on her, of course, but not Israel. If he'd been aware of that, he'd have put him off the *Katipo* years ago.

But, despite Haunui and his gut feelings, he didn't think Israel had Amber now. Longwei had a fearsome reputation as a pirate and some, well, rather unusual ideas, but Rian had trusted him, even though Kitty had asked if he was mad. He didn't believe Longwei would have given Amber to Israel just because Israel had said he should. Not five minutes after they'd boarded his junk during their first visit Longwei had worked out the hierarchy aboard the *Katipo*, and he knew damn well that Israel was nowhere near the top of it. No, Amber would still be with him today, and this visit would prove it. Haunui was usually pretty wily when it came to determining others' deeds and the reasons for them, but this time he was wrong.

'Yes, I do. I'm just not sure what,' he said.

Battling the wind, Kitty swept her hair back off her face and tied it with a length of ribbon. 'You know, I really am quite shocked, but more at myself than by anything else. How did I not see that Israel is in love with Amber?'

'I suppose we weren't looking for it.' Rian altered the wheel slightly and called to Ropata and Gideon to brace the yards.

'But is he? Really?'

Rian glanced at her. 'What do you mean?'

'I know Haunui's convinced he is, and Ropata, and God knows why he's disappeared, but do we actually know what he feels for her?'

'Well, no one's found his diary confessing everlasting love, if that's what you mean. You've just got a soft spot for him.'

'And you don't like him because you think he's got Amber.'

'I *don't* think he's got her, actually. I think we'll find she's still with Lee Longwei. And I do like him. Well, I did.'

'If he doesn't have her, why did he run off?'

'I don't know and I don't care, but whatever the reason, he's deserted and won't be welcome back aboard this ship.'

Below them Wing and Ka, who was carrying a sizable bundle of wet laundry, appeared on deck. As Rian watched in growing amazement, Wing pointed out to her servant where she wanted her clothes hung on the rigging to dry.

'For God's sake, Kitty,' Rian exploded, 'get them below. And their bloody washing. We're not on a bloody day trip up the Thames!'

The *Katipo* was fast approaching the headland that concealed Hung Shing Yeh Bay. They'd be a laughing stock if they arrived with women's clothing flapping all over the place.

He watched sourly as Kitty shooed the women below again, Wing as usual going with bad grace. Although the servant girl was a pleasant young thing, Wing was a pain in the arse and he couldn't wait to be rid of her. Possibly the only person aboard the *Katipo* who might be sorry to see her go would be Mick, who'd taken quite a shine to her. But then Mick took a shine to every woman who wasn't outright ugly, and Lai Wing Yan definitely wasn't that.

Hawk appeared at his side, his watch in his hand. 'We have made good time with the wind behind us.'

'Means a slower trip back, though,' Rian said.

He shouted instructions as the *Katipo* rounded the headland and sailed in a graceful arc into the wide mouth of Hung Shing Yeh Bay.

Which was empty.

Lee Longwei and his squadron had gone.

⋆   ⋆   ⋆

The *Katipo* returned to Hong Kong, the entire crew bitterly disappointed and angry, Kitty in tears. At Lamma Island, on discovering that Longwei had weighed anchor, Bao had told Wing and Ka to go to their cabin and stay there until she informed them they could come out. For once Wing, unnerved by the crew's mood, obeyed without an argument.

Having moored this time in the harbour to avoid Yip Chun Kit discovering that they were hiding Bao, his runaway primary concubine and her servant, they gathered around the mess table to talk about what to do. Wing had condescended to hang out her own laundry while Ka worked in the galley washing the supper dishes so Pierre could sit in on the meeting.

At first he'd insisted she wasn't allowed. 'The lovely shiny pots, she will scratch them.' He mimed vigorously scrubbing a pot then staring at it in abject horror. 'See? *Ruined!*'

'Oh, for God's sake, Pierre, she's a servant,' Rian said. 'She knows how to clean a bloody pot.'

'Non, she is the *lady* servant, not the scullery servant.'

Ka put her small hand on Pierre's arm, looked into his eyes — which she could do quite comfortably as he wasn't much taller than her — and said something in her own language.

'She be saying?' Pierre demanded of Bao.

'She says she will wash your pots with the same love and attention that you would employ bathing your first-born grandchild.'

Pierre's hand flew to. his mouth. 'Oh! Beautiful!' He took Ka gently by the elbow, led her to the washing-up bowl, pointed to the kettle on the galley stove and showed her where the soap was kept. 'My apologies, ma chérie.'

Rian rolled his eyes. 'Can we get started now?'

Finally everyone was seated.

'As you all know, I think Longwei still has Amber,' Rian said.

'And I don't,' Haunui interrupted.

'And we can't find out who actually does have her because Longwei and Israel have both disappeared,' Rian went on. 'Now, I'm not prepared to sit here on my backside and do nothing, so which one of them are we most likely to track down?'

'Israel,' Hawk said. 'Haunui has seen him here in Hong Kong, or he thinks he has seen him, and Longwei could be anywhere at sea by now.'

'Don't say that,' Kitty said.

'I am sorry, Kitty, but it is true.'

Haunui said, 'We should go back to where I saw Israel, and I'm sure it was him . . . ' His finger shot up. 'And don't forget Lily, the little bar girl at the Red Lantern. She definitely saw him, eh? We should go back to where I last saw him, spread ourselves out and start knocking on doors. Or knocking them down. I reckon he's got lodgings round there somewhere.'

Rian gave him a look. 'Do you know how

many doors there are in that area? Only about a third of Hong Kong's Chinese live there.'

'Rian!' Kitty snapped. 'Do you want to find Amber or not?'

'Of course I do.'

'Well, stop being such a damned doom-monger and do as Haunui says. At least *listen* to him. You *have* been sitting on your backside. All you've done to get Amber back is talk to that bloody Cixi woman, and what a waste of time that was.'

'That's not true. I — '

Kitty slammed her hand on the table so hard it hurt. 'It *is* true. You've been dithering around for days. I don't know what's wrong with you.'

Rian stared at her. Everyone else stared at anything but Kitty and Rian.

'Well?' Kitty prompted. She was shaming Rian, her precious, beloved husband, in front of his crew and friends, but she didn't care. In her opinion he'd been prevaricating, refusing to listen and generally wasting precious time, and it was worrying and scaring her.

Sighing hugely, Rian rubbed his face with his hands. 'I was worried that if I pushed Longwei too hard, or defied him, he'd hurt Amber. Or kill her. He was civil to us when we met him but he's a ruthless bastard. I've asked around. That reputation of his is deserved. So I've been trying to tread gently and humour him. And as for Israel, I really can't believe he'd have the brains to convince Longwei to let Amber go. I really can't.'

'Tahi,' Kitty said. 'Would Amber go with Israel?'

He nodded. 'They're friends, as far as Amber's concerned. She'd want to get away from Longwei, too, of course.'

'Does she have any idea about how he feels about her?'

'If she does she's never said anything to me about it.'

Wing appeared then, her elegant little shoes silent on the companionway steps. Mick leapt to his feet to help her down the last few.

'Where is Ka?' Wing asked.

'In the galley washing pots,' Bao replied. 'She might need some help.'

Pierre cringed but Wing ignored Bao and disappeared towards her cabin.

'Anyway,' Haunui boomed, making everyone jump. 'About trying to find Israel. We could start with lodging houses.'

'There are dozens down that end of the city,' Simon said. 'It's where a lot of the sailors stay, and some of the less well paid British civil servants.'

'But dozens isn't hundreds,' Haunui said. 'So that's all right.'

'You're all forgetting something rather obvious,' Kitty said. 'If Amber's staying at a lodging house with Israel — '

'She won't be *with* him,' Tahi said fiercely. 'She'd never do that.'

'Oh, love, you know what I mean,' Kitty said soothingly. 'I know she wouldn't. But if she's at a lodging house here in Hong Kong, why hasn't she just come here, to the *Katipo*? So perhaps Longwei does still have her.'

Haunui drew a small circle on the table with his tumbler of brandy. 'I've been thinking about that. Maybe she can't come.'

'What do you mean?' Kitty asked. A nasty little finger of dread crept up her spine.

'She doesn't know where we're berthed,' Simon pointed out. 'There are hundreds of ships tied up along these wharves, and three times as many at anchor in the harbour. Perhaps she couldn't find us. And we've moved twice now.'

'But only once from Pedder's Wharf,' Kitty pointed out.

'Maybe Israel is keeping her prisoner,' Haunui said.

'Why?' Kitty asked, baffled. 'Why would he do that?'

'To stop her from coming to us.'

They all thought about that for a moment.

'That means he's either planning to stay here with her,' Simon said, 'which is unlikely because Victoria's not a big city and he must know we'd find them eventually, or he plans for them to leave for some other destination.'

Rian said, 'He'd never be able to keep Amber prisoner, not somewhere like a boarding house. Can you imagine it? She'd be a nightmare.'

Haunui glanced at the ship's clock on the wall. 'Time for less thinking and more doing. We've done enough thinking. Do we start tonight or tomorrow?'

Rian looked at Kitty. Her desire was to tear straight out and start banging on doors now, but her instinct told her they'd be more successful with a planned approach tomorrow after a good night's sleep, if such a thing were possible. 'Tomorrow,' she said, 'but early.'

Ka stepped out of the galley then and said something to Bao, which was followed by a short conversation between the two.

Bao said, 'Ka says she grew up in the west end and knows quite a lot of the families living there. If you will allow her, she would like to help tomorrow.'

Smiling properly for what felt like the first time in days, Kitty said, 'Tell her yes, thank you, we'd appreciate that very much.'

★　★　★

Mick knocked on the door of Wing's cabin. Ka opened it.

'Er, evening. Can I talk to Miss Wing, please?'

He could see her sitting on her bunk, her glorious, shining hair falling like a waterfall down her back.

Ka didn't answer, probably because she didn't have a clue what he was saying, he thought, and then they were both staring, with him standing at the door like a mutton-head.

He looked over the top of Ka. 'Miss Wing? Can I talk to you?'

She frowned slightly, her pretty lips pursing, and he thought she was going to say no. The disappointment settled like a great rock in his chest.

Finally she said, 'Yes, Mr Doyle, you may.'

His heart soared. Victory! 'In private?'

Again her porcelain-smooth brow wrinkled

slightly. She wasn't wearing any of that white stuff on her face tonight. He liked her better without it. It looked like confectioners' sugar but he bet it didn't taste like it.

She said something to Ka, who flitted next door to visit Bao in what was Israel's cabin.

Again that tremendous leap of his heart. This was ridiculous; he hadn't felt like this since he was about fifteen and didn't know any better. She beckoned and his feet moved into the cabin of their own accord, then she patted the bunk's mattress, but had to lean to do it which meant he wasn't sitting as close to her as he would've liked. Still, early days.

'Yes?' she said.

'Eh?'

'You wanted to speak to me.'

'Ah.' Shite. Now he was here he felt tongue-tied. He cast about, grappling for something intelligent to say. 'D'you like your cabin?'

'My cabin? No. It is far too small. I am accustomed to much bigger accommodations than this. And far more luxurious. My apartment at the house of Yip Chun Kit had two-hundred-year-old wall-hangings of silk velvet embroidered with gold thread.'

'Did it?'

'Do you have such luxuries in your home?'

'Not quite.'

'Where is your home?'

'You're sitting in it.'

'You do not own property ashore?'

'Me mam and me own a lot of houses in Sydney, Australia, 'cos we're in business

351

together,' Mick lied. 'We're landlords, so we are.'

His mother, Biddy, owned the property — he slept on her sofa when he was on shore leave.

'How many houses?'

Mick waved a dismissive hand. 'Can't remember off the top of me head. Me mam's always buying houses. I'd have to consult the books.'

Unlikely. Biddy never let him anywhere near her ledgers, and kept an even tighter rein on her purse strings.

Wing leant towards him. Her hair slid over her shoulder and he could smell her perfume, something lovely and flowery, just like her. She was like . . . an exotic orchid. God, he was getting poetic in his middle age.

'And does your wife help your mother run the business, Mr Doyle?'

'Me wife? I'm not married. Never have been.'

'And why is that?'

'Never found the right lady, I suppose,' Mick said. And why should I buy the cow when I can have the milk for free?

'What would constitute the right lady?'

Mick hesitated. What the hell did 'constitute' mean? What if he gave a stupid answer and made a fool of himself? 'In what way?' he asked.

He loved 'in what way'. It got him out of all sorts of shite — ignorance of words, not listening, needing more time to think.

'What would her personality be like, I suppose,' Wing said. 'Her attributes.'

Fuck. He wasn't entirely confident about 'attributes' either, and he couldn't say 'in what way' again. But 'personality' was easy.

'Well, I'd want, I mean I'd *like* her to be pleasant, happy, kind, generous. Willing to please her husband. You know, all those things that make a good wife. Things that every man wants.'

'Of course,' Wing said. She laid a pale hand on his knee, her touch electrifying him. 'I am sad that you have not yet found marital happiness. You are a handsome man, Mr Doyle, and obviously kind and generous. Who knows? Perhaps the woman you seek is closer than you realise?'

Ah God, Mick thought with a wild surge of hope, does she mean her?

$$\star \quad \star \quad \star$$

Israel popped another small spoonful of rice into Amber's mouth, thinking, This must be what it's like feeding a baby. He'd never done that. There was only him, though he suspected his mother might have had children in England before she was transported.

Amber had eaten rice yesterday as well, the day he'd talked to Longwei and then been chased by him, so that was two meals she'd had now, last night and this morning. He'd waited until she was waking up from the opium and was sure she wouldn't choke, then hand fed her. She'd talked a little, well, mumbled and said words that didn't make sense, and he'd told her what he'd said right at the beginning — that she was unwell. She definitely *looked* unwell now. She had big dark shadows under her eyes and her face was really quite pale, and halfway through last night's rice she'd been sick, but he'd caught it all in the bowl, which he'd been quite proud of, and had simply served her another lot in the other bowl. Then, when it seemed like she'd had enough, he'd given her more opium and off she'd gone. This morning, though, she wasn't showing any signs of wanting to be sick and had eaten nearly all her rice. He might even give her a drink, she'd been so good not wetting the bed in the night.

He'd left the jug of ale in his room so he shot next door and was just pouring a little into a tumbler when someone knocked on the door. He stopped dead, hardly even breathing. Mrs Whittle? No one else knew they were here. He put the ale and the tumbler down and went to the door.

'Who's there?'

No reply but he could tell someone was outside. He could . . . *feel* them.

'Mrs Whittle?'

Nothing.

He put the chain on, which he'd stupidly left off, carefully slid open the bolt and cracked the door an inch. It flew open, breaking the chain, and hit him full in the face.

Staggering backwards, he fell over a chair and scrambled to his knees, Ip To looming over him. He raised his hands to ward off the blows he knew were coming. Instead, a note was shoved at him: he clutched at it with a shaking hand and stared in terror up at Ip To, who turned and left.

Israel remained on his knees for a moment,

then collapsed forward onto the palms of his hands like a dog, watching as drops of bright blood from his battered nose dripped onto Mrs Whittle's carpet. His face felt as though it were on fire and he wanted to lie down and cry. But he bit the inside of his cheek so he wouldn't: anyone worthy of marrying a girl like Amber didn't cry just because they'd banged their face and things were going a bit wrong.

He reached for his old, grubby shirt, held it to his face and tipped back his head. After a while the flow of blood slowed, then finally stopped. He wondered if he'd have black eyes tomorrow.

Opening the note and leaving bloody fingerprints all over it, he smoothed it against his knee. It said:

Monday, the 26th of October, 1863
To Israel Mitchell,
I have decided that I wish to accompany you and the girl to your meeting with William Eastwood. However, Tuesday evening is not convenient for me. Please consult with Mr Eastwood and change the meeting time to this evening, at eight o'clock at the Lotus Pond Gardens. I am sure, if he is as eager for the meeting as you have implied, he will agree.

Failure to make the above arrangements will be taken by me as confirmation that you have reneged on our contract. You are aware of the consequences.
Your Obedient Servant
Lee Longwei

My obedient servant? Israel thought in dismay. You rotten bloody bastard. This was going to ruin everything!

He clambered to his feet, feeling dizzy and hoping his nose wouldn't start bleeding again, and crept to the door, peeping out to make sure Ip To really had gone. No sign of him.

Shit, shit, shit. What was he going to do?

He went next door, gave Amber a drink, half of which ended up running down her chin, and sat on the end of her bed to think.

12

By midday, Rian, Kitty and the crew had knocked on possibly three hundred random doors and talked to the proprietors of seven lodging houses. It was an interesting exercise but not a fruitful one: nobody who cared to answer either the door or the crew's questions had seen a couple answering to Amber's and Israel's descriptions. Ka, Simon and Pierre had even gone to the Lotus Pond Gardens, an edge of which was bordered by Queen's Road, and approached people there — Chinese and a few British women enjoying the beautiful, peaceful surrounds and the autumn sun — until a pair of sour-faced soldiers from the 31st Regiment told them to move on.

They all met at twelve-thirty for a meal at an eating house and to regroup before they began again in the afternoon. The last section to be searched was the most heavily populated, a warren of houses packed together over a square mile and threaded with narrow lanes and thoroughfares that could only be accessed on foot. It would take them hours if they were to try every address and there was no reason to think that would be of use anyway. It hadn't been this morning. So they decided to limit their questioning to the lodging houses, markets, shops and hotels.

Kitty was beginning to suspect their task was hopeless. She'd woken that morning after, frankly, a dreadful night's sleep, but nevertheless feeling quite optimistic about finding Amber, but that enthusiasm had dwindled as the morning hours had passed and nothing had changed except her feet were sore from walking and she'd grown tired of getting doors closed in her face and blank stares from people who couldn't speak English.

She and Rian were now on a street about a quarter of a mile back from the waterfront that seemed unable to decide whether it was commercial or residential: on it were houses, some small shops, houses *above* shops, several lodging houses and a pub.

'We'll try in here first,' Rian said, reading the sign on the lodging house wall saying *British Patrons Welcome Only*. 'This looks likely.'

They went in. A man stood behind a counter in a poky little foyer, writing something in a ledger. He wore enormous mutton-chop whiskers, a rather snug three-piece tweed suit that had seen better days, and a bowler hat that was also too small for him.

'Afternoon,' he said. 'Arnold Whittle at your service. After a room, are you?'

'No, information, actually,' Rian replied.

Mr Whittle's eyebrows went up. 'Sounds mysterious.'

'Do you have an Israel Mitchell and an Amber Atuahaere registered as staying here?'

Mr Whittle pointed at them as though he were aiming a pistol. 'Hang on, I'll just have a look in the trusty registrations book, shall I?'

What an idiot, Kitty thought.

The trusty registrations book was consulted, then slammed shut. 'No, no Mitchells or Atooraras here.'

'They might be using false names,' Kitty said, and described Amber and Israel in some detail.

'Waste of time telling me all that, dear,' Mr Whittle said cheerfully. 'It's usually the wife here behind the counter, not me. It's her fortnightly day off. You'll have to come back tomorrow if you want to speak to her.'

Kitty lost her temper. 'Then why didn't you say that before I spent five minutes giving you descriptions, you *fool*?'

'Here now — '

'Kitty,' Rian warned.

'You've behaved extremely flippantly regarding our request and I can assure you, *it is not a flippant matter!*'

'There's no need to get on your high horse, missus.'

Kitty glared at him, then spun on her heel and marched outside.

'Women, eh?' Mr Whittle remarked to Rian.

Rian shrugged noncommittally and followed Kitty out.

On the street he said, 'Look, I know you're upset but I'm not sure that was the wisest thing to do.'

'That's good, coming from you.'

'It's just we'll have to come back there tomorrow and speak to his wife.'

'Well, he was being a complete bloody

imbecile. He deserved it. Anyway he won't remember in an hour's time. That stupid bloody hat he's wearing will squeeze it out of him.'

'Probably. Let's try the pub, shall we?'

So they did. They went into the pub, with no success, the shops, which were all owned by Chinese people who didn't speak English, and the other lodging house also with a disappointing result. There was a Chinese lodging house on the street but neither Rian nor Kitty imagined Israel would have taken rooms there, so they didn't bother going in. For a convict's brat he could be a little particular about what company he kept.

By sunset they'd been along all 'their' streets, Rian was as disheartened as Kitty, whose feet were really sore now, and it was time to meet up with the others.

At the agreed meeting place, another eating house at the very western end of Queen's Road, the others arrived in twos and threes, all with demoralising news: Amber and Israel were nowhere to be found. Haunui felt awful.

'I'm really sorry,' he said. 'I was sure we'd find them, eh? I still think they're here somewhere.'

Rian clapped him on the shoulder. 'Maybe they are and we just didn't ask at the right places.'

'Or maybe I'm talking rubbish,' Haunui said gloomily, 'and Longwei's had her all along.'

'Well, we'll go to the shipping office tomorrow and see if passage anywhere has been booked under their names,' Rian said.

Their meals arrived and they ate more or less in silence. No one knew what to say and, far worse, what on earth to do next.

Israel had spent the day trying to get Amber to sober up.

After sitting on her bed thinking about what to do about the meeting tonight, he'd finally decided, but she'd have to be pretty well free of the effects of opium. Thank God he hadn't dosed her again before Ip To had given him that bloody note.

But sobering her up had turned out to be far more difficult than he'd expected. First of all she'd just gone back to sleep, as though he *had* given her more opium. So he'd woken her, which had been tricky because she hadn't wanted to wake up and had grumbled and grizzled and burrowed under the bedclothes, and then he'd tried to get her to sit, which had been *hopeless*. He'd prop her up, let go and she'd flop over sideways or onto her face, her hair getting tangled with everything. So in the end he'd slapped her across the face quite hard, which, he was sure, had hurt him more than it had her. That had certainly jolted her awake. Well, awake but still groggy, because she didn't know where she was or seem to recognise him.

He'd really been quite shocked because he'd thought opium would be like rum or whisky: you drank it, you got swattled and went to sleep, then you woke up sober, albeit with the horrors. But the effects of opium seemed to drag on and on. Mind you, he'd given her a fair bit over a couple of days. Maybe it just needed time to wear off.

The trouble was, he didn't have time.

As the day had passed, though, she'd become more lucid. Getting her to eat and drink had helped. By mid-afternoon she seemed in charge of her arms and legs again, though she was moving very slowly, like a creature called a sloth he'd once seen in the London Zoo. She'd used the chamber pot, and she'd recognised him, though she was still having trouble remembering where she was and why they were here. That, he hoped, would also pass in the next few hours.

He'd told her she'd been very ill and that he'd been caring for her.

'Ill with what?' she'd asked, frowning. Though whether she'd been frowning at the thought of being ill or at the way her words had come out, he didn't know.

'An ague, I expect. You got quite wet and cold in the sampan when we came back from Hung Shing Yeh Bay.'

'Why isn't Ma looking after me?'

So he'd had to remind her yet again: 'They're not here. The *Katipo*'s gone to Shanghai, remember? Lee Longwei asked your father to talk to the British customs and excise men there about the opium. It's one of the conditions of your release.'

'Opium's bad,' Amber said.

'Yes, it is.'

'And Tahi's gone too?'

Israel had had to clench his fists then, because no matter what state she was in, no matter how drugged or distressed, she always remembered who *he* was. 'Yes, he's gone as well. They all have.'

But the more Amber improved, the worse he felt. The dread had returned, churning in his belly and making his mouth so dry he could barely speak. When he'd gone out for food, locking her into her room, he'd shot into the pub down the street for another jug of ale, which was nearly all gone. He might have to go out for another.

Now, he looked at his watch: a quarter to seven. God. He'd tell her the first part shortly — he'd have to, to get her to the Lotus Pond Gardens — but he couldn't quite decide whether to tell her the second part tonight or in the morning. Either choice would mean hysterics, but he had the opium. Tonight, probably, to give her a chance to get used to the idea.

Then he stood in front of the mirror on the wall, inspecting the damage the door had done to his face. He did indeed have a pair of black eyes, and he was sure his nose was crooked. It was definitely swollen, and there was blood crusted around his nostrils, but they felt like they were packed with broken glass and were too sore to clean properly.

'What happened to your face?' Amber asked.

'I walked into something.'

'Looks sore.'

'It is.'

'Amber, I have to tell you something.' He sat on the end of her bed. She drew up her knees to give him room. 'You know how the *Katipo*'s gone to Shanghai? Well, I'm sorry to tell you this but they're in trouble.'

'Who are?'

'The crew. Your mother and father.'

She looked alarmed. That was good.

'What do you mean?'

'Your father failed.' Oh, it felt good to be able to say that, even if it wasn't true. 'He couldn't talk the customs authorities around. They wouldn't agree to stop letting the opium through at Shanghai.'

'I'm not surprised. Pa's not God, you know.'

'No. Anyway, Longwei must have spies in Shanghai because on the way back the *Katipo* was run down by his ships and everyone aboard taken captive.'

Amber's hand flew to her mouth.

'As far as Longwei's concerned the deal's off. If I don't return you to him, they'll all be killed.'

'No!'

Israel grabbed her hands. 'No, Amber, please, it's all right. We'll think of something. It's not the end of the world.'

'It is!' Slowly her hands slid out of his. 'How do you know all this?'

He was prepared for this question. 'When I went out before, I saw Ip To on the street. He was coming to speak to us. He told me.'

'But he doesn't speak English.'

Whoops. 'He had a letter, from Longwei.'

'Can I see it?'

Israel made a show of patting his pockets, thinking that Amber's mind had sharpened up a lot in the last hour. 'I think I threw it away.'

'You don't seem very upset,' Amber said.

'Of course I'm bloody upset but I'm thinking of you. And someone has to keep a cool head.'

'There's nothing wrong with mine.'

'You haven't been well.'

'I feel fine now.'

'You might *feel* fine, but you could easily relapse.'

Israel didn't want her to think herself too capable. She might do something using her own initiative, which wouldn't do at all.

'What, exactly, did the letter say about what I have to do to get him to release Ma and Pa and the others?' Amber asked.

'We're to meet him at the Lotus Pond Gardens tonight at eight o'clock. After that I'm not sure what will happen. The letter didn't say.'

He *was* sure, actually. He and Amber were going to run like hell. He knew the area reasonably well, no doubt better than Longwei did, a man who spent most of his time at sea, and he, Israel, was clever. Cleverer than most, in fact, even if he did say so himself. Then they would spend the night holed up somewhere out of sight. One night hiding in an abandoned, flea-ridden shack was nothing compared to a lifetime of happiness with Amber. In the morning they'd board the *Ann Marie* and then they'd be gone, leaving all the lies he'd told behind them. Well, except for the biggest one of all.

There was no other way. She just wouldn't leave Hong Kong with him otherwise. It would break her heart, and probably his to see her so upset, but she'd mend after a while. And he'd be the one to care for her and ease her grief and soothe her fears and help her to forget the life she used to have, and eventually she'd come to see that he was the one she should have been in love with all along, not bloody Tahi. He'd get a job ashore somewhere in England — no more sailor's life for him — and when they could afford it they'd buy a little cottage with a garden in a village far away from any ports the *Katipo* might visit, and one day children would come along and he'd give them the childhood he'd never had. And, yes, Amber might have strange, modern ideas about doing things for herself but that would all change once she realised how content she could be as his wife, and after he told her it would *have* to change. She'd stay at home and wear pretty dresses and cook good, plain English food for him and raise the children, and if anyone ever asked him why her complexion was a little dark, he'd tell them she was from Italy. They sometimes had dusky skin. It might not do to admit she was part native New Zealander. He was so close now to his dream he could smell the beef roasting in the range and the roses climbing up the wall outside the cottage.

'Will Ma and Pa be there? At the gardens?' Amber asked.

Christ, I bloody well hope not, Israel thought. 'I wouldn't think so, not if he's holding them prisoner.'

'So I'll have to go with him?'

'I don't know.'

'And then he'll let everyone go?'

'I said I don't *know*!' She was asking questions about a situation that wasn't even real, and it was starting to irritate him.

'Well, you read the letter.'

'And all it said was we're to meet him.'

'What time?'

'Eight o'clock.'

'What's the time now?'

Israel looked at his watch. 'It's just past seven. We should have some supper.'

'I don't want any supper.'

'You've hardly eaten anything for four days.'

He didn't want to tell her that they might not get the opportunity for food until they were aboard the *Ann Marie*. She didn't know they were going to England at all, yet.

'Well, I'm not hungry.'

Israel sighed. He was. 'You need to get dressed. Why don't you put on your new gown?'

Longwei thought Amber was coming to the gardens to meet William Eastwood; it wouldn't do for her to turn up looking like a drab.

'What for? I'm probably only going to end up in Longwei's cabin again, aren't I? I'll wear the tunic and trousers you bought me.' She frowned. '*Did* you buy me those or did I just dream it?'

'I bought them but you can't wear them. They're dirty. You slept in them.'

Amber looked down at the nightgown she was wearing. 'I've been sleeping in this, haven't I? This isn't mine. When did I get this?'

'I bought it for you.'

'How did . . . ' Outraged, Amber exclaimed, 'Israel Mitchell, did you look at me naked?'

'No! I didn't, I promise. I made sure I didn't.'

Amber spied the chamber pot. 'And . . . what

about that? God, Israel!'

'You used that yourself,' he lied. It would be too complicated to explain how he'd managed to get her on it without looking. He decided not to mention the wet bed sheet.

'I don't remember that.'

'You've been very ill.'

'Stop *saying* that!'

'Well, you have.'

'What about the clothes I had on when we came back from . . . ?' Amber screwed up her face, obviously trying to recall. 'Christ, I can't remember that either. Wherever it was Longwei's ships were.'

Israel thanked God he hadn't got around to having any laundry done. 'They're still dirty too. It'll have to be the gown.'

He was beginning to think she didn't like it.

'Oh well.' Amber folded back the bedclothes, put her feet on the floor and looked at him.

'What?'

'Can I have some privacy, please?'

'Oh. Right. I'll go next door and pack. You should, too.'

'What do you need to pack for?'

'Well, we don't know what's going to happen, do we?' Israel said.

While her back was turned he slipped the half-empty bottle of opium into his pocket. He'd need it tonight when he gave her his bad news, which raised the question: how was he going to drag her around the city when she was insensible? He'd have to dose her after they'd found somewhere to hide, then go easy on the amount in the morning when they boarded the ship, just enough to keep her calm and quiet. Once she was in her cabin he could give her more and she could sleep for a day or two, then he could help her get used to the idea that everything had changed for her. He'd tell the others on the ship her tragic tale. They'd understand and leave them alone.

In his own room he gathered together his few possessions and tied them in the shirt he'd used to staunch his bleeding nose. They were woefully underprepared for the time they'd be at sea but they could go ashore at their first port of call and do some shopping. At Singapore, probably, which was full of Chinese and Indians but was owned by the British and was a good-sized trading port. He looked around to make sure he hadn't forgotten anything, then went next door again.

Amber had put on the gown and she looked absolutely beautiful. The shape and size suited her perfectly. So much for her mother saying that clothes bought ready-made never fit properly.

'You look lovely,' he said. 'Really lovely.'

'Thank you.'

On her feet Amber wore the shoes he'd bought with the Chinese outfit, which he could see weren't quite right, but they'd have to do. She'd brushed her thick hair so energetically that now it was lifting up as though it had a life of its own.

She caught him eyeing it. 'I know, it won't behave. It needs a good clean. *I* need a good clean. I'm quite smelly.' She pulled out the neck of the dress, sniffed and made a face.

'We'll get you a decent wash on the — ' He

stopped himself just in time. 'I'm sure we can get you a decent wash somewhere. You still look beautiful. Are you ready?'

'I think so.' She pointed to her own little swag, made from her nightgown and holding her hairbrush and bits and pieces, then hesitated. 'Israel?'

He waited.

'I don't want to go back to Longwei again, but I will for Tahi and Ma and Pa. And the others.'

'Well, let's wait and see.'

He turned down the lamps and closed the door behind them.

★ ★ ★

Kitty, Rian, Bao, Ka and the crew were making their way back to the wharves, trudging along Queen's Road, feeling tired and dispirited. The moon was full and bright and hung in the sky like a glorious pale gold pearl, but they barely noticed it, except to be grateful that it lit their way. Traffic on the road was busy but soon most of it would be gone as the city's Chinese population retreated indoors in reluctant observance of the curfew, leaving only British subjects and other foreign visitors out and about.

Kitty's feet were so sore she was almost tempted to hail a sedan chair but refused to. She had principles, and the grumpier she got the more rigidly she stuck to them. Even Rian had suggested a chair.

'No! I don't need one.'

'Then why are you limping?'

'Because my feet hurt!'

'Then hire a damn chair.'

'I said *no*, Rian.'

'Well, shall I carry you?'

'Don't be so stupid!'

'Is it blisters?' Simon asked.

Kitty gave him a withering look. 'No, actually, it's gout.'

'I didn't know you had gout.'

'Of course it's bloody blisters.'

'You could take your boots off,' Simon suggested.

Kitty said, 'And walk all the way home in bare feet?'

'Well, no. You could have my socks. Not the freshest, I'm afraid, but better than nothing.'

'Mine, too, chérie,' Pierre volunteered.

Tahi said, 'And mine.'

Mick kicked off his boots, inspected his socks, and kept quiet.

Rian also offered, but no one else was wearing socks. Haunui was barefoot.

Kitty sat down at the edge of the road and started to unlace her boots.

'Not here,' Rian said, pulling her up by an arm. 'You'll get run over. Let's cross the road and sit down.'

They all trooped across Queen's Road to a public garden, its gravel paths, trees and shrubs, lotus ponds and pavilions receding into shadow, where Kitty sat on a wooden bench and took off her boots. By the moonlight she could see black patches on her heels where blisters had broken and bled.

'Painful, eh?' Haunui said. 'You want some of

Hawk's stinky bear grease. Fixed mine.'

Kitty made a face: Hawk's ointment really did reek, but it seemed to help most wounds heal. She dabbed at the blisters with her own socks to wipe away the blood and ooze, then pulled on Rian's. They didn't smell the best, but then neither did hers. Then she tugged on all the rest until she had a thick layer of wool beneath her feet, almost as good as boots but with very little pressure on her heels. She only hoped no one else got blisters now from going without socks.

'Hey,' Ropata exclaimed. 'Isn't that Israel?'

They all turned to follow his gaze.

'Where?' Rian demanded, squinting into the darkness.

'Going into the gardens, down there by that pine tree. About a hundred yards away? I just saw the shape of his hat. I'm sure it was him.'

Kitty's heart was thumping so violently she could barely hear herself think. 'Was Amber with him?'

'I didn't see her. I only just caught sight of him.'

Kitty grabbed Rian's hand and yanked. 'Come on, we have to catch up with him!'

'Hold on, hold on, let me think.'

'No, come on!'

Rian twisted his hand out of her grasp and grabbed her wrist. 'No, Kitty, wait! What if she isn't with him but he knows where she is? If we all go pounding after him and lose him, we lose her as well. No, we'll follow him and find out where he's going.'

'Rian!' Kitty couldn't believe what he was saying.

'If she's with him we'll see her soon enough. And keep your voice down. He might hear us.'

Kitty felt like she'd been slapped. 'You keep your bloody voice down.'

Rian cupped his hands around her face. 'Please, Kitty, just do as I say, just this once. We might only get this one chance. I know you're frightened. So am I. Please?'

She gazed into his eyes, silver in the moonlight, and nodded.

'Good,' he said. 'That's my girl.' He picked up her boots, then handed them to Simon. 'Here, take these, will you?'

They entered the gardens following a path that crunched alarmingly loudly beneath their feet. Rian held up a hand; somewhere farther into the gardens they could hear other footsteps, so the owner could probably hear them.

'Move onto the grass,' Rian said quietly.

They all did. Coming to a little arched bridge spanning a pond filled with lotus plants, their flowers closed for the night, they crossed one at a time, Kitty feeling ridiculously like one of the billy goats gruff. They paused on the other side and listened again. They could still hear the original footsteps but now they thought they could hear more, approaching from a different direction.

Rian raised his eyebrows at Hawk, whose face, as usual, remained impassive. 'Sounds to me like quite a lot of feet,' he said.

'More than us?' Rian asked.

Hawk nodded. 'Perhaps. We are eleven but the women cannot fight.'

'I will,' Kitty said fiercely. 'I'll fight for my daughter.'

Rian settled a calming hand on her arm. 'It could be nothing, just soldiers going back to the barracks. We might not even pass them.'

'Hush,' Hawk said.

They all fell silent, and listened.

★ ★ ★

'Are you sure this is the right way?' Amber asked over her shoulder.

Israel was feeling slightly hysterical and had a terrible urge to laugh. Of course it wasn't the right way. How could it be? He'd made the whole fucking thing up! He slipped the opium bottle out of his pocket and took another sip. He shouldn't, he knew he shouldn't, but it was definitely taking the edge off his nerves, and God knew they needed the edge taken off them.

He hadn't told Longwei where they were allegedly meeting William Eastwood in the gardens, and Longwei hadn't asked, which, now that he thought about it, was a bit odd, so he supposed they should keep walking until they came to a spot that looked suitable for a tryst. If Longwei couldn't find them, he, Israel, would be euphoric. They'd wait for ten minutes, just in case, then get out of this horrible place as fast as possible. Amber would be full of bloody questions, of course, she always was, but she'd forget them as soon as he told her she was now an orphan.

'It is,' he said. 'Keep going.'

'I can hear other people walking around,' she

374

said. 'Quite a few, actually.'

That'll be Longwei, Israel thought, feeling suddenly sick with disappointment. Somewhere deep inside himself he'd harboured a desperate hope that Longwei wouldn't actually turn up, but obviously he had.

They walked through a pavilion paved with wide flagstones, passed a pond, then crunched along yet another path that opened through an arch onto a wide lawn.

Israel's heart sank into his boots when he saw that Longwei was standing in the middle of it. With him were Ip To and perhaps a dozen of his shifty-looking pirate cronies.

He and Amber had no choice but to approach them. Amber dumped her swag on the ground, which annoyed him because she was bound to waste precious seconds grabbing it when it came time for them to run. And then he remembered that she didn't know yet that they would be running: he should have told her before they'd got here.

Longwei produced a ridiculously expensive-looking watch from the depths of his tunic and tilted the face towards the moon.

'Are my mother and father well?' Amber snapped. 'And my husband? And what about the rest of the crew?'

Israel nearly fainted from an overwhelming surge of panic. Why couldn't she just keep her mouth shut?

Longwei stared at her. 'I assume so.' He looked back at his watch. 'Mr Eastwood appears to be late.'

'Who — ' Amber began before Israel stepped on her foot, hard.

Sweat popped out on his brow and in his armpits. He'd planned to suggest to Longwei that William Eastwood must have developed cold feet, to explain his failure to appear, but he'd also completely forgotten that Amber didn't know anything about the fictitious arrangements involving Eastwood. But perhaps he could still get away with it, if he was careful with his words.

'Maybe he thought better of it,' he said. 'Or changed his mind?'

Longwei smiled. 'It is only five minutes past the hour. Let us give the man a little more time, shall we?'

'I really don't think he'll be coming,' Israel said, hearing the desperation in his own voice. 'He said he'd be here exactly on the dot of eight.' Then he had a spectacularly brilliant idea. 'Maybe he *didn't* fancy being outdoors. Why don't I take Amber to his house?'

Amber demanded, 'Whose house? Why would I want to go to someone's house?'

Israel caught her gaze and tried, with all his will, to convey to her that she had to play along with him. 'William Eastwood's. You know.'

'Who the bloody hell's William Eastwood?' Amber exclaimed, her voice getting louder with every word.

Longwei said, 'Oh dear. It seems that the spinner of yarns may well have been exposed.'

'*What* yarns?' Israel flinched as Amber punched him on the arm. 'Israel, what the *hell* is going on?'

'Look,' he said to Longwei as he furiously tried to think. 'There's a reason for all this.'

'I have no interest in your reasons,' Longwei said flatly. 'You are a dead man. And you, Mrs Atuahaere, are coming with me.'

* * *

'Like hell she is,' Rian called out, stepping from the shadows.

There was an ominous *shiiiing* sound as a dozen sabres were unsheathed simultaneously.

Kitty swallowed nervously. They hadn't come heavily armed, having not started the day expecting that they'd need to, but she knew Rian was carrying his revolver and that the others would have knives tucked away somewhere. No match, however, for the pirates' weapons, which could take your head off with one stroke.

But her worry about how well armed they were, or weren't, was subsumed by her delight at seeing Amber. She rushed forwards, only to be jerked back by Rian's hand gripping her forearm. 'Just wait,' he hissed.

Haunui had been right, she thought: Amber must have been with Israel. How could he? How *could* he, after all she and Rian had done for him? She glanced at Tahi, whose face was set in rigid lines of absolute fury.

Longwei took a firm hold of Amber's wrist and the two groups approached each other warily. Israel, Kitty noted, was now surrounded by Longwei's men.

Close up she could see that Amber didn't look

particularly well. There were great shadows beneath her eyes and her face seemed pale. It might just be the moonlight but she feared it wasn't. Israel certainly didn't look too chipper with two black eyes and a swollen nose, and a good job, too.

'Tahi!' Amber said, 'are you all right?'

'Yes, but are you?'

'Fine. Ma and Pa? You haven't been harmed?'

Kitty glanced at Rian. What was she talking about?

'Thank you for letting them go,' Amber said to Longwei.

He frowned at her. 'I beg your pardon?'

'Thank you for letting my family and friends go. I didn't realise they'd be released so quickly.'

Longwei looked contemplative, then reached out and hauled Israel forwards by an ear. 'Explain to us what it is you have been telling her.'

'I haven't told her anything.'

'I think you have.'

He drew his own sabre then and held the tip to Israel's throat. It moved as Israel swallowed and said, 'I told her you'd taken the crew of the *Katipo* prisoner.'

A terrible silence fell over the little crowd. Even Longwei's men were engrossed — at least those who could understand English were.

'Why?' Longwei demanded.

'To get her to come here tonight.'

Longwei nodded again. 'Because the story you told about William Eastwood was a lie, too, yes?'

Israel admitted that it was.

'And all this so you could take this girl for yourself?'

Israel was silent for several seconds, then burst out, 'She *should* be with me! Not with him,' he rasped, pointing a shaking finger at Tahi. 'Me! I'm the one who can look after her. *I* know what she likes, *I* can make her laugh, *I* can make her happy. I've just never had the — '

Amber flew at him, punching up at his already damaged face and kicking his shins and doing her best to ram her knee into his balls.

'You bastard!' she shrieked. 'You bloody, bloody *bastard*. You told me they'd been taken captive! I was worried *sick*! And all because you were jealous and felt *sorry* for yourself! You . . . *fucker*!'

'Bravo!' Pierre exclaimed, applauding.

Tahi stepped forwards but Longwei got there first and pulled her off Israel, then Haunui steered Tahi back the way he'd come, for fear that a killing might occur.

'We'll take Amber and go now but you can keep him,' Rian said, nodding at Israel. 'We don't want him.'

'I do not think so. He made a contract with me, and so did you. Neither contracts were executed. The girl comes with me. You have lost her.'

'No!' Kitty cried.

Longwei ignored her and turned away. Amber booted him in the leg but Ip To simply picked her up and carried her.

Rian drew his pistol. Out came the sabres again.

'Stop!' Bao commanded, her voice ringing through the clear night air.

She moved between the two groups and uttered a sharp order to Ip To, who glanced at Longwei, then put Amber down.

A rapid conversation in Cantonese ensued between Bao and Longwei, then Bao said to Rian, 'Please excuse us. I wish to discuss a proposition with Longwei that I hope will secure Amber's release, and I would prefer to speak in his language. Do I have your permission to proceed?'

'Christ, of course you do, Bao. If you need money, for God's sake, say so. If it's something else he wants we can get him practically anything.'

Bao gave a small nod. 'Thank you.'

She and Longwei walked away, into the shadows, though the sounds of their voices carried. Not their words, however, to the disappointment of all those who could speak the the language.

At one point the conversation became very heated and Kitty despaired, her heart thudding painfully as she feared that all might be lost, then the voices resumed their calm cadence and hope flooded her chest once more.

Bao and Longwei returned thirty minutes later.

'A contract has been made,' Longwei announced to Rian. 'I will release your daughter.'

Her knees feeling wobbly with relief Kitty hurried to Amber and wrapped her arms around her, horrified to find that she could feel her ribs beneath the fabric of her dress. 'Oh, my darling, didn't he feed you?'

'I was sick. I slept most of the time.'

'You *slept*? Why?'

'I had some really strong medicine. It knocked me out.'

Bao's lips flattened into a straight and very forbidding line as she marched over to Israel, spun him around and, to his shock, tore off his jacket.

'Give me that, that's mine,' he complained, trying to snatch it back.

Bao leapt away from him, digging through the pockets. In a moment she'd produced the opium bottle, and a ring that glittered faintly in the moonlight.

Amber stepped closer. 'That's my wedding ring!'

Passing it to Amber, Bao wrenched the cork from the bottle and licked it. 'You gave her *this*?' she accused, furious. 'How could you? Opium is death! You could have killed her!'

'Yes, but I was *careful*. I *love* her!'

Dropping the bottle, Bao jumped straight up and kicked out with a foot that connected very solidly with Israel's already broken nose, then performed a half turn in the air and let fly with the other foot, collecting him across the side of the head. He went down, hard. A cheer erupted from both groups.

Astonished, Kitty realised that her mouth was hanging open. She shut it with an audible click of her teeth. Longwei, she noticed, was staring at Bao with undisguised admiration.

Israel struggled to his feet, holding his jaw, his eyes wild. He shoved his way past several of

Longwei's men and ran, sprinting madly across the grass, his moon shadow streaking behind him.

Longwei turned to Rian and gave a formal bow, divesting himself of any claim to Israel.

Rian, in turn, exchanged a glance with Haunui, who nodded, and they both stood aside to let Tahi past. He took off after Israel like a cat after a mouse, catching up with him just before he ducked into a stand of bamboo, which would have been a mistake anyway, Kitty thought, because he'd have been caught in it like a bug pinned to a board.

She watched what followed with almost complete indifference, except to wonder briefly what had happened to the cheeky lad she'd met outside that hotel in Melbourne. He'd been full of life and full of himself, but it was true that he'd been light-fingered, and it was clear he'd not learnt to keep his hands off what didn't belong to him. She had no sympathy for him, and tried to recall when she'd become so hard-hearted. Not when she'd killed Amiria, because she'd had no choice about that. Probably, she thought, when she'd shot Avery Bannerman.

She decided it didn't matter anyway, not when her family were concerned.

★   ★   ★

Tahi grabbed Israel's collar and jerked him backwards, unbalancing him. Israel spun on one leg, raising the knee of the other and withdrawing a long, curved, Chinese fighting knife from

382

the ankle of his boot. The handle snagged on his cuff and Tahi heard him swear as he tore fabric extricating it.

Tahi fell back, drawing a knife of his own from his waistband. His, however, was shorter, though its blade glinted malignantly in the moonlight. It wasn't a mere, a patu, a taiaha or tewhatewha, a musket or a rifle, the weapons Haunui had trained him so thoroughly to use, but he knew how to handle it. He was confident, and he was angry.

They faced each other, turning in a slow circle.

'Did you touch her?' Tahi demanded.

'What do you think I am?'

'A lying, stealing arsehole. *Did* you?'

'Only when I had to.'

Tahi didn't believe him. 'She was drugged, you filthy bastard.'

Israel stumbled and righted himself. 'I swear I didn't. Ask her.'

'She wouldn't know.' Tahi adjusted his grip on the knife. 'Why, Israel? Why did it have to be her? She's mine. She always has been. Was *that* the reason?'

Israel sneered. 'You're so bloody arrogant. No, it was her. I've always loved her, ever since Melbourne. And I've had to watch the pair of you flirting with each other for nearly ten bloody years. It's just about made me sick.'

Tahi took a step closer: Israel moved back. 'Well, bad luck. It was *me* she wanted, not you. Why didn't you find yourself someone else?'

'God, you're stupid. I didn't *want* someone else. I wanted her.'

Tahi shrugged, which seemed to enrage Israel. He lunged at him, his knife slashing at the air where Tahi had stood a moment earlier.

'Were you ever my friend?' Tahi asked.

' "Were you ever my friend?" ' Israel repeated in a silly voice. 'No, not really. But it was the only way to get close to Amber.'

'She didn't particularly like you, you know,' Tahi remarked. Amber hadn't told him that, but she'd never said she was terribly fond of him either, and he knew that saying so now would provoke Israel. 'She only put up with you because we're the same age. She thinks you're a fool.'

Israel risked a desperate glance across at Amber standing between her mother and father. 'That's not true!'

'Well, you must be. How did you think you'd get away with abducting her? Where did you think you were going to go?'

'England.'

Tahi snorted. 'And what did Amber think about that?'

'I hadn't told her yet.'

'You don't think she might have been a bit homesick for everyone? Especially me, her *husband*.'

'*You're* the fool. There wasn't going to be any 'everyone'. I was going to tell her Longwei had killed you all.'

It took a moment for Israel's words to sink in, and when they did, the magnitude of what they meant took Tahi's breath away. Stunned, he slowly straightened from his fighting crouch and stared at Israel. 'But . . . that would've destroyed her.'

'No. She'd have had me.'

'You . . . *lunatic!*'

In a fit of cold rage, Tahi launched himself at Israel, but Israel was ready. He sidestepped and Tahi's knife flashed past his ear. He responded with a swing of his own and also missed, Tahi ducking out of the way. Again they faced each other.

Israel lunged forwards with a great backhand sweep of his arm, which Tahi blocked, using his knife against Israel's forearm as though he were striking with the long edge of a patu. The blade sliced into Israel's flesh and his arm flew upwards, releasing his own knife.

Tahi grabbed him by the front of his shirt and hauled him to within kissing distance.

'Do you have anything to say before you die?' he asked.

Israel's eyes were wide, his breath short. 'Tell Amber I — '

Tahi didn't want to hear the rest and stabbed him in the heart before he could finish.

Israel sank to his knees, black blood pumping down his chest, then tipped over onto his side. 'Tell her I'm sorry,' he whispered.

Tahi wiped the blade of his knife on the grass, and walked away.

Part Three

GOING HOME
NOVEMBER–DECEMBER 1863

When I am dead, my dearest

13

The return voyage south was reasonably uneventful, bar high winds, big seas and blinding rain in the Solomon Seas, but the *Katipo* sailed neatly through the heavy weather without sustaining damage. Wing and Ka, however, were horribly seasick for the first week, and the other women aboard were kept busy mopping faces with damp cloths, washing bed linen (always a performance when the *Katipo* was under sail) and rinsing out sick buckets. The crew used their down time during the first day or two to put the finishing touches to Tahi and Amber's cabin, so that by the time the ship had reached the Philippines, the couple were enjoying the luxury of a double bed.

Or at least they should have been.

On their first night at sea they'd fallen into bed exhausted and gone straight to sleep, but the following night Amber brushed her hair until it shone like treacle, put on her prettiest sleeveless white voile nightgown and waited in bed for Tahi to come off his shift on deck. When he had, however, he sat for half an hour in the mess room talking to Mick and Pierre, and when he finally came in she could smell booze.

'Have you been drinking?' she asked.

'Just a bit of whisky.'

'Why?'

'I felt like it,' he said, kicking off his boots.

'Oh.' She was surprised. He hardly ever drank for the sake of it. 'Well, come on then, hurry up and hop in.'

'Christ, Amber, wait a minute, will you?' he said wearily. 'I've only just got in. I need a wash. I stink.'

Blinking at his mild rebuke, she drew her knees up to her chest and hugged them, watching as he stripped off his jacket and shirt. Catching her gaze, he turned his back, which stung her even more.

He poured too much water from a ewer into a bowl, swore as a roll of the ship spilt some over the rim, and splashed about with a piece of soap.

'What's the matter?' Amber asked.

'Nothing.'

Amber knew this was a lie. He'd been touchy and out of sorts since he'd killed Israel, which she expected was a good enough reason. After all, for the last six years he'd thought Israel had been his best mate, but best mates didn't go about stealing your wife, did they? Privately Amber thought Israel must have been fond of Tahi at least some of that time. Who could keep up such a pretence for that long? Not Israel — she just didn't think he was that clever.

She knew Haunui had taken Tahi aside after the killing and had a long talk to him about it, because Haunui had told her father, who had told her mother, who had told her. Tahi hadn't said anything to her, though. Not a word. She knew they'd discussed utu, which of course she knew was the Maori custom of rebalancing — in this case — a serious wrong that had been committed, because Haunui had taught her all about it, but Haunui's conversation with Tahi hadn't seemed to have alleviated his strange mood at all.

It wasn't as though he was being mean to her, he wasn't. But the intimacy they'd shared before she'd been taken from the hotel at Cebu had disappeared — which was grossly unfair, because it wasn't the fault of either of them that she'd been abducted. She thought if she could just bring him back to her, make him look at her properly again, everything would be fine. And the best way she could think of to do that was to offer herself to him, because he'd never been able to resist her.

'Did anything happen on watch?' she asked, changing the subject.

'No.'

'You didn't catch Mick and Wing sneaking about?'

'No.'

'Ma says Mick's keen on her.'

That made Tahi pause, a soapy facecloth to his armpit. 'True?'

'Well, he's been having little chats with her in her cabin. Without Ka.'

'He'll just be wanting a leg over. You know Mick.'

'Ma says he's serious about her.'

Tahi snorted, rinsed his cloth and washed his face. Amber sat back, pleased that he seemed to have relaxed a little. He should be bloody well relaxed, judging by the whisky she could still smell.

'Where's the tooth powder?' he asked.

She told him. He dipped his toothbrush into the tin, cleaned his teeth, rinsed and spat into the bowl. When he'd finished his ablutions he opened the window and threw out the contents.

Then he sat on the side of the bed.

Amber threw back the bedclothes. 'Aren't you getting in?'

'In a minute.'

A minute passed, then another.

'Amber?'

'Mmm?'

'I'm quite tired.'

'Well, hop in and we'll see what happens.'

Tahi took off his trousers and slid into the bed, and Amber thought it was possibly the first time he'd got that close to her without an erection. She pulled up the bedclothes and snuggled next to him, settling her arm and leg across him.

'Oooh, you're freezing.'

That was always his cue to say, 'Then warm me up,' but he didn't.

She kissed him, tasting the chalky soap of tooth powder and an underlying hint of whisky. The whisky was much nicer. He returned the kiss briefly, then gently pressed her head against his shoulder.

Didn't he want to kiss her? she wondered. Had she remembered to clean her own teeth?

She slid her hand over his belly and down to his groin but he took hold of her wrist and turned away from her, trapping her arm against his chest. She tried to pull free but he wouldn't let go.

'Tahi!'

'What?'

She yanked her arm away, whipped the bedclothes back and straddled his legs so he had to turn onto his back. Slowly, she lifted her nightgown off and tossed it on the floor. Now they were both naked.

She ran the fingernails of both hands lightly from his chest to his groin, something he loved, but still his penis lay flaccid. Crawling backwards down his legs she took him in her mouth, but even that didn't work.

'What's the matter?' she asked.

'Nothing.' He wouldn't look at her.

Amber didn't know what to do. This had never, ever happened before.

'Tell me,' she said.

'Nothing's the matter,' he snapped. He closed his eyes for a moment then opened them again, staring at the ceiling. 'I told you, I'm just tired.'

'Shall I get on my knees?' That was his favourite position.

'No! Look, let's just leave it. Put your nightgown back on. Let's just go to sleep.'

Amber felt a twinge of panic. 'I don't want to leave it. I want to know what's wrong. I want us to fix it.'

'Well, I bloody don't. Come on, hop off.'

Amber got off. *Why* didn't he want to fix it? The panic was stabbing at her now like a long, sharp knife. 'If we talk about it we — '

'I said no, Amber!'

'But — '

Tahi lunged out of bed, snatched his trousers

off the floor and slammed out of the cabin.

Staring after him, Amber burst into tears.

★ ★ ★

Tahi tapped on the door of Hawk's cabin, his mood not improved by the time he'd spent standing in the short passageway trying to work out where the hell everyone was sleeping. Haunui was in with Ropata so no room there, Simon was bunking in with Pierre because Wing and Ka were in his cabin, although Wing might be with Mick tonight so he was out. Bao was in Israel's old cabin, though he wouldn't have slept in there anyway, which only left Gideon and Hawk, and Gideon snored like a walrus with chronic catarrh. Hawk, however, hated being woken up for no good reason.

He was about to knock again when the door opened. He'd forgotten what a light sleeper Hawk was.

'Is there trouble?' Hawk asked.

His long hair hung unbound from its customary plait to his waist and he wore nothing at all but a very sour expression.

'No, but — '

Hawk shut the door in his face.

Tahi knocked again. When it finally reopened he said quickly, 'Can I bunk in with you?'

'Why?'

'I just need somewhere to sleep.'

After a long stare, Hawk let him in. He climbed back into bed and threw a pillow up onto the top bunk. 'Do not snore. I cannot stand snoring.'

Tahi got himself settled and lay with his hands behind his head, his face barely two feet from the ceiling, convinced he'd never get to sleep. He'd never in his twenty-three years been unable to perform sexually and now he couldn't, but he knew the reason for it and he felt profoundly angry. It was all Israel bloody Mitchell's fault. He was glad he'd stuck that knife in him and killed him. The satisfaction had been immense, but not, apparently, enough to drain the bitter poison of jealousy and resentment from his heart.

Israel had raped Amber, he knew he had. She insisted he hadn't, but he knew Israel and he went with whores and treated them like shit. He had no respect for women at all. Why would he not have raped Amber when he had all that opportunity? He'd fed her that opium for days, for God's sake. She wouldn't have known what the hell he'd been doing to her.

Tahi swallowed a retch. Honestly, just the thought of it made him want to vomit. It was truly sickening. He tried not to think about it but he couldn't help it, as though he were constantly picking away at a deep, painful scab until it bled.

He was astonished that Amber expected him to make love to her, to put his ure where Israel's had been. He didn't think he'd ever be able to have sex with her again. And she couldn't see it, how much it was upsetting him, what it meant. That was making him angry, too. Didn't it matter to her that she'd been raped? He couldn't just go on as if things were normal when he knew they weren't, not any more.

His mind had been going round and round like this since he'd got Amber back, and after what had just happened it would be even worse. He knew he'd still be awake by morning, turning it over in his head, feeling the pain, reliving the humiliation, planning revenge against a man he'd already killed.

But he did fall asleep, and while he slept he had a vision.

He was back in the Lotus Pond Gardens in Hong Kong, though it wasn't night time any more, it was day, the light bright and white. Israel lay on the ground, dead in a pool of congealed black blood, and a great cloud of flies buzzed all around him.

Tahi was holding someone's hand and thought it was Amber's, but it felt odd, and when he looked he saw it belonged to Lily Pearce, the nasty prostitute who'd been a thorn in everyone's side at Ballarat. Her arms and face were all melted, as though she were made of wax, and most of her hair was burnt off. He hurriedly let go of her and she laughed.

'You should have come and seen me, love. Boys were my speciality. I could have fixed your problem.'

'Leave him alone, Lily.'

Tahi's mother stood on the far side of Israel, her long hair lifting in a gentle breeze Tahi couldn't feel.

Lily took two steps backwards and disappeared.

'Mama,' Tahi said. 'I need help.'

'Yes, you do.' Wai walked through Israel's corpse, not even disturbing the flies.

'I need to talk to him,' Tahi said, pointing. 'Make him come alive.'

'I cannot do that. In any case, he is not your dilemma. That lies inside you.'

'But I have to know what he did.'

'Do you really?'

'Yes!'

A procession appeared, led by a Chinese man scattering small pieces of paper, followed by a horse and cart on which lay a coffin. Dressed all in white, Bao rode on the cart and behind walked the crew of the *Katipo* and perhaps a hundred and fifty Chinese and European mourners. They passed in complete silence, until Tahi lost sight of them among the garden's trees.

'All you need to know is what truly matters between you and your wife,' Wai said.

'I just said that.'

'You did not.'

'I *did*. I said I have to know what happened.'

'That is not the same thing. It does not matter what happened. You must continue to love her regardless.'

'But — '

Wai held up a small hand. 'Be quiet, boy. If you do not continue to love her, he *will* have stolen her from you.'

Tahi glanced down at Israel. He was propped up on an elbow now, grinning at him, his teeth and chin covered with sticky blood.

'You said you couldn't make him come alive,' Tahi said to his mother.

'And I have not. You have done that. You are keeping him alive.'

'Well, we'll see about that,' Tahi said.

He ran up to Israel, kicked his head as hard as he could and watched with immense satisfaction as it separated from his neck, sailed off and landed many yards away in the middle of a bamboo stand.

★ ★ ★

The next morning Tahi woke early. He felt physically ragged, but mentally far more at peace than he had for many weeks. He trotted up on deck for a few minutes to see if dawn was coming yet and to greet Ropata on watch, then went down to the galley to visit Pierre.

'You up early,' Pierre said, up to his elbows in flour.

'Couldn't sleep.'

Pierre had a good stare at him. 'Happy boy, though?'

Tahi grinned. He was.

'Très bien. Happy is good. Hungry?'

'Starving.

'Yesterday's biscuits in the barrel. Kettle just boiled.'

Tahi laid out a tray with a teapot, two cups and a plate for the biscuits.

'Ooh, the romantic breakfast tea in the bed?' Pierre asked.

'Something like that. I don't suppose we've got any fresh flowers?'

'In the middle of the Tasman Sea?'

'No, thought not.'

Pierre's face lit up. 'But one moment.' Dusting

down his hands he rushed from the galley in a haze of flour.

Tahi spooned tea leaves into the pot and added hot water, sniffing as the rich, dark aroma rose upwards.

Pierre returned clutching a handful of beautifully made red and white satin roses. 'I buy them in Cebu. They for the Spanish ladies' hair.'

'And for yours?' This was odd even for Pierre.

'Non, you fool, to *give* when there are no fresh.'

'Perfect! Now all I need are Samson and Delilah.'

'What . . . ah! Pierre knows!'

Pierre took the little triangle he used to summon the cats for their meals and gave it a good few whangs with the beater. It wasn't long before Tahi heard the thud of little feet along the deck and down the companionway, and Samson and Delilah tore across the mess room and into the galley.

'Good morning, mes petites,' Pierre cooed as they wound around his legs, divesting fur over his trousers. 'Uncle Tahi has the little job for you.'

Taking a white rose he bent down and threaded it into Delilah's collar, then did the same with Samson, except her rose was red. She'd always been the more aggressive of the two females, hence she'd received the male name. It wouldn't have done to have a mating pair aboard — there would have been kittens everywhere.

'Very nice,' Tahi said. Sort of, but he knew Amber would think it adorable.

Pierre picked up the cats, one jammed under each arm, both furry faces registering surprise and indignation at the lack of breakfast. 'You bring the tray.'

At his cabin door, Tahi balanced the tray on one hand and opened the door, peeking inside.

'You awake?' he asked.

Amber nodded. He thought she looked miserable.

'Can I come in?'

Another nod. Tahi gave Pierre the signal: he put the cats down and they scampered into the cabin wearing their roses, and jumped onto the bed. Amber giggled. Tahi followed, closing the door with his foot, and set the tea tray on the floor.

'Thought you might like an early-morning cup of tea.' He sat on the bed. 'I'm sorry, Amber. I've been an idiot. And a pig.' He waited, then, for her to say he hadn't.

She sat up, bunching a pillow against the wall behind her. 'You have, actually. I didn't ask to be kidnapped, you know, not by any of them. How do you think *I* feel? It was bad enough being passed from pillar to post by sodding Lo Fang and then Longwei, but Israel! How did we not know he was mad?'

She still didn't know *how* mad, Tahi thought. He hadn't told anyone except Haunui what Israel had said at the end, and though it had been truly shocking, he would have killed him anyway.

'We weren't looking for it, were we?'

'He could have *killed* me with all that opium, he could have done anything.'

400

Tahi steadied himself. 'But he didn't.' It wasn't a question.

'Of course he didn't. I've *told* you. I woman knows these things. And he was such a gentleman.' She gave a short yap of a laugh. 'He stole me, lied horribly to me, nearly poisoned me to death, and showered me with gifts and was a perfect gentleman. Poor Israel. What a mess.'

'Poor Israel be buggered. He deserved what he got.'

'I don't deserve what *I'm* getting. It wasn't my fault, Tahi.'

Tahi scooted up the bed and took her hand. 'I know. That's why I said I'm sorry. For behaving like I have.'

Tears brimmed in Amber's eyes. 'He's ruined it for us, hasn't he?'

'No, he hasn't. But I nearly did.'

There was an ominous ripping sound as Samson tore off her rose.

Tahi leant forward and kissed Amber. Her arms came up and wrapped tightly around his neck.

The tea went cold.

★ ★ ★

They arrived in Sydney Harbour on the twenty-sixth of November and planned to stay only a few days at most, Wong Fu's state of health being uppermost in everyone's minds — just long enough to see Wing and Ka settled and for Bao to speak with her uncle. Kitty expected she was going to tell him exactly what she thought of him, but who really knew with

401

Bao these days? She really had grown into the most extraordinary young woman.

The matter of Wing and Ka had been worrying her. She'd imagined they might find lodgings with the Chinese community in Sydney but apparently Mick had other plans. According to him his mother would be more than happy to take them in; Kitty, who knew Biddy well, wasn't so sure. Mick, she knew, had ulterior motives, and she doubted Biddy would be keen on the idea of keeping Mick's fancy woman, and her servant, while he was away at sea. She wondered if Wing even liked Mick, and asked her as the *Katipo* was being towed into a berth.

'He is a fine man,' Wing said, her gorgeous hair fluttering like a black silk banner in the sea breeze and a beautifully painted parasol open to keep the sun off her face.

For about the twentieth time Kitty marvelled at how she managed to keep her hair looking so lovely and shiny.

'Do you think so?' she asked after she'd swallowed a mouthful of the biscuit she was eating. Mick had been called many things, but 'fine' was very rarely one of them.

'Yes. He is handsome, kind, thoughtful and he has excellent manners.'

'Mmm.' She hadn't seen him drunk, of course.

'And he is very wealthy, but you would know that.'

'Is he?'

Wing turned to her, the morning sun lighting her perfect, pale skin. She tilted the parasol to block it. Her eyes were the loveliest brown colour, like the inside of a pine cone.

'Yes, the business he has with his mother. All of the properties?'

'Oh. Of course.'

'Does she have a lovely house?'

Kitty thought about Biddy's two-storey tenement in Carahers Lane, which, although very clean and beautifully kept, was undeniably modest. It was all she'd ever aspired to, despite the wealth she'd accumulated in her later years, and, by all accounts, far better than what she'd come from.

'It's comfortable. Folk have a different way of living in Australia. You might find it takes a bit of getting used to. And you came from the house of a *very* wealthy man, remember.'

'But not a kind man. Not like Mick. He is looking for a wife, you know.'

Kitty nearly choked on her biscuit. Mick, married? What was she talking about? Mick was the original sailor with a woman in every port, and proud of it. He'd never settle down. He was too selfish.

'Has he said that?'

Wing's parasol blew inside out. Scowling, she dropped it overboard. 'He has said that so far he has not found the right lady. During our conversations over the past weeks he has strongly hinted that I am she.'

Kitty said, 'Yes, well. It's been very nice talking to you, Wing, but if you'll excuse me I've got so much to do before we go ashore.'

'And I cannot stay in the sun without my parasol.'

Kitty watched her as she went below, then

hurried along to the bow where Mick was preparing the ropes for berthing. It was a warm morning and he'd taken off his shirt, but she was immune to the sight of his muscled chest and arms. He was still very fit, and undeniably handsome if you liked dark-haired' Irishmen with twinkly eyes. She preferred blond Irishmen, one in particular.

'Mick?'

'Mmm?'

'I've just been talking to Wing and she tells me you want to get married.'

'I do.'

'To her?'

'Who wouldn't? Look at her. She's like a perfect little doll, so she is.'

'But you're awful to women.'

'Ah, Kitty, that's cruel.'

'You are. Why the sudden change of heart?'

'I'm in love.'

'Oh, grow up.'

Mick set the coiled rope tidily on the deck. 'That's the thing. I finally have and me heart tells me she's the one I want.'

'Do you know what she's really like?'

'We've had lots of nice chats.'

'You haven't bedded her yet?'

Mick gave her a look of mock disapproval. 'Kitty Farrell, is that all you ever think about?'

'Me? That's good, coming from you!'

'I'm saving meself for the wedding night.'

'She was a concubine, you know.'

'Well, we all have our secrets.'

Kitty was starting to lose her temper. 'Mick, she's after your money, which you don't actually have because you've lied to her.'

'Not really. Mam'll leave some of it to me when she dies, so she will.' Mick stared at the deck for a moment. ''Cept she probably won't die for another hundred years, the tough old boot.'

'And she isn't going to put up with Wing living in her house. Or at all, probably. She'll see straight through her.'

'There's nothing *to* see. She's a lovely girl.'

'You're a fool, Mick Doyle,' Kitty said, and stomped off.

★ ★ ★

Bao went straight from the *Katipo* to the Chinese quarter, not far from the wharves.

'Good morning, Mr Sun,' she said in Cantonese as she entered the furniture shop.

'Miss Wong, good morning,' he replied, smiling broadly then bowing. 'Do you wish to speak with your uncle?'

He didn't appear surprised to see her, Bao thought, so perhaps he wasn't aware that she was supposed to be in Hong Kong.

'Thank you, I do.'

'One moment, please.'

The gong sounded and a minute later So-Yee appeared through the curtain at the rear of the shop. His eyebrows lifted and he smiled, revealing half a dozen gold teeth, a very rare display of emotion for him.

'Miss Bao, you have returned.' To Sun Lee Sing he said, 'You may go outside briefly.'

Sun Lee Sing went, digging in his trouser

pocket for his pipe tobacco.

'I am *delighted*,' So-Yee added. 'You are well?'

'Yes, thank you, and yes, I have come back,' Bao replied, 'which I sincerely hope gives my uncle the fright of his life.'

'I am sure it will. Were the arrangements in Hong Kong not to your satisfaction?'

'No they were not, and you know that. They would not have been even if Yip Chun Kit had been the kindest, most handsome man in all of China. Which he was not.'

'Did he tire of you or did you escape?'

'I escaped.'

'Well done.'

'Thank you.'

'And your transport here?'

'Rian Farrell.'

'Ah. A reliable fellow, Captain Farrell.'

'Very. Have you news of my father?' Bao asked.

'Our last correspondence, received on Tuesday, advised that he was failing but still with us.'

Bao nodded. That would have been sent over two weeks ago. Her father could well be dead by now.

'Will you take me up to Kai?'

'Be warned, Miss Bao. He will not be pleased.'

'*I* am not pleased, So-Yee.'

Another small smile as he gestured to her to follow him.

Wong Kai stood at the window of his office looking down at the street below, and turned as Bao knocked and entered. For a moment expressions of confusion, dismay then rage chased across his face, then he composed himself.

'Bao, I did not expect to see you. You should be the wife of Yip Chun Kit by now.'

'No, Uncle, I should not, and you should not have schemed to give away money that belongs to our family. You should not have schemed to give away my *life*.'

She hadn't spoken to him during the few days she'd been in Sydney on her way to Hong Kong — he hadn't allowed it — and this was her first chance to tell him how she felt about what he'd done.

Kai spread his hands. 'It was for the good of the family that I did scheme. When we are given power, such as I have and such as you will soon receive, we must make sacrifices.'

'What sacrifice were you going to make? You were going to help yourself to the office of Cloud Leopard while I was to be stuck with a man who looks like a frog and smells like ten cloves of raw garlic.'

'These are tumultuous and changing times, both abroad and at home in China. *Especially* at home. Our tong needs a strong leader, a figurehead who can lead by example, in both word and deed. You are not that figurehead.'

'I am, by birth and by training. And *you* trained me, if you care to recall.'

'Only at the behest of your father. I had hoped he would see sense by now.'

'There is nothing to see sense about, Uncle. My father has always known exactly what he is doing.'

Clearly growing frustrated, Kai said, 'Bao, you are a woman!'

'What difference does that make? The Empress Dowagers Cixi and Ci'an are women, and they are co-regents of all of China.'

'That is different.'

'How?'

'They are merely babysitting.'

Bao looked at her uncle in disgust. He'd never change. He'd been this way for as long as she could remember, and he'd continue along the same arrogant, bullying path until he died.

He sat down on his ridiculously ornate chair and set his hands flat on the desk in front of him as though about to inspect his fingernails. 'There are those on the tong committee who say they will not tolerate a woman tong master,' he remarked. 'There will be insubordination. There will be subterfuge.'

Bao sat down herself. 'There *will* be? Do you think I do not know what has been happening? Do you think my father has not told me? He has struggled to preside over it for years.'

Kai shrugged. 'I am simply telling you that you must expect more.'

'It has been the death of him. He is not an old man.'

'I agree.'

Bao fixed her gaze on a large jade bowl on her uncle's desk, then said quietly, 'And I have decided that I do not want it to be the death of me.'

Kai looked at her sharply. 'What are you saying?'

To calm herself Bao took a deep, slow breath. 'I am saying that I consent to passing the office of Cloud Leopard to you.'

Kai stared at her in astonishment. 'But you have just vigorously argued about why it should be yours.'

'I have argued about the *principle* of why it should be mine.'

Recovering quickly, Kai asked, 'And what do you want in return?'

'Two matters. Firstly, I want you to say nothing about this conversation to anyone until my father has died. Agreed?'

'Yes, but why?'

'As I am *sure* you know, it is Tam Chong Ho who administrates during the succession of one Cloud Leopard to the next, and I will need to declare officially in writing that I do not wish to take up the office after my father dies. Chong has my father's ear but, I fear, is not his friend. I do not want Chong to know until he has to.'

It was possible that news of her decision might reach Lawrence before she did and the truth was she didn't trust Tam Chong Ho not to tell her father out of pure spite, and she didn't know how her father might feel about her decision. She couldn't bear the idea of him going to his grave disappointed with her.

'And the second matter?'

Bao pushed a piece of paper across the desk. 'I want you to send this amount of your personal money, *not* tong money, to China, to this address, as soon as possible, and I want the bank and postal receipts to prove it.'

Kai looked at the note. 'This is a lot of money.'

'Do not tell me you cannot afford it.'

'Oh, I can afford it. What is it in aid of?'

Bao hesitated, then decided there would be no harm in telling him. 'To cut what is quite a long story short, Rian and Kitty Farrell's daughter, Amber, was abducted by a man named Lee Longwei, a pirate.'

Kai looked confused. 'But — '

'Yes,' Bao interrupted, 'that was *after* Lo Fang took her. I said it is a long story.' She pointed to the note. 'I negotiated her release from Longwei for that sum. With your money.'

'That was very generous of you.'

'I knew you would pay it if I offered to relinquish my claim to the office of Cloud Leopard. And I am right. You will.'

'Captain Farrell must be grateful indeed to have a friend with ready access to such an amount.'

'He does not know.'

'More secrets?' Kai looked amused.

'I do not have half as many as you.'

'What if I do not pay this money?'

'Then I will not stand down.'

'And you will be left owing this . . . *pirate* all this money.'

'Yes, I will. But I will also have access to the tong's coffers.'

Outraged now, Kai said, 'You cannot use tong money for personal debt!'

'Why not? The committee help themselves whenever they feel like it. And you spend family money that does not even reach the coffers.'

Kai didn't have to think for long. He tugged his snow-white cuffs from beneath the sleeves of his jacket so that they were perfectly even and adjusted one of his onyx and gold cufflinks. 'I will make arrangements to have the money sent this afternoon. Come back in the morning for the receipts.'

'Thank you.' Bao stood.

'One minute! How do I know you will keep your part of the bargain?'

Bao had suspected he was going to say that: there were very few people Kai trusted, and she clearly was no longer one of them. 'Give me paper and a pen.'

Kai opened a drawer and produced a pristine, pale yellow sheet, passed it across the desk and indicated a pen and ink. Bao wrote a short sentence, signed and dated it and handed it back.

'Will that suffice?'

Kai read it and gave one of his unpleasant smiles. 'Yes.'

★　★　★

Mick knocked once and opened the bright blue door to his mother's house. Kitty glanced nervously at Rian, both anticipating with alarm what was about to happen but compelled to watch it all the same.

'Mam, I'm home!'

A voice from inside replied, 'Mick, is that you?' A moment later Biddy Doyle appeared, wiping her hands on a tea towel. 'My boy!'

She gave Mick a great big hug, followed by equally generous embraces for Kitty and Rian. When she came to Wing and Ka she stopped, her hands planted on her wide hips.

'And who's this?'

Wing had outdone herself, wearing the best silk embroidered robe and skirt she had, plastering on face powder and rouge and drawing on her eyebrows, dressing her hair with fancy combs and artificial flowers, and tottering on high platform shoes. In contrast Ka wore her usual tunic and trousers, flat shoes, and a simple bun. Side by side they looked like a starling out walking with a peacock.

'Mam, meet Wing. She's from China. She's come to stay with us.'

'Has she now?'

Though Wing looked a little confused she bowed low. 'I am very happy to meet you, Mrs Doyle.'

'Happy to meet *you*, dear. I think.'

'And this is Ka,' Kitty said, embarrassed because no one had introduced her. 'She doesn't speak English.'

Ka bowed deeply and Biddy, clearly still confused, gave a little bob back.

'Well, come on, come inside, don't stand around cluttering up my doorstep,' she said. 'The kettle's on and I've just made a nice batch of buttermilk scones.'

She led them into the room that served as parlour and kitchen, of which she was immensely proud, and urged them to take a seat at the table, dressed with a lace cloth and a vase of spectacular coral and pink dahlias. Kitty could see that Biddy had just finished her morning cleaning routine as every surface gleamed and the smell of furniture polish was heavy in the air, but before she sat, Wing surreptitiously wiped the seat of her chair.

Unfortunately, Biddy saw her.

Kitty tensed but Biddy merely crossed to the stove and removed the kettle. Ka got up to help but Biddy shooed her back to her seat. 'Tea, everyone?' she asked.

'Green, thank you, if you have it,' Wing said.

Biddy replied, 'Oh dear, you'll have to forgive me, I only have black, so I do. And it's nothing fancy.'

'In China we have more different types of tea than you can count,' Wing said. 'We believe that growing and producing tea is an art.'

'Is that so? Well, here it's bloody expensive so, believe me, paying for it's an art.'

Here we go, Kitty thought. She dared not catch Rian's eye.

While Biddy bustled about preparing the tea and scones, Mick recounted their adventures in China. Biddy was agog, especially when he got to the part about Tahi killing Israel.

'Holy Mary!' she exclaimed. 'Lucky you were in a Godless country where the law doesn't apply.' She frowned, her head on one side. 'Mind you, he probably could have done that *here* and got away with it.'

'English law does apply in Hong Kong,' Rian said. 'To British citizens, anyway. I expect some poor person out for an early morning walk through the gardens must have found him the next day, but we'd sailed at daybreak. And he had nothing on him to tie him to the *Katipo*. All the same, we

413

might not go back there for a while.'

'And Amber's quite all right after being passed from pillar to post?'

'She wasn't 'passed', Biddy,' Kitty said. 'She was abducted. Kidnapped. She must have been terrified. And I think the worst of it was when Israel had her. He drugged her with opium for days. He could have *killed* her.'

Biddy looked appalled. 'He didn't . . . ?'

Mick looked deeply uncomfortable and Kitty could see Rian's jaw muscles tense and the cords in his neck tighten.

'He said no, and she doesn't think so,' Kitty said, 'but would you ever really know?'

'Is this your servant's house?' Wing asked Biddy.

Biddy slowly and very carefully set the tea tray down on the table. 'No. Why, does it look like it should be?'

'It is very small. Mick said you and he own a lot of property. I thought, because you are so rich, you would live in a wonderful big house.'

Biddy looked at her son. 'He said that, did he?'

Mick reddened. 'I'm not sure those were me exact words.'

His mother stared at him piercingly a moment longer, then sat down, urging, 'Help yourselves, everyone.'

She took a scone for herself, cut it in half and spread a slab of butter onto each half. When she bit into one, there was so much butter it squeezed out through the little gaps between the tops of her teeth.

Rian plastered almost as much butter onto his own scone, took a huge bite and said, 'These are

414

delicious, Biddy. You must give Pierre the recipe.'

'He gave it to me.' Biddy turned to Wing. 'What are you planning to do in Sydney, dear?'

Wing said nothing, simply batted her eyelashes at Mick.

You cunning witch, Kitty thought.

Mick cleared his throat and took a quick sip of tea then flinched, having obviously burnt himself. His eyes watering, he swallowed furiously. 'We thought, Wing and I, that is, well, *I* thought I might ask Wing to marry me.'

Biddy's eyes narrowed just as Rian's scone broke, scattering crumbs everywhere. 'What?' he said.

'Well, you know, I'm getting on, so I am. It's time I thought about finding meself a decent woman. And I think I have.'

'Christ, you mean leave the *Katipo*?'

'Maybe.'

'And where do you think you're going to live?' Biddy asked.

'In one of his houses,' Wing said.

Mick said, 'I thought we could stay here.'

Biddy carefully placed her teaspoon in her saucer. 'I think it's time you and I had a talk, son.'

'I don't. I've made up me mind.'

'Oh, well, that's that then, isn't it?' Biddy rose, went to a cupboard and retrieved a broom, which she handed to Wing.

Wing stared at it. 'What is it?'

'It's a broom. If you're going to live, here you can make yourself useful by sweeping up those scone crumbs.'

'Ka will do that. She is the servant.'

'Oh no you don't. I won't have any of that nonsense in my house.'

'But I do not do sweeping.'

'You do now. I can lend you an apron if you want one. And while we're getting a few things straight, *I* own all the property round here in the name of Doyle, not Mick. Mick can barely lay claim to the clothes on his back.'

Alarmed, Wing said, 'What is she saying, Mick?'

But Mick was extremely busy lining up his butter knife with his plate.

'Time to go, I think!' Rian said rather too cheerfully. He stood, brushing crumbs off his trousers. 'Sorry about the mess, Biddy.'

'That's all right, Captain. Wing can clean it up.'

'No, wait,' Wing said. 'I will come with you. I do not wish to stay here after all.' She barked something at Ka, who sprang to her feet.

'Actually, I might have a job for that one,' Biddy said. 'She speaks no English at all, you say?'

Kitty shook her head. 'But she's sweet and a hard worker. And, er, extremely tolerant.'

'I lease two or three houses and two business premises to Chinese folk, and I'd like to lease more. They're good customers but most land-lords won't lease to them and I can see a gap in the market. I need someone who can talk to my current tenants and drum up a bit of trade in the Chinese community. Except how would *I* talk to her?'

'She would not be suitable,' Wing snapped. 'She is only a servant.'

Biddy said, 'I'll be the judge of that, thank you.'

'I could get Bao to talk to her,' Kitty suggested, glancing at Ka and wondering if she realised they were talking about her. 'Perhaps someone could teach her to speak English. She seems bright.'

'She is not,' Wing said. 'She is quite dull-witted.'

'We'll ignore the fact that she puts up with you,' Biddy remarked. 'That's a good idea, Kitty, so it is.'

Wing said, 'But I cannot go without a servant. What will I do?'

Brush your own hair? Kitty thought. 'You might find another Chinese girl here willing to work for you.' Very unlikely, though.

'But I do not have any money.'

'Then how are you going to pay Ka?'

Wing burst into tears. Kitty realised that, mercenary though the young woman's behaviour was, she was only trying to look after herself the best way she could — by using her feminine attributes to get what she wanted. And genuinely needed.

'Look,' she said, 'forget about Mick.'

Wing withdrew a handkerchief from her little silk bag and daintily blew her nose. 'I have.'

'Oh. Thanks very much,' Mick said.

Biddy muttered, 'Shut up, son, and be grateful.'

'You're clever, you're young and beautiful, and you're safe from Chun here,' Kitty went on. At least, she hoped that was true. 'You can start

417

again. Make the most of it. Life *is* different in Australia, but you can adapt. Bao knows some of the Chinese people in Sydney. Perhaps she can introduce you tomorrow and help you find a place to live and some work.'

Nodding, Wing dabbed at her eyes, though she looked less than enthusiastic at the idea of actually having to work. Her tears had worn a track through her face powder. 'I just . . . it is just so *daunting*.'

'I know.' Kitty could barely recall her first months in New Zealand without a faint shudder. 'But you'll get used to it. You will, I promise.'

'But I need Ka, for company.'

'Then stop treating her so badly.'

'She does not mind.'

Snorts from Rian *and* Biddy, even though Biddy had known Ka for less than an hour.

'That's because Chun paid her not to mind. And I suspect she hasn't left you now because she's loyal. She doesn't have to stay, you know. *You* can't pay her.'

'I do have *some* money,' Wing admitted, 'but it is in Hong Kong currency. And not enough to pay Ka, only enough for food and other necessities. I did not have much money in my apartment when we had to run from Chun.'

'The bank might be able to change it into English money for you,' Biddy said. 'Or a money exchange in the Chinese quarter.'

'They can,' Rian said. 'Thanks, Biddy. We'll leave you to console Mick, shall we?'

'Console him? I'll bloody well knock him into next week, the lying little shite. Let me know when you've talked to Bao, won't you?'

'We will,' Kitty said. 'We're sailing again on Saturday, if not tomorrow afternoon. We'll see you before we go.'

★ ★ ★

The next morning Bao and Ka hurried along the lower end of George Street until they came to the premises of Lau Chi Ho, the draper and tailor.

Outside, Bao explained to her, 'Mr Lau is Cantonese but he speaks English and knows several other dialects. He has lived here for some years with his wife, Lok Yi, and their son, Kan Kuen. Their shop is always very busy and I am hoping they may have a job for you. Mrs Doyle's offer is very kind but you will not be able to start work for her until you can speak at least some English. Mr Lau has taught other Chinese people and he is very good at it. English is a tricky language because whenever there are rules there are always times when they must be broken, which is not sensible, but you are a clever girl. What is the matter?'

Ka looked worried. 'I will not be able to pay him. I do not have any money. I gave all that I had to Miss Wing.'

'Then we will just get it back. Stand up for yourself, Ka. In any case, that is why I want to discuss the possibility of a job. You can work in lieu of payment. Now, Mr Lau can seem quite stern and formal, but really he is a very nice man. It is just that he has quite a lot of European

419

customers and he does not wish to give them reason to criticise or mock him. Once you come to know him, should everything go to plan, you will find he is very kind. And so is Mrs Lau.'

'I do not know anything about the business of drapery.'

'You do so. You have been dressing Wing for how long? You know about how to look after fabrics, you know how they behave, you know about what colour goes with what and what sort of fabric wears best in winter and what is more comfortable in summer. You know everything there *is* to know about silk. And what about flowers and ribbons and what have you for the hair? You dress Wing's every day.'

Ka smiled, her face lighting up. 'I do, too.'

'You see? Now, shall we go in and see how we get on?'

Lau Chi Ho and Lau Lok Yi, were both at the counter, Lok attending to a customer while Chi, it seemed, was busy adding up a list of figures. Bao and Ka hung back until the customer had left the shop and Chi's pencil was parked behind his ear.

'Miss Wong,' he said in English, 'how wonderful to see you. It has been a very long time.'

Preferring to continue in English and thereby save Ka from embarrassment in the event that Mr Lau declined to either teach or employ her, Bao said, 'It is wonderful to see you, too, Mr Lau. And you, Mrs Lau. Yes, we have been in New Zealand, in Lawrence, gold mining.'

'Any luck?'

'We have been moderately successful.'

'And how is your esteemed father?' Chi asked.

'Not well, I am afraid. He has a cancer of the stomach. He is not expected to live much longer. I am on my way to Lawrence now.'

Chi and Lok both looked genuinely distressed: Bao knew they liked Fu, even though they didn't know him well.

'Please convey our best wishes,' Chi said. 'His loss will be deeply felt.'

'I will.'

Bao noted that Chi hadn't asked where she'd been. Perhaps he already knew. The Chinese community was as susceptible to gossip as any other.

'And who is your friend? Lok asked.

'This is Chan Ka Yee, who has recently come from Hong Kong.'

Chi and Lok bowed. Blushing, Ka bowed back.

'She speaks Cantonese and would like to learn to speak English. She has been offered work here but requires English for it, and obviously cannot take up the position until she is at least moderately fluent.'

The door to the shop opened and several European women entered, briefly interrupting the conversation to ask where the hat notions were.

'The English language cannot be learnt overnight,' Chi warned.

'Of course not. Fortunately, the offer will remain open to her.'

Chi said, 'I would be happy to teach her. My rates are a shilling per two-hour lesson, or eight pence for one hour.'

The shop door opened again: a party of three this time. Lok left the counter to assist them.

Bao said, 'Ka had to leave Hong Kong under less than happy circumstances. She does not have funds to speak of.'

'Are you suggesting that she defers payment?'

'No, but I will ask you if you are willing to take her on as an assistant. You do seem to be quite busy. Does Kan not work here any more?'

'Yes. And no wife yet,' Chi said gloomily. 'No grandchildren. He is at the wharves picking up a shipment of cloth. What does your friend know about drapery?'

'Until very recently she was personal servant to the concubine of a very wealthy hong. She knows about clothing, and about silk. And she is honest and a very hard worker.'

'Which hong would that be?'

'I feel that it would be indiscreet to name him,' Bao replied, but couldn't resist adding, 'but he is known to some as the Frog.'

Chi barked out a laugh, startling the lady shoppers, who turned to look.

'Yip Chun Kit!' Chi declared, grinning.

Startled, Bao asked, 'Do you know him?'

'I know of him. My sister-in-law, who lives with my brother in Guangzhou, has a sister whose elder daughter is a concubine of Yip's. Her name — ' He clicked his fingers. 'What was her name?'

'There were three,' Bao said, 'and they were called Lai Wing Yan, Yu Peijing and So Mei Yan.'

'So Mei Yan, that is it. In my sister-in-law's letters we hear stories about Yip passed on via her sister about how fat, rude and arrogant he is. Apparently Mei only stays with him because she likes living in his luxurious compound and it is close to good shopping.' Switching to Cantonese he said to Ka, 'No wonder you left Yip's employ, Miss Ka. I gather he was not the most generous or pleasant of employers.'

Startled, Ka blinked and visibly struggled for something positive to say. 'We ate well. And the gardens in his compound were beautiful.'

'What a sweet-natured girl,' Chi said.

Lok returned with three huge rolls of black fabric balanced across her arms, trailed by the three shoppers. Bao and Ka stood aside. Chi took the rolls from Lok and set them at one end of the long counter, asking how much of each the women wanted. Someone had died so a considerable amount of the grosgrain and the barathea were required, along with a slightly lesser amount of the foulard silk.

'Is madam sure she wants the grosgrain?' he asked.

Madam said, 'Of course I am. I wouldn't have asked for it if I didn't want it.'

'As you wish.'

Chi cut the lengths with shears sharp enough to amputate a limb, then carefully folded the fabrics, wrapped them in brown shop-paper and tied the parcels with string.

Their purchases paid for, the women departed.

'Would you have recommended the grosgrain?' he asked Ka.

'Was that the heavy ribbed silk?'

'Yes.'

'What did she want it for?'

'A funeral costume.'

Ka frowned. 'Black, for a funeral?'

'It is the European custom.'

'No, I would not, not if the funeral is to be held now. The weather is warm and the grosgrain will cause the wearer to sweat, which will damage the fabric. Perhaps also the other material, in the medium weight. What was that called in English?'

'Barathea. A mix of silk and worsted wool.'

'Yes, that too, but the lighter silk the woman chose will be suitable.'

The door opened yet again and Bao looked up, expecting yet more customers, but it was Kan, the Laus' son. Outside she could see the shop's cart parked in the street, their faithful old horse with her head in her feedbag, munching away. On the cart sat three wooden crates the size of armchairs.

'Hello, Miss Wong,' Kan said in English as he took off his hat.

It was indeed warm at the moment and his black hair was stuck to his head, except for a jaunty tuft that stuck up at the back. He was a nice-looking boy of twenty or so, not devastatingly handsome but even-featured and clear-skinned and always quick with a smile.

'Hello, Kan. How are you?

'Very well, thank you. What brings you to Sydney?'

'A bit of business,' Bao replied, but Kan's gaze had already slid away to rest on Ka, who had turned the colour of plum blossom.

'Oh. Good,' Kan said, a bit inanely.

At the counter his mother nudged Chi quite hard with her elbow.

'You are just in time,' Chi said in Cantonese.

'What for?' Kan asked, turning his head though his gaze remained on Ka.

Bao felt very pleased with herself.

'To meet Miss Chan Ka Yee, who will be starting work with us tomorrow. It is rude to stare, son. Say hello.'

'Pardon me. I am pleased to meet you, Miss Chan.' The colour of Kan's face now matched Ka's.

'And I you, Mr Lau,' Ka replied in a voice hoarse with embarrassment.

'Do you have lodgings, Miss Chan?' Lok asked.

'Not yet, Mrs Lau,' Ka said, 'but I am sure I will find something.'

Shut up, Bao thought frantically.

'Nonsense. You will stay with us. We have the room and I do not mind cooking for one more. You will earn more in a day working here than one English lesson's worth of pay. Your board should be included at the very least.'

Ka bowed deeply. 'Thank you very much, Mr and Mrs Lau. I am honoured and very much in your debt. I have a few things I need to collect and then I will return.'

'You are welcome, Miss Chan,' Chi said. 'We look forward to having you.'

On the street, Bao said, 'See? I told you that he is a very kind man.'

'I liked his wife, too.'

'And his son?' Bao prompted.

Ka blushed again, then her expression grew

pensive. 'What will happen to Wing? I feel as though I cannot just leave her.'

'Do not worry about Wing. I have just the job for her.'

★　★　★

Kai was reading a letter and scowling ferociously when So-Yee ushered Bao into his office. Before the door had even closed behind her he shook the pages at her and exclaimed, 'You are responsible for this.'

Bao took a seat and waited for the tirade of bad-tempered accusations, refusals and denials she knew were coming. She knew him well and was familiar with the format of his tantrums.

'This,' he hissed, 'is a letter from Yip Chun Kit. It arrived this morning. He is demanding compensation. Compensation!'

'What for?' Bao asked, though she knew.

'What *for*? Breach of contract on my behalf, that is what for, because *you* absconded from Hong Kong and his marriage to you failed to take place.'

'He did not love me, and I certainly did not love him.'

'Do not be so childish. What does that have to do with anything? He was to receive a significant payment from me as your dowry and now he wants *twice* that amount in compensation.'

'How much were you going to pay him to marry me?' Bao asked, curious.

'None of your business. You are worth what I say you are worth.'

'I am very fond of you, too, Uncle.'

'What?'

Bao shook her head. No, he would never change.

Kai tossed the letter onto his desk. 'He is also demanding compensation for the loss of his favourite concubine and,' he leant over the letter to check that he'd read it correctly, 'one female servant. He claims that they were involved in your escape. Is that true?'

'It is.'

'Why would they choose to help you? Did you coerce them?'

Now was the time to start weaving the magic. 'You have not met Chun. I meant what I said yesterday when I stated that he is neither kind nor handsome. Nevertheless, Lai Wing Yan, the favourite concubine referred to in that letter, loved him, but she carried a heavy burden: she wished to become his wife. And she deserved to be as she is stunningly beautiful, very dainty and refined and with the most charming manners. It is true that in turn Chun adored her, as I suspect most men would, but his sole wife is a termagant who would not allow him to take another.' Not, of course, quite true, but Kai wasn't to know that.

'And he lets his wife dictate his personal life?' Kai was astonished.

'She tried to. She loathed me and did her best to have me sent away. Wing also wanted me gone so *she* could marry Chun, so she helped me to escape. Her motivations for helping me were, I believe, pure love for, and loyalty to, Chun, even if that loyalty was a little misplaced. She is a very loyal woman. But he turned on her when he discovered that she was involved with my escape, and she and her servant were forced to run for their lives. Wing was utterly heartbroken.'

'How do you know all this if you had already escaped yourself?'

'Because before I left I offered them sanctuary aboard Captain Farrell's ship, which I knew was berthed at the Victoria wharves, should they need it. And, as it happened, they did.'

'So where is this Lai Wing Yan now?'

'Oh, here in Sydney,' Bao said casually. 'So you can see why Chun is demanding compensation for breach of contract *and* loss of his concubine. Beneath his anger he is probably heartbroken himself at losing her.'

'Well, I am not paying him compensation for either, or for his servant. *I* am not responsible for you running off, especially when members of his own household assisted you.'

'And especially when you have not lost out, have you?' Bao said. 'You have what you wanted now anyway.' She decided to give Kai a fright. 'Have members of the Yip tong travelled as far as Sydney? I know they were in Ballarat when we were there nine or ten years back.'

Kai glared at her. 'Yes, they are here.'

'Then perhaps you had better pay Chun something.'

'Bah!' Kai swept the letter off his desk with a wild swipe of his hand.

'And speaking of payments, may I please have the receipts we spoke of yesterday?'

Kai found them and gave them to her.

'Thank you.'

Kai stood, tugged at the hem of his waistcoat and went to his window. Over his shoulder he said, 'If I am to pay Chun compensation for this concubine of his I want to meet her. Can you arrange that?'

Bao smiled to herself.

14

The *Katipo* arrived at Dunedin on the thirteenth of December and nosed into a berth at the wharf. There was no time to waste so Rian bought tickets for the overnight Cobb and Co to Lawrence, pleased to discover that once again Ned Devine would be their driver. Everyone wanted to make the trip. No one said it aloud but they all knew it would be the last time they'd see Wong Fu alive, and they wanted to say goodbye. Rian understood this and, out of respect for Fu, paid a couple of reasonably trustworthy-looking men to guard the *Katipo* until they returned.

They set off at six in the evening, seven of them wedged inside the coach, Haunui and Tahi on the driver's seat with Ned, and Gideon, Ropata and Hawk balanced on the roof. Five miles out of Dunedin, Ned stopped and Tahi changed places with Gideon, as the black man's enormous bulk jolting about was affecting the coach's progression. Gideon happily obliged, his face sheened with terrified sweat.

'It is worse than being in the crow's nest in a hurricane,' he confided to Haunui.

They arrived at Lawrence a little before eight o'clock the next morning, sore, tired, grumpy and hungry, but rather than stopping for breakfast they hired a cart and went straight on to the Chinese Camp.

At least this time the weather was far more pleasant than it had been during their last visit. The snow had receded to the mountain ranges to the west, the hills were green with summer grasses, and the morning air was still and warm.

'Ow,' Kitty said, slapping at an enormous mosquito.

No one came to meet them at the entrance to the camp.

Bao had already noticed this, and the empty streets, and the eerie silence that draped over the little settlement like a fine silk veil. The ember of dread she'd harboured for so long in her belly flickered into a flame. Were they too late?

She walked under the archway at the entrance to the camp, then broke into a run. She pelted down the street until she came to the small house she shared with her father, her feet kicking up small puffs of dust. Not stopping to knock, she pushed open the door and burst in.

Her father lay on his bed as still as stone, surrounded by six of the camp's elders, their heads bowed. She was too late.

Stifling a sob, she walked to the bed on legs she could no longer feel and gazed down. His hair had turned completely white, his face had wasted to the point where his cheekbones jutted like knife edges, and his closed eyelids were tissue thin.

'Oh, my beautiful father.'

Tam Chong Ho took her shaking hand. 'Bao,' he said in Cantonese, 'you are just in time. He does not have long.'

'He is alive?'

Wong Fu's eyes slowly opened. 'Bao, my child. Is that you?'

His voice was feeble, and Bao could barely hear him. She collapsed onto her knees and lay her head on his bony chest, tears coursing down her face.

'He cannot see you,' Chong said. 'He has lost his sight.'

'Yes, it is me, Father,' she said in a shaky voice into the sheet drawn up to her father's chin. 'I have come home.'

'You are well?'

'Yes, I am very well.'

Bao felt her father's bird-like hand pat her head as he said, 'That is good.'

She knew that would be enough. She wouldn't have to tell him the long story of her abduction at the hands of Lo Fang, her incarceration in Chun's house and how Wing helped her escape, and everything else that had happened. He understood that she was back, that she was fit and healthy, and that was enough.

'Father, there are some people who would like to see you. To say goodbye.'

'Rian?'

'Yes, and the crew.'

'I do not think that is wise,' Chong said. 'They will tire him.'

Bao shot him a sharp look: meddling old devil — Rian and the crew were his friends.

'Do not fuss, Chong,' Fu said. 'I will see them.'

So out trooped the elders and in came the

crew of the *Katipo*, but two at a time, hats in hand. Kitty and Rian went first, followed by Amber and Tahi, then Pierre and Simon. Pierre wept copiously and emerged with a damp moustache, and by the time they'd all spent a few precious minutes with Fu, they all felt morose. Chong took them off for a meal in the camp's dining room, though Bao refused food and settled in beside her father. Tsun Hin, the camp's resident herbalist and physician, told her that he expected Fu to pass at any time, and that in fact he'd lived longer than the course of his disease had led everyone to predict.

'Now that you have come,' he warned, 'he may go very quickly.'

'Is he in pain?' she asked.

'Yes, but the opium helps.'

'May I have some time with him in private?'

'Of course,' Tsun Hin said, and left quietly.

The room was almost silent now. Her father's breathing was laboured and tiny beads of sweat stood out on his brow.

'Are you too hot?' she asked.

'No. I am cold.'

She unfolded a blanket and laid it over him, tucking the sides beneath the thin mattress.

Time passed. She watched, waited and listened.

'Are you ready, my child?' he asked eventually.

'Yes.' And she was, though not for what he imagined. She felt immeasurably sad at the thought of letting him down.

More silence. Then: 'Do you want the responsibility?'

'No, I do not. Did you?'

'No. Sometimes I wish you had been born a boy. Life might have been easier for you. But you have been the best daughter a father could have wanted, Bao.'

She found his hand and squeezed it. 'And you have been the best father.'

Fu sighed, a long, stoical letting go of breath. 'You may choose not to take on the office of Cloud Leopard, Bao. There is always a choice. You must do as your heart desires.'

Relief washed across Bao like a tidal wave. Nevertheless a great pain swelled in her chest and she lay her cheek against her father's hand.

'The world is changing,' Fu said. 'The family may want someone like Kai at its head. I have been accused of being old-fashioned.' A pause while he caught his breath. 'Perhaps I am. Perhaps my time has passed.'

Bao knew he was talking about more than just his physical life: he was referring to the traditional lifestyles and culture of China. 'Father, no.'

'Everything must change, child. Nothing stays the same. In any case, you must choose.'

★ ★ ★

Fu died the following morning at five minutes past three o'clock, having slipped gently into a coma the evening before. The grief throughout the camp was muted as his death was expected, but it was genuine, even among those who no longer supported him as head of the Wong family. As the camp organised his funeral, his

434

body lay in state until the afternoon to allow mourners to pay their respects, then he was taken by cart into Lawrence to be prepared for burial by one of the few Chinese businessmen there, the undertaker Kwan Siu Hong. The funeral would be held the following day and Fu buried in the Lawrence cemetery — in the non-consecrated section for heathens, suicides and unbaptised babies — and there was much to do.

The camp butcher had slaughtered and dressed two pigs and purchased and wrung the necks of three dozen chickens and one and a half dozen ducks; the camp vegetable garden was denuded of produce and a party was sent into Lawrence to buy extra supplies of rice, eggs, cooking oil and spices, and to exchange pound notes for silver coin; and the shelves of the camp's general grocer were raided of spirits for the mourners and for the funeral rituals, and of candles, writing pads (with which to make imitation paper money) and playing cards (to suppress evil spirits). Some preparations had already been made in advance, however: a coffin had been ordered weeks earlier and a new suit of white burial clothes had been made for Fu.

Every member of the camp was busy doing something, so when Bao slipped off into Lawrence for an hour to visit Mr Kwan after dark, no one even noticed.

Very late that night Fu's body was brought back to the camp, on the same cart but in a solid rimu coffin. He was carried into his little house and the coffin placed on a stand, which creaked under its weight. Bao refused to allow the lid to be opened as she no longer wished to see her father's body in death, despite the appropriate cloths draped over him, and no one complained. A white sheet was hung over the door, candles and incense were lit, and Bao began a vigil so that her father would not be alone during his final night. Mourners drifted in and out to make their last visits, but by two o'clock in the morning, and for the last time, Bao finally had her father to herself.

★   ★   ★

The next morning, at exactly ten o'clock, Wong Fu began his penultimate journey. If the family could afford the expense, after seven years or perhaps even sooner, his body would be exhumed and sent back to lie for eternity in the soil of his beloved village in China, but for now a New Zealand resting place would have to do. The procession from the Chinese Camp to the cemetery was long as, together with the Chinese and everyone from the *Kapito*, about fifty of Lawrence's European inhabitants also attended. These people were mostly shopkeepers and miners, and women who'd bought vegetables from the camp garden, all of whom had met Fu and liked him, plus a few who were merely attracted by the spectacle.

Fu was transported on the cart near the front of the procession, Bao sitting on the seat beside the driver. She wore white, while others wore a strip of white cloth around their hats. Ahead of the cart walked an elder, tossing small pieces of imitation money. At the cemetery, before Fu's coffin was lowered into the ground, the white hatbands were removed, collected in a pile at the foot of the grave and set alight. Apples and biscuits were handed around to the mourners, then wine and spirits from tiny cups were poured onto the ground three times. At last the coffin was lowered.

'Goodbye, father,' Bao murmured.

'Be strong,' Kitty said.

'I will. Thank you.'

'I can't believe he's not allowed to be buried in the consecrated section,' Kitty then said, loud enough for the Lawrence contingent to hear.

'Father will not mind,' Bao replied.

At the cemetery gate every mourner was given a little paper packet containing a one-shilling coin, even the white people. Bao thought her father would approve.

★　★　★

That night, Bao formally advised Tam Chong Ho that she didn't wish to be the next Cloud Leopard. He was not displeased.

'I think you have made a wise choice, my dear. Your father was a very good tong master in his time, and he has trained you in accordance with his values and beliefs, but that time has passed. It is time for change.'

'So you have been one of those undermining my father and lobbying for Kai to take over?'

'I would not say that, but I believe I have the

437

family's best interests at heart.'

'The family's, or your pocket's?'

'There is no need to behave in a churlish manner, Bao. We must all stand aside for change.'

'Then why not you? You must be at least fifty-five by now. Why are you still on the tong committee?'

Chong's eyes narrowed. 'I am repeatedly voted on by the men here in the camp.'

'After you have bribed them. With their own money.'

Sighing, Chong sat back. 'Why do you care, Bao? You just said yourself you do not wish to be Cloud Leopard.'

'I have said that, and I mean it, but I do care about the family. What does it matter who sits at the head of the table as long as we prosper and work together cohesively and happily, and everyone receives their share? Kai can take my place, if it means an end to all this disharmony.'

'It is what the people want.'

'A greedy and manipulative tong master?'

'A tong master who can use our money to its greatest potential.'

Bao stared at him. 'Well, then they will get what they deserve.'

'You have definitely made up your mind?'

'I have.'

Chong slid a document across the table towards her. 'Sign this.'

Bao took up a pen, dipped it into the ink pot and wrote her name and then the date across the bottom.

'Thank you,' Chong said.

★ ★ ★

The next morning Bao stood with the others outside the Oasis Hotel, waiting for the Cobb and Co driver (who wasn't Ned Devine this time) to finish loading luggage onto the coach.

Bao had known she wouldn't be staying at Lawrence, but the others hadn't and she couldn't tell them why not: at least not this instant. Also, she had another favour to request of Rian, and felt dreadful asking him to oblige her family yet again.

'Do not put too much on the roof,' she instructed the driver.

'Why not?'

'We have to sit up there.'

'Plenty of room,' the man said, whose name was Bart.

At the moment there was, Bao thought. They set off, using much the same seating arrangement as they had for the journey out. No one was looking forward to the long, bumpy trip back to Dunedin, but at least this one was taking place during daylight hours.

A mile out of Lawrence, as the coach entered a stand of bush, Bao rapped hard on the wall, a signal for the driver to stop.

'What's the matter?' Kitty asked as the coach jerked, lurched and creaked to a halt.

'Let me out,' Bao said.

Pierre, Mick and Simon dived out of the way in case she was about to throw up.

Jammed between Amber and Rian, Kitty struggled to her feet. 'Are you not well?'

439

'I am fine.' Bao opened the door and jumped to the ground.

'What the hell's going on?' Rian demanded.

Bao stuck her fingers in her mouth and whistled piercingly. Somewhere nearby a horse whinnied: several of Bart's animals responded by nickering, their ears up. Then came a fair bit of rustling and a very audible Chinese curse, and after a moment a horse and cart appeared out of the trees. The driver was the undertaker Mr Kwan, and on the cart lay a rimu coffin.

Turning to the coach, Bao said, 'Come on, give me a hand.'

They all stared at her.

'Who's in it?' Simon asked.

'My father.'

Looking extremely confused, Mick said, 'Didn't we just bury him?'

'We buried a pile of rocks. I am not leaving him here.'

'Ah,' Rian said.

Bao could see by his expression that he was piecing at least some of the picture together, and had realised what she would shortly be asking him.

'Who will help me?' she asked. 'I cannot lift him by myself.'

By this time Bart had climbed down from his seat. 'Here now, you're not putting that on my coach. I'm not licensed to carry dead bodies.'

Bao put her hands on her hips. 'Why do you need a licence?'

'In case . . . er.'

Bart clearly didn't know. Bao thought he was

probably making it up anyway.

'In case it falls off and the bits go all over the road!' Bart declared, pleased with himself.

Rian got out his purse and handed him a five-pound note. 'Here, buy yourself a coffin-carrying licence. Is that enough?'

''Spect so. But it's not going in the coach. You'll have to tie it on the roof.'

'Fine,' Bao said. 'Father always liked fresh air.'

Mr Kwan hopped off his seat and he, Gideon, Haunui, Rian, Hawk — all the men, in fact — almost gave themselves hernias getting Fu's coffin off the cart and on top of the coach.

'Christ almighty, Bao, have you got rocks in this one as well?' Simon asked, his face beet red.

'No, gold.' Finding herself the centre of attention once again, she explained, 'I stole all the gold we've mined here, which would have only been spent by Kai and his cronies now that he is Cloud Leopard, and I'm taking it home to my family in China, where it should be anyway.'

'You put it in with the body?' Amber looked both fascinated and faintly ill.

'Yes, but it is all right. Father has been preserved. Mr Kwan has packed him in salt and the coffin is lined with lead.'

'And, er, are we taking you back to China?' Rian asked.

Bao felt her face burn. 'If you possibly could. My family will be forever in your debt. And I can pay. There is plenty of money now.'

'To Hong Kong?'

'No, Zhaoqing. If you make port at Macau I can go inland by the Shenwan River.'

Rian took off his hat and scratched his sweaty head. 'Well, I can't see why not. And we can take on a cargo while we're there. But — ' He held up a finger.

Bao's heart, which had sprouted wings, plummeted like a dead bird.

'I won't hear another bloody word about payment, all right?'

Blinking back tears, Bao said, 'Thank you. Father will be so happy to be going home.' Impulsively she hugged Rian who hugged her back, this time with no discomposure whatsoever.

It took another twenty minutes to lash Fu's coffin securely to the roof of the coach and say goodbye to Mr Kwan, and then they were on their way again, Bart driving more cautiously now. It wouldn't do to rein in quickly and have the coffin shoot off the roof and take off a horse's head.

However he was travelling too slow for Bao, who leant out the window and urged him to increase the horses' speed, which he did, slightly.

'Just in case Chong realises the gold is missing,' Bao said as she resumed her seat, her hair blown all over her face. 'I do not think he will, not for a while. It was locked in a strongbox hidden beneath Father's bed. I replaced the sacks of gold with pebbles, and I have taken both sets of keys. Of course, Chong may have had another set made,' she added. 'I would not put it past him.'

On reflection, she stuck her head out the window again and shouted, 'Faster, Bart!'

As a result they made very good time back to

Dunedin but arrived almost crippled. Bao asked Bart to deliver them to the wharf, which he did for a fee everyone suspected would not see Cobb and Co's coffers. Tumbling from the coach onto the street, they were relieved to see that the *Katipo* was still tied up where they'd left her. While Fu's coffin was wrestled down off the coach, Rian went aboard to pay the two men he'd hired the remainder of their fee, on the way greeting Samson and Delilah, who sat tidily on the gunwale near the bow, apparently waiting patiently for everyone to come home.

When he rejoined the others they were all staring out to sea.

'What?' he asked.

Hawk pointed.

Rian looked and saw it himself — a large, fearsome-looking junk, her dragon sails furled, at anchor in the harbour. 'Christ, is that Longwei's ship?'

Nodding grimly, Hawk said, 'I think so.'

'What the hell's he doing here?'

Bao stared out at the harbour in dismay and disbelief, though not fear. She wasn't frightened of Longwei and had in fact found him disturbingly attractive. He was, however, also undeniably dangerous. She crouched and dug with shaking hands through the little bag in which she kept her papers, and found the bank and postal receipts Kai had given her for the money he'd sent Longwei — or allegedly sent him. They appeared genuine but they could easily be forgeries, couldn't they? Then, chiding herself for being such a fool, she realised that if

Longwei had been at sea for a month, he couldn't have 'not' received the money, so that wouldn't be the reason he was here. Had he changed his mind about their contract and come to take Amber back? Surely not.

'What's that you've got there?'

She looked up to see Kitty eyeing the receipts in her hand. Quickly, she shoved them into a pocket. 'Nothing.'

'Excuse me for prying, Bao, but that amount of money seems quite big to be 'nothing', and why is Wong Kai's name on them?' Kitty asked. 'What have you been up to?'

A wave of heat washed over Bao. She'd not planned to tell Rian and Kitty the details of the arrangement she'd made with Longwei. At first, this was because she hadn't wanted them to feel beholden to her, though she knew they did anyway. She suspected they thought the deal had been struck as a result of some esoteric Chinese code of honour, and, rather guiltily, she'd let them. She'd taken quite a risk when she'd made the deal as she didn't have anywhere near the amount of money Longwei had demanded. But she'd explained to him that as Cloud Leopard, which she would become on her father's passing, she would have access to the tong's coffers. By then, however, she was already seriously considering declining the office, as she knew there were ways she could help her family without having to preside over a committee of recalcitrant and greedy old men. If Kitty and Rian knew she'd swapped the money for her inheritance, however, they would think she'd sacrificed

444

her future as Cloud Leopard just to save Amber, and although she had, it was more complicated and a little less altruistic of her than that.

And now Longwei was here in Dunedin, and Bao didn't know why.

As they watched, a tiny ship's boat was lowered from the junk and headed for the shore.

Bao's mouth went dry and in her mind she ran through several versions of the truth, and some outright lies, that might satisfy Kitty. She couldn't bear their guilt if they thought she'd thrown away her life for them.

'Rian, look what Bao's got,' Kitty said.

He moved closer. 'What?'

'Show him, Bao.' Kitty gave her best stern look. 'Please, dear.'

Reluctantly she fished the receipts from her pocket and gave the creased papers to Rian.

'Christ, that's a fair amount,' he said. 'What are you doing with these?'

Wishing she were anywhere else but where she was, even back in Yip Chun Kit's compound — well, no, perhaps not there — Bao moved from foot to foot, crossed her arms, then sighed. 'Amber!' She beckoned. 'You too, Tahi.'

And she told them.

When she'd finished, both Amber and Kitty were crying. Amber threw her arms around Bao's neck.

'You're so clever, Bao. And so brave. And such a friend. Thank you.'

Kitty blew her nose. 'Why didn't you tell us this before? Not that we're not grateful. We'll always be grateful.'

'See, this is why. I did not want you to feel beholden.'

Tahi kissed her on the cheek. 'Won't you miss being the Cloud Leopard?'

'No. I have thought about it a lot, and no, I will not.'

'What did your father think about your decision?' Rian asked. 'Mind you, knowing Fu, I think I know the answer.'

Bao glanced out to sea: the ship's boat was a lot closer. 'I did not tell him outright before he died, but I think he knew. He told me to follow my heart.'

'Sounds like him. So why is he here?' Rian inclined his head towards the harbour.

'I do not know.' Bao decided there was no time to be anything but blunt. 'I am very worried that he has come for Amber.'

Rian's eyes narrowed and he looked suddenly far more alert. 'But I thought all that's over and done with?'

'So did I.'

Turning, Rian ordered, 'Hawk, get everything aboard ship and stowed *now*, including Fu. And have the crew wait on deck. There could be trouble.'

'I will stay here,' Bao said.

Rian said, 'No, you'll go aboard.'

'No. I will speak to him.'

'I'll do that. Go aboard.'

'No!' Bao's voice was close to a shout, something she rarely did. 'It was my contract with him, I will speak to him.'

She and Rian glared at each other, then Rian

gave in. 'I'll be on the wharf if you need me. If there's trouble, Bao, run.'

'I never run away.'

'No, I don't think you do, do you?'

As the crew carried their bits and pieces onto the *Katipo*, Bao waited alone on the polluted, fish-guts-strewn beach.

The *Kaili*'s boat arrived, and Ip To scrambled out and hauled it up onto the sand. Everyone on the *Katipo* lined up along her gunwale to watch, ready to race back down to the wharf if necessary.

Longwei stepped out of the boat, scowled at the filthy surrounds, and picked his way across to Bao. A low-flying gull shrieked overhead and Bao, taut with apprehension, started badly.

He bowed. 'Miss Wong, we meet again.'

Her heart thumping, Bao returned the bow. 'Captain Lee. You have travelled a long way.'

'Yes, I wished to speak to you.'

'You could have sent a letter.'

'I did not know your address.'

'Is this about our contract?'

Longwei looked faintly surprised. 'No.'

Bao felt so faint with relief she suddenly needed a seat, but certainly wasn't going to sit in stinky fish guts. And sitting down would only make her appear weak. 'Then why are you here?'

'To enquire about your circumstances.'

'My . . . circumstances?'

'Yes. When we last spoke you told me that your father was very ill.'

'Oh. Yes, he died several days ago.'

'He passed peacefully?'

'He did.'

'I am glad. And you are now tong master?'

'No, I am not. I relinquished my claim to the office last night.'

Bao waited for him to ask about his ransom money, but the question didn't come.

Instead he said, 'And now?'

'I am taking my father home. I am sailing with Captain Farrell.'

Longwei glanced over at Rian. 'I would be honoured to escort you and the body of your esteemed father back to China.'

'Oh, but — '

Longwei had already marched off towards the wharf. She hurried after him.

'Captain Farrell,' Longwei said.

'Captain Lee.'

'I understand that Miss Wong is sailing with you to China.'

'She is.'

'I would be very pleased to take her. It will save you a trip.'

'Why?'

Longwei frowned. 'Why what?'

'Why do you want to take her?'

'Because I wish that we may learn more about each other so that I can ask her to be my wife, and I cannot do that if she is aboard your ship, can I?'

Bao nearly died of embarrassment — and excitement.

'Is that so?' Rian said. 'Why should you be trusted? You stole my daughter.'

'I do not care if you trust me,' Longwei

replied. 'It is whether Miss Wong trusts me that matters.'

'Do you trust him, Bao?' Rian asked her. 'And do you want to go back to China with him?'

He'd stopped short of asking her if she wanted to be Longwei's wife, Bao noticed, and what a relief, too. She thought she might but she wanted time with him before she decided.

'Yes, I do trust him,' she said. 'He has not proven devious, has he? And I would like to accompany him back to China, if you do not mind, although I am very grateful for your offer, Rian. I think Father would enjoy the trip home on the *Kaili*.'

Rian said, 'You should probably follow your heart. Isn't that what Fu would say?'

'It is,' Bao agreed. 'It is exactly what he would say.' To Longwei she said, 'Thank you, Captain Lee, I accept your offer. Of passage home to China,' she added hastily.

Clearly extremely pleased, Longwei said, 'I should warn you, Miss Wong — '

Interrupting, Bao snapped, 'Really, if we are to sail together, I would much rather you called me Bao. 'Miss Wong' will get very irritating quite quickly.'

'Very well, then. I should warn you that aboard the *Kaili* you must be prepared to fight for what is right, to put yourself in the path of danger, and to defy the law.'

'That sounds like sailing on the *Katipo*,' Kitty said, who'd appeared at Rian's side.

'Is that acceptable to you?' Longwei asked.

'It is,' Bao replied, 'and I would be

disappointed in you if it were not the case.'

'See?' Longwei said. 'We are already coming to know each other.'

Then he took Bao in his arms and kissed her. Aboard the *Katipo* a great cheer went up. Ip To glanced over at his captain and rolled his single eye.

'I need to say goodbye,' Bao said. 'I do not know when I will see my friends again.'

'Of course.' Longwei turned to Rian and Kitty and bowed. 'We will meet again, Captain and Mrs Farrell.'

'I hope not,' Rian muttered under his breath.

Longwei gave a small, amused smile. 'Oh, we definitely will.'

As Fu's coffin was unloaded from the *Katipo* and wrestled into the *Kaili*'s boat, Bao said goodbye to everyone.

'Congratulations — I assume?' Amber said happily.

'Perhaps. I will have to see how everything goes. I would say come and visit but I do not know where we will be.'

'No, I never know where we'll be, either.'

They laughed.

'But I am sure we will see each other again,' Bao said.

'So am I.'

Bao gave Amber an extra hug, then she was running back down to the beach. She took off her shoes, threw them into the boat, splashed through the scummy waves and jumped in.

'Poo. She will need the proper bath after that,' Pierre remarked.

They all waved madly as Ip To leant into the oars and the boat rounded the end of the wharf and headed out into the harbour.

Rian took Kitty's hand and squeezed.

She squeezed back. 'I like a happy ending.'

Author Notes

Not knowing much about the history of China in the nineteenth century, I needed to do quite a bit of research for this book. Unfortunately the more I did, the greater became my realisation that I was barely scratching the surface, to use a cliché (which writers should avoid), and that it would take me much longer than I had to really appreciate the complexities of recent Chinese history. Even worse, I was only seeing a Western perspective on that history, but I suppose I should be used to that by now. I didn't go to Hong Kong, either, but perhaps I will one day.

Here is an extremely brief and simplified summary of China's so-called Opium Wars. The problem was essentially an unbalanced market. China had tea, for which Westerners were desperate, plus lots of gorgeous silk and delicate porcelain, but Britain had nothing the Chinese wanted to buy or trade, except gold and silver, both scarce in China. So the British reluctantly paid for their pekoe, teacups and bolts of silk in bullion, but, concerned at the amount of silver in particular leaving England, soon realised that there was also a market for opium in China. They hadn't introduced the drug there — that had apparently been the Arabs, for medicinal purposes, then the Portuguese — but the British East India Company discovered how to grow opium cheaply in Bengal and by the 1770s they were the leading suppliers to the Chinese market via the one port open to foreign trade — Guangzhou, known as Canton to Westerners, on the Pearl River near Hong Kong.

Over the years, millions of Chinese became enslaved to opium, severely disrupting the Chinese way of life. Understandably, successive emperors banned its import, sale and use, but demand was rampant and the British East India Company sidestepped the bans by licensing private 'country traders' — that is, anyone willing to sail the fast, specially fortified and armed opium clippers and risk being raided by pirates — to ship the opium from India to China, where the traders sold the opium to smugglers and pirates along the Chinese coast who took it ashore. The profits then went back via the traders to the British East India Company to purchase Chinese tea and the like.

In 1839 the emperor's special emissary, Lin Zexu, ordered the port of Guangzhou closed to all foreign merchants in a determined effort to eliminate the opium trade. British warships retaliated, destroying the Chinese blockade on the Pearl River, and by 1841 British land forces controlled the vast rice-growing lands of southern China. By the following year the 'foreign devils', as the Chinese called the British, occupied Shanghai and therefore commanded the mouth of the Yangtze River. The Chinese were forced to sign the Treaty of Nanjing, ceding Hong Kong to the British and, in addition to Guangzhou, open the ports of Amoy, Foochow,

Shanghai and Ningbo to foreign trade. Worst of all, the Chinese had to agree to Britain being given 'most favoured nation' status and to Western merchants no longer being accountable to China's laws, only to those of their own countries.

War broke out again in 1856 after two years of Britain's insisting that China legalise the import of opium from British cultivations in India and Burma, exempt British goods from all import duties, allow the establishment of a full British embassy in Peking, and open all Chinese ports to foreign trade. Again unsurprisingly, China didn't want to do any of that, and when a fracas arose involving the British-registered ship the *Arrow*, British — *and* American, French and Russian — forces descended on China. The defeated Chinese signed the Treaties of Tianjin in 1858 but refused to ratify them, until further military pressure from the British forced them to sign the Beijing Convention in 1860, ratifying the Treaties of Tianjin and opening the ports of Hankou, Niuzhuang, Danshui and Nanjing, and the Yangtze River, to foreign trade. Other conditions included ceding the port of Kowloon near Hong Kong to Britain, agreeing to the export of indentured Chinese labourers to the Americas, and allowing foreign missionaries to preach throughout China.

Jardine Matheson and Company was, and still is, a real entity, founded in 1832 by Scotsmen William Jardine and James Matheson. Aside from the British East India Company, Jardine Matheson and Company are historically the firm most closely associated with the importation of opium into China. William Eastwood, mentioned in the story, however, is fictional.

The Lotus Pond Gardens, where Israel meets his stabby end, are also made up.

I have tweaked history a little in this book. As mentioned above, the British import of opium into China from India and Burma was legalised in 1858 after the Second Opium War, but in this story it's still being smuggled in by the country traders and pirates. The story doesn't quite work in places if it isn't.

Another tweak: the Tongzhi Emperor and the Empress Dowager Cixi (pronounced Tsee-Chee) did not travel to Hong Kong in September 1863. In fact Cixi spent most of her life in the Forbidden City and the Imperial Summer Palace, both in Peking (also known as Beijing).

And just in case anyone's wondering, Kwangtung, Guangdong and Canton are all different versions of the same name. Canton or Kwangtung Province, now known as Guangdong, is where most Cantonese people come from.

Chinese people are not all the same, as of course you'd expect in such a geographically large country with a very long history. For example, the Cantonese, Hakka and Manchurian peoples were all culturally different, spoke distinct languages, and didn't necessarily see eye to eye all of the time.

Chinese naming conventions: the family name comes first, followed by the primary given name, then the second given name if there is one; for example, WONG Bao Wan. Thanks S.C.C.

Overton! http://www.sccoverton.com/uploads/2/
8/3/5/2835504/cantonese–name–generator.pdf,
for help with creating Chinese names.

The details of the Empress Dowager Cixi's
costume, as I've described it in the scene at the
governor's residence, come from a photograph
taken of her by a Chinese photographer named
Xunling, a diplomat's son. There aren't many
photos of the empress dowager, but apparently
she allowed him to take a series of very carefully
managed images in 1903 and 1904. The empress
dowager was suffering from particularly poor PR
by then, having backed the Boxers (who called
themselves the Righteous Fists of Harmony)
during the Boxer Rebellion against her own Qing
dynasty in 1900, and possibly hoped, it's alleged
anyway, that the photographs would rehabilitate
her reputation. It seemed they didn't, as in the
West, at least, she remains portrayed as the
quintessential Dragon Lady. She died in 1908 at
the age of seventy-three, and I should point out
that in the story, when she wears the described
costume, she is only in her late twenties.

A note on Lawrence, in Otago, New Zealand.
On 20 May 1861, Gabriel Read found gold in an
Otago valley — Gabriel's Gully. A rush soon
followed. By July the population of the new
goldfield surpassed eleven thousand. A perma-
nent settlement, named The Junction, grew at
the head of the valley, where the Weatherston's
and Gabriel's gully streams united and flowed
into the Tuapeka River. The town was surveyed
in 1862, a post office was opened on 1 April
1863 and the name Tuapeka adopted. In 1866,

however, the name was changed yet again to Lawrence — after Sir Henry Montgomery Lawrence, who died heroically during the Siege of Lucknow in 1857. I've gone with Lawrence in the story for the sake of modern geographical clarity, and in case anyone wants to google it.

And here I have to confess to another historical tweak: Otago was not settled by Chinese until 1866 — gold miners who arrived at Dunedin from Victoria, Australia, late in December 1865. Some went to Lawrence (then known as Tuapeka), but as the good citizens of Tuapeka passed a bylaw in 1867 prohibiting Chinese from living or operating a business within the town, the newcomers were relegated to living on an acre of soggy ground a kilometre away, which came to be known as the Chinese Camp. For more on the Chinese experience in Otago, see the Bibliography.

The snippet of poem at the beginning of Part One comes from a work by Chinese poet Shijing, called 'Guan! Guan! Cry the Fish Hawks'. The line at the start of Part Two is from William Shakespeare's Sonnet 147, 'My Love is as a Fever, Longing Still'; and the fragment of poetry at the start of Part Three comes from 'When I Am Dead, My Dearest', by Christina Rossetti.

Bibliography

As mentioned, I did some interesting new research for this book. Jung Chang's *Empress Dowager Cixi: The concubine who launched modern China* (Vintage, 2014) was really useful. On the front cover is the image I used in the governor's residence scene. Jung Chang also wrote *Wild Swans: Three daughters of China*. Also helpful was *Tea: A history of the drink that changed the world* (Andre Deutsch, 2011) by John Griffiths. Who knew there was that much to know about tea? I bought the book after a very pleasant afternoon at the Zealong Tea Estate at Gordonton. Helpful, too, were Frank Welsh's *A History of Hong Kong* (HarperCollins, 1993); *The Hong Kong Story* (Oxford University Press, 1997) by Caroline Courtauld and May Holdsworth; *The Chinese Opium Wars* (Hutchinson, 1975) by Jack Beeching; and an interesting working paper by Jeffrey A. Miron and Chris Feige from the (American) National Bureau of Economic Research titled 'The Opium Wars, Opium Legalisation and Opium Consumption in China' (May 2005). Go to www.nber.org/papers/w11355

For Chinese costume I found a really useful book by Verity Wilson (photographs by Ian Thomas) called, imaginatively, *Chinese Dress* (Victoria and Albert Museum, 1996) — full of lovely pictures and really detailed descriptions. Another little book I used, also produced by the V&A Museum (2010) and which already happened to be on my bookshelf, was *Chinese Textiles* — image after image of gorgeous antique Chinese silk fabrics. Sadly, some of my descriptions of said fabrics have been edited out of *The Cloud Leopard's Daughter*, and quite rightly, too, but I had fun writing them.

As for the Otago bit of the story, Stevan Eldred-Grigg's beautiful book, *Diggers, Hatters and Whores: The story of the New Zealand gold rushes* (Random House, 2008) was no end of helpful, as was *Dirt: Filth and decay in a new world arcadia* (Auckland University Press, 2005) by Pamela Wood, which is about why and how Dunedin got so disgusting in the later nineteenth century, and what was done about it. Well worth a read. Also pleasingly useful was a spiral-bound book I picked up at an antiques fair, which was written for 'Social studies and technology units level 3 & 4' (would that be eight-year-olds?) and is called *Coaching Days in Otago* (Otago Settlers Museum and the Ministry of Education's Learning Experiences Outside the Classroom Programme, 1998) by John Neumegen. Handy! It has a diagram of a Cobb and Co coach and old Otago maps and coaching trails and everything! Possibly best of all, though, was James Ng's work, *Windows on a Chinese Past* (Otago Heritage Books, 1993), a collection of four volumes on the history of Chinese immigrants to Otago. Sadly, they're as rare as hen's teeth (another cliché) and I had to photocopy the bits I wanted at the library because they're reference only. Annoying and expensive.

Finally, there were all the many other odd bits and pieces that go into my research and which are too numerous to list. I'd be here all day. A few highlights, though, are Papers Past at the National Library (of New Zealand), which I dip into all the time. Great for ideas on what people were buying in the shops, eating in restaurants, furnishing their houses with, making their clothes out of, ship's names, etc. Go to https://papers-past.natlib.govt.nz/ for New Zealand newspapers, and to http://trove.nla.gov.au/newspaper/about for Australian newspapers. I do use the Internet a lot. I know, you shouldn't trust the Internet, but you shouldn't trust a lot of books, either. The Internet's okay, if you check the sources.

Acknowledgments

Producing a book is team work. A writer might think they've done it all themselves, but they rarely have. Unless they self-publish, of course, and I don't. So thank you once again to the HarperCollins Australia team: to Mary Rennie, my (very patient) editor this time round, and to Shona Martyn, ever supportive and always willing to listen. Thanks also to freelance editor Kate O'Donnell, font of awesomely good ideas and endless enthusiasm, and to my agent, Clare Forster, for level-headed advice and constant encouragement.

A big 'mwah' as well to the entire team at HarperCollins New Zealand, for working so hard on behalf of my books and being so rah-rah every time I see them. Thanks, guys. I really do appreciate it.

I think a general blanket thank you needs to go out to my friends and family for being so tolerant during the writing of this one. I did spend a lot of time in my office, putting people off and not going to things due to deadlines, so perhaps a change of some sort could be in order. After all, you're not likely to get rich, vivid stories out of a boring worn-out writer.

Kerrie Ptolemy, of Ptolemy Consulting, Australia, also deserves a shout-out for doing my new website. Not only is it lovely but it works really well. Thanks, Kerrie!

Last but never least, thanks to my husband, Aaron Paul, who, as usual, made the dinners and cups of tea while I worked, even though sometimes the rubbish didn't get put out. But that's okay.

We do hope that you have enjoyed reading this large print book.

Did you know that all of our titles are available for purchase?

We publish a wide range of high quality large print books including:
Romances, Mysteries, Classics
General Fiction
Non Fiction and Westerns

Special interest titles available in large print are:
The Little Oxford Dictionary
Music Book
Song Book
Hymn Book
Service Book

Also available from us courtesy of Oxford University Press:
Young Readers' Dictionary
(large print edition)
Young Readers' Thesaurus
(large print edition)

For further information or a free brochure, please contact us at:
Ulverscroft Large Print Books Ltd.,
The Green, Bradgate Road, Anstey,
Leicester, LE7 7FU, England.
Tel: (00 44) 0116 236 4325
Fax: (00 44) 0116 234 0205

BAND OF GOLD

Deborah Challinor

When dashing Irish sea captain and part-time gunrunner Rian Farrell spontaneously buys the deed to a claim at Ballarat, where reef gold has recently been discovered underground, his wife Kitty is dismayed. Not only is mining dangerous work for the crew, who are seamen rather than labourers, but the desolate goldfields are no place for their adopted fourteen-year-old daughter Amber. As the headstrong and passionate Kitty endeavours to embrace the challenge by opening a bakery and building a small community of friends, she still yearns for life on the sea. But disaster strikes when the Yarrowee River bursts its banks and Rian disappears in the flood. Believing herself widowed, Kitty's heart is left in tatters. Alone and grieving, she turns to Rian's long-time shipmate Daniel, who has loved her from afar for many years.

KITTY

Deborah Challinor

When eighteen-year-old Kitty Carlisle's father dies in 1838, her mother is left with little more than the possibility of her beautiful daughter making a good marriage. But when Kitty is compromised by an unscrupulous adventurer, her reputation is destroyed, and she is banished to the colonies with her dour missionary uncle and his wife. In the untamed Bay of Islands, missionaries struggle to establish Victorian England across the harbour from the infamous whaling port of Kororareka, Hell-Hole of the Pacific. There Kitty falls in love with Rian Farrell, an aloof and irreverent sea captain, but discovers he has secrets of his own. When shocking events force her to flee the Bay of Islands, Kitty takes refuge in Sydney — but her independent heart leads her into a web of illicit sexual liaison, betrayal and death . . .

AMBER

Deborah Challinor

When Kitty Farrell is offered a trinket by a street urchin, her impulsive response will change both of their lives forever, and place an unexpected strain on Kitty's marriage. For the past four years, she has sailed the high seas on the trading vessel *Katipo* with Rian, her wild Irish husband; but when they return to the Bay of Islands in 1845, they find themselves in the midst of a bloody affray. Their loyalties and their love are sorely tested, and Kitty's past comes back to haunt her when she encounters the bewitching child she names Amber. As the action swirls around them, Kitty and Rian must battle to be reunited as they fight for their lives and watch friends and enemies alike succumb to the madness of war and the fatal seduction of hatred.